THE
FLYER

STUART
HARRISON

1

NORTHAMPTONSHIRE, ENGLAND. 1901

A swirling cloud of fat black flies rose like a veil. Sally Wright squatted down, her dirty brown knees showing below the hem of her skirt. She poked at the bloody mess with a stick. 'What is it?'

The animal had been torn apart, skin and fur violently separated from the flesh. The blood on the ground was still tacky.

'A hare, looks like,' William said. 'Come on or they'll find us.'

Sally poked at the corpse again, reluctant to abandon it without a proper examination, before she got up and followed.

They made a hiding place in a hollow of flattened wheat. A small, roofless cave that smelt of the dust and the sun scorched wheat. William peered across a half-cut field that shimmered in the heat haze. He could hear the others from beyond the hedgerow, where the ground sloped to a brook at the edge of the woods.

'They'll never find us,' he said, though his triumph was tainted by the suspicion that they had been forgotten. He imagined the others splashing in the brook, where the water ran silvery and clear over the pebbled bed. He sat down again. Sally watched him, her freckled face smudged with dirt, twisting her straw coloured hair in her fingers.

'Do you remember yer mam, then?' she asked.

'A bit.'

'My mam says she never came to the village much. I saw her once though when me and Jess was looking for mushrooms. Jess said she thought she were better'n the rest of us 'cause she talked like the lady from the manor.'

'Your Jess dun't know anything!' William replied hotly.

'I know, Will,' Sally said quickly. 'I didn't say I thought yer mam were stuck up. It were just Jess. I thought she were nice. I didn't mean to make you angry at me.'

'It's alright,' he said relenting.

'Do you think she's watching us now from heaven?'

William tried to imagine his mam in heaven. Reverend Yates said that's where she had gone after she died, but when William asked his dad what it was like there his dad confessed he didn't know, 'cept that nobody was unhappy and no-one was rich or poor. In the church there was a big window made of stained glass, with a picture of Jesus on the cross and the angels looking down on him. William wondered if his mam was an angel like them. He wished Sally hadn't asked about her because it made him feel sad. He wished she hadn't died.

'I'm going to lie down for a bit,' he said without answering Sally's question. He put his hands behind his head and closed his eyes.

Sally plucked an ear of wheat and tickled her chin with the cat's whiskers. 'Shall we go and find the others?'

'It's too late now. They'll be starting again soon anyway.'

She peered over the top of the wheat, at the adults lying about under the shade of the trees after having their dinner. She sighed and lay down beside William. 'I s'pose you're right.'

It was hot. The ground was baked hard from the long summer. As if from a distance they heard the occasional stamp of a heavy horse's hoof and the ringing note of metal buckles on a harness, the muffled voices of the adults. Before long they both fell asleep.

*****

William woke to the sound of a storm. He'd been dreaming of his mam, though her face was hazy. She'd died four years ago when he was only six, and now he could only really remember her voice. She used to read to him from her books. He'd liked the sound of her voice. None of the women in the village talked a bit like her.

The storm thrashed the wheat into a frenzy. He opened his eyes. The sky was blue, not a cloud in sight. Sally stirred.

'What's that?'

Her voice was thick with sleep. He didn't answer her, still trying to wake up properly himself. He was puzzled because the treetops along the hedgerows weren't moving at all, yet as the sound grew louder the walls of their hollow began to tremble and he felt a vibration in the earth.

Suddenly William knew what it was. 'Sal! The harvester!'

Already his voice was drowned by the noise of the blades, but Sally saw the heads of the leading horses, their blinkered eyes and their broad chests like towering walls and she scrambled like a frightened rabbit out of the way of those giant, iron shod hooves. Startled by the unexpected flash of movement, the beasts strained against their harness in panic, catching the driver unawares. He only saw a glimpse of her blue dress, and even as he stood and hauled back on the reins and shouted a warning he felt a bump under the iron rim of the wheels. It was followed by a piercing scream. People ran to see what had happened, and there were cries and confusion when they saw the wet blood vivid against the wheat.

*****

At the hospital in Northampton, John Reynolds waited anxiously for news of his son's operation. When the surgeon came he stood up, clutching his cap in his hands.

'Your boy is extremely fortunate, Reynolds,' the surgeon said. 'I managed to save the leg.'

Relief made William's father feel giddy. 'Thank you, sir. Can I see him now?'

'Yes, he's been taken back to the ward. But he won't wake up for a little while yet.' The surgeon looked around as if he expected to see somebody else. 'Is the boy's mother here?'

'She died, sir. Six year ago now. There's only me and Will now.'

'I see. You're from somewhere near Brixworth aren't you?'

'Scaldwell, sir.'

'What sort of work do you do?'

'I'm a blacksmith.'

The surgeon frowned. 'You must understand that you shouldn't expect your son to follow in your footsteps. He may walk with the aid of a crutch, it's too early to say, but he'll never be able to manage any sort of manual work. Is he good at his schoolwork?'

For a moment Reynolds was too shocked to reply. If William couldn't work, how would he live when he was older?

'Reynolds? Did you hear me? I asked you if your son is good with his schoolwork.'

'Sorry, sir. Yes, he is. His mam always said he were a bright lad.'

'If that's true things may not be so bad. Perhaps when he's older the boy will get a position in an office, where he won't have to be on his feet all day.'

'Yes, sir.'

'Well, good luck. Doctor Easton will tell me if there are any complications. Make sure he gets as much exercise as possible, that's the best thing.'

'I will, thank you for everything you've done, sir.'

When the surgeon had gone, Reynolds went to the ward to see his son, but at the door he had to stop for a little while and compose himself. The weight of the surgeon's prognosis had crushed his spirit. William would be a cripple for the rest of his life. He might never be able to work and marry and have a family of his own. It didn't seem fair that it should happen to a boy who had already lost his mother, and had no brothers or sisters to look after him or make him feel less lonely.

Eventually he went inside. Will was sleeping. He was pale and thin, his hair stuck to his scalp. Tears welled in Reynolds' eyes.

*****

That winter, a buggy with gleaming lacquered coachwork splashed with mud from the lane, was driven into the yard. Reynolds came out of the forge, wiping his hands on his apron. A man climbed down from the buggy. Rain dripped from the brim of his hat, missing his white-whiskered face and splashing onto the cloth of his coat. He regarded Reynolds with loathing. They spoke briefly, and then Reynolds led the way to the cottage.

When they came inside William looked up from the book he was reading by the window.

'This gentleman is Mister Gardner, Will. He wants to talk to you,' Reynolds said.

Gardner said nothing, only looked pointedly at Reynolds who, reluctantly it seemed, turned to go.

'I'll leave you for a bit then.'

After Reynolds had gone, Gardner looked all about the room at the simple wooden chairs and table by the fireplace,

5

and the open door into the cramped kitchen. Eventually he turned to William and studied him intently. His eye fell to his crutch, and then he noticed the book on his lap and came closer.

'What is this you are looking at?'

'It's called Kidnapped.'

'You can read it?'

'Yes.'

Gardner frowned. 'Hasn't anyone told you to address your elders as 'sir'.'

'No... sir'

'That's better. How old are you, boy?'

'Eleven....sir.'

'Will you read some of that page to me?'

William hesitated. He wished his dad would come back, but he had gone inside the forge. He began to read, and when he was halfway down the page Gardner stopped him with a gesture.

'You read well for a village boy.' He sounded faintly surprised. Even pleased.

'My mam taught me...sir.'

Gardner's expression changed. A look of pain mingled with anger flashed in his eyes. 'Do you remember your mother....William?'

'Not really, sir.'

Gardner looked disappointed. His gaze wandered, and rested on the shelves that were full of books.

'They were my mam's,' William said, sensing his interest.

Gardner went over and took one of the books down. He opened the cover and stared at the page for such a long time that William thought he'd forgotten where he was. 'Have you read very many of them?' Gardner asked finally.

'All of them, sir.'

Gardner returned the book to the shelf and came back to look more closely at William's injured leg. 'Does your leg hurt you very much?'

'Sometimes it does, sir. Especially when I do my exercise. Dad says I have to though, to make my leg strong again.'

'Can you walk for me now?'

William struggled to his feet, and with his crutch managed to limp across the room.

'Do you remember your accident?' Gardner asked when William sat down again.

'No, sir.' Sometimes though, he has a dream. He is falling under the horses hooves, and he can feel them thudding on the ground all around him. They say one struck him a glancing blow and crushed his thigh, and he was lucky it wasn't his head because if it was he would've been killed. Then the sharp metal tines of the harvester pierce his flesh. It wasn't really a memory though, it's only from what he was told afterwards. But there was one thing he remembered. One night he woke up in the hospital and found a woman sitting beside him. She stroked his hair and spoke softly to him and he recognised his mam's voice. When he told Gardner this the old man stiffened.

'What did she say to you?'

'I can't remember. Dad said it must have been a nurse.'

'Do you think he's right?'

William shook his head. 'No, sir.'

Gardner didn't stay much longer. After he said goodbye he went outside and spoke to William's dad again, before he climbed back into his buggy and drove off down the lane.

That night when they were eating their supper, William asked who Mister Gardner was.

'He's your granddad, Will. Your mam's dad.'

This news surprised William, because until then he hadn't known he had a grandfather.

'When me and her first met we lived in a place called Birmingham,' Reynolds said. 'We never told you about any of this 'cause you were too young. Your mam was rich, you see. Least her family was. I worked in a factory then. A printers it were. I looked after the machines and mended them when something broke. I was always good with my hands. I met your mam at a meeting.'

'What sort of meeting?'

'It were about politics. Your mam was a socialist.'

William wondered what a socialist was, but he didn't want to interrupt. He wanted to hear about his mam

'I were in the union, and that's how we got to know each other. After a bit we started walking out together, only she couldn't tell anybody about me.'

'Why not?' William wanted to know.

'Because I were poor. People wouldn't have liked it. Especially her family. But her dad found out in the end and he told her she couldn't see me anymore. Your mam had to decide if she wanted us to be together or if she would do what her dad wanted. She decided to stay with me, and that's why we had to move away and we came to live here.'

Reynolds got up from the table and cleared away their supper things, and then he sat by the fire and lit his pipe.

'Why did my granddad come today?' William asked. He'd been thinking over everything his dad had said, trying to work out what it meant.

'I wrote him a letter to tell him what happened to you.'

'Did you write to him when mam were sick too?'

'Yes,' Reynolds answered heavily.

'Did he come then?'

'No.'

'Why not?'

'Why are you asking these things, Will? Did he say something to you about your mam?'

'He wanted to know if I remembered her. I think he wanted me to.'

Reynolds smiled sadly. 'I 'spect you remind him of her. You take after your mam, you know.'

They didn't talk about Gardner's visit again for a week, though William could tell it was on his dad's mind. A week later a letter came. William guessed who it was from because his dad never got letters otherwise.

'Your granddad has said he'll pay for you to go to school at Oundle,' Reynolds announced at supper.

'Where's Oundle?'

'It's a town not too far away. There's a train from Brixworth.'

'But what about the school in the village?' William wanted to know.

'This is a different sort of school. It's much bigger than the one in the village. The boys live there. They eat their meals and sleep there and everything, and they go home in the holidays. You'll learn things you wouldn't ever learn in the village, and when you're grown you might even go to university, and then one day you can work in business or in a bank or even be a doctor.'

'Then won't I learn to be a blacksmith like you?' William asked. He'd always assumed this is what he would do when he was older. He could already sharpen tools and keep the furnace hot without being reminded.

'It's better for you to learn at a proper school, Will. It's what your mam would've wanted for you. She always said you were clever.'

'But I don't want to live there,' William protested. 'I won't know anybody.'

'You'll soon make friends.'

'I want to stay with you.'

'You'll come home in the holidays, Will, I promise, and then it'll be like old times. You and me. It'll be grand, you'll see.'

William blinked back his tears because he knew his dad wanted him to be happy.

Reynolds put his big, calloused hand gently on his son's shoulder. 'There you are, see. It'll be alright in the

end. I know it will.' He turned and pretended to tap his pipe
into the fire so William wouldn't see him wipe his eyes.

2

It was September when the train took them to Oundle. They passed by the River Nene, and from the carriage windows saw the town looking out over the water meadows and the fields of the surrounding farmland.

Reynolds was uncomfortable in the collar and tie he wore beneath a heavy jacket. It was a warm day. The smells of sweat and work and tobacco lingered about him, though he had filled the bathtub in front of the fire that morning and scrubbed his skin until it was raw. He gripped the rim of his hat in both hands, twisting it with fingers darkened with grime that no amount of scrubbing would remove.

William felt equally uncomfortable in his new clothes. His granddad had sent instructions about what would be needed and the name of a shop in Northampton where an account had been arranged. As well as his school uniform, William had been fitted with an entire wardrobe of clothes and shoes. He hadn't been allowed to bring any of his old things at all. Not even his socks or underwear.

They hired a cart and driver to take them up the hill. A pair of tall iron gates stood at the entrance to the school. It was the day before term began and other boys were arriving too. A motor car stopped at the foot of the steps and the driver, who wore a chauffeur's uniform and cap, went to find somebody to help unload a trunk from the back. A boy of thirteen climbed out and waved to somebody he knew.

'Hello Pritchard, how are you? It's awfully good to see you again. When did you get here?'

'I came on the train this morning. We're in the same dorm by the way, I've already checked.'

'Good show! Where's Griffin, have you seen him yet?'

'Yes he was over by the quad earlier.'

The two wandered off. It was all very strange and new to William. The boys spoke in a grown up way, and they all sounded like the boy and girl who lived at the manor in the village. Sometimes William and the other children used to climb the big chestnut tree on the green so they could see over the manor wall and watch the boy and girl playing games on the grass. If the boy saw them he would turn to his sister and say that those dirty ruffians were spying on them again, and that they ought to fetch Jones the gardener to see them off. The boy was away at school except in the holidays. William supposed he must go to a school like this one. Perhaps he might even be here, though William hoped not

Reynolds looked around for somebody to ask where William should go, and spoke to a boy of perhaps seventeen who appeared to be directing people.

The boy consulted a list, and ignoring Reynolds said to William, 'You must be a new boy. Let's see... Reynolds, yes here you are. You're in Lakston, first year dorm. It's over there, the last building by the playing fields. Have your man take your trunk over there and get yourself settled in.'

William realised that the boy thought his dad was a servant, but the boy strode off before William could correct his mistake.

'Come on, Will,' Reynolds said quietly.

When they found Lakston house, the cart driver helped to carry William's trunk to the dorm on the third floor where William would sleep. It was difficult to climb the stairs with his crutch, but eventually he managed. He passed other boys who looked at him curiously, but nobody spoke to him. The dorm was deserted. Each of the beds was surrounded by a curtain and wood panelling to form a small cubicle. Some had already been claimed. Trunks had been placed inside and in some cases partially unpacked. As Reynolds paid the cart driver, a boy of about eleven came in.

'Hello, are you a first year too?' he said to William. 'I'm Thompson, how do you do?'

William shook the proffered hand uncertainly.

'What's your name?'

'William Reynolds.'

Thompson looked at him in puzzled surprise, and William knew it was because of the way he spoke.

'We don't know which bed he should have,' Reynolds said, though it sounded much more like '*We dunt know whuch bed he should 'ave.*'

Without acknowledging Reynolds at all, Thompson addressed William directly. 'I think you can take any one you like, so long as nobody has beaten you to it.'

William decided on the one closest to the door, which appeared untouched, and his dad dragged over his chest.

'I'll help you get unpacked, Will.'

'It's alright, I can do it,' William said, aware that Thompson was watching them curiously.

'I'll say goodbye here then shall I? So you don't have to come down the stairs.'

William nodded. He didn't trust himself to speak. His throat felt tight and tears swam in his eyes. He wished more than anything in his life that his dad wouldn't leave him there.

'It will be alright, Will, you'll see,' Reynolds said. He would have liked to bend down and put his arms around his son and hold him tightly, but instead he held out his hand. 'You won't forget to write to me will you?'

William shook his head.

'I'll see you in the holidays, then.'

As soon as his dad was gone, William began to unpack his trunk. He didn't want the other boy to see the tears that were blurring his eyes.

After a minute or so, Thompson sauntered over. 'I say, Reynolds?'

He turned around. 'Yes.'

'That chap just then, who was he?'

'My dad.'

Thompson regarded him incredulously. 'Oh, I see,' he said at length.

By the end of the afternoon the dormitory had filled with boys. Some were quiet and uncertain in their new surroundings, others took it in their stride and went around introducing themselves to one another. At five o clock an elder boy, who was their dormitory prefect, came to tell them they had to go to the hall for tea. Hundreds of boys of all ages arrived at about the same time, and there was a good deal of pushing and jostling. William self-consciously negotiated his way to his dorm table with the others, aware of the attention his crutch was attracting. He noticed that Thompson avoided sitting near him, and the place next to him was taken by a thin, nervous boy.

'I'm Carmichael,' the boy said. 'What's wrong with your leg?'

'It were caught in a harvester.'

'Why are you speaking like that?' Carmichael demanded, looking puzzled.

William didn't know how to respond. He felt himself blush.

'I saw his father earlier,' Thompson said. 'I thought he was a porter at first.'

The boy next to him was intrigued. 'Who are you talking about?'

'Reynolds here.'

The boy, who was big for his age and had red hair, stared at William belligerently. 'What are you doing here if your father's a porter?'

'He isn't,' William protested.

'What is he then?'

'He's a blacksmith.'

The boy, whose name was Yardley, addressed the table in a loud indignant voice. 'I say, did you hear that? Reynolds here says his father is a blacksmith. What do you think of that?'

'Is he pulling your leg?' somebody said.

'He must be. My father wouldn't be very pleased to know they were letting common boys come here now. How can he afford it anyway?'

'It's a damn cheek if you ask me.' Yardley gave William a threatening look. 'We'll teach you a lesson later.'

'Yes, we ought to thrash the blighter,' agreed Thompson enthusiastically.

William looked in alarm at the faces all turned towards him. Carmichael shifted further along the bench.

'Do you know, I think he smells?' he said and with a smug look turned to William. 'Do you ever wash?'

The others laughed, and before William could respond they were all joining in.

'I bet he's never seen soap, have you, Reynolds you dirty little rotter?'

'His father certainly had a bit of an unpleasant whiff about him,' Thompson said.

'That's what we'll do then,' Yardley announced with authority. 'We'll give him a thorough wash afterwards.' He grinned malevolently, then picked up a slice of bread and butter and spat on it before putting it on William's plate.

William spent the rest of the meal in isolated silence. He was miserable, and felt desperately lonely. Wherever he looked he was met with sneers and hostility. Carmichael took to kicking him in the shins underneath the table, emboldened by the idea that by being cruel to William the others might not think of bullying him.

After tea was over, the younger boys were allowed an hour to themselves before they had to go to bed. William spent it alone in the dorm. He was terrified of what would happen when the others returned. He washed and put on his pyjamas, then climbed into his bed and drew the curtains around his cubicle, hoping that they would forget about him. He heard their voices when they began to return, and then the dorm prefect came and told them to hurry up. Eventually the gas was turned off, and they were left in darkness with a threat from the prefect that he would return to beat anybody who made a noise.

William lay in his bed listening to whispers in the dark. After a few minutes the curtain was pulled aside and Yardley came into his cubicle, followed by Thompson.

'Let's have a look at your leg,' he demanded.

Though Yardley was big, William had decided that he would not let himself be bullied. 'No,' he said.

'What a cheek!' Thompson said indignantly.

'I'll soon show you some manners.' Yardley grabbed William's bedclothes to try and turf him out of bed, but as he leaned over, William hit him as hard as he possibly could on his nose, and Yardley stepped back with a yelp. Blood dripped onto the floor. For a moment he was too stunned to react, but then he leapt on William and began pummelling him furiously about the ears. Though William did what he could to protect himself, it was hopeless. He tried to get up, but Thompson pushed him down again. Suddenly a voice bellowed from the door.

'What the devil is going on in here?'

When the dorm prefect lit the gas light again he was confronted with the sight of Yardley with his pyjamas covered in blood.

'What on earth happened to you?'

'It was Reynolds. He punched me on the nose.'

The prefect looked doubtfully at William.

'It's true,' Thompson chimed in. 'These common boys are all ruffians.'

'Common? What are you talking about?'

'Didn't you know? His father's a blacksmith. Ask him

to say something if you don't believe me.'

The prefect clearly didn't believe a word of it. 'What have you got to say about this nonsense Reynolds?'

William didn't answer. He knew as soon as he opened his mouth he would be condemned, but his silence made the prefect angry.

'I say, are you going to answer me, you insolent brat?'

'I told you,' Thompson said. 'They don't know how to behave. We've a stable boy at home who's just as impudent.'

'You'd better answer me, or it'll be the worse for you,' the prefect threatened. He pointed at Yardley. 'Is it true that you gave this boy a bloody nose?'

In the end William decided he had no choice. 'Yes,' he said. 'But I only did it because he tried to see my leg.' *I only did ut 'cause 'e troid to see my leg.*

The prefect regarded him with fascinated revulsion. 'Good Lord.' He fetched a stick from his room, and when he came back told William to get out of bed and bend over, but when he did, William's disability became obvious and the prefect hesitated.

'Well, I suppose I can't hit a cripple. You'd better do some extra work instead. Come and see me in the morning. The rest of you get back to bed immediately, and if I hear another sound I'll punish you all.'

As Yardley returned to his bed he scowled at William, furious that he had escaped a beating, and William knew that sooner or later Yardley would get his revenge. He spent the rest of the night unable to sleep, worried by the slightest sound. In the morning, when he got up and went to the bathroom, some of the other boys were waiting for him. Two of them seized his arms at once, and though he struggled and managed to kick one of them with his good leg he was easily overpowered, and they dragged him to the floor and pulled off his pyjama bottoms.

'Look at his leg. That's disgusting,' Yardley said and

all the boys crowded closer to examine the ridged and scarred tissue.

'He's a freak,' Thompson declared.

'He's a dirty, common, freak,' Yardley said. 'Have you cleaned your teeth, Reynolds? I bet you haven't. I expect you don't even know what a toothbrush is, do you, you disgusting oaf.'

From behind his back Yardley produced a toilet brush. He grinned as William began to struggle violently.

'Hold him tight,' he said, and grabbing William by his hair he thrust the brush at his face. William kept his mouth resolutely clamped shut and twisted his head from side even, though he could feel his hair being torn out by its roots.

'Hold him still, damn it!' Yardley said angrily, but it was no good. William bucked and twisted with all his might. Suddenly Yardley drew back his fist and thumped William hard on the side of his head. It felt like he'd been hit with a brick, and for a moment he saw specks of silver floating before his eyes, and his ears rang.

'That's better,' Yardley said, then sat down on William's chest and clamped his head between his knees and pinched his nose so that he couldn't breathe. He felt like a sack of potatoes, and William was sure that he would suffocate and die. His heart pounded and blood pulsed in his temples.

'Open up, you little peasant,' Yardley demanded, waving the brush in front of William's face.

Still William refused. Yardley's face swam and blurred before his eyes, but he decided he would rather die than surrender. But then, without even realising what he was doing, he gasped for breath, and straight away Yardley thrust the brush into his mouth and jerked it vigorously back and forth.

'This is all you're good for, Reynolds, eating a gentleman's shit.'

William gagged, and when they let him go he turned

over and vomited onto the floor, crying tears of rage and utter humiliation. And while he lay there, beaten and helpless, one by one the boys all took turns to kick his bare, pale arse.

3

The Latin master at Oundle was Mister Norris. He was a thin man with a nose like a blade, and small grey eyes which he would fix on his pupils with a withering, contemptuous stare if they displeased him in the slightest. The boys were all afraid of him.

Norris disliked being a schoolmaster, and disliked his pupils even more. In his youth he had studied classics and philosophy at Oxford, and dreamt of becoming a great poet. In his final year, however, his father died owing a great deal of money. Norris found himself without the means that he'd imagined would always allow him to live comfortably without the necessity of having to work for an income. He became a school master instead of a poet, briefly convincing himself of the worthiness of teaching the classics to boys who reminded him of a younger version of himself. But a failed romance and disillusionment with school life made him bitter. Instead of seeking some other means of making a living, he became increasingly resentful at the change in his circumstances, and as he became older whatever redeeming qualities he might once have had became atrophied. He hated the world.

As the first year boys filed silently into his class he stood beside his desk and regarded them with a cold glare. They kept their eyes lowered and walked briskly, but without hurrying, to their allotted desks. The last of them closed the door behind him and joined the others waiting for permission to sit down. Norris looked over them, ready to pounce on any boy who had dared come to his lesson improperly attired. His gaze lingered on William, who stood with his crutch at his side. That wretch, he thought! That he should be forced to endure a village dolt studying Horace and Virgil. It was an insult.

'Sit,' he commanded.

The boys obeyed, but the scraping of chairs against the floor irritated Norris intensely and he scowled at Yardley, who, it seemed to Norris, made more noise than was necessary. It gave him a small measure of satisfaction that the boy visibly paled and averted his eyes.

Norris went to the chalkboard and wrote a line from Horace's Odes. *Dulce et decorum est pro patria mori*. He turned to the boys who were now sitting with their hands clasped on their desks, looking at what he'd written. They were like statues, none of them moving so much as a muscle in case he should pick them out.

'Reynolds,' he said, 'be so kind as to translate the phrase to English.'

William stared at the words on the board and desperately attempted to make sense of them from the rudiments of Latin grammar he'd managed to learn during his first weeks at Oundle.

'I am waiting,' Norris prompted impatiently.

But the little William had learned, fled from his mind. The complexities of noun declensions, verb conjugations, and of ablatives of means or manner or absolute, meant nothing to him.

'What is the tense, boy?' Norris demanded. 'Surely even you can tell us that.'

'The tense, sir?'

'Yes the tense! You know what that is, don't you? They must teach you something at a village school. There are only three possibilities for goodness sake.'

'We wasn't taught any Latin, sir,' William mumbled. *We wasn't tart any Latin, soir.*

'Weren't, Reynolds! The subject is plural. Of course you weren't taught Latin, you dolt! What on earth would a farm boy need with Latin? Unless, perhaps, you rear an extraordinarily educated breed of pig.' Norris looked around at the other boys, wearing a thin, sarcastic smile, inviting them to enjoy his mockery. 'I am referring to English grammar, boy.' He fixed his eye on Yardley. 'You boy, be so kind as to enlighten our ill-educated friend in the mysteries of tense.'

'Sir?'

'Tense, boy! For goodness sake, it is not a difficult question. There are three of them! What are they?'

'Past, present and future, sir,' Yardley stammered as understanding dawned.

'Precisely. Now, Reynolds, surely even you can discern which of those applies in this case.' Norris strode to the board and took up a short cane which he used to point at the fourth word. 'What is this?'

'Est,' William said. *Ust*.

Norris rolled his eyes. 'Est Reynolds! The word is est. You are not in the fields now, boy. And what does it mean?'

Silence. Norris advanced on him, his gown flapping like crows' wings. He rapped his cane down hard on William's desk, making him flinch.

'Get up, boy! Get up and come here!'

William obeyed, limping on his crutch to the board, where Norris made him face the rest of the class.

'The phrase translates as; "It is sweet and becoming to die for one's country." It is. Present tense. Repeat it, Reynolds.'

William did as he was told, though he didn't sound anything like Norris. *'Ut is sweet und becoming to doi fer one's country,'*

At the stifled sniggers from the other boys, William's face burned with humiliation. Norris muttered furiously under his breath, as if to himself, though loudly enough for

22

the entire class to hear.

'Good Lord, listen to him. Am I meant to perform miracles?' Out loud he said, 'Do you understand what it means, Reynolds?'

But William didn't. Tears pricked his eyes and his throat was tight, strangling his voice.

'Horace is speaking of honour and duty to one's country, noble sentiments that extend far beyond the notion of the individual. I don't expect you to comprehend the subtle beauty of the idea, Reynolds, such things are beyond a person of your class. However it has fallen to me to drum into your cabbage-like brain some knowledge of the Latin language, though what good it will do you is beyond me. Hold out your hand.'

William obeyed, and Norris raised his cane and brought it down sharply three times, each stroke causing a vivid red welt to appear. It irritated him that William uttered no sound, even though Norris hit him harder with every stroke. Frustrated by his stubbornness, Norris ordered William to take a chair and sit in the corner with his back to the class. 'And before you return to this classroom, you will write the phrase with its English translation a hundred times.'

With difficulty, William dragged his chair from his desk, and for the remainder of the lesson the room was silent except for the scratch of nibs against paper as the other boys faithfully copied down a translation of a passage from Ovid's Metamorphoses.

*****

During the week the boys attended chapel within the confines of the school, but on Sundays they went to morning services at St Peter's church by the market square. The sonorous tones of Reverend Beamish filled the great empty space above the stone arches on either side of the nave. He was preaching a sermon, reminding the congregation of the love of Christ for mankind, and emphasising that it was the duty of all men to do unto others as they would have others do unto them. William had quickly realised that God and duty were themes that often cropped up at Oundle.

The masters sat apart from the boys, and as the Reverend's sermon continued, William's thoughts wandered. He found himself watching Mister Watson, who was the youngest master at the school. He taught English language and literature and came from Edinburgh, though you wouldn't have guessed it from looking at him. Though he was British by birth it was rumoured that his father was Indian, from Calcutta. His skin was quite dark.

Mister Watson was unlike his fellow masters in ways other than his appearance. He was quietly spoken and seemed to enjoy teaching. During his classes he encouraged the boys to ask questions and was happy to wander from the text of whatever they were studying if a discussion arose, something Mister Norris would never have done. He told them that he wanted them to learn the skills required for intelligent debate, an idea which he had once joked was quite probably considered anathema to some people. William had looked up the word anathema in the dictionary later to see what it meant, and when he found it he wondered if Mister Watson might have been talking about Mister Norris.

William had noticed that Mister Watson was hardly ever seen with the other masters outside of the necessities of his school duties. He had the feeling that the other masters regarded Mister Watson with vague suspicion, as if he was a slightly exotic but unpredictable curiosity.

The sermon ended and the reverend announced that they would sing hymn number forty seven. The first dusty notes of Come All Ye Faithful wheezed from the organ, but as the congregation rose to their feet the boy next to William shoved him with his elbow so that William staggered and almost fell. As William steadied himself, Mister Norris glared at him, an angry flush rising in his cheeks.

After the service, the boys trooped outside into the cold. The masters stood with their wives, chatting pleasantly in small groups, though Mister Watson lingered on their periphery. As the boys filed past, Norris fixed his eye on William, limping along the path towards the gate. Norris waited until William had almost reached it before he called out to him.

'Reynolds!' he barked. 'Come here, boy!'

Slowly, William limped the twenty yards back along the path, past the smirking grins of the other boys.

'Why were you were playing the fool during the service,' Norris demanded.

'Excuse me, sir, but I weren't playing the fool, sir,' William replied.

'Wasn't, Reynolds! The subject is singular. Your grammatical butchering aside, however, you certainly were playing the fool. I saw you with my own eyes, or do you think I'm blind, you impudent oaf?'

'No, sir.'

'No sir, what?'

'I don't think you're blind, sir.'

'Indeed?' Norris said scathingly. 'Then you think I'm a fool?'

'No, sir.'

'But you must think I'm a fool if you believe you can deceive me when I clearly saw you larking about with my own eyes.'

William felt trapped, certain that whatever he said would be twisted and used against him.

'Answer me, boy! Do you think me a fool?'

'No, sir.'

'Then you are calling me a liar!' Norris declared with glittering malice. 'But I suppose we should expect no better from you. It seems to me that we cannot make a gentleman out of a turnip. Nevertheless, we must do our best. You will translate the first one hundred lines from book one of Virgil's Aeneid by tomorrow morning.'

'Yes, sir,' William replied with his eyes downcast.

As Norris returned to join his fellow masters, William followed the other boys back to the school. He knew he was incapable of carrying out the task he'd been set, though he would spend the only free day of the week trying, and in the morning his failure would earn him six strokes of the cane. He had almost reached the school gates when somebody called his name.

'Reynolds!'

He turned around to see that Mister Watson was behind him. 'Yes, sir?'

'I wondered where you're off to.'

'The library, sir.'

Watson smiled as he fell into step beside him. 'I see. To translate from Virgil for Mister Norris I expect?'

'Yes, sir.'

'I think I've something that might help you with that in my rooms. There's a fire lit so it should be warm, and I daresay I could manage a cup of tea if you'd like?'

William wasn't sure if he had heard correctly. 'Sir?'

'I'm offering to help you, Reynolds,' Watson said kindly. 'But of course the decision is entirely yours. I shan't be offended if you prefer to decline. What do you say?'

'Thank you, sir,' William managed to say. 'I mean, I'd like it if you could help me.'

'Good. Come along then.'

Like most of the masters, Mister Watson lived on the school grounds. When they reached his rooms, he invited William to have a seat beside the fire. 'Mrs Hedges usually looks after me, but I have to fend for myself on Sundays I'm afraid. Still, I think I can manage a cup of tea and a plate of biscuits.'

He left William, alone promising to return in a few

minutes. While he was gone, William looked at the paintings that hung on the walls. There were several Scottish landscapes done in watercolour, the empty hills purple with heather. There were also numerous paintings of different types of birds. He got up and looked closer at one of a kingfisher. Every feather on its back seemed to have been individually painted, the colours delicately bleeding from slate grey to turquoise, the eyes bright and sharp with life. He wandered about the room looking at Mister Watson's things. There were shelves full of books, many of them ornithological, but there were also novels and poetry in English, and others in Greek and Latin.

'Do you enjoy reading, William?' Watson said as he returned with a tray which he put down on a small table.

'I used to, sir.'

'You mean you don't anymore. Why not?'

'There's no time to read, sir.'

'Surely you have time to yourself after you've done your prep?'

'It takes me longer than the other boys,' William said. 'There's lots they didn't teach us at my other school.'

'Ah, yes, I see. Like Latin you mean?'

'Yes, sir.'

'Sit down and have your tea.' Watson offered a plate of biscuits, and told William to help himself. He took down a leather bound book from a shelf. 'This is The Aeneid,' he said. 'You'll find it contains both the original Latin version of Virgil's epic, and also John Dryden's English translation. 'The first one hundred lines, I believe Mister Norris said.' He put the book down on the table and winked. 'I think you'll find this useful.'

William looked through the pages, both pleased and astonished.

'I think,' Mister Watson added, 'that it might be wise to make one or two deliberate errors. Just so that you don't arouse Mister Norris's suspicion. You can stay here and copy it out this afternoon if you like. It will be quite peaceful as I usually go for a walk on Sunday afternoons. Have you ever been to Fotheringhay?'

'No, sir.'

'It's a village about four miles from here. There used to be a castle there, though now there's only a mound left where it stood. A pair of hobbies were nesting in a hollow tree by the river during the summer.' Watson fetched a watercolour he'd done of a pair of the little falcons. 'I'm something of a birdwatcher in my spare time as you can see. There's a path that follows the river, you know. It's quite a pleasant walk if you ever feel like doing it.'

'I can't walk very far because of my leg, sir.' *Oi carnt wark very far because of moi leg.*

'Of course, I'm sorry, I forgot.' Mister Watson regarded William thoughtfully. 'This painting reminds me of my summer holidays,' he said. 'I spent several weeks watching another pair of hobbies near my parents' house in Scotland. I used to take long walks every day, whether it was fine or wet. I always took my sketch pad and binoculars with me.'

William didn't know what to say to this, though Mister Watson didn't seem to mind his silence.

'Do you know, William, my father is a Hindu,' he went on. 'You don't mind if I call you by your Christian name do you? And you must call me Mister Watson rather than 'sir' all the time. Do you know what Hindu is, by the way? It's a type of religion practised in India where my father comes from.' Watson paused to light a cigarette.

'I was quite a lonely child at school. The other boys made fun of me because of the colour of my skin. They called me a half-breed. That's why I became interested in bird-watching. It was a way of escaping, if you like.'

William understood that Mister Watson was telling him that they had something in common. It made him feel better to know that he wasn't quite as alone as he had thought.

'I would like to propose something to you, William,' Watson said. 'I suggest that you come here every day for extra tuition. I will teach you the things that the other boys have already learnt. That is to say, I will give you lessons in English grammar and also Latin and Greek. I think you'll find that you will catch up with the other boys quite quickly. Between you and I, there are no geniuses among them.' He smiled. 'The other thing I will teach you is how to speak like them. It will take time, but I'm sure that if we are both prepared to put in the effort we will succeed. What do you think?'

A clock on the table ticked.

'Thank you, sir,' William answered. 'I'd like that.'

'Good,' Watson said. 'Now, why don't you have another biscuit.'

*****

William's life at Oundle changed. Every day after lessons ended he went to Mister Watson's rooms for extra tuition, where for half an hour he practiced his elocution, and then for another hour either English grammar or Latin and Greek. Mister Watson was a patient teacher and William looked forward to his lessons. The young master's rooms became a kind of sanctuary where William could escape the taunts and bullying of Yardley and the other boys. The process of learning itself was an escape from his misery. He became interested in the wider scope of the subjects he was learning. He not only wanted to be able to translate the Latin poets and Greek philosophers, but wanted to understand them too, and in Mister Watson's rooms, William's love of reading English novels was rekindled.

The speed with which William improved surprised both himself and his teacher. Encouraged by his success, William practiced alone whenever he could, and for once his disability worked to his advantage since it precluded him from fagging, and gave him more time than he might otherwise have had. He spent it in the library, where he absorbed everything he read.

As the weeks passed and William gradually lost his country burr, he noticed that he was less often the victim of derision and bullying because of the way he spoke. He began to think that with determination and work there was nothing he couldn't overcome, and one afternoon Mister Watson discovered him trying to walk without his crutch. William was unaware that he was being watched until he fell to the floor as he tried to take a few steps across the master's living room. He got up and reached for his crutch, burning with humiliation and anger at his own weakness.

Mister Watson put down the tea tray he was carrying and left the room, returning a few moments later with a cane.

'Would you like to try with this?' he offered.

He cleared a space between two chairs, and when William tried again, this time he didn't fall down.

'You can keep it if you like,' Mister Watson said. He took William's crutch and leaned it against the wall. 'Why don't we leave this here, and then you'll know where it is anytime you want it. Now, shall we have some tea before we get back to Virgil?'

From that day, William began to take daily walks around the school grounds using his new cane. Though progress was initially slow, he endured the muscle cramps and blisters that formed on his feet, and ignored the cruel mockery of the other boys. At first it didn't seem to make any difference. In fact the pain and swelling he suffered made walking more difficult than ever, but he persisted. Sometimes at night he cried silently in his bed, something that Yardley and Thompson and the others had never been able to make him do. The pain became so terrible that Mister Watson was afraid that he would do permanent damage to himself. He tried to persuade William that he should relent, at least for a little while, but stubbornly William refused. Eventually, by small degrees, he began to notice an improvement, though rather than welcome the easing of his discomfort, William's response was to ask Mister Watson if he would give him permission to leave the school grounds so that he could lengthen his daily walks.

'I want to see if I can get as far as Fotheringhay by the end of term,' William explained.

'But it will take you hours to walk that far,' Mister Watson said. 'Where will you find the time?'

'I can go early in the morning,' said William, having already thought it through.

Mister Watson was dubious, concerned that William was pushing himself too hard on all fronts, but he agreed to speak to his house master. In the end, since physical ability was admired at least as much, if not more than academic prowess at the school, permission was given. For the rest of the term William got out of his warm bed at half past four every morning and went out into the freezing dark. He walked down through the town to the path along the river that led eventually to Fotheringhay, increasing the distance a little bit every day. He steeled himself against the frequent cold and the wind and rain. Since he was used to being alone the solitude didn't concern him at all, and by degree he was rewarded as his leg became stronger with every passing week.

Towards the middle of December, William received a Christmas card from his grandfather. Inside was a short note expressing the hope that William was working hard at his studies and reminding him that his mother would have wanted him to do his very best, and that he should endeavour to do justice to her memory. Before term ended and the boys went home for the Christmas holidays, Mister Watson gave William a copy of Homer's Odyssey translated into English.

'It's the story of Odysseus. After the Trojan wars he

struggled for many years against great hardships to return to his kingdom of Ithaca. I think you might enjoy it, William. It seems to me that you share Odysseus's spirit.'

'Thank you, Mister Watson.'

Inside was written; *For William, happy Christmas from your friend E. Watson.* He turned the book over in his hands. It was bound in dark blue leather with gold lettering, the pages inside crisp and white. It had a distinct smell of libraries; of learning and history, and immediately the book became William's most treasured possession. He vowed that he would keep it always, and that one day he would fill an entire room of the large house he would live in with other books just like it, though this one would always hold a special place. He felt that the packet of tobacco that he had bought for Mister Watson was a poor gift in comparison, though his teacher seemed very pleased and surprised.

'Enjoy your holiday, William. I'll see you when you come back,' he said as they shook hands.

The following day, William caught the train to Brixworth and was met at the station by his father, who hugged him tightly and said that he was glad that he was home. The familiar smells of his father's clothes evoked a sudden, unexpected welling of homesickness. There in his father's strong embrace was the forge with its smoky heat, the ring of hammer on red hot iron and the stamp of a horse's hoof, the snap of meadow grass underfoot and the dew frozen white by a hoar frost. There were the scents of the cottage too, of the stove in the kitchen where a rabbit or pigeon cooked in the oven, the sweet tang of hops from a glass of beer his father drank after his work and the smell of the pipe tobacco he smoked by the fire.

When they parted, William tried to hide his tears, but his father's eyes were as wet as his own and they sniffed and laughed at one another with awkward love.

'You've grown, Will,' Reynolds said when he could look properly at his son and then his brow creased in puzzlement. 'Where's your crutch?'

'I can manage with a cane now,' William told him proudly. 'At least for a little way. My leg feels much stronger.'

He explained his regime of walking, and talked about the encouragement Mister Watson had given him. As he spoke, William's father looked increasingly bemused until in the end William had to ask what was wrong with him.

'It's how you talk, Will. You sound like a proper gentleman already. Your mam'd be proud as can be if she heard you.' He smiled, though there was a shade of sadness in his eyes too.

On the way back to the village in the cart, William answered his father's questions about the school, elaborating on what he had already told him in his letters. He said that he was doing well in his classes, though Latin and Greek were difficult. He had a lot to catch up on, as the other boys already knew quite a lot, though he was getting better now that Mister Watkins was helping him.

'Who are your friends, Will? You never write about them,' his father wanted to know.

'Oh, there are lots of them. All the boys in my dorm. There's Thompson of course, you met him when you took me to Oundle on my first day, and then there's Carmichael and Yardley, they're in my dorm too.'

His father seemed reassured, and if he noticed that William never mentioned any of their names again during the holidays he didn't say anything. After he'd painted a rosy picture of his life at the school, William asked all about the village and his friends, and how things were at the forge, and for the rest of the journey they didn't speak about Oundle again.

William could hardly wait to see the cottage. During the months he'd been away it was the thought of home that he'd clung to when he felt most miserable, but when they came around the corner and through the gate he felt vaguely disappointed, though he wasn't sure why. Nothing had changed. A broken wheel stood leaning against the wall, half of one of its spokes missing, just where it had been the day he left. A corner of the thatch still needed repairing, and there was a puddle in the yard where a pothole needed to be filled. He was glad to be home, but the cottage bore a faint air of neglect that he'd never noticed before.

He went inside while his father saw to the horse. A fire was lit and the room was warm, and something was cooking on the stove. His mother's books were on the shelves against the wall, and the scarred table where they ate their meals was where it had always been. William thought of his father there alone while he was away at school, imagined him reading the letters he wrote. Walking to the pub in the village in the dark to find the warmth of company.

The following morning after breakfast, William told his father he was going to walk into the village. His father looked doubtful, but William assured him he could manage. He took his cane, and all the way there he imagined how surprised his friends would be when they saw him. He went to the cottage where Jim Coleman lived and found him and some of the other boys throwing stones at some jars they had put on the wall. When they saw William they stopped what they were doing.

'I thought you were livin' at that posh school,' Jim said.

'Yes I am, but everybody goes home at the end of term.'

The boys all looked at him silently. He wondered what was wrong with them because they were so quiet.

'Where's your crutch then?' Jim asked.

'I can manage without it now. For a bit anyway.' He demonstrated by walking a little way along the lane. When he turned around the boys were smirking and nudging one another.

'I say chaps, I can manage without it now,' Jim

suddenly said, parodying William's new way of talking. He began to walk with a grossly exaggerated limp, one shoulder down, the knuckle almost trailing on the ground. The others laughed cruelly, and in a moment they were all trying to outdo one another while William's face burned with confusion and the pain of being rejected by boys he thought were his friends. When Jim came close to him, all the humiliation William had endured over the past months erupted in anger. He lashed out with his fist and caught Jim in the mouth, splitting his lip. In a second they were rolling on the hard, cold ground, throwing punches and kicking one another while the other boys crowded round egging them on.

'Get 'im, Jim!'

'Garn, smash 'is face!'

Finally, a woman came out of her house and chased them off. Jim and the other boys ran away. They called William a 'snot-nosed bastard' and threatened to get him if they caught him in the village again.

'Bugger off back to yer posh school.'

William remembered how they used to climb the chestnut tree by the manor wall and shout the same insults at the boy and his sister when the boy threatened to set the gardener on them.

After the fight with Jim Coleman, William spent the rest of the holiday with his father. He helped him in the forge and went for long walks in the woods. They set snares for rabbits and shot pigeons and pheasants to cook for their supper, and in the evenings while his father smoked his pipe, William read The Odyssey, or studied Latin grammar.

When it was time for William to return to school his father hitched the horse to the cart, and they drove to the train station in Brixworth. Neither of them spoke very much. On the platform they hugged one another tightly. When the train pulled away, William opened the window and waved until his father was out of sight. He felt as if he was leaving one life behind and returning to another, but he was no longer sure to which of them he really belonged. As the carriage swayed and the wheels rattled on the tracks with a hypnotic rhythm, he wondered what it would be like to stay on the train and never get off. And then before long he saw the spire of St Peter's, and apprehension formed a tight ball in the pit of his stomach.

In the dorm, on the evening of the boys' return to school, Yardley grew bored with tormenting Carmichael, who had quickly become a victim because he could be relied on to blub and beg for mercy. When William went to the bathroom, Yardley was sitting on one of the basins as if it were a throne.

'I think we neglected you a bit last term, Reynolds, you despicable little peasant,' he said unpleasantly as two other boys grabbed William's arms. 'We don't want you to forget your place, after all.' He slid down and adopted an arrogant pose, his hands in his pockets. 'By the way, what is your place, Reynolds?'

As always William refused to speak, which did not surprise Yardley, who expected nothing more. Yardley grinned. 'I say, you chaps, it seems we're just in time, Reynolds has forgotten already.'

'Gosh, we'd better remind him then hadn't we?' Thompson piped up, taking his cue.

They began to drag William towards a toilet cubicle, and though he struggled as much as he possibly could it was no good. He lashed out with his feet, but they had learned to keep well clear of him now and his attempts were ineffectual. As he was dragged by an open cubicle he glimpsed Carmichael inside, sitting on the floor crying. His hair was soaking wet and he was naked, his thin, pale body smeared with shit.

When they reached the next cubicle William redoubled his efforts to escape, or at least to inflict injury on one of his tormentors. Yardley put a meaty arm around his neck and squeezed tightly, bending him towards the toilet bowl where a large turd floated in the water.

'I saved this for you especially, Reynolds,' Yardley said.

He and the other boys thrust William's head into the bowl. William screwed his eyes shut and held his breath. His heart pounded and he heard the rush of blood in his ears. Just when he thought he would suffocate, they pulled him out gasping for air.

'Yum yum, eh Reynolds,' Yardley gloated. 'I expect that reminds you of having your dinner at home doesn't it?'

They went off laughing among themselves, while William wiped the shit from his face. He threw up every morsel in his stomach, retching until his stomach ached and his throat was raw. Eventually he cleaned himself up, and when he went back into the dorm he went straight to Yardley's cubicle. When Thompson nudged him, Yardley turned around and was surprised when he saw William.

'What do you want, Reynolds? I say, chaps, perhaps he's come for his pudding.'

They all laughed, but then William bunched his fist and hit Yardley on his chin with every ounce of strength he could muster. The force of the blow snapped Yardley's head back and knocked him onto the floor. For an instant there was stunned silence, and then with a bellow of pained rage Yardley leapt to his feet and threw himself at William with a flurry of fists and feet. The fight was over quickly, and Yardley's size and weight combined with William's lack of agility meant William didn't stand a chance. Nevertheless, he managed to land one or two decent punches and at the end of it they both had bloody noses.

After that Yardley and the other boys contented themselves with snide insults where William was concerned.

4

1908

At five o'clock in the morning the course of the river could only be discerned by the trees along its banks. They stood gaunt and grey above the mist veiling the water meadows below the town.

Pausing to lift his gaze to the lightening sky, William watched a hobby, one of a pair that nested nearby each year. He remembered a painting Mister Watson had done of one of them, though it has been three years since Watson left the school. The little falcon rose with rapid wing beats, searching for an unwary blackbird or thrush and was lost from sight.

William began to run down the hill. At seventeen he was tall and lean. To begin with he favoured his left leg very slightly, but as he settled into a familiar rhythm this became less obvious, so that a casual observer would not even register it. Nowadays, it is only in the winter when there is a particularly cold spell that he feels an ache deep in his thigh that will cause him to limp, and very occasionally he has to use a cane for support.

He climbed a stile to the path that led across a field to the river. There was nobody else about. Sometimes he would see a figure herding cows to the milking shed, or later in the year when there was hay to be cut or crops to harvest he would see people working in the fields, but they are only distant glimpses. He had followed this route every morning since his first term at the school all those years ago now, though of course he could barely walk then. It was the solitude he liked more than anything.

As William descended to the meadow the mist cloaked him from the world. The grass was wet with dew. An animal dashed in front of him, a blur of brown fur, perhaps a hare or even a fox. When he reached the river the mist was thick between the reeds along the bank. His breath clouded before him. A pair of stately swans appeared gliding silently on the water and vanished again, like pale ghosts.

By the time he reached the ruins of Fotheringhay castle the temperature had risen and the mist was lifting, though a few shrouds still lingered around the mound. Sometimes, William imagined he could feel vibrations in the atmosphere, a humming below the pitch at which things could be heard or felt in the ordinary sense. Mary, Queen of Scotland, had been imprisoned in the castle a little over three hundred years ago, and eventually she was exectued there. Did such things somehow leave their indelible mark on the fabric of time and space? An imprint of melancholy, the extremes of the range of human feeling. It was said that when the castle was demolished the staircase was used in the Talbot Hotel, and that Mary's ghost has been seen walking down them on the way to her execution. William had seen a figure on the mound more than once. He was sure it was a woman. She stood gazing out across the field, though he sensed she couldn't see him. An aura of loneliness surrounded the place, a feeling he understood.

He turned away and began the run back towards the town, where the spire of St Peter's was visible for miles around, pointing towards heaven, if there was one.

Before he reached the square he passed a large Georgian house built from the local stone. He paused and bent down on one knee, pretending to tie a loose lace. He saw a figure looking out from a window on the uppermost floor. Her name was Emmaline, a girl of sixteen with long chestnut coloured hair and wide, dark eyes. He had seen her several times about the town before he'd spoken to her in the cake shop one day. She knew he ran along the river every morning and she was always at her window when he came back. He raised a hand to her and she waved in return. When he stood up he felt as if he could run on air, and he sprinted the rest of the way back to the school.

On Sunday afternoon, William saw Emmaline walking across the square. He caught up with her and asked where she was going.

'I was bored indoors, so I decided to come out for a walk.'

'Can I walk with you?'

She smiled. 'If you'd like to.'

When they reached the church gates, Emmaline suggested they take the path through the churchyard. There were few people about and they walked slowly.

'Where's your aunt today?' William asked.

'She's gone to visit Mister Barnes and his wife. I didn't want to go so I told her I wasn't feeling well.'

Emmaline lived with her father and his sister. Her mother had died when she was young.

'Is your father at home?'

'No, he's away on business,' Emmaline said.

'If you're not in a hurry then,' William suggested, 'we could sit and talk for a little while if you like.' He gestured to a seat.

'My father would be furious if he knew I was here alone with you.'

'I'm sorry. I don't want to get you into any trouble.'

'Well, I suppose it'll be alright. You are an Oundle boy, after all.' She smiled to show that she was teasing him. 'Anyway, I don't care what he thinks.'

It was the first time they had been alone. They sat a foot apart from one another.

'I expect you're going home for Easter aren't you?'

Emmaline said.

'Yes.'

'Where do you live?'

'In a village called Scaldwell.'

'Do you like living there?'

'There isn't much there really.'

'Where will you live when you finish at Oundle?'

'I'll be going to Oxford.'

'You're lucky,' Emmaline said. 'My father doesn't approve of girls attending university. He wouldn't even let me go away to school. Instead I've had to put up with Mister Willis. He's my tutor. What will you be studying at Oxford?'

'I haven't decided yet. Perhaps law.'

'Is your father a barrister?'

'No.' William faltered. He didn't want to tell her that his father was a blacksmith. 'Actually it was my grandfather's idea. He lives in Birmingham.'

He told Emmaline that his grandfather owned several businesses, and that he'd advised William to study law because it provided a sound basis for almost any career. He knew he was giving the impression that he was much closer to his grandfather than was really the case. In fact, William only saw him twice a year, and always felt that his grandfather's visits were undertaken more in the spirit of somebody who was keeping an eye on his investment than for any other reason. However, when William was offered a scholarship to Oxford his grandfather had promised to provide an allowance to enable him to take it up, and for that, William was grateful.

'I wish I could get away from here,' Emmaline said enviously. 'It's even worse during the holidays. The town seems so quiet and empty.'

She looked away, her face shaded by her hat. William thought she was beautiful. 'I wish I could stay here,' he said.

'Why on earth would you wish that?'

'Because while I'm away I'll miss you.'

'Will you really?'

'I think about you all the time. When I go for a run in the morning I can't wait to get back, just so that I can see you in your window.'

'I always make sure I get out of bed early and wait for you,' she confessed.

They laughed at themselves. He longed to touch her, just to hold her hand. If he could do that, he thought he'd be happy to sit there for ever. Neither of them spoke. William's mind was completely blank. He couldn't think of anything at all to say to her and was sure she would think he was a fool. All the time his heart was pounding so hard he thought she must be able to hear it. Suddenly she made a frustrated sound and turned away from him a little.

'What is it?' he asked.

'You must think I'm an idiot!'

'Why?'

'Because we're alone at last and I can't even carry on a conversation. I've dreamed about being together like this, just the two of us, and now it's happened and I can't think of a single word to say.'

He was almost delirious with happiness to hear her say that she had dreamed of being with him. 'I was thinking the same thing myself. I was afraid that you must be trying to think of an excuse to leave. I've never met anybody like you,' he told her. 'Or felt like this.' He wanted to kiss her, and as he looked into her eyes he was sure she felt the same way. He leaned towards her and as she closed her eyes their lips met for a few moments.

When they parted, somebody came along the path and they moved away from each other. William longed to kiss her again, but he was afraid they would be seen.

'Shall we find somewhere else to sit?' he asked.

'If you like.'

They got up and followed a path towards the back of

the graveyard, where the bushes and trees grew thickly near the wall. They paused to read an old, worn gravestone.

'I'm sorry,' Emmaline said eventually. 'I don't know how you should kiss somebody. I've never done it before.'

'I don't know how to either. But I do know there's nothing I'd rather do than kiss you again.'

William placed his hands on Emmaline's waist. She turned her face up to him and closed her eyes, and this time they kissed for longer. He was overwhelmed with feeling for her, drowning in sensations of touch and smell and he moved closer, drawing her against him. She acquiesced willingly. When at last they parted, they held one another tightly, breathless with emotion.

Later, when he walked her home, he thought of the holidays coming up and wondered how he would stand to be away from her.

Near her house they parted. 'I'll write to you every day,' he said but she told him he mustn't.

'My father doesn't know anything about you. When you come back we'll think of a way for you to meet my aunt, and then you can come to the house and meet my father.'

William's spirits sank.

'What is it?' she asked.

'I'm not sure your father would approve of me.'

'What do you mean? Why shouldn't he?'

Suddenly, he didn't know what to tell her. Every perception she had of him was wrong. No doubt she imagined he came from a reasonably well-to-do village family, that his father was perhaps a doctor or something. How would she react when she discovered that he was the penniless son of a blacksmith? And what would her father think?

William was ashamed of himself for concealing the truth. He was certain that Emmaline wouldn't care about his background. After all, he would have a degree from Oxford one day, and then he would be able to begin a respectable career. Perhaps once her father met him and saw what sort of person he was he wouldn't care where he came from. He decided that he would tell Emmaline the truth about himself, but he would wait until he had the time to explain everything to her properly.

'I simply mean that I shouldn't think any father approves of a fellow his daughter wants him to meet,' William joked.

'Well, he'll just have to get used to the idea,' Emmaline laughed.

*****

During their final two years at Oundle the boys were given a room of their own. William's was small, just large enough for a narrow bed and a desk at which to study. A few days before the Easter holidays there was a knock at the door, and when he opened it a third year boy told him that there was a gentleman to see him.

When he went to the office where the daily running of the school was managed, he was asked to wait. Shortly a man in his forties emerged from the headmaster's rooms.

'Ah, there you are Reynolds.' The headmaster turned to his guest. 'I'll leave you to introduce yourself, shall I?'

'Yes, thank you.'

The man regarded William curiously for a moment. There was no warmth in his expression.

'This is rather a strange situation, William,' he said. 'My name is Mark Gardner. I'm your uncle. Your headmaster tells me the library is generally empty at this time of day. Why don't you show me where it is and we can talk there.'

In the library they sat at a reading table beside the window. William was still trying to get used to the idea that he had an uncle.

'I imagine this has come as something of a surprise to you,' Gardner said.

'Yes, sir, it has.'

'I take it my father... your grandfather, didn't discuss his family with you?'

'No, sir.'

'I see. Well, your mother was my sister. You take after her in your looks,' Gardner said. 'My father said that you did. In fact, he's the reason that I'm here. I'm afraid I have some rather bad news. Your grandfather died last month.'

Though he couldn't claim to have had any great feeling for his grandfather, William was surprised at the effect his uncle's news had. His grandfather had been a tangible connection to the memory of his mother, and his death already seemed to make her more distant. William realised his uncle was watching his reaction, and he put his own feelings aside, remembering that Gardner had lost his father. 'I'm very sorry for your loss,' he said.

'Thank you.'

An awkward silence fell between them. Gardner looked about the room. 'This place reminds me of my own schooldays. Your headmaster tells me that you've done very well here. I understand you've been offered a scholarship to go up to Oxford. Have you decided what you would like to study?'

'Your father suggested law.'

'Did he? You wish to become a solicitor?'

'I'm not certain. But your father thought that a law degree would be a good basis for whatever career I choose.'

'I see. And will your scholarship cover all your expenses?'

'No, I would need money to live on. Your father had generously promised me an allowance.'

'He told you that?'

'Yes.' William began to feel uneasy about his uncle's questions, wondering where they were leading.

45

Gardner got up and stood looking out of the window. 'My father didn't come here very often did he?'

'I saw him twice a year.'

'Did you love him, William?'

William hesitated, uncertain how to answer or why the question had been asked. In the end he could only answer truthfully. 'I hardly knew him, but I've always been very grateful for everything he's done for me.'

'At least you're honest,' Gardner commented. 'Tell me, have you enjoyed your time at Oundle?'

'I don't know that I would use that term.'

'What term would you use then?'

'If I hadn't come here there's a great deal I would never have had the opportunity to learn. I'm glad that I've had that opportunity.'

'I understand that your first year was very difficult. Your headmaster told me the other boys gave you something of a bad time because of your background and so on.'

'I suppose some of them made fun of me for a while,' William admitted at which his uncle gave a thin smile.

'I expect it was a little more than that. Your headmaster holds you in quite high regard you know. He considers you to be intelligent and exceptionally determined. On the other hand he says you have never made friends here. That you are a solitary type. I went to a boarding school myself, William. Even at the best schools young boys are savages beneath it all. They gang together against the weak. Especially those they perceive as being different in some way. Would you say you've really fitted in here, William? I know you've done well with your studies, but I mean in other respects.'

'I'm not sure what you mean.'

'School isn't only about getting an education. It's about forming bonds... friendships, with people of one's own type. The sort of network that can help you in later life, both socially and with one's career. Without those bonds one has to wonder if it was really a good idea to send you here. I may as well tell you I was against it. My father felt obliged to do something for you because you were my sister's child, but I believe that she made her choice when she turned her back on the family. He agreed I think, but he always had a soft spot where my sister was concerned. A blind spot, perhaps I should say.'

Gardner's tone was resentful, and William wondered if his uncle had been jealous of his sister. He didn't say anything, knowing that he wasn't expected to.

'You should know that before my father died he made provision in his will for your education to continue here until you leave at the end of next term, so you needn't worry about that,' Gardner continued. 'However, there was no mention of an allowance to enable you to attend university. Perhaps he had decided against it. Possibly he wondered if you would fit in any better at Oxford than you have here.'

William knew his grandfather had not changed his mind, though if his intentions hadn't been made clear in his will, William also knew he couldn't prove it. He could feel his place at Oxford slipping from his grasp, and with it, any hope of a future profession.

'However,' his uncle said. 'Now that I've met you for myself I shall give the matter some thought. I'll let you know my decision by the start of your last term. There's still plenty of time to apply for a place.'

He looked at his watch and said that he had to go or else he would miss his train.

'There's no need to show me out.'

He didn't offer to shake William's hand before he left, and as William watched him leave he knew his uncle's decision had already been made, and that he wouldn't be going up to Oxford.

*****

When William went home for the Easter holidays he thought his father looked ill, and asked him if he was feeling alright.

'I had a bit of a cold in the winter, that's all,' Reynolds said. 'I get a bit tired still.'

They finished supper, and while William cleared up his father lit his pipe. He began a deep hacking cough from deep in his lungs that left him breathless and red in the face.

'You shouldn't smoke with a cough like that,' William warned.

'I 'spect you're right,' Reynolds agreed and tapped out the tobacco.

'There's something I have to tell you,' William said. 'My grandfather died.' He told his father about his uncle's visit, and that there would be no money for him to go to Oxford.

'He were always a nasty bit of work, that one,' Reynolds said. 'Him and yer mam never saw eye to eye. What will you do if you can't go to university, Will?'

'I haven't really thought yet. Perhaps I'll get some sort of position in business.'

He tried to sound optimistic, but the truth was that he was bitterly disappointed. Without a degree, and with no money to article himself in some sort of profession, the best he could hope for was a job as clerk in an office, where in time he might be able to work his way up.

'You could always stay here, Will,' his father suggested. 'But I don't 'spose you'd want to learn to be a blacksmith now.'

'I wouldn't mind. Perhaps I will stay here.'

But his father knew it wasn't what Will wanted, and he shook his head sadly. 'It don't seem fair. I sent you off to that school because I was worried about your leg and you've done better'n anyone ever thought, but still you might end up stuck back here.'

'It's alright, dad,' William said, though the irony of the

situation hadn't escaped him. He had been given a glimpse of a future that might be his, a future of possibilities that a boy with no money would never have, and it had been taken away from him.

He thought of Emmaline. He hadn't told her yet that he wouldn't be going to Oxford. He hadn't told her anything. What would she think of him now? Not only did he have no money, he had no prospects either. He was in love with her, and the thought of losing her made him sick with worry. He would have given anything to hear her say that none of it mattered, that she loved him for who he was. It struck him that his mother must have said something like those words once to his father. She had given up her family for him and come to Scaldwell to be the wife of a village blacksmith. He wondered if she had ever regretted her decision.

He persuaded his father to go to bed early, concerned that he looked unwell, and in the morning William went to the doctor in the village and asked if he'd come. When the doctor arrived that afternoon he was driving a motor-car he'd recently bought, but as William admired it the doctor grumbled that there was something wrong with it.

'I'll have a look if you like while you're in with my father,' William offered.

The doctor was surprised. 'Do you know about motor mechanics?'

'A little bit. One of the masters at school brought a Renault last term.'

The master had started up a motoring club, which William had joined. He'd always known there was a practical side to his nature, which he thought must come from having spent his early childhood years around his father. It turned out he enjoyed taking the Renault to bits to see how it all worked, and when something went wrong he had a knack for getting it going again. By the time the doctor returned, William had cleaned the spark plugs and adjusted the carburettor, and the car was running smoothly again.

'I say, well done,' the doctor said, very pleased. 'You know, you ought to teach your father about mechanics. There are several motors in the district now, and there are bound to be more of them around as time goes by, but the nearest garage is in Northampton. We could do with somewhere local that could do repairs and so on.'

'I'll mention it to him. How is he?'

'Oh, he'll be alright, just a touch of phlegm on the chest. He ought to stop smoking that pipe so much. Don't forget what I said.'

'I won't,' William assured him. He did mention it later, but his father said he was too old to be learning new tricks.

'By the time there's enough of them motors to make it worth my while, I'll be dead,' he joked.

Over the following week Reynolds' cough improved, and when it was time for William to return to Oundle his father was feeling much better. As they drove to the station they talked about what William would do at the end of term now that he wasn't going to Oxford. William tried to reassure him that everything would be alright, and that he would think of something.

'You just look after yourself,' William said.

They shook hands on the platform, and when the train pulled away from the station William leaned out of the window and waved until his father was out of sight. Alone in the carriage, he gazed out of the window at the passing fields. Part of him was looking forward to going back so that he could see Emmaline again, but during the past few days he'd become increasingly anxious. It had been terrible being unable to write to her, and after three weeks he was convinced that she would have forgotten him, or even worse - that she had somehow discovered the truth about him before he could tell her himself, and now she despised him.

When the train arrived at Oundle station he looked eagerly out of the window to see if Emmaline might be waiting for him on the platform. He was disappointed that she wasn't there, as he'd told her before he left which day he would be returning. He was sure it was a sign that she was lost to him, and as he walked into the town he felt miserable. A black mood descended over him. He wished he'd never seen Oundle. The constant loneliness he'd endured over the years he'd been there seemed pointless now. As did everything he'd learnt. Without money none of it meant anything.

He was close to the square when he saw Emmaline walking towards him. His spirits soared for a moment, and then plummeted again when she faltered as soon as she saw him. There was no happiness in her expression, only a kind of trepidation at having to face him. There wasn't much else he could do but continue and so he tried to put on a brave smile.

'Hello,' he said when they met.

Her eyes darted from his. 'Hello.'

'How are you?'

'I'm very well, thank you. Did you enjoy your holiday?'

Her manner was polite, but no more than that and he saw at once what would happen. They would exchange bland pleasantries and go their separate ways, and he would never know what had changed her mind about him. He shook his head.

'Not really. I couldn't stop thinking about you.'

To his surprise, Emmaline suddenly smiled. 'Did you really? I thought you would have forgotten about me.'

'I could never do that.'

'I've been worrying continuously. I thought you'd meet some girl at home who's far cleverer and prettier than me.'

'I've never met anybody even half as pretty as you,' he told her. He was deliriously happy, and it struck him that the misery he'd endured while he was away was almost worth it just to feel like this. 'Where are you going?' he asked.

'To the station. I've been looking for you on every train from Brixworth.'

'Shall I walk you home?'

'Yes. But let's go by the river where it's quiet.'

As soon as they were within the shelter of the trees they fell against one another and kissed.

'I could kiss you all day,' Emmaline said when they parted.

He kissed her again and decided that he would tell her about Oxford tomorrow.

Several weeks of the summer term passed. They met as often as they could, but time was always short and William never felt it was the right moment to tell Emmaline the truth. As time went by she talked increasingly about introducing him to her father, but William always found a reason to put the occasion off. One day she told him her birthday was approaching and she'd asked her father if she could invite a friend for lunch.

'Do you mean me?' he asked her, alarmed.

'Yes, of course. I've already told my aunt that I've met a young man from the school and we've become friends. She promised not to say anything until after she's met you herself. Actually she's been wonderful about it. My father needn't ever know that we've been meeting like this.'

They were lying in the grass together in a field near the river. William didn't say anything.

'What is it William? Don't you want to meet my father?' Emmaline asked.

'It isn't that.'

'Then what is it? Every time I mention it you find some excuse not to. You're not afraid of him are you? He's quite alright really, and I know he'll like you.'

William sat up. 'It isn't that. The thing is, there's something I have to talk to you about. I should have said something before, but I didn't know how to. I suppose I wasn't sure what you'd think.'

'What is it?' Emmaline said sounding worried.

'It's just that I'm worried your father won't approve of me.'

'Of course he will. He'll love you as much as I do. Well perhaps not that much.' She kissed him, glad that his concern was nothing serious. He was nervous, that was all.

'I love you too, Emma. More than I can tell you. And I know none of this will matter to you, but I'm not sure about your father. Perhaps if I was still going up to Oxford it wouldn't matter so much.'

'What do you mean - if you were still going up to Oxford?'

'The fact is I can't go. I can't afford it. The only reason I'm at Oundle is because my fees were paid by my benefactor, but he's dead now and there's no more money.'

Emmaline stared uncomprehendingly. 'But you have a scholarship...'

'It doesn't cover my living expenses.'

'Surely your family will give you an allowance.'

'My family don't have any money, Emmaline. That's what I'm trying to tell you.' He told her how his mother and father had met, and how they had loved one another despite their different backgrounds. It struck William that the similarities between his parent's situation and his and Emmaline's was somehow a good portent.

'Your father is a blacksmith?' Emmaline repeated.

He saw at once that she was taken aback, but he didn't blame her for that. It must be difficult for her to absorb it all at once. He should have told her before. He wondered if she was thinking about his parents too, trying to picture herself married to a blacksmith, and William wanted to explain that their own situation was different. His father hadn't been educated at a public school. He'd never had William's advantages.

Emmaline was very quiet when they walked back towards the town. They separated before they came in sight of the first houses. William kissed her, but when she turned her face up to him he was sure she hesitated, and when they parted she seemed less reluctant than usual.

'I'll look for you in the morning,' he said.

'Yes. I'd better go or I'll be late.'

He kissed her quickly again, though she was less responsive than usual. As she left he wanted to call out that he loved her, but he managed to stop himself. When she was gone he thought his heart would break from the feeling of loneliness that broke over him like a wave.

In the morning, when he ran to Fotheringhay, he felt anxious the entire time. He didn't linger at the ruin as he normally did. He couldn't think of anything but getting back to the town, hoping desperately that Emmaline would be at her window as usual. He even prayed to a God he wasn't sure he believed in. When he reached the place where he always stopped, he bent down to pretend to tie his lace. He couldn't look at first. He told himself she would be there, and then everything would be alright. His heart was racing and his hands shook. Finally he looked up at the house, to the rows of symmetrically placed windows, among them Emmaline's; as empty as he'd known it would be.

He only ever saw her once again. He lessened the chance of it by rarely going into the town, and he changed the route of his run in the morning. He reverted to his studies for solace, and spent long hours in his room reading Homer and Ovid. He ended the academic year with distinction, though he didn't know what good it would do him. On his way to the station, when he finally left Oundle for the last time, he saw a familiar figure come out of a shop door in the square. His heart leapt when he saw it was Emmaline, but she was with a young man he didn't recognise. They seemed to know each other well. Then the cart turned the corner and they were lost from sight.

*****

William's father met William at the station in Brixworth, and they drove home along the narrow lanes between hedgerows thick with rosehip and blackberry bushes, to the plodding clop of the horse's hooves.

'Will you take the reins, Will?' his father asked. He looked unwell again, though he claimed to be alright. 'I feel tired, that's all,' he said.

'Lean against me and close your eyes if you like,' William offered.

He had no idea what he was going to do. He supposed he'd help his father at the forge. He'd been thinking about what the doctor had said about there being a need for a local place to mend the motorcars in the district. It wasn't what he'd envisaged doing with his classical education, but he admitted he was interested in mechanics, and who knew what opportunities there might be if he put his mind to it. The world was changing quickly. He thought he would do better in a town though, perhaps somewhere like Northampton. He decided he'd talk to his father about the idea of them both moving away from Scaldwell, though he'd wait a few weeks and allow things to settle.

Before they reached the village, William stopped the horse because his father had fallen asleep. He was slumped heavily against him and in danger of toppling off the cart. But when he tried to wake him, William realised that his father had died. Gently he laid him down in the back. He looked peaceful. William wiped away the tears that came to his eyes. A feeling of profound loneliness descended over him.

5

John Reynolds was buried in the churchyard beside his wife's grave. After the funeral one or two of the mourners approached William to say they were sorry and he thanked them, and then neither they nor he could think of anything else to add. A young woman with hair the colour of straw lingered until the others had all gone.

'D'you remember me, Will?' she asked.

For a moment he was at a loss, but then he did. 'Yes, you're Sally,' he said. A vivid memory of that day in the wheat field came back to him, and he thought that if he had moved a moment sooner how different his life might have been.

'I'm sorry 'bout yer dad.'

'Thank you.' He was grateful to her for staying behind. He asked how she was, and she told him she worked for a farmer and his wife as a housemaid.

'It's hard work and I don't get much time off, but they treat me well.'

'Would you like to go for a walk?' he asked, thinking that they could reminisce about when they were young and he could avoid returning to the empty cottage.

'I can't,' she said. 'I've got to get back.'

'Of course,' he said, disappointed.

There was an awkward moment, then Sally brightened. 'I'm gettin' married next year.'

He congratulated her, though she seemed young. She told him her fiancé worked on a farm at Lamport.

'Now you're back again, will you come to the wedding?'

He thanked her, but said he didn't think he would be staying in Scaldwell. He didn't belong there anymore, he thought, though he didn't say that.

'Good luck then,' she said.

'Thanks. Good luck to you too.'

As she left, she looked back and smiled. He almost called out to her, but he didn't know what he would say, and so he simply watched her go down the path until she was lost from his sight.

A week later he left the village. He had given up the rented cottage and the forge, and sold most of the contents. The only things he kept were some of his mother's books and a framed photograph of his parents taken on the day they were married.

He took the train from Brixworth to Northampton, and though he had to be careful with the little money he had, he decided to take a room for the night at the Station Hotel. When he was told the price of a single room was five shillings he almost changed his mind, but it was getting late and he doubted he'd find anywhere much cheaper. That evening he went out to a café for his supper, and later went back to his room and read from the Odyssey. As he turned the well-thumbed pages to follow Odysseus's trials he thought of Mister Watson, and wondered where he was now. When he felt his eyes drooping he turned off the gas and got into bed. For a long time he lay awake in the dark, wondering where his life would take him.

In the morning, William bought a newspaper and looked in the advertisements for lodgings. He found a place offering clean rooms in a respectable house for thirty shillings, with breakfast and supper included if required. He was alarmed that he couldn't find anything cheaper, but he supposed if he managed to get a job quickly he wouldn't have to eat into too much of his limited capital. After paying for his hotel room he had just over eight pounds left. It seemed like a very small amount.

He left his trunk at the hotel and took a cab to the address given in the paper. The house turned out to be an ordinary looking brick villa in a terraced row. When he knocked at the door it was answered by a maid, who showed him into a living room. A few minutes later the woman who owned the house appeared. She was middle aged and thin, with dark hair pulled severely back from her face.

'Good morning,' William said. 'I've come about a room.'

She looked him up and down quite openly, but seemed uncertain of him, perhaps because of his age.

'I usually only let my rooms by the week. I prefer my guests to be long term lodgers really, you see,' she informed him.

'I'm afraid I can't really say how long I'll be staying, but I'm happy to pay for a week in advance.'

His offer to pay, coupled with his general manner and appearance seemed to persuade her. 'Well, I have got one room that's available. I'll show you where it is and then you can decide.'

She led the way up the stairs to a room on the top floor, and stood aside to let him see it properly. It was small, furnished with a narrow bed and chest of drawers. A window looked out over the roofs of the houses across the road, and a single bad watercolour hung on one wall. William found it depressing.

'Your advertisement said your rooms are thirty shillings a week, is that right?' He wondered if such a small room might be let for a cheaper rate.

'I provide breakfast and clean sheets once a week for that price,' she replied firmly.

'Alright, I'll take it,' he decided, thinking that it wouldn't be for long anyway.

'If you'd like supper it's an extra ten shillings a week,

58

which I think you'll find is very reasonable,' she told him. 'If you don't want it every evening it's two shillings casual rate, but you have to tell me in the morning.'

William took out his wallet and counted out a week in advance. 'I might make my own arrangements about supper, if that's alright,' he said. 'Though I'll take it tonight.'

The woman took his money and put it away in a pocket of her dress, and as they went back down the stairs she told him her name was Mrs Hall. 'There's a bathroom downstairs on the next floor. You'll meet my other gentlemen this evening when they come back from their work.'

'Thank you.'

He sent the cab back to the hotel for his trunk, and when it arrived the driver helped him carry it up the stairs. Mrs Hall apologised that there was nobody else to help, him but she only employed a cook and a girl for cleaning and serving the evening meal. After he'd unpacked his things, William went out again and caught a tram into the town. He walked along Gold Street looking at the shop windows. The streets were busy with trams and motorbuses, as well as horse drawn carriages and the occasional motorcar, and the pavements were full of people. After Scaldwell, and even Oundle, the town felt thriving and prosperous, and William began to feel more optimistic about his situation. Though he was alone in the world he was well educated and well dressed, and he had a little money in his pocket, enough to get him started in his new life. He decided that he would begin looking for a position straight away. Within a few weeks, he thought, he would be earning a regular income, responsible to nobody but himself. He would find rooms, which he would make comfortable with books and pictures on the wall that were to his taste. No doubt he wouldn't be able to afford anything very grand to begin with, but it would be his home, and he would make it as pleasant as he could. He resolved to put his recent disappointments and the sorrow of his father's death behind him and look forward to the future instead.

He still had the paper he'd bought earlier, but when he looked at the section advertising vacant situations he was surprised at how few there were. Though nothing appealed particularly, he was aware that his money wouldn't last very long and he resolved to take any kind of work to begin with. Once he'd had a chance to settle down he would think about his longer term plans. Most of the advertisements were for manual work in factories or warehouses, but there were some vacancies for office clerks which William thought he might be more suited to. Though all of them seemed to require relevant experience, he was sure that his education - coupled with a willingness to learn - ought to do instead.

At the first place he went to he was told the position had already been filled, and the same thing happened when he arrived at the Northampton Boot Company, where a position as a clerk in the stores was advertised. As he left, William was glad the job had gone. The firm occupied a number of high, dirty brick buildings with a grim and forbidding air about them, and the air smelt unpleasantly of blood and the chemicals used in the tanning works.

The third place he tried was a brewery, where the position of clerk in the purchasing office had been advertised. When he arrived he joined a dozen men lined up in a corridor, all waiting to be interviewed. They were all older than William. He took his place next to a man who was perhaps in his mid to late twenties, who wore a suit that didn't quite fit him properly, and whose shirt collar was beginning to fray at the edge. All of the men had a similar sort of appearance, and William realised that in the clothes he wore, paid for by his grandfather before he died, he stood out from them. The man in front of him nodded.

'I 'aven't seen you around before.'

'I only arrived today,' William said, wondering why the man would expect to have seen him in a town the size of Northampton. The man seemed taken aback by the way

William spoke, and afterwards didn't speak to him again.

Eventually it was William's turn to be called into a small, cramped office where a fat, balding man sat behind a desk dictating a letter to a young woman who sat in front of typewriter at a small desk in the corner.

The man paused mid-sentence and looked curiously at William. 'Are you here about the position then?'

'Yes, sir. My name is William Reynolds.'

'What sort of experience have you got?'

'None really, I'm afraid. I was at Oundle school until recently.' He was beginning to realise that there were a lot of people looking for work, and that he would have to sell himself to stand out from them, especially given his lack of experience. 'I passed English and Mathematics with distinction,' he added thinking that they were both subjects that would be useful in a purchasing office.

'Did you now?' The man leant back in his chair and cast an amused look towards the typist. 'What's a young man from a school like Oundle doing coming here for a clerk's position, is what I'd like to know.'

'I need to work,' William said. 'My parents are both dead, so I have to look out for myself. I think I can assure you that if I'm given a chance you'll find me extremely keen to do my best.'

'I expect you would be keen. Keen to get on too, I should think. You'd want to better yourself, a well-educated young man like you.'

'I'd certainly try to ensure that my work was thought well of,' William agreed.

The man's attitude abruptly changed. He jabbed a finger in William's direction. 'What I want is someone who's going to work hard and do what's expected, young man, that's what I want! Not somebody who thinks they know everything there is to know five minutes after they've started!'

The man's belligerent attitude took William aback. 'I

apologise if I've given you the wrong impression,' he said. 'I only meant that I'm very willing to learn.'

The man took no notice. 'I've seen that type before, you know. They think they're a cut above. No respect for those who've done their work steadily over the years without giving cause for complaint. It takes time to learn things properly, you see.'

'Yes, of course,' William agreed.

The man pushed a ledger across the desk, open to a page on which there was a column of figures. 'Let's see how long it takes you to add them up.'

William ran his finger down the list and gave the answer. The man frowned, and looked at the figures again as if there was something there he'd missed. He didn't comment on whether or not the answer was right, but waved a hand in dismissal.

'You're not what I'm looking for, young man. Not at all. Send the next one in when you go.' Without another glance at William he went back to the letter he had been dictating, and the young woman's fingers began clattering over the keys of her typewriter.

That evening William was exhausted by the time he returned to his lodgings. He went upstairs to wash and change, and when he came down found the other lodgers were already seated at the table. He greeted them and took the only remaining seat. There were three men besides himself; two in their early fifties or thereabouts, and another of perhaps thirty five. The older men sat on either side of Mrs Hall, who presided at the head of the table. They nodded vaguely when William was introduced, and afterwards ignored him completely, but the younger man, whose name was Carter, winked at him.

The food, which was plain and not very well cooked, was served by a sullen maid.

'I hope everybody likes mutton,' Mrs Hall said in a tone that implied that if they didn't they ought to.

'My absolute favourite, Mrs Hall,' said the man on her left obsequiously. His name was Johnson. 'You can't beat a good bit of mutton I say. Completely under-rated it is. You spoil us, you do, and no mistake.'

As the maid served him with a glutinous piece of the fatty grey meat he frowned, however. 'Now, Maureen, dear, I think I'll have that piece if you don't mind.' He indicated the biggest slice on the platter. 'I can't tolerate too much fat with my teeth, you understand. Not that there's anything wrong with a bit of fat, mind. Very tasty it is.'

'You're quite right, Mr Johnson,' Mrs Hall agreed. 'There's some that don't appreciate mutton, but I always think it's very flavoursome. The trouble is some people don't know how much it costs me to put good food on the table, though I try my very best.' She looked directly at William as she spoke, as if it was to him she was referring.

'You're right, Mrs Hall,' declared the man on her other side, whose name was Hodges. 'I never heard a truer word spoken, nor by a finer woman than yourself, as I've said many a time before and meant it, every word.'

Across the table, Johnson glared at him.

William was the last to be served, by which time all that remained on the plate was a piece of fat with a few slivers of meat attached to it. The vegetables were pale, overcooked cabbage and grey mashed potato. The meal looked worse than anything he'd experienced at school, but he was so hungry he ate it anyway, and listened with fascination to the duel of words between Johnson and Hodges, who both seemed determined to outdo one another in the amount of lavish praise they heaped upon their landlady. To William's ears not a word of it sounded genuine, but Mrs Hall appeared to regard the flattery both as justified and entirely sincere.

During the lulls, the younger man, Carter, kept up a continuous account of his day, even though the others seemed largely disinterested. He was a travelling salesman for a firm of ironmongers whose job took him all over the county. He explained to William that since he travelled so much, it was convenient for him to reside at Mrs Hall's whenever he was in his home-town.

'I like to stay in 'omely sort of lodgings when I'm travelling,' he said with a wink. 'Though there's none to compare with Mrs Hall's 'ospitality. And bein' a regular I can count on getting looked after, isn't that true Mrs Hall?'

'I daresay it is,' she agreed.

Carter was drinking wine from a bottle that was brought to the table half full, though everyone else drank water. He offered some to William, and before William could respond, poured him half a glass.

'I always like a bit of wine with my supper, I do. The French 'ave wine with their meals, you know. I travel to the continent sometimes you see, with my work. I expect you know about all that sort of thing anyway, William. I can see you're a young man of refinement, like myself.'

He winked and glanced at Johnson and Hodges, who were both concentrating on their meals and pretending not to listen.

'Yes, I 'ad a very good day,' Carter went on as if somebody had asked him. 'I always do well around Northampton, I 'ave to say. Why, I expect my commission was at least twenty five bob if I worked it out. Not bad for a day's work eh, William?'

Johnson cleared his throat. 'I'm always surprised you don't stay at The Grand, Carter, since you're doing so well,' he said acidly.

'What, and miss Mrs Hall's 'ospitality? I shouldn't think so. I think of this place as like my own 'ome, in a way.'

He winked at Mrs Hall, who pretended not to notice though the faintest trace of colour touched her cheeks.

'One of these days I might just stay here permanent, like. Get myself a position in a local firm,' Carter added.

This remark was greeted with pained silence by Hodges and Johnson. After supper was finally over, Carter went outside to smoke in the evening air and invited William to join him. They stood on the step by the front door.

'What are you doin' here then, William, if you don't mind me asking?'

William found himself telling Carter about his father's death, and how before that he'd been at Oundle. 'Now I'm looking for some sort of work.' He told him about the interview at the brewery. 'The man I saw said it was because I didn't have experience, but I'm sure I could have done the work easily enough. He just didn't seem to like me for some reason.'

'Course you could do the work,' Carter said. 'That's what he was worried about. A young man like yourself, with a proper education and manners like a gentlemen, he'd have been scared that if he took you on you'd 'ave your eye on his job before he knew it.'

Carter advised him to try and make himself look a bit more ordinary. 'Look at that suit your wearin' for instance. I'll wager you didn't get that off the rack. Anyway, you don't want to get yourself stuck in some office like that. A salesman, now that's the life for a young feller,' he said. 'Look at me. I do very well thank you very much, and I'm not stuck in one place with a boss lookin' over my shoulder all the time like Johnson and Hodges in there. They've been 'ere for years, you know. Both of them think one day they're going to marry Mrs Hall.' He laughed cynically. 'That's why I come 'ere to tell the truth, just to butter her up a bit. It gives me a laugh to see their faces.'

'Do you think I could get a job as a salesman somewhere?' William asked.

'Course you could,' Carter said. 'I'll tell you what, I'm off again in the morning, but I'll see if there's anything going in my firm and I'll drop you a line. You'd 'ave to start at the bottom of course, but you'd soon work yourself up.'

William thanked him, his spirits suddenly rising after the day he'd had.

'Don't mention it,' Carter said. 'I always like to give an 'elping hand if I can, me.'

For the next two weeks William went out every day to look for work. He took Carter's advice and spent some of his money buying a cheap suit that made him look more ordinary, and whenever he got an interview he didn't mention that he'd been to Oundle. There wasn't much he could do about the way he spoke, however. It struck him as deeply ironic that he had spent years learning how to behave and sound like a gentlemen, and yet now it worked against him.

His efforts however, were to no avail. Jobs were hard to find, and without experience, it seemed almost impossible. Wherever he went there was always a queue of men applying for the same position. He came to recognise people he saw at various places, but though he'd nod and say hello he avoided any closer relationship, aware that they were his competitors. Each evening when he returned to his lodgings, he asked Mrs Hall if there was a letter for him. He kept hoping that Carter would write to say that he'd arranged a position in his firm, but when nothing came he realised that Carter probably exaggerated everything he said. When he thought about it, the fact that Carter lodged at Mrs Hall's made no sense really if he could afford somewhere better. The food was awful, and everything about the way Mrs Hall ran her house was designed to squeeze the last penny she could from her lodgers. There was often only a sliver of soap in the bathroom, and she complained constantly about the cost of employing people to wash and cook and clean.

'I really ought to put my rates up to cover it all,' she would say. 'I'm too generous for my own good, that's my trouble.' At these times Hodges and Johnson would remain uncharacteristically silent.

As the end of his third week at Mrs Hall's approached, William worried constantly. Though he never ate supper there, and lived as frugally as he possibly could, he only had fifteen shillings left. He contemplated asking Mrs Hall to allow him to stay until he found a job, on the understanding that he would then repay his debt, but most of the jobs he applied for paid less than thirty shillings a week anyway. He hated going back to the house each evening. Though there was a sitting room for the guests, Johnson and Hodges made it clear they resented William's presence when he went there. They hardly ever spoke a word to him unless it was to ask if he'd found a position yet, and when he said he hadn't, they exchanged looks that seemed to indicate that the fault somehow lay with him.

Instead he'd taken to spending his evenings in the café where he ate his meals. He would linger over cups of tea until eight or nine at night when the café closed, and then he would return to his lodgings and slip quietly inside in the hope of avoiding Mrs Hall. Whenever he ran into her she asked if he had found a position, and then made a point of reminding him that she needed advance warning of his intentions regarding his room.

'In case somebody should enquire whether there is a vacancy'.

He resented her constant badgering, especially as Carter's room had remained empty since he left, and William doubted that there were people clamouring for his own tiny room. Worry made him irritable, and he became short with her and told her he would let her know in plenty of time. He did his best to avoid her completely, and in the mornings he left without breakfast, even though he was hungry.

The optimism with which William had faced his first day looking for work was gone. With every penny he spent and every position he was turned down for he became increasingly depressed. The loneliness of his existence began to eat at him. He was used to being alone, but to be faced with such uncertainty over his future and to have nobody to turn to made it much worse. Sometimes he dreamed of his father and the cottage. At other times he thought of Emmaline and the anguish and pain of loving her came back in full force.

Eventually the day came when he was due to either pay for another week at Mrs Hall's, or give notice. He left the house early and went out to look for work, though as usual he was unsuccessful. That evening he ate supper at the café he frequented. The special meal for the day was liver and onions with potato for ninepence. It was warm inside and the food was plentiful. He was a regular by then, and the woman who ran the place always put a bit extra on his plate because she said he needed some meat on his bones. He only ate this one meal each day, other than a bun and a cup of tea in the mornings, and he had lost weight over the past few weeks. The café was busy. There were always people like himself who wanted somewhere cheap they could eat. A young woman, a girl really, who he thought couldn't be older than seventeen caught his eye. She was thin, but pretty in a washed-out kind of way. He looked away, and when he saw her again she was leaving with an older man who put his arm around her and said something quietly in her ear, and then laughed out loud.

William stayed until the café closed. He was dreading going back to Mrs Hall's. When he arrived, Mrs Hall came out of the sitting room. He had the feeling she had been listening for him.

'There you are, Mister Reynolds,' she said feigning surprise.

'Good evening, Mrs Hall.'

'Since I've bumped into you, I might as well ask if you intend staying another week. Only you haven't said, and I must know for when people come asking for a room.'

'Actually I was going to come and see you,' he said. During the walk from town he had been rehearsing what he would say to her. He'd decided to swallow his pride and throw himself on her mercy to stay another week. If he had to, he was going to tell her that he was expecting some money from a relative which he thought she would probably believe, but suddenly he knew he couldn't do it. If all he had left was his pride he would at least hang on to that.

'The thing is I've managed to get myself quite a good position,' he told her. 'They want me to start straight away, but I'm afraid it's on the other side of town so I've decided to find lodgings somewhere a bit closer.'

'You must do as you like, of course,' she said tersely.

'It's a question of expense, you see. There's the cost of catching a tram every morning, and then there's the extra time.'

'I daresay that's all very well, but I would have thought you would give me more notice of your intentions,' she said. 'If I had known I could have let your room.'

Though he doubted that was true, William wondered if he might get her to give him a cheaper rate. Even if he could stay a few more days it would be something. 'I could always stay on for a little while if it would help,' he offered. 'Perhaps you could give me a reduction for being a regular.'

Though William was sure Hodges and Johnson didn't pay as much as he did for their lodgings, Mrs Hall seemed annoyed by his request, however she appeared to reconsider.

'Well, since you are a regular I suppose I could let you have five shillings off the usual price. Though I don't know how I'll make anything out of it if I do, and I have to live.'

William's heart sank. Five shillings wasn't enough. 'I was hoping you could let me stay for ten shillings,' he said. 'The thing is, I won't get paid straight away, and I'm a bit short of money.'

'I couldn't possibly let a room for that amount,' Mrs Hall said flatly. 'It simply wouldn't be worth it.'

'Then I'm afraid I'll have to leave tomorrow,' William said, angry that she should reject him out of hand and sound so offended when he'd paid over the odds for three weeks.

'I expect rooms to be vacated first thing in the morning so they can be cleaned,' Mrs Hall snapped.

He turned on his heel. He would have said something, except that he realised that he couldn't take his trunk with him and would have to ask her to look after it. That night he hardly slept. His leg ached as it often did after walking for miles around the town every day, but it seemed worse than usual. His future seemed bleak. He thought of his years at Oundle and everything he'd endured there, and asked himself what had it all been for? He had seen the poorest parts of the town where people lived in squalor and poverty.

Without money or position, people lived miserable lives, and he had neither.

6

By the time morning came, William knew he had to stop feeling sorry for himself. He was worn down by the constant failure and rejection, but he reminded himself that during his time at Oundle he'd learned something other than the classics and how to behave like a gentleman. He had learned to overcome whatever difficulties were placed in his path by drawing on nothing more than what was inside him, and with that in mind he went downstairs to find Mrs Hall and asked to leave his trunk.

'I'll send for it when I can,' he said, ignoring the look in her eye when she realised he had made up his story of having found a position.

Later that day, after he'd tried unsuccessfully for a position at a firm of accountants, William began to think about the night ahead. He remembered seeing some signs stuck onto walls and lamp-posts in Criterion Street that advertised beds for sixpence a night. It was one of the worst parts of the town, a maze of cramped houses and alleys near the canal, where sweated workers eked out a living of sorts. The entrance to the house was through an alley that led to a tiny yard hemmed in by the buildings that rose oppressively all around. The revolting stench from an outhouse was enough to persuade William not to go any further, but before he could leave, a fat old woman with greasy grey hair and rotten teeth came out of a door and asked if he was looking for a bed.

'Come an' 'ave a look if yer want,' she said.

Unwillingly, he followed her into a gloomy passage and up a set of stairs. On a landing he passed an open door leading to a room where several mattresses that were stained and filthy beyond belief were stacked against a wall. Otherwise, every inch of floor space was completely covered in piles of paper cut into squares, and amidst them sat a woman and four children, all of them busy in a sort of production line of pasting and sticking together the edges of the paper to form bags. One child was mixing the paste while another applied it, and the woman and the other two children made the folds and arranged the finished bags to dry. One of the girls looked at William as he passed. She must have been about eight or nine years old. She was pale, with lank hair and bad skin, and her arms were as thin as sticks. The filthy window was firmly closed and the air inside was stuffy and fetid.

He hurried after the fat woman, who showed him another equally filthy room containing eight narrow cots all squeezed together. A man lay sprawled on one of them snoring drunkenly.

'Don't mind 'im,' the woman said. 'Soon as he wakes up 'e'll be off out again to the boozer.'

William mumbled some excuse and hurried out as quickly as he could. That night he went to the café where he usually had his supper, and stayed there until it closed at nine. He saw the thin girl there again, and when he left she appeared from the dark shadows of an alley.

'D'you want a bit of fun?' she said to him. Though she smiled, her grey eyes were hard.

'No, I'm sorry,' he said.

She turned away without a word, looking for somebody else to approach.

For the rest of the night William walked the streets of the town. He wasn't alone, there were others like himself with nowhere to go. He saw dozens of people moving like aimless shadows. He would have gone to the park and found somewhere to sleep, but the gates were locked and he was afraid that if he was caught trying to climb the fence he'd end up in prison.

Down by the canal he saw a group of people gathered around a fire. He heard voices arguing. They sounded drunk. After watching them for a little while he turned away, and as he went back along the path he passed a man who looked at him with sharp, narrowed eyes. When he looked back, William saw the man had turned around and was following him. He walked faster, and when he turned a corner ran to an alley where he hid until the man gave up looking for him. After that he kept away from the area by the canal.

For the rest of the night he wandered the streets near the centre of town alone. The night seemed interminably long, and in the early morning it was cold even though it was summer. It made William wonder what would happen if he still had nowhere to go by the time winter came. He went back to his usual café, and when it opened he brought a mug of hot tea and a bun and sat at a table, grateful to rest his aching leg while he read the advertisements in the paper to decide which position he would apply for first.

*****

After six nights without a place to sleep, William was constantly hungry. Each morning he would go to the public lavatories in Gold Street to wash and make himself look as respectable as possible. Later, when he had applied for all the jobs he could, he would go to the park and find a place to sit where he could sleep for an hour or two. He felt light headed and disoriented half the time. It was worse in the early hours of the morning, when he could barely drag his feet to keep moving. When it rained one night he felt so miserable that he wasn't sure he could keep going.

One morning in the newspaper he read about a man who'd been found dead by the railway siding. The article said he'd fallen from a bridge in an accident, but he had no home and no work, and William wondered if it was true that he'd fallen. There were times when the idea of a fall and then sudden and final oblivion appealed to him. The only thing that kept him going was a promise that he made himself, that one day he would make something of himself by his own means, and when he did he would never allow anybody to have control over his life again.

That evening he walked past a church. The door was open and there was a welcoming light inside, though there appeared to be nobody around. He went inside to sit down for a few minutes and looked up at a stained glass window behind the altar. The scene depicted Jesus, and presumably some of the disciples gathered underneath a leafy tree on a grassy bank beside a stream. There was something distinctly pastoral and familiar about it, as if the artist who created it had exchanged the landscape of Palestine for that of England, and it reminded William of Blake's poem taken from the preface to Milton.

> *And did the Countenance Divine*
> *Shine forth upon our clouded hills?*
> *And was Jerusalem builded here*
> *Among these dark Satanic Mills?*

A voice startled him, and William realised he must have nodded off for a few seconds.

'What are you doing here? The church is closed.' A man wearing an ecclesiastical collar regarded him indignantly. He took in William's dishevelled appearance.

'I'm sorry, I must have closed my eyes for a moment.'

The clergyman seemed surprised at the way he spoke. 'You shouldn't be here.'

'The door was open,' William said. 'I just wanted to sit down for a little while.' He looked at the window again where Jesus wore an expression of serene benevolence. He felt dizzy from hunger and tiredness, and couldn't collect his thoughts.

'You must leave at once,' the clergyman said, becoming vexed again. 'If you don't I will have to fetch the police.'

William stared at the small gold crucifix the man wore, and then when he got up the clergyman quickly stepped back as if he was afraid William intended to steal it.

He reached into his pocket. 'Take this and leave,' the clergyman said in a high voice, holding out two pennies in his hand.

William ignored him and began to walk back along the nave towards the door. As he went along the path outside to the street, the man came to the door and called out to him.

'If you pray to God he will help you.' Then he closed the door firmly and turned a key in the heavy lock.

Without knowing where he was going, William walked back towards the town. Across the road he saw a girl approach a man who was passing by, but the man spoke to her brusquely and shoved her aside so that she stumbled and fell. She shouted after him.

'Piss off then, you bastard!'

He recognised the girl from the café, and went over to help her up.

'What about you, luv? D'you want to have a bit of fun?' she said.

'I just wanted to make sure you're alright.'

She peered at him closely. 'I know you, don't I? I know! You was the one in the café.'

'Yes, that's right.'

She came closer and pressed her body against him. 'Since it's you, and you was nice to me, I'll do yer for sixpence if you like.'

He shook his head. She was younger than he'd thought. Perhaps as young as fifteen. 'Sorry.'

She shrugged. 'Suit yerself.'

They heard the sound of footsteps as somebody came towards them. The girl frowned when she recognised who it was. 'It's only you,' she said disappointed.

'That's right, only me, luv.'

William recognised the voice straight away. It was Carter, the salesman he'd met at Mrs Hall's.

'Hello there, it's young William isn't it?' Carter said sounding surprised. 'What are you doing 'ere? After a bit of sport with Lucy are you?' He winked lewdly.

'He just 'elped me up after some bloke pushed me down,' the girl said. 'I don't think 'e's got any money.'

'Are you staying at Mrs Hall's again?' William asked, though even as he spoke he noticed that Carter's suit was stained and his shoes were scuffed.

'Lost me position,' Carter said. 'Some business about expenses, or some such thing.'

'I wondered why you never wrote to me,' William said, though from Carter's blank look it was obvious he didn't know what William meant.

'What's this about not 'aving any money then, William?' Carter said.

'All I've got is five shillings,' William said. 'I had to leave Mrs Hall's because I couldn't find a job.'

'Five shillings is it?' Carter said. 'You'd better let me look after that for you. You don't know what sorts you might run into out 'ere.'

'It's alright,' William said, suddenly not liking Carter's menacing undertone. 'Actually I ought to be getting on.' He started to turn away, but Carter produced a knife from his pocket; the blade a dull flash of steel.

'You'd better give it to me, William,' Carter said again, all the cheerfulness gone from his voice. He stepped closer with his hand outstretched, but William knocked it away and stood back warily. Eyeing the blade of the knife he took a few coppers from his pocket and dropped them on the ground.

'Take that,' he said. 'But I warn you, I won't give you anymore.' As the coins hit the pavement he began to walk away, looking back over his shoulder as he went. For a moment Carter hesitated, then the girl pushed past him to pick up the money and he grabbed her by the arm.

'What do you think you're doin' then?' he demanded.

William hurried on, and left them to argue between themselves.

In the morning he read of a position in the stock department of Ballantynes, which was the largest shop in Northampton. When he arrived he was directed to the goods yard at the back, where as usual a line of men were waiting. He took his place and waited to be called.

Some men were loading furniture into the back of a lorry that was painted green and had the name of the shop written on the side in gold lettering. One of the men went to crank the starter handle, but after several unsuccessful attempts he leaned against the radiator breathing heavily, his face red and sweating.

'You'd better tell Mister Wilkins the bloody thing won't start again,' he said to his younger helper.

'Let me 'ave a go,' the young one said, and took over cranking the handle until he too was sweating and breathing hard. He gave up and gave the wheel a savage kick. 'Bloody thing,' he muttered under his breath. 'You can tell Wilkins,' he said to the older man. 'He's in a right mood already, and if we don't get this lot out he's going to get a right earful from upstairs.'

The older man glanced toward the open doors, clearly reluctant to be the bearer of bad news. 'Let's 'ave another go first.'

As he bent to the handle again, William spoke up. 'You ought to check the contact breakers, that's often what the problem is.'

Both men looked at him in surprise. 'What's that when it's at 'ome then?' asked the younger man.

'I'll show you if you like,' William offered. 'Open the bonnet.'

The two men glanced at one another, and the older one shrugged. 'Can't 'urt to let him 'ave a look.'

The younger one lifted the bonnet and fetched some tools. William took the distributor cap off and saw the problem at once. 'It's this here, you see, it's dirty. Have you got a rag or something to clean it?'

Within a few minutes he'd cleaned and re-set the gap which looked too big. 'Try it now,' he said, and this time when the older man cranked the handle the engine started straight away. 'You ought to do that regularly,' William said as he closed the bonnet. 'And the plugs could do with a clean to by the sound of it.'

'Lucky you was 'ere,' the younger man said. 'You come about the position then?'

'Yes,' William replied.

'You'll be seeing Mister Wilkins then. That's 'im now.'

A man in his fifties wearing a dark brown suit came out the door. He wore a harassed expression when he saw how many men were still waiting to be seen. 'I 'aven't got time to see all of you,' he said. 'So anyone who 'asn't worked in a stock room before might as well not wait.'

About three quarters of the men turned away with disconsolate expressions, and William began to follow them.

'Where're you off to?' the young man asked.

'I've never worked in a stock room,' William explained.

The young man looked at the older one. 'We should tell Mister Wilkins he fixed the lorry.' Without waiting for the other man's opinion, he went inside while William lingered, unsure what to do. A few moments later the man in the brown suit reappeared and gestured for William to come over.

'I 'ear you mended the lorry,' he said.

Though he was about to say that it was only a matter of cleaning a dirty contact breaker, William changed his mind. 'Yes, sir,' he said instead.

'What's your name then?'

'Reynolds, sir. William Reynolds.'

'You know about engines and mechanics, do you, Reynolds?'

'A bit, sir, yes.'

'Where do you live?'

'Nowhere presently, I'm afraid. I was lodging in Cumberland Road, but I ran out of money.'

'Any experience in this sort of work?' Wilkins asked.

'I'm afraid not,' William admitted his heart sinking.

Wilkins studied him doubtfully, and William waited for the usual dismissal, but for once it didn't come straight away. Eventually Wilkins turned and beckoned for William to follow.

'You can start tomorrow if you want,' he said. 'Your wages are ten shillings, but that's just pocket money. You get your board and lodgings on top.'

William could hardly believe what he'd heard. Though ten shillings sounded a pitifully small amount, he was too tired and relieved to care. 'Thank you,' he said gratefully. 'I won't let you down, Mister Wilkins.'

'I'll give you the address of the place where you'll be living. You can go there tonight if you want. The doors are opened at half past six. Ask for Taylor, 'e'll show you 'round.'

Five minutes later William went outside again. The other men waiting had already been told the position was filled, and he was aware of the envious looks they gave him and the dull despair in their eyes. He couldn't look at them. He could hardly believe that a few short minutes ago he had been like them and now, suddenly, by a stroke of good fortune, everything had changed.

7

The first weeks at Ballantynes passed quickly. Besides William there were half a dozen people working in the stockroom in the charge of Mister Wilkins. They were responsible for taking delivery of goods and distributing them to the appropriate departments, and also for arranging delivery of items to customer's homes. They were kept busy most of the time, but the work wasn't particularly strenuous or difficult, and they kept the same hours as everybody else in the shop, which meant they started at half past eight in the morning and finished at half past six.

William's mechanical knowledge stood him in good stead. The Hallford lorry, which was the pride of the shop's manager and a symbol of the firm's determination to keep abreast with the times, frequently broke down. Since nobody else knew anything about mechanics it became William's unofficial responsibility to maintain the lorry and keep it on the road. He didn't mind because he found it interesting, and during his first week he subscribed to an automotive magazine so that he could learn more. A month later, an opportunity arose to improve his knowledge further when the manager of the shop bought a new Sunbeam and asked if William would look after it for him. William accepted gladly, and afterwards the manager would occasionally ask him some question or other and they would end up discussing the latest developments in the automotive industry, their relative positions in the shop briefly forgotten.

The other advantage of looking after the lorry was that it got William away from the shop. After his initial relief at having found a position that also gave him a place to live, he found that his life was almost completely given over to Ballantynes. The firm owned several houses where many of its employees lived. William shared a room with four other men, and one of the first things he had to do was learn the rules that governed the arrangement. He discovered that there were set times when they were allowed to come and go, and everything had to be done in the manner laid down. Beds had to be made in a certain fashion, possessions kept tidily and to a minimum, and if any rule was infringed there was a fine. Their meals were taken at work, half an hour for dinner at midday, which would be a hot meal, and another half an hour for tea which might be bread and butter and jam, while they had to provide breakfast at their own expense.

Employees also had to provide for themselves the clothes they wore to work, though Ballantynes had strict rules governing those as well. William discovered that many people spent almost all of their meagre wages on either the food they bought to supplement the basic fare they were given, or on items of clothing. Since the slightest infraction of the many rules they lived under earned a fine, some people ended up paying over as much as half of what they earned back to the firm. The whole system seemed designed to ensure that their lives were not their own.

Every second Wednesday evening, a staff social was held in the basement restaurant where they ate their meals. It was an opportunity for everybody to gather together informally; the shop girls and departmental buyers and assistants, the people who worked in the offices on the top floor, the floorwalkers, the people who did the window displays and also the stockboys. At all other times, especially during the working day, a definite hierarchy operated. The buyers considered themselves above

81

everybody else, as did their assistants, and the office people thought the same of everyone except the buyers. William observed that even the shopgirls differentiated themselves from one another according to the department they worked for. Those in Ladies Fashions imagined themselves at the pinnacle of all the salespeople, while for some reason that William couldn't fathom, anyone who worked on the housewares counter was at the very bottom. Beneath them all, the lowliest of the low, languished the stockboys as they were universally called, even though Frank, who drove the lorry, was in his fifties.

It was Taylor, the young man who'd helped William get his job, who introduced him to his first social. The tables had been put aside and everyone was dressed in their best. The men wore lounge suits, and the women and girls wore elaborate dresses. Since nobody really spoke to the stockboys, even on these occasions, Taylor kept up a running commentary in a low voice, so that William would know who was who.

The evening began with people volunteering some sort of entertainment. A young woman played a popular tune badly on the piano, and when she finished turned to the applauding crowd and inclined her head graciously, as if their acclaim was her rightful due and they were at the Albert Hall.

'That's Miss Worth from Perfumery,' Taylor said. 'If you take a delivery to 'er department she won't speak to you directly, but tells 'er girls anything she wants to say instead, even if you're standin' right in front of 'er.'

A man in his late thirties with a thin and serious face stood up next to recite a poem.

'Mister Cook from Gentleman's Hosiery,' Taylor said. 'Does the same thing every time.'

The poem was Tennyson's *The Charge of the Light Brigade*, and was rendered with much gesticulation and overly dramatic emphasis. Mister Cook's voice swelled and thundered to give the impression of galloping horses and booming canons, but was so overdone and with such seriousness that William wasn't sure if it was meant to be parody.

> *Canon to right of them,*
> *Canon to left of them,*
> *Canon in front of them*
> *Volley'd and thunder'd:*
> *Storm'd at with shot and shell,*
> *Boldly they rode and well,*
> *Into the jaws of Death,*
> *Into the mouth of Hell*
> *Rode the six hundred.*

At the end, the man was red-faced from the effort and the emotion of it all. He looked down at the floor and absorbed the rapturous cheers and applause, mainly from the young men in his department.

A very large woman, who wore lace gloves and too much glittering jewellery, sang excruciatingly out of tune. Another man did a tap dance. Mrs Ferris did palm reading with much oohing and aahing and melodramatic pronouncements of tall dark strangers, unexpected surprises, long trips abroad and other banalities, though she herself had a different perception.

'It's a curse, you know, the gift. Sometimes I see such terrible things, I do.'

Afterwards there were sandwiches and coffee and tea. Alcohol wasn't allowed. Then the tables were arranged for progressive whist.

'That's Ruth Hodges, there,' Taylor said about a blonde girl of about eighteen. 'And that's Catherine with her. They're on Haberdashery.'

Catherine was small and dark, but had a haughty look about her. Taylor took William over to introduce him and started talking to Catherine. He asked if she was enjoying herself.

'I daresay it's alright,' she answered barely looking at him.

Taylor looked at her desperately, trying to think of something to say. 'I like that frock you're wearin'. It really suits you.'

'Thanks,' she said coolly.

'If you wanted, I could take you to a place I know one evenin',' he suggested suddenly. 'We could 'ave a drink and a bit of a laugh.'

She looked at him in astonishment, then turned to Ruth. 'I think I'll join in the whist. Are you going to come?'

'In a minute I will,' Ruth said, at which Catherine threw a withering look at William and walked off, completely ignoring Taylor, who stared disconsolately after her and then wandered off to talk to Sayers, who was one of the others who shared their room.

'Catherine can be a bit stand-offish sometimes,' Ruth said to William. 'You mustn't take too much notice of her. She don't really mean anything by it. Is this your first time to a social then, William?'

'Yes, it is,' he said.

'They're quite good fun really if you haven't got anything else to do. I don't usually come myself, of course,' she added unless he should think the caveat applied to herself. 'Who did you like the best anyway?'

'I thought the lady who played the piano was very good,' William said to be polite.

'Miss Worth? Oh yes, she's lovely, and ever so talented.'

They talked for a little while longer and then the tables were cleared away again and Miss Worth returned to the piano. She began to play a waltz, and very soon there were couples dancing. Ruth and William looked on, and he felt she was waiting for him to ask her to dance. When the second tune began he asked her.

'I'd love to,' she said.

It was hot in the room. Ruth danced well, much better than he did, William thought. He apologised, and explained he'd only danced with the boys at his school before, when they were made to.

She giggled. 'What sort of school was that then?'

'A boy's school at Oundle.'

'Was it very posh then?'

'Why do you ask that?'

She looked at him in surprise. 'Well, nobody else I know talks like you do. And I bet that suit you're wearing didn't come off the rack either did it? I saw Mister Porter looking at you before. He was quite jealous, I could tell.'

'I suppose it is a good school,' William admitted.

'So what are you doing working here then?'

'I didn't have a choice. I haven't got any money.'

'Oh well, it doesn't matter does it. I expect you'll do very well here. Somebody told me you're already in well with Mister Dodd, and I never heard of him taking notice of a stockboy before.'

'I only look after his motor,' William said.

'Perhaps you do now, but it's bound to lead to other things, you mark my words.'

A few weeks after the social, William asked Ruth if she'd like to go to for a walk with him one Sunday, and perhaps have tea later. She agreed and they spent most of the day together. Though they didn't really have a great deal in common, William enjoyed the time he spent with Ruth. He hadn't realised until then how lonely he had become. He liked her and she seemed to like him too, and it became a regular thing for them to spend Sundays together. They often went to the park or took a tram out to the edge of town and walked along by the river. Sometimes William read to her from The Odyssey, and though he didn't think she was really interested she didn't say so. When Mister Wilkins gave him the job of helping with the stock ledger, Ruth surprised him by throwing her arms around him and kissing him.

'We should have a celebration,' she said. 'Why don't we have a meal somewhere?'

He agreed, even though he was trying hard to save his money. Ruth teased him because he was careful never to get fined for even the smallest thing and because he was so frugal.

'I have to be if I don't want to end up working in the stockroom for the rest of my life,' he told her.

'You don't have to worry about that,' she laughed. 'I bet you'll end up a buyer one day, you wait and see.'

He wanted to explain that he meant he didn't want to work for Ballantynes for ever in any position, but then she would want to know what he was going to do, and since he didn't have any idea he decided not to say anything.

To celebrate, they went to a restaurant where they had dinner. Afterwards Ruth held William's hand as they walked along the street, and when they took a short-cut through the park he kissed her against a tree.

'Have you ever done it?' she asked as they stood together in the dark.

'No,' he said, embarrassed by his admission.

'Neither have I. But I will with you, if you want me to.'

He did want to, and he kissed her again, but after a minute she pushed him away.

'You'll have to get something so I don't get in the family way,' she said, straightening her clothes. 'Then you can take me to the country next Sunday. We'll have a picnic somewhere nice.'

She was very practical, he thought.

8

At the beginning of May, during William's second year working for Ballantynes, a wooden chest of drawers had to be delivered to a farm-house on the Kettering Road. On the way back to Northampton, William stared out at the countryside. After the long winter the trees were green again and the hedgerows by the side of the road fat with spring growth. Though there was still a chill to the air, and the sky that day mantled the land with a dull grey hand, there was a freshness in the breeze and birds wheeled about the woods, returned from warmer climes.

Frank was whistling tunelessly, his hands on the wheel as the lorry jolted along on its inadequate springs. William imagined the summer ahead, long days in the shop when he would rather be… rather be where, he wondered? Doing what? They were familiar questions, the scope of his answer narrowed by lack of money.

From underneath the bonnet, amidst the intricate machinery of the engine, came a sound of clanging metal. Frank, oblivious, continued to drive. Perhaps it had only been a stray stone flung up by the wheels William thought. But a mile from the town, Frank cursed and with much grinding of metal teeth and tugging on the stubborn lever he changed gear.

'Bleedin' thing's playin' up again.'

The lorry slowed and a trail of steam issued from the bonnet. The radiator hissed, leaking what was left of its boiling contents. They stopped, and William lifted the bonnet to find that a hose had split, probably caused by the stone he'd heard earlier.

'I can't do anything until it cools down,' he said. 'Anyway, one of us will have to fetch water.'

'My back's killin' me,' Frank said immediately. 'You'd better go, Will.'

'Yes, alright.'

William didn't mind a walk anyway, and it meant they would be out a bit longer. Lately he'd begun to dislike his work, though on reflection it wasn't so much the work as the way he was living. He had the feeling that life was rushing past and he, with eyes dulled from boredom, was a spectator to it all.

He remembered a cross-roads just beyond the edge of town, where new houses were springing up all around. There was a pub there that had once been a coaching inn. When he reached it he asked if he could fill his can with water and the landlord directed him to a tap in the yard. As water splashed into his can William noticed an empty building with a sign on the door offering it for rent. He thought it must have been part of the old stables once. A motor went past on the Kettering road, and then another turned out of the cross-roads. They weren't exactly a common sight, at least not outside of the main towns, but their numbers were certainly increasing. Manufacturers were springing up all over the place, growing from small engineering firms or bicycle shops. William read about them in the magazines he bought. Names proliferated, more every week: Wolsely, Riley, Clement-Talbot, Morris. There were races at Brooklands and on the Isle of Man, capturing the public's imagination. Cars were no longer only for the rich. Smaller, cheaper motors were being made for the ordinary man, like the American Ford.

Water splashed from the can over William's feet, and he turned off the tap and went back to the pub to look for the landlord. 'I couldn't help noticing your sign on the building next door,' he said. 'Have you had much interest?'

'Trouble is, it's too far from the town,' the landlord said. 'I thought mebbe a saddle-maker or some such might want it, but I 'aven't 'ad much luck yet.'

'How much rent are you asking?'

'It's reasonable enough, if I say so myself. Only twenty five pounds a year.'

William thought it was still too much, though it was much cheaper than anything that could be had in town. He asked to have a look inside and the landlord took him out and unlocked the door. There was just a large open space with stalls partitioned off along one side. It wouldn't take much to adapt it, William thought.

When he got back to the lorry, Frank was sitting on the grass leaning against one of the wheels, sleeping contentedly. William cut off the end of the split hose and re-clamped what was left before filling the radiator. When he cranked the handle, the motor chugged into life again and Frank jumped up.

'You might've bloody told me you was back!' he exclaimed indignantly.

'Sorry,' William said, smiling.

A few minutes later when they passed the pub again, he looked carefully at the building, his mind spinning with possibilities.

*****

On Sunday, William got up early, before it was properly light, and quietly gathered his things. Taylor and the others were still asleep, but Brown's bed was empty. The bathroom was on the floor below, but William found the door locked. He waited on the landing outside, listening to Brown vomiting. Brown had come back drunk the evening before though he'd managed to conceal it from the house superintendent, or else he'd slipped him a bottle of beer to keep quiet. They were thick as thieves.

The door opened and Brown appeared wearing a dressing gown over his pyjamas. A miasma of stale cigarettes and beer mingled with last night's regurgitated supper clung to him. His eyes were bloodshot and his complexion sallow. His mouth curled when he saw William.

'Oh, it's you is it, Reynolds. Sneaking away early again, I see. What plans have you got today, I wonder? An afternoon at the museum is it? Or a tea dance at The Grand with your Miss Hodges? I expect you'll read Greek to her from that book you're always carrying around.' Brown's expression twisted in a sarcastic leer. 'I'll bet she's impressed with all that education and your fancy talk. Gets you into her pretty little drawers, I'll wager.'

'Have you finished in there?' William said, used to Brown's unpleasantness.

'No need to get sniffy with me, lad. You've got ideas above your station, that's your trouble. Bloody stockboys reading Greek. It's like shit with strawberries. No fucking point to it at all.'

'I'd appreciate it if you'd let me in,' William responded calmly.

'Appreciate it would you?' Brown echoed nastily. 'And what if I choose not to let you in, eh? What'll you'll do about that?'

Brown had a cruel, sardonic manner which he used like a knife on those he thought he could intimidate. It was worse when he drank, which he did as often as he could afford to. It brought up, in more ways than one, all of his pent up bile, his hatred of the world that he imagined himself unfairly treated by. He was middle aged, a man without a home or family of his own, dependent on his employer for everything.

William stood his ground, and though anger flashed in Brown's eye, William was young and tall. On consideration, Brown's ire quickly withered and expired and he pushed past with a scowl. When Brown was gone, William bathed and dressed, and by seven-o-clock he was walking in the park. He mulled over the idea that he'd been thinking about all week, going over the figures he'd jotted down, such as they were. At eleven he was waiting for Ruth by the statue of Prince Albert, where he'd arranged to see her.

She waved when she saw him and when they met she kissed him. 'Hello, have you been waiting long?'

'No, I've been walking around.'

She tilted her head to one side. 'You are a deep one aren't you, Will.'

'Am I?'

'Yes.'

It was a sunny day and people were out walking with their families. A couple went past with three children, the youngest in a baby carriage. The woman looked at Ruth and they smiled at one another.

'Have you heard anything about Mister Barnett, Will?' Ruth asked him, referring to one of the assistants in the Gentleman's Clothing department who had given his notice. Ruth had encouraged William to put his name forward for the vacancy, and though he wasn't sure he wanted to work on the shop floor, he'd agreed when she pointed out that he would earn half as much again as he did in the stockroom.

'Not yet,' he answered. 'Anyway, I'm not sure I'd accept the position.'

'What on earth d'you mean?' she said sounding shocked.

'I've been thinking about giving my notice.'

From Ruth's expression he might have said he was considering committing murder. 'You can't mean it, Will!'

He told her about the building he'd seen for rent. 'It's away from the town, but it's right beside the crossroads. I think it would be a good place to start a garage. I couldn't afford somewhere right in town, but the landlord's only asking for ten shillings a week, and I think he might take less.'

He asked her to sit down on a bench, and he showed her the figures he'd done. Though she listened, her expression was set disapprovingly, but he hardly noticed. The more he talked, the more excited he became. It was as if speaking about his ideas out loud made them seem more real.

'I've got a bit over twenty pounds saved,' William told her, though she already knew. 'I'm sure if I look around I could find some second-hand tools and equipment. If I can get an account with one of the bigger places for parts I think I could manage. I imagine I'd need a bit to live on while I get established, but once people get to hear about me, well, it's not very far to go really, and there are new houses being built all the time out that way.'

He went on, thinking ahead into the future. His first aim would be to make a living, but as time went on and he established a proper reputation with the bank he thought he might start selling cars as well as repairing them. 'Second hand to begin with. I could buy them cheaply and fix them up so I can sell them on for a profit.'

Eventually he became aware that Ruth had said almost nothing. 'Well, what do you think?' he asked her. He realised that he wanted her approval, or perhaps her encouragement. He wanted somebody to believe in him, perhaps because he wasn't certain that he did himself. At the back of his mind was the constant memory of what it had been like when he first came to Northampton, and he'd wandered the streets without anywhere to live and without any money. He remembered his feelings of hopelessness and despair.

'I suppose it's all very well for somebody who wants to do that sort of work,' Ruth said.

'You sound as if you don't approve.'

'It's not for me to approve or not, I'm sure,' she said.

'Motoring is the future, Ruth. There will be wonderful

opportunities for anybody who wants to take them.'

'Well, I wouldn't know anything about that,' she said, though he thought he detected a glimmer of interest. 'Where would you live, anyway?'

'At the garage to begin with, so that I can save money. I don't need much. A bed and a table. I expect I'll manage. At least I won't have to answer to anybody. I'll be able to come and go as I please and I won't have to sleep in a room with other people.'

'You wouldn't always have to live like that if you stayed at Ballantynes,' Ruth said. 'If you got Mister Barnett's position I bet you'd do well. I wouldn't be surprised if you was made a manager in a year or two, Will, and then one day you'd be a buyer. Everyone knows you're clever, and you've got such nice manners and you speak so well. It seems wrong to throw it all away and waste all the money you've saved up all this time just to work in a dirty garage. Look at Mister Samuels,' she went on, referring to one of the buyers. 'Him and his wife have got a lovely little house and two little children who're ever so sweet...'

She continued painting the picture she had obviously been carrying in her mind, and William realised that Ruth had different expectations than he did of their relationship. He knew he wasn't in love with her, though he was very fond of her. She was kind and pretty and not unintelligent, and she had ambitions, even if they were not the same as his own.

'Will you think about it, Will?'

He looked at her, realising she'd asked him a question. 'Yes, of course,' he said, not knowing what else to say.

'Good, I knew you would.' They got up, and she slipped her arm through his.

A few days later Mister Wilkins told William that Mister Dodd wanted to wanted to see him. On his way through the shop, William passed the Gentlemen's Clothing department. An assistant approached a customer who had paused in front of a display mannequin.

'Good morning, sir, how may I help you?' the assistant said.

'I was just admiring this jacket. Have you got it in my size do you think?'

'A very good choice, if I may say so, sir. If you'll step this way I'll just take your measurements.'

The customer made an impatient gesture. 'I haven't time for all that now. Surely you ought to be able to make an estimate.'

'Of course, sir, you're quite right. I expect you're about a forty two. If you'll excuse me, I won't be a moment.'

'Alright, but be quick about it.'

As the assistant scurried away, William tried to imagine working on the shop floor instead of where he was. At least he got away for a little while on most days and usually spent an hour or two working on the lorry or Mister Dodd's motor.

When he arrived upstairs he was told to wait. After a few minutes he was shown into the manager's office. He realised he'd never been there before. Mister Dodd sat at a large desk beside a tall window that looked out onto Gold Street.

'There you are, Reynolds. Sit down.' He waved to a chair. 'Did you manage to sort out that leak by the way?' he asked referring to oil that had been seeping from the engine of his car.

'Yes, it was just a worn seal.'

'Good. Thanks. Now, I wanted to talk to you about this vacancy in Gentleman's Clothing. Of course, working on the shop floor, dealing with customers and so on, is quite different from working in the stock room, but in your case I'm quite certain you'll do very well. After all, you went to Oundle, didn't you?'

'Yes, Mister Dodd.'

'I imagine you did well in your studies there?'

'I believe so. I was offered a scholarship at Oxford.'

'Why didn't you go?'

'I couldn't afford it. My benefactor died before I finished school.'

'I see. Well, I think you'll find your education will stand you in good stead, Reynolds. In fact, if you apply yourself I don't see why you shouldn't do very well here. Perhaps in a year or two we might move you up. You might be a buyer by the time you're twenty five. I myself was once a buyer, in fact. You can take up your new position next Monday.'

Dodd sat back with a benevolent smile to wait for William's reaction.

For a moment William hesitated. 'I'm very grateful for the faith you've shown in me, Mister Dodd. But I'm afraid I'm unable to accept your generous offer.'

'I beg your pardon?'

'The fact is, sir, I've decided to give my notice.'

As he spoke, William's heart thudded in his chest. He felt a mixture of apprehension and elation. He hadn't known he would resign, but now that he had, he already felt as if he'd cast off invisible chains.

'Do you realise what you are saying, Reynolds?' Dodd said, completely taken aback.

'Yes, sir. I've thought about it carefully.'

'I see,' Dodd said coldly, his manner abruptly changed, as if William's decision was a personal affront. 'Frankly, I think in that case I may have overestimated you. Obviously you are not suitable after all. Good afternoon, Reynolds.'

At the door William turned to say goodbye, but Dodd was already busy with the papers on his desk and he made no response, as if to his mind William had ceased to exist.

That evening after the shop closed, William told Ruth what he'd done. Disappointment flooded her eyes. 'We'll still be able to see each other on Sundays if you like,' he said. 'You can come out and see the place once I'm settled.'

'I'll have to see what I'm doing, won't I?' she responded. 'Anyway, I hope you don't think I'd want to spend my time off in some dirty garage.'

He knew then that he wouldn't see her again. 'I'm sorry, Ruth,' he said.

She looked at him sharply, and without another word turned on her heel and walked away.

9

1913

At the sound of an approaching engine, William looked towards the trees across the road, his brow creased in a puzzled frown. There was something peculiar about the noise. The pitch rose and fell as if somebody had put on the accelerator and then let it off again.

'Can you hear that?' he said to Arthur Hawkins. Arthur was twenty four and had been working for William for six months. He looked up from the engine of the Vauxhall he was bent over, and when William went outside Arthur followed.

The road was empty. The sound was coming from a field beyond the trees. The engine roared again, suddenly loud, but after only a second or two it faded away. Over the tops of the elms came a lumbering apparition.

'Bloody 'ell!' Arthur said, gaping in astonishment.

It was no more than fifty yards away. The machine had two pairs of wings connected by a maze of braces and wires and in the middle was a sort of seat where a man wearing a cap and a pair of goggles appeared to be desperately wrestling with the controls. An engine was positioned behind him, and was connected further back to a blurred disc that was rapidly slowing down so that it was possible to make out the two arms of a propeller. It was the first aeroplane that William had seen first-hand. He watched in fascination as the machine dipped towards them. The engine now seemed to be barely idling. A set of wheels underneath the thing clipped the uppermost branches of one of the trees, causing the plane to wobble dangerously as it passed directly overhead at a height of about eighty feet. It continued to glide towards earth, losing speed with every second, and then at a height of twenty or thirty feet, the nose dropped and the whole thing vanished from sight into the field behind the garage. They heard the crash, which sounded like kindling snapping, and then silence.

William and Arthur ran behind the garage to help. When they climbed through a hedge they saw that the plane had crashed halfway across the field. One set of wings pointed to the sky, while the other set lay in splinters on the grass. A small herd of frightened cows huddled in a corner of the field underneath a chestnut tree.

As William reached the wreck, the pilot staggered out and fell to his knees. There was blood on his face. His goggles were broken and his hat was gone, as was one of his shoes.

'Are you alright?' William asked. 'Here, you'd better lie down, you look a bit shaky.'

Wordlessly, the pilot did as he was told. He gazed up at the sky, his eyes unfocused and confused. He was bleeding from a cut on his forehead, but when William wiped it with his handkerchief the gash didn't appear to be very deep.

'Are you hurt anywhere else?'

'I don't think so.' The pilot closed his eyes. He was breathing normally and didn't appear to have broken any bones. After a little while the colour began to return to his face. He opened his eyes again and when he saw William he began to sit up. He looked at his wrecked aeroplane.

'Did I crash?' he asked.

'Yes. You were lucky to get out of it. Can you stand, do you think?'

'I'll try.'

'We ought to get somebody to have a look at that cut. I

can take you to the hospital.'

The pilot gingerly felt his head. 'I think I just got a bit of a knock. Did you see what happened by any chance?'

'Don't you remember?'

'I was coming towards some trees when I started having trouble with the engine. Damn thing kept losing power for some reason.' The pilot looked around, trying to get his bearings. 'The next thing I knew you were telling me to lie down.'

'Your wheels caught the top of those elms.' William pointed. 'You came over the top of the garage and then you just seemed to drop like a stone and we heard the crash.'

'Yes, I remember now. I saw a sign and a petrol pump. Anyway, I'm jolly grateful to you. I'm sorry, I ought to introduce myself. My name is Christopher Horsham.'

William shook the proffered hand. 'William Reynolds.' He gestured towards Arthur, who had gone to have a closer look at the wreckage. 'And that's Arthur Hawkins. He works for me.'

William and Horsham were about the same age. William picked up a shoe that was lying in the grass. It was handmade from the finest quality leather. He recognized the maker's name as one of the very best in the county.

'I think this is yours.'

'Oh, thanks.'

While Horsham sat down to put his shoes on, William went over to examine the plane. 'Have you had trouble with your engine before?'

'Yes, actually. I had a chap at Sywell have a look for me, but he couldn't find anything wrong.'

'Sywell?'

'Yes, a few of us have got together to start a flying club there.'

'It sounded as if it was starved of fuel,' William said. He stepped in amongst the confusion of broken wood and canvas. The propeller was intact, though the shaft linking it to the engine had snapped. He found the fuel tank fixed to the upper wing with a gravity line leading to the carburettors, and when he undid the plug at the bottom he caught some of the petrol that ran out and rubbed it between his fingers.

'It feels as if there's water in here.'

He stood up and looked at the broken wings and trailing wires, trying to work out how it had all gone together. What puzzled him was that, even after the engine stopped, the plane appeared to glide perfectly well for a minute. 'Why do you think it suddenly came down?' he asked.

'Not enough speed I expect,' Horsham said. 'It's one of the things they tell you to look out for when you're learning. After a certain point the thing simply won't fly.'

'How do you land it normally then?'

'You have to keep your speed up until the wheels touch the ground.' He pointed to a shattered flat section of canvas and wood at the front of the machine. 'That's called the elevator. There's another at the back. You control them with a pedal attached to a wire. It's broken now of course, but it's what makes the plane climb or descend.'

'And what's this?' William wondered, looking at the large fin-like arrangement at the back.

'It's the rudder. You use it for turning, like on a boat.'

Fascinated, William knelt down and moved the parts with his hands so that he could see it for himself. He wondered what it would feel like to fly above the earth, how things would look. He'd read about the Frenchman Bleriot reaching heights of as much as ten thousand feet. After a minute he remembered Horsham's injury and got up again.

'Sorry,' he said. 'We ought to go and clean up that cut.'

When they got back to the garage, William asked Arthur to carry on with the Vauxhall he was working on. He took Horsham to the room he'd partitioned off at the back of the building which he used as an office and his living quarters, and fetched some disinfectant to clean Horsham's wound.

'You're going to have quite a bruise,' William said. The skin was already turning a dark red colour and beginning to swell. 'Are you sure you don't want to see a doctor?'

'Honestly, I feel alright. It's a bit sore that's all. I'm used to a few knocks and scrapes anyway.'

'Have you crashed before?'

'In my plane, you mean? Good lord, no. But I've had a few prangs in my cars when I've been racing.'

William suddenly realised he'd heard of Christopher Horsham. 'I thought your name was familiar. You won at Brooklands last year didn't you?'

'Actually I came second. Luke Ashbury managed to get me on the final straight.' Horsham flashed a disarming smile, and with a careless gesture pushed his hair back from his forehead. All at once William was reminded of photographs he'd seen on the front page of the Northampton Gazette after Horsham had entered some race or other; the dashing and yet slightly diffident son of the Earl of Pitsford.

'I had my first time up in a plane at Brooklands, now you mention it,' Horsham said. 'Tommy Sopwith was giving joy-rides in his machine for a pound a go. I was hooked straight away, I must say. I'd never done anything so exhilarating. It even beats roaring around a track at eighty miles an hour, and that's saying something.'

'Have you given up motor racing now then?'

'I don't really know, to be honest. The thing is there's going to be an air-race at Sywell in May. I was going to enter, but I doubt that I'll be able to get another plane in time now.'

Horsham took a cigarette case from his pocket and offered one to William. He looked around at the neatly made bed and William's desk where William did his accounts. On the other side of the room was an area William used as a kitchen, where he managed to produce simple meals on a wood stove that also warmed the place during the winter months. Against the wall was a small bookcase, where alongside William's treasured copy of the Odyssey, were Ovid's Metamorphoses and some of Virgil's works in Latin and a smattering of novels by English writers that he liked.

'I say, do you mind if I ask you something?' Horsham asked curiously. 'Do you live here?'

'Yes.' William wondered what Horsham made of his home, and supposed it didn't compare favourably to Pitsford House, glimpses of which could be seen from the Market Harborough road amid its vast, tree-studded parkland surrounds. 'When I started the garage I couldn't afford anywhere else. I suppose I've become used to it.'

'How long have you been here?'

'Nearly two years now.'

'You seem to be doing well enough,' Horsham commented.

'It's getting busier all the time. The first year was difficult, but there are more cars about now and people are beginning to know about me.'

Horsham gave him a quizzical look. 'I hope you don't mind me saying so, but you don't actually strike me as the usual sort of chap you find running a place like this. Where did you learn about mechanics?'

'I picked up a bit at school to start with. One of the masters started a motoring club. But I suppose I'm self-taught really. I don't know half of what Arthur knows. He used to work for a garage on the other side of town before I persuaded him to come and work for me.'

Horsham glanced through the open door where Arthur was busy with the innards of the Vauxhall. 'Where did you go to school?'

'I was at Oundle.'

'I know a chap who was there. Lilly, his name is.

Roger Lilly. Do you know him?'

'I don't think so. Look, can I give you a lift somewhere?' William asked, eager to change the subject.

'Of course, I expect you're busy aren't you. It's very decent of you. My car's at Sywell. If you could drop me off there I'd be very grateful.'

'I'll just tell Arthur where I'm going.'

The aerodrome at Sywell was little more than a large open field, accessed through a gate in the lane. A small wooden building served as the clubhouse, and another much larger structure was where Horsham said people kept their aeroplanes. There were several cars parked on the grass, including a large, eight-cylinder Fiat that belonged to Horsham, and two more bi-planes stood on the field looking like gigantic dragonflies.

'Look here,' Horsham said when they arrived, 'I've been thinking about my machine. I was wondering whether you'd be interested in helping me fix her up? The thing is, with somebody who knew what he was doing I think we could resurrect her in time for that race I mentioned. I'd be quite willing to pay you, naturally. What do you say?'

'But I don't know anything about aeroplanes,' William said, taken aback by the proposal.

'Perhaps not, but you've an eye for practical things, I could see that straight away, and with the little that I've managed to pick up I think we might manage quite well together.'

William was tempted by the opportunity to learn about aeroplanes, but the garage was busy, and since that was his living it had to be his priority. He also had reservations about becoming involved with Christopher, who reminded him of his Oundle days, which he thought of with very mixed feelings. 'Let me think about it,' he said.

'Yes of course. But, look I've an idea, why don't you come here on Sunday? I'll borrow Wentworth's machine and take you up for a ride if you like. It might help you make your decision. There'd be absolutely no obligation. After all, it's the least I can do after all the help you've given me.'

William looked at the two ungainly looking planes nearby. If nothing else, he thought, he would find out what it was like to fly. 'Alright, thanks.'

He agreed that in the meantime he would salvage the wreckage and put it in the barn behind the pub, which he knew was unused, so long as Christopher would pay whatever rent the landlord asked for.

'Absolutely,' Christopher said as they shook hands. 'I'll see you on Sunday then. Wear something warm, it can get quite chilly once you're in the air. And thanks again for everything.'

*****

Four years had gone by since William first arrived in Northampton. He was twenty two years old and he owned his own business, which was now doing well. He could have afforded to rent a cottage somewhere if he wanted, but instead he'd put the money he made back into the garage to buy equipment like the old Hallford lorry and a Wolsely motor car that he used to get about in. He had increased his business by selling the occasional second-hand car, but he had bigger plans which involved opening a second garage near the town centre, which was why he'd brought Arthur to look at the site.

'What do you think?' William asked as they stood outside the building, which had once housed an engineering firm. 'It's a busy road, so there's plenty of passing trade.'

Arthur regarded the building doubtfully. 'I don't know, Will. It seems very big to me. Won't a place like this cost a lot? Where will you get the money from?'

'I've already spoken to the bank. They're happy to give me a mortgage, and I've got enough saved to get the place started. We'll only need part of the building to begin with, but I've got some ideas for the future.'

He showed Arthur some sketches he'd drawn, showing the building as William imagined it could look one day. Most of the front wall would be replaced by glass windows and the interior converted to a showroom to house new motor-cars. 'We'll continue to do servicing and repairs of course, but that will all move around the back. There's another entrance there. Here is where we'll present our face to the world.' In a moment of whimsy he'd even drawn a sign over the front of the building which read; W. Reynolds Ltd. Purveyors of Fine Motor Cars.

'It looks grand,' Arthur said, though William could see that he still had his doubts.

Arthur was only two years older than William, but in some ways the difference in their ages seemed greater than that. Arthur was a down-to-earth, practical man who had been involved with the fringes of the trade unions and the Labour party. To Arthur, business and the means to finance it belonged to a world that was not only foreign to him, but was populated with the kind of people he regarded as the enemy of the ordinary man.

'You don't like it, do you?' William said.

'It's not that. It just seems funny that's all.' Arthur compared the drawing to the reality before him, trying to imagine the transformation. 'I s'pose I always thought you'd build up the place you've got now,' he said.

It was a question of vision, William thought. Arthur couldn't imagine using the bank's money to create something like this. But William wanted to change Arthur's attitude. He recognised that Arthur could do more with his life than work as a mechanic if he wanted to. He was the kind of solid and capable person William needed.

'I'll keep the other place too,' he said. 'I've spoken to the landlord about buying the building already, and there's land next door that I can get cheaply if I buy it now. It'll be a good investment. In the future, once the town grows a bit more, the Kettering Road garage can look like this too.' He gestured to the drawing. 'One day I'll have a whole chain of them.'

Arthur looked at the drawing again, trying to make William's ideas seem real.

'The thing is, Arthur, I need you to help me. If I go ahead with this it's going to take up all my time. I'll need you to run the other place. You'll have to hire somebody to help you of course, and I'd pay you a manager's salary. You could take shares in the business if you like and pay for them out of what you earn.'

'A manager?' Arthur said in astonishment. 'Me?'

'Yes, why not?' William laughed. 'Come on, we'll talk about it again later when you've had time to think.'

On Saturday morning they had to return a Clement-Talbot to a customer in the town. William followed Arthur in the Wolseley to bring him back to the garage, but when they turned onto Gold Street they were confronted with a group of people carrying banners and placards marching along the middle of the road. William pulled over and they climbed out to watch. The crowd were mostly women. There were about a hundred of them, flanked by twenty policemen on either side to keep an eye on them, though the march seemed peaceful enough. Their placards demanded votes for women, and a banner carried in front bore the legend; Northampton Women's Society for Political Union. They were chanting slogans, and some of them were calling out to spectators who either supported or denounced them.

'Emily's girls,' Arthur commented, referring to Emily Pankhurst, the suffragette.

A pair of well-dressed women nearby looked on disapprovingly. 'Don't these women realise they are doing more harm to our cause than they are good?' one of them questioned loudly in a haughty tone.

A group of men on a corner called out insults, which

some of the suffragettes responded to in kind. One man wearing a top-hat came out of a shop, and seeing the women became outraged.

'Go home!' he shouted angrily. 'Go and learn how to be decent mothers to your children and wives to your husbands! Women have no business in politics!'

One of the leaders, an intense looking woman, met his eye and held it. 'You are living in the past, sir,' she said loudly. 'You and your kind have had your day, and it is time you realised it. Women will have the vote whether you like it or not.'

Her words had the ring of prophetic certainty, which only enraged the man further.

'No woman will ever vote in this country while I draw breath, Madam,' he said, to which she only offered a grim smile.

'Then I look forward to that day coming.'

Then she was past him and he was left spluttering impotently in her wake.

'What do you think, Arthur?' William said. 'Is she right?'

'He'll have more to worry about than just women gettin' the vote when there's a Labour government,' Arthur replied. 'People are fed up bein' treated no better'n animals. They want decent wages, a decent bloody place to live. Things are changin' everywhere so he might as well get used to it.'

'I suppose you're right,' William agreed, though he felt guilty that he couldn't muster Arthur's righteous anger. He wondered why that was. Whereas Arthur saw himself as being on one side of a struggle between the rich and the poor, William wanted to make his own way in the world.

As the last of the marchers passed them by there was a commotion among the suffragettes. At a prearranged signal they reached into their coat pockets and bags, and before the police realised what was happening they broke ranks and ran towards the shops on either side of the road. A hail of missiles filled the air and as they struck the plate glass windows the sound of smashing glass mingled with the shouts of women and the piercing blast of police whistles.

Bystanders looked on in shock and some of them ran away, fearing a riot, but in fact once the women had achieved their objective they were content to allow themselves to be arrested.

'More publicity for the cause,' Arthur commented wryly. 'The papers'll report their speeches from the dock.'

Change was everywhere, William thought. Every day the papers carried stories of strikes by miners and rail-workers and acts of vandalism and civil disobedience from suffragettes. People were prepared to go to prison for their beliefs.

In the melee of the disturbance William and Arthur were separated, but when it had petered out and many of the women had been taken away by the police, William saw him talking to a young woman. She was perhaps nineteen or twenty, with striking looks. Her slightly olive complexion and large dark eyes gave her an almost exotic look.

'Will, this is Sophie Yates,' said Arthur when William joined them. 'Me and her used to live in the same street when she were little, didn't we Sophie? I just turned 'round and there she was. We 'aven't seen each other for years.'

'I'm pleased to meet you, Miss Yates,' William said.

'Arthur has been telling me that he works for you, Mister Reynolds.'

He was surprised by the way she spoke. There were none of the rough edges that gave away Arthur's background, and by her manner and the way she was dressed he never would have thought they'd grown up in the same area.

'I was lucky to find him,' he said. 'I doubt there's a better mechanic in Northampton.'

She smiled in a polite, but faintly disinterested way.

'Were you watching the marchers?' he asked.

'I just came out for a minute to see what all the fuss was about.' She gestured to a door behind her that opened to a flight of stairs. A brass plate revealed that it was a firm of solicitors. 'That's where I work.'

'They 'ave their meetings at the Union Hall,' Arthur said to her, referring to the suffragettes. 'You should come and see if you're interested.'

'I haven't really got the time for that sort of thing, with my position,' Sophie said. 'In fact I ought to get back to work now. Goodbye Mister Reynolds, it was nice to meet you. And it was nice to see you again too, Arthur.'

'Goodbye Miss Yates.'

Arthur said goodbye to her, and as she left he shook his head in wonder. 'You wouldn't 'ave looked at her twice when she were a girl, honest, Will. Her arms and legs was like sticks. Now look at 'er, and working in a solicitor's office.'

'It just shows you then, Arthur. You can do anything if you want to badly enough.'

'I suppose you're right,' Arthur agreed thoughtfully.

As they drove off, Arthur looked back at the office where Sophie worked, and William guessed it wouldn't be the last time Arthur saw Sophie, though privately he had the feeling that she was less interested in Arthur than he appeared to be in her.

10

When William arrived at Sywell on Sunday, Christopher and another man were looking over the plane that was standing on the field. Christopher waved and came over.

'Hello. I'm glad you came,' he said as they shook hands. 'It's a perfect day for flying. Do you still want to go up?'

'Yes, I'd like to,' William said.

'Good man. Come and meet Wentworth. He's already said I can borrow his machine. Nigel, I'd like you to meet William Reynolds. He's the chap I was telling you about.'

As they shook hands, William was aware of Wentworth's subtle appraisal. It was done in the blink of an eye, registering the cut of William's clothes and the slightly battered Wolseley. Wentworth wore a striped blazer and baggy white trousers, and he drove a large, expensive Napier that was parked next to Christopher's Fiat. For a moment William wondered why he'd come. These were the sort of people who had always provoked antipathy in him; the privileged elite with their cars and country homes, and now their aeroplanes, and yet he admitted there was a part of him that was attracted to it all.

'I must say, I admire you for going up with a fellow after he almost crashed into your garage the other day,' Wentworth commented jokingly.

'Don't listen to him,' Christopher said. 'Come and meet Liz before we go. She's in the clubhouse making drinks I think.'

The clubhouse consisted of two or three rooms used for storage, and a main area where there were some comfortable chairs and a rudimentary bar where a young woman was mixing drinks.

'Better get another glass, Liz,' Christopher called out. 'By the way, I'd like you to meet William Reynolds. William… do you mind if I call you that?'

'Not at all.'

'And you must call me Christopher…. meet Elizabeth Gordon.'

'How do you do Mister Reynolds?'

William shook her hand. She had long, fair hair and startlingly green eyes, the colour of which made him think of coloured glass shot through with sunlight. They were unusually vivid and at the same time almost transparent.

'We're all having whisky and soda, but I can find something else if you prefer.' She peered into a box that hadn't been unpacked yet. 'Let's see, there's gin here, I think.'

'Whisky is fine, thanks.'

'I hear you're going to go flying.' She handed him a stiff drink. 'This ought to steady your nerves.'

There was something about her that William felt was vaguely familiar, though he was certain they'd never met. He realised that she reminded him of Emmaline. Not so much because of her looks, but because of her poise and manner. Wentworth and Christopher had it too, he thought. People like them were brought up imprinted with an innate confidence that in some became arrogance, but in most it was simply a sort of careless expectation of life. Having always had money and material things, they didn't think about them in the same way that ordinary people did.

When Elizabeth came out from behind the makeshift bar, her body flowed beneath the long dress she wore. Her figure was slender and long legged. The word coltish came to William's mind. He supposed she was about twenty or so.

Wentworth took out his cigarettes and offered them around. 'Christopher mentioned that you were at Oundle,' he said casually to William. 'Do you know a chap called Foulkes? J. R.'

'I don't think so.'

'I haven't seen him for a few years, actually. He was at Oxford I think. Although I remember somebody mentioning that he went to South Africa.'

There was a brief pause, an opportunity for William to say that he had been at Oxford himself, or else to say where he had been. But he left it unfilled.

'Are you from Northampton, Mister Reynolds?' Elizabeth asked. She was sitting on the arm of Christopher's chair, a drink in one hand, the other holding a cigarette. William wondered what their relationship was.

'No, I came here after my parents died,' he said.

He didn't really mind their questions. He supposed somebody who'd attended Oundle and now owned a small garage, where he lived like a gypsy, aroused their curiosity. He didn't offer anything more about himself and politeness prevented them from asking. He caught Elizabeth looking at him, perhaps faintly intrigued by his reticence.

As they talked he discovered a little about her, none of which surprised him. She had brothers and sisters and lived nearby with her family. He gathered that her father owned land, though perhaps not as much as the Horsham's, who owned half of the county. He understood that she and Christopher had known each other since they were quite young.

When they'd finished their drinks, Christopher announced that they ought to go while the weather held.

'Good luck,' Elizabeth said as they went outside. William smiled, not sure which of them she was talking to.

Christopher gave William a pair of goggles to wear and asked him to help turn the plane around. 'Always point into the wind for take-off. You get more lift that way. Now, I'll have to get you to help me get her started.'

He climbed up into the pilot's seat and asked William to go behind and take hold of the propeller. The machine was a pusher type, as most were, with the engine and propeller mounted behind the pilot's position. 'Give it half a turn to prime the engine,' Christopher instructed. 'Then I'll switch on and you give her another turn. She ought to start then.'

'Right.' William did as he was told, and though nothing happened on the first attempt, the second time they tried, the engine fired and caught and a cloud of smoke drifted across the grass.

Christopher gestured for William to climb up behind him. Since the engine was just behind William's position and almost completely exposed, the noise was deafening. He glanced back at the propeller as it blurred to a shining disc, and then the machine began to move quickly forward across the field. For a few seconds it was bumpy and uncomfortable, and then as the hedgerow rushed towards them Christopher pulled back on the wheel to operate the elevators and suddenly, miraculously, the jarring ceased and they were airborne.

William gripped the edge of his seat as the ground fell away underneath them. His heart was pounding and his mouth was dry, but as the machine climbed inexorably into a sky of drifting stacks of cloud and vast oceans of blue, he gradually forgot his nerves. Beneath them the countryside unfolded to the far horizons. William was amazed at how far he could see, and he began to look for landmarks that he recognised to help him put it all into some sort of perspective. He looked back towards the aerodrome and the clubhouse, where two tiny figures stood watching, and then he found the lane that led to the village of Sywell; which was no more than an insignificant cluster of cottages and the church, like a handful of pebbles. Further afield,

Northampton was reduced to a blur of brown rooftops. From there he found the garage by following the line of the Kettering Road, but there was nothing to see, and it struck him that so much of his life revolved around a place of such little consequence.

Soon, William's attention was taken by the wider vista. Roads and lanes connected villages and towns across the county and beyond, traversing valleys and skirting woodlands. He followed the course of a river to Ravensthorpe Reservoir, which became a puddle of blue merging with a surrounding pattern of shades of green and brown as the land lost definition and perspective, and then it was no longer the earth that fascinated, but rather the sky. Clouds drifted at different heights, some towering tens of thousands of feet into the air, others a fraction of that. The sky became a realm of depth and substance, a vast three dimensional entity through which they sailed in a flimsy contraption made of canvas and thin pieces of wood, all held together with tensioned wire and powered by a noisy, rattling engine that it seemed at any moment would shake itself free and send them tumbling to the distant ground.

After forty five minutes in the air they returned to the aerodrome. The grass field rushed towards them and the wheels hit the ground with a jolt, then the roaring engine quietened as they slowed and finally came to a stop. When the engine was switched off the silence seemed strange.

'What did you think?' Christopher asked when they'd climbed down.

'Wonderful. Like nothing I've experienced before.'

Christopher grinned. 'I had a feeling you'd feel like that. I could teach you to fly yourself, if you like,' he offered.

William regarded the plane, trying to imagine himself at the controls, but then he thought of the cost. 'It must be expensive, isn't it?'

'I've thought of that. If you decided to help me fix up

my plane, we could look on flying lessons as my end of the bargain.'

They started back to the clubhouse, where Wentworth and Elizabeth had come outside again to wait for them. William thought of his plans for the garage. He couldn't afford the time to help Christopher. 'The trouble is I've rather a lot on at the moment. Besides there must be plenty of people who could help you.'

'I suppose I could find somebody or other if I have to, but there isn't much time to be honest. Anyway, I've been thinking about it since the other day and I think we'd get on well together. I'd pay you for your time of course, as well as the flying lessons. And I don't think I mentioned it, but there's a five hundred pound prize up for grabs. If you agree to help me, if I win, we'll split it down the middle. What do you say?'

Christopher's manner was both disarming and flattering, and William admitted to himself that he was tempted. He was excited by the idea of learning how to fly.

'How was it?' Elizabeth asked William as she joined them. 'Did you enjoy it?'

'Yes. It was incredible.'

'Perhaps you can persuade Liz to go up with you one day, William,' Christopher said. 'I've tried, but she always refuses, so I've given up. I'm going to teach William to fly,' he added in explanation. 'At least I hope I am.'

'That's wonderful,' Elizabeth said, smiling warmly at William. 'That means we'll see a lot more of you.'

All at once William knew he would accept. He was aware that he was being subtly manipulated, and that Elizabeth was part of the reason he would agree to help. Almost despite himself, he was attracted to the idea of entering their world, even though he felt a little like the moth that flies helplessly toward a flame, or perhaps like Icarus who had flown too close to the sun.

'Alright,' he agreed.

Christopher grinned and shook his hand. 'Good show! I knew you would.'

'But only on the condition that if we're going to share the prize money I won't accept any payment,' William added.

'Agreed.'

Elizabeth and Christopher exchanged a quick, complicit look, and then unexpectedly she positioned herself between them and took both of their arms. 'We ought to have a drink to celebrate,' she said. 'I think there's a bottle of champagne in the clubhouse.'

11

In the offices of S. T. Walker, Solicitor, Sophie Yates was typing a letter to one of the firm's clients. Her desk was by the window in an office she shared with Mrs Fisher, who had been with the firm for twenty years. Sophie's fingers few across the keys, never missing a beat, the rapid clackety-clack rhythm of her typing assured. When she finished, she took the sheet from the roller and read it through looking for mistakes, but she couldn't find any. She put the letter in Mrs Fisher's tray to be checked and then returned to her desk. She glanced at the clock. It was half past five. Looking out of the window to the street below, she frowned when she saw Arthur Hawkins waiting for her.

'Didn't I see you speaking to that young man the other day?' Mrs Fisher said at her shoulder.

'Yes, you might have.'

The older woman peered through the window, her thin mouth pursed disapprovingly. 'Mister Walker wouldn't like your young men loitering outside the office at all hours you know.'

'He only comes when I finish work,' Sophie said. 'Besides, he's not my young man. I've asked him before not to come.'

'But you know him? You must know him if you were talking to him.'

'Yes. At least I knew him when we was... were... growing up.'

'He looks rather common,' Mrs Fisher sniffed. She

gave Sophie a pointed look that lasted for several seconds. 'Make sure you put the cover on your typewriter before you leave.'

Cow! Sophie thought, though her expression revealed nothing of her feelings. She consoled herself with the reminder that she had her revenge for Mrs Fisher's constant unpleasantness simply by being there each day. She was a reminder to Mrs Fisher that her youth, and whatever attractiveness she'd once possessed, were long past. She probably wasn't very old really. Forty perhaps. She'd never been married though. Sophie sometimes wondered if Mrs Fisher was in love with their employer. Unrequited love. She'd read the word in a book and looked it up in a dictionary to see what it meant. Not reciprocated. Not returned in the same way or to the same degree. Perhaps that was why she was such a sour old biddy.

The door to Mister Walker's office opened, interrupting Sophie's thoughts, and Mister Walker peered at her over his glasses. 'Sophie, do you think you could type a letter for me before you go home? It's rather urgent.'

'Of course, Mister Walker.' She began to take the cover off her typewriter again, but Mrs Fisher put on a false smile and twittered like a girl.

'Oh, Mister Walker, you should let me do that for you. Sophie's young man is waiting outside for her already and I'm sure she wants to get away on time.'

'Oh... I didn't realise,' he said.

'I was just telling Sophie that she mustn't encourage young men like that to loiter outside or they'll put off your clients.'

Mister Walker automatically looked out of the window as if he expected to see a ruffian frightening passers-by. Sophie wished that Arthur hadn't come, or at least that he was better dressed.

'It's alright, I don't mind staying behind,' she said. 'He's not my young man, and I've already asked him not to wait for me.'

'Well, if you're sure you don't mind, Sophie.'

She smiled prettily. 'Of course I don't.'

'Very well.' He gave her the letter. 'You get off home, Mrs Fisher, and we'll see you in the morning.'

Mrs Fisher scowled at Sophie and got up to fetch her coat. She didn't even say goodbye when she left, but shut the door behind her with a bang.

It only took Sophie ten minutes to finish the letter. She knocked on Mister Walker's door, and when he called for her to go in she found him sitting at his desk. He put his pen down and gestured to a chair.

'Sit down, Sophie.'

He read over what she'd typed, and then put his signature on the bottom. It hadn't been urgent at all, Sophie knew.

'I've been meaning to speak to you,' he said. 'You seem to have settled in very well. Are you enjoying your work?'

'Yes, Mister Walker. Though I worry sometimes that my work isn't good enough.'

'Really? I don't know why you should think that. This letter, for example, is very good. There isn't a single mistake anywhere and you were very quick.'

'Then you don't have any complaints about me?' she asked hesitantly.

'Complaints? Not a single one.' He laughed in an avuncular fashion. 'Why would you imagine that I have?'

She looked down at her lap. 'I thought perhaps Mrs Fisher might have said something,' she said quietly.

For a few moments he didn't say anything, and Sophie wondered if she'd overplayed her hand. But then she looked up and he gave her a sympathetic smile.

'You mustn't worry about Mrs Fisher, Sophie. You see, she's rather stuck in her ways. She's been with me a very long time and sometimes, well, it's difficult for people to get used to changes, new people and so on. I expect she's still getting used to the idea, that's all.'

'I wouldn't want to give you the wrong idea,' Sophie said. 'Most of the time Mrs Fisher is very good to me.'

He nodded, pleased. 'There you are then.'

He stood up and went with her to the door. As he opened it he placed a hand on her shoulder. 'You know, I'd like to take you for supper one evening, to make up for Mrs Fisher. Would you like that?'

'I'd love to, Mister Walker. It would be lovely to meet your wife,' Sophie said, deliberately misunderstanding him.

His smile wavered. 'Yes, well, perhaps when things are not quite so busy then. Goodnight, Sophie.'

'Goodnight, Mister Walker.'

When she went outside, Sophie found that Arthur was still waiting for her. She ignored him, but after a moment he fell into step beside her.

'Hello, Sophie. I thought I'd missed you.'

'I had to work later today,' she said and threw him an irritated look. 'Why are you here Arthur? I asked you not to come to my work, didn't I? Now Mrs Fisher has seen you and she's complaining to Mister Walker.'

'What is she complainin' about? All I was doin' was waiting for you.'

'She doesn't like me. The point is I've asked you not to come,' she snapped.

They walked in silence, but after a little while Sophie felt guilty for being so short with him, especially as he wore such a hangdog expression. The trouble was she was angry with Mister Walker, though she supposed she shouldn't be really. If it had been left to Mrs Fisher, Sophie knew she never would have got a job there, but when she went for her interview she had been introduced to Mister Walker, and she'd used her looks to charm him. Men were simple creatures, really. All it took was a pretty face and a sweet smile and to listen to them talk as if every word they uttered was fascinating. Men believed women are susceptible to flattery, but they didn't realise that they were no better. And flattery had worked with Mister Walker because he had given her the position. The trouble was he wanted more from her now. Men always wanted more.

'Arthur,' Sophie said in a softer voice. 'What is it you want?'

'I just want to see you, Sophie, that's all.'

'No it isn't. You want to walk out with me, don't you?'

'Well, what if I do? What's wrong with that?'

'Nothing,' she said. 'Except…'

''Cept what?'

She didn't know how to explain it to him without hurting his feelings. He was a kind man, and though she rarely went back to the street where she'd grown up or wanted to see anybody there she'd known, she sometimes missed people. Her mum. Her sisters. Arthur reminded her of them.

'Have you had your supper?' she asked him.

'Not yet.'

Sophie normally made something for herself in her rooms. But it was lonely by herself and she didn't like living there. She could hear the other tenants in the rooms either side of her, the sound of voices arguing or other equally unwelcome sounds. It was all she could afford on her wages.

'The King's Arms does a good roast supper,' she said. 'We could go there if you like.'

Arthur agreed happily, and even insisted that he would pay for her, though she told him that she didn't want him to.

'I've got my own money.'

When they arrived at the pub they ordered their meals, and Sophie allowed Arthur to buy her a drink. She asked him how things were going at his work.

'Alright,' he said. 'The garage is busy. 'Specially now Will's helpin' Mister Horsham mend his aeroplane.' He told her about the crash and how they'd gone to help.

She looked at his hands on the table. His nails were black with oil around their edges, even though she could see he had scrubbed his hands. The cuff of his jacket was frayed.

'Are you doin' anything on Sunday, Sophie?' Arthur asked. 'I thought if you're not we could go somewhere.'

'Do you know how I left the terrace, Arthur?' she said

He looked confused at her abrupt change of subject. 'Someone told me you went into service.'

'That's right. I got a position as a maid at a house in Victoria Gardens.'

She was thirteen then. Since she'd finished school she had been working in the boot factory and living with her mum and three older sisters. They shared a single room in a house with families on either side. It was her eldest sister who got her the maid's position. Sophie hated working in the factory, but she didn't want to be a maid either. She took the job because she knew her mum wanted her to. At least she'd have somewhere proper to sleep and get her food.

'It was the best thing that ever happened to me,' Sophie said. 'The work was hard because I did everything except the cooking, and I didn't get paid much. But the family were kind to me. I've seen some girls treated like slaves, but I was lucky.'

The family she worked for were respectable. The husband was a surveyor called Edwin Wallace, and his wife had been a teacher before she married. They had three children of their own but they were all boys.

'I think she was nice to me because I was a girl. She gave me books to read and helped me to practice my writing, and she taught me how to speak properly and how to behave like a respectable lady. She said I was clever and that I shouldn't settle for being in service all my life, and when I was sixteen she helped me get a job as a shop-girl in a drapers.'

To begin with Sophie hadn't liked her new position very much. She was on her feet all day and the food they were given wasn't very good, and she had to share a room with three other girls. At least at the Wallace's she had a room of her own in the attic. But she met people, and that was why she took the position.

'I decided I wanted to make something of myself, you see,' she explained. 'I met somebody there who sent me to lessons so I could learn how to type, and then he got me a position in the office.'

His name was Percy, and he was the son of the man who owned the shop. He was married with two children. In return for the things he did for her she became his mistress. He told her that she was beautiful, and she had the sort of looks that men liked. He took her to the theatre and taught her about music and art, and encouraged her to read books. He said that she was everything a certain type of man wanted, which was not submissiveness, but was what society said they couldn't have. They wanted a woman who turned other men's heads, but was respectable and behaved like a lady except in the bedroom. In the bedroom they wanted a woman who knew how to fuck. Those were the words he used. And that is what he taught her.

But in the end Sophie left Percy and left her position as well, because she didn't want to be anybody's mistress. She was grateful for what he'd taught her and she intended to use it to make her own way.

Sophie didn't tell Arthur about Percy. Instead she said, 'I don't intend to work in an office all my life, Arthur. And I'm not going to marry a man who doesn't want the things I do. I don't want to be poor. I don't want my children to be servants.'

And neither was she going to become a whore for Mister Walker or for anybody else, Sophie thought to herself. Percy was the only man she'd ever slept with. She'd liked him, but she hadn't loved him. She'd slept with him because he'd helped her, but she would never do it again. When she slept with another man it would be because she wanted to, for love. She still believed in love. She believed in love more than ever.

'You mean you won't 'ave me because I'm just a mechanic?' Arthur said.

'It isn't that, exactly.'

'Yes, it is.'

Their meals arrived, but Arthur didn't notice. She felt sorry for him. He was nice looking really. He had a strong face, and though he hardly knew her, he cared for her more deeply and genuinely than Percy ever had.

'Eat your supper before it gets cold,' she said.

As they ate she noticed he didn't know how to hold his knife and fork properly, and once he wiped his mouth with his sleeve.

'Oh no, she would never do that. But it would be embarrassing for her, I suppose. Anyway, I'm glad she's gone. Do you mind if we get my cigarettes somewhere else in case she comes back?'

A few days later, Christopher mentioned his near encounter with Anne Donaghue to Elizabeth.

'I don't know why you're worried about seeing her,' Elizabeth responded with surprising acidity. 'It's her own silly fault that she made an ass of herself.'

Christopher threw William a wry look. 'In case you haven't noticed, old man, Liz tends to be of the sort who does not suffer fools.'

'I won't apologise for that,' Elizabeth retorted. 'I told you that girl had every intention of marrying you the moment she laid eyes on you. She let everyone know that you had as good as proposed before you went to France, and then that picture appeared and made her look rather silly.'

'Which wasn't true, by the way,' Christopher said. 'I never said anything to make her think I was going to marry her. Anyway, I told her the first night we met that I'd already promised to marry you.'

'Yes, but you probably also mentioned that I was only eight at the time, so I shouldn't imagine she took much notice.'

They laughed, but William wondered if there had been something more between them once, however innocent. He knew from experience that first love left a lasting impression. He still thought of Emmaline occasionally. There were other occasions when Christopher joked about girls he'd known, comparing them unfavourably to Elizabeth, as if she were the standard by which he judged them. It was very light-hearted, but underneath it all there was an undercurrent like a shared secret and William always felt a prickle of envy that he was excluded.

One evening Elizabeth came to the barn, and after the three of them had eaten the supper she'd brought,

Christopher put on a gramophone record and lay on his back listening to the scratchy notes drifting across the field.

'It's such a beautiful evening, I feel like going for a walk,' Elizabeth announced. 'Who wants to come with me?'

'Alright,' William said, though Christopher only waved a languid hand.

'I think I'll stay here.'

They walked through a field of long grass flecked with poppies like sparks, not hurrying, relishing the swish of grass and the chatter of birds in the trees gradually falling quiet as the twilight faded. Their hands brushed accidentally and Elizabeth glanced at him, smiling, her eyes a deeper green in the dying light

'How are you getting on with your plane, you two? Will you be finished in time for the airshow?'

'Yes, I think so.'

'Christopher says he couldn't have done it without your help, you know.'

'I expect he could have found somebody if I hadn't happened along.'

'Perhaps. But he likes you. And he says your ideas will make a big difference. He thinks you're very talented.'

'I didn't realise the two of you spent so much time discussing me,' William said, not sure whether he was pleased by the idea or not. He decided he was.

'Christopher talks about you a lot,' Elizabeth said. 'You've become good friends, haven't you?'

'Yes, I suppose we have,' William agreed. 'I hope that you and I have become friends too.'

'Of course we have.'

'Can I ask you something?'

'If you like.'

'How long have you and Christopher known one another, exactly?'

'For ever. We practically grew up together. I remember as children we used to climb trees in the woods. I fell out of one once when I was seven and broke my arm. I've been afraid of heights ever since.'

'Is that why you won't fly?'

'Yes.'

She was quiet for a moment. 'Is that what you really wanted to ask me?'

He was surprised at her intuitiveness. 'I'm not sure what I wanted to ask really. No, that's not true. It's just that I'm not sure how to, or if it's even any of my business.'

'Why don't you tell me what it is, and then if it isn't any of your business I won't answer you.'

He saw she was joking and smiled. 'Alright, I suppose the truth is, I wonder sometimes about your relationship. Yours and Christopher's I mean.' She didn't comment and he wished he'd never said anything. 'Are you offended?' he asked her eventually.

She shook her head. 'Of course not. I suppose I was trying to think how to answer you, that's all. The truth is, Christopher and I are friends. Very good friends. But we've never been lovers. That's what you meant, isn't it?'

'I told you it's none of my business.'

'I don't mind,' she said, and as if to prove it linked her arm through his. They didn't speak again for a little while, though the silence between them was comfortable.

'You're very different from Christopher, aren't you?' Elizabeth mused eventually.

'You mean that Christopher is rich, and that compared to my life, Christopher's life is exciting and glamorous?'

'You're being flippant, and no, that isn't what I mean.'

'Sorry.'

'Christopher can be impetuous. When he gets excited about something he pursues it with all his attention, whether it's motor racing, or aeroplanes or even women. He gets caught up in things, and then something new comes along and suddenly everything changes. But you're not like that are you? You're more steady. More serious about things.'

'You make me sound dull.'

'No, no you're not at all. Of course you're not. I didn't mean that. I like the way you are. I'd bet that if you say something you've thought it through and you mean it. I imagine that once you've decided to do something you see it through to the end. I think those are admirable qualities. I admire them anyway.'

William was pleased by her compliment, though he wasn't sure everything she said was true. What she'd said made him think of the garage. He couldn't avoid the fact that ever since he'd met Christopher he'd neglected his business, and certainly his expansion plans had been put to one side. But then a degree of flexibility was important. His goal remained the same, which was to make his own way in the world and become successful, but he was no longer certain of the means.

'You know, I think that's the reason you and Christopher get on so well,' Elizabeth said, evidently having thought about it. 'You're opposites in many ways, and yet very alike in others. Two sides of the same coin. Perhaps that's why I feel so comfortable with you. I feel as if I've known you for years.'

'I'm glad you feel that way,' he said.

They had reached the far side of the field. The gramophone had stopped playing and the evening was hushed. They could hardly see the barn anymore. William wondered how Elizabeth would react if he tried to kiss her. He had the felling she wouldn't object. For a moment it seemed like the most natural thing in the world to do. He knew he was falling in love with her, but at the same time he didn't want anything to change. He wanted life to go on like this for ever. The three of them listening to music and talking and laughing at the end of the day.

He knew that wasn't possible. In a few weeks the plane would be finished and then there would be the race and afterwards... What, he wondered? What happened then?

Elizabeth had just told him that Christopher's life was a series of adventures and passions, one after the other. Had she been warning him? After all, their lives were very different. He had the garage to think of - his future. All of these thoughts went through his mind, and he realised there was no point in wanting everything to stay as it was. Nothing ever did.

They were standing very close to another, Elizabeth's face pale in the darkness folding around them. His heart was thudding. He moved closer to her, but as he did a sound reached them from across the field, the faint, scratchy beginning of a tune and suddenly the moment was lost.

'We ought to get back,' Elizabeth said.

'Yes.'

Several times a week William and Christopher would drive to Sywell, and William would have an hour's lesson using Wentworth's machine. After a few attempts at piloting with Christopher sitting behind him, William took his first flight alone, and soon afterwards applied for his license from the British Aero Club. Elizabeth sometimes came to the aerodrome to watch, and it was there one day after William had taken a forty minute solo flight that Christopher suggested they ought to go to Brooklands.

'What do you think, William?'

They were sitting outside the clubhouse on deckchairs. It was late afternoon. William was watching the way the sun struck the tops of the trees in the hedgerows so that they seemed almost to be ablaze. He came to, realising belatedly that Christopher had asked him something.

'Sorry, I was miles away.'

'There's no use trying to get anything out of William when he's like this,' Elizabeth teased.

'What do you mean?' he asked.

'You always go off into this dreamy state after you've been flying. It makes me quite envious.'

'Do I? I hadn't realised. I suppose it's because when

I'm up there I can appreciate how beautiful everything really is. You know what it's like when you look at something closely... I don't know what... a flower perhaps, like those, what are they called?' He gestured to a clump of pale mauve wildflowers growing nearby.

'Mallow, I think.'

William went over and picked one. 'You see these all the time. So often that you hardy notice them. From any distance they appear to be one colour, but if you look closely you can see they have these dark purple veins. See how delicate they are.'

Elizabeth smiled. 'Yes, they're actually rather beautiful.'

'Well flying is like that, only in reverse. Suddenly you have this entirely different perspective. You see all the places... villages, towns, roads and so on... as a small part of the countryside as a whole, and all at once you realise that there is so much more to it than you appreciated.'

'William's right, you know Liz. You ought to see for yourself,' Christopher said. He was always trying to persuade her to go up but she never would.

When William sat down again he noticed that Elizabeth kept the mallow, and every now and then he saw her gazing at it thoughtfully. He had the feeling she was thinking about what he'd said about seeing things with new eyes. Since that evening when he had almost kissed her something had changed between them. A subtle difference existed in their relationship - an awareness or perhaps even an expectation of things to come. The world changes, William thought, whether we want it to or not.

'Anyway, what I was saying before was that we ought to go to Brooklands,' Christopher continued. 'We could see what Tommy Sopwith and all those other fellows there are doing. We're bound to learn something we can use to make sure we beat Wentworth here in the race.'

'I say, that's not very sporting of you,' Wentworth

protested mildly.

'Why don't you come with us? Any number of firms have set up to build aeroplanes there now. There's a real push on to try and catch up with the French.'

'Let me know when you're going and I'll see what I'm doing.'

'What about you William, what do you think?'

'I think it's a good idea,' he said.

'Good, we ought to go soon. What about this weekend? You could come too, Liz, if you like.'

'I can't,' she said. 'It's Joanna's birthday on Sunday and I can't miss it,' she said referring to her youngest sister.

'I can't make it either, I'm afraid,' Wentworth said. 'Prior engagement with Maureen Hampton.'

'Looks as if it's just us then, William. I'll find out what time the trains are and let you know tomorrow.'

The following morning, when Arthur arrived for work, he said that a man had come in the previous afternoon to say he had broken down on the Wellingborough road.

'What did you tell him?' William asked.

'I said he'd have to leave his car and we'd fetch it today. I couldn't do it on my own, Will,'

'No, of course,' William agreed guiltily. There were already three cars waiting for repair besides the one Arthur was working on, and though Arthur hadn't complained, William thought he must feel resentful at being left to cope alone such a lot. 'We might as well go and get it now then,' he said.

They took the lorry to tow the broken-down car back with. On the way, William asked Arthur how Sophie was, as he knew they'd been seeing one another occasionally.

'She's alright.' Arthur said glumly.

He didn't seem willing to talk about Sophie, and William wondered if things were going alright between them. When Arthur had first begun seeing her - after they met on the day of the suffragette march - Arthur had talked about her constantly, but lately he'd barely mentioned her. William had to admit he wasn't really surprised. He'd never believed Sophie was the sort who would settle for somebody like Arthur.

When they found the car that had broken down at the side of the road, they attached a chain to the front axle so they could tow it back to the garage. Arthur barely spoke and seemed distracted.

'Will,' he said finally. 'There's something I want to ask you. Are you still thinkin' about opening another garage like you talked about?'

'To be honest, I haven't had time to think about it lately,' William said. 'Why do you ask?'

'I just wondered because you 'adn't mentioned it, that's all. Do you want me to drive the lorry?'

'Yes, alright.'

William thought about what Arthur had asked him on the way back and brought the subject up again when they arrived. 'Have you thought about what we talked about if I did open another garage? That you might run this one?'

'Yes,' Arthur said immediately. 'If you thought I could do it, I'd like the chance.'

'There's no question of that. You're already running it more or less by yourself.' William had the feeling there was something else on Arthur's mind, and asked him what it was

'You said something about me buying a share in the business.'

'That's right,' William agreed.

'Do you think the bank would lend me the money to do that if I asked?'

'I don't see why not,' William said, surprised. 'You seem very keen all of a sudden.'

'I've just been thinkin' about it, that's all. When do you think you'll decide what you're going to do?'

'We'll talk about it again when I get back from Brooklands,' William promised.

On Saturday morning, Christopher arrived to pick William up and they caught a train from Northampton to London, and from there took another to Weybridge, which was the closest station to Brooklands. A taxi took them the rest of the way, and as it turned out there was a motor-race meeting on that afternoon. When they arrived there were already crowds of people in the stands opposite the finishing straight. Near the track itself bookies were taking bets on the afternoon's programme.

'It could almost be a meeting at Ascot,' William observed. There were even changing rooms for the competitors and a clubhouse and restaurant.

'Yes, I suppose you're right,' Christopher agreed. 'The thing is, nothing had ever been built like this before, so I suppose they had to model it on something.' He looked at his watch. 'Why don't we have something to eat? We can watch the first race if you like.'

'They went to the Blue Bird restaurant to see if they could get a table and found they were in luck. The table they were given offered a view of the track and the crowds of people, and they could hear the sound of powerful engines being given a final tune-up before the first race.

A waiter bought their menus, but after a glance at the wine list Christopher put it aside. 'I don't know about you, but drinking wine at lunch makes me awfully sleepy. I think I'll stick to whisky and soda.'

'I'll have the same. Have you eaten here before?'

'Yes, a couple of times. The food's not bad really.'

After they'd ordered they lit cigarettes, and Christopher pointed out the landing strip in the middle of the track. 'This is where I had my first flight, did I tell you? I was racing my Renault here about a year and a half ago. Tommy Sopwith had set up a flying school the year before, after he won four thousand pounds for flying a British made machine the longest distance from England to the Continent. He travelled a hundred and sixty nine miles in something like three and a half hours.'

'Yes, I remember reading about it,' William said. He'd been at Ballantynes then.

'The flying school is still operating as far as I know, though I suppose they don't operate while there's racing on.'

The first race of the day took place while they were eating lunch. About fifteen cars took their places at the start line, all of them great, powerful machines like Christopher's Fiat, with long bonnets to accommodate their huge six litre engines. When the flag dropped and the cars roared off, the noise even in the restaurant was deafening, and they could see a pall of smoke drift across the spectators.

The track was two and three quarter miles long in total and a hundred feet wide, with thirty foot high banked corners at either end. The longest straight ran alongside the London to Bristol railway for half a mile, and it was there that the drivers got the fastest speeds out of their cars. After two laps the field was well spread out, and several cars had been forced to pull out altogether with engine trouble, but there were three cars at the front all competing closely for the lead. First one would be in front, and then another would edge ahead, finding a moment to get on the inside as they roared out of a bend, only to be beaten on the straight by the third. It was clearly a duel of driver skill as much as it was a competition between the cars themselves.

'That's Kerridge in front now,' Christopher said as the cars came out of the banked turn onto the long straight. 'He's driving a Bentley. He's a marvellous driver. I raced against him once myself, and I don't mind admitting he was impossible to catch. He takes enormous risks, but he's got the skill to carry it off.'

'Who's that coming up behind him now?' William asked as one of the two cars closely following, gained quickly. They seemed to be going at a fantastic speed, the sound of their engines shattering the tranquillity of the countryside.

'Clarke,' Christopher said, looking at his programme. 'I don't know him, but he's driving a Peugot. It looks very fast. I'd say he's got the edge on the straights, but Kerridge is holding him off on the curves.'

As the race continued it was the two lead cars that put up a determined battle for first place, the third one gradually dropping further back until it was out of contention.

'They must be getting up to eighty or ninety miles an hour along that straight,' Christopher commented.

'We ought to be able to build an aeroplane that can go as fast as that,' William said.

'I don't see how. It's a question of weight surely. Can you imagine one of those engines on my kite? It would never get off the ground.'

'You're right. But there are new types being developed all the time. It's no good using engines that are made for cars.'

A chorus of excited shouts went up from the crowd as the leaders came down past the stands again, this time with the Peugot in front. William imagined Christopher out there, hanging grimly onto the wheel as his car hurtled around the track, while in the clubhouse with its green domed roof, people looked on as they drank champagne.

'Will you race again, do you think?' he asked.

'I don't know. I hadn't really thought about it to tell the truth,' Christopher said. 'I might stick to flying, but it depends how we get on at the airshow.' He thought for a moment. 'I suppose I could do both, actually.'

'Did you win many races before you started flying?'

'A few.'

'Is that why you did it? To win?'

Christopher looked at him in surprise. 'Yes, of course. Though I suppose that wasn't the only reason. It's exciting to go out there and drive as fast as you possibly can and try to beat the other fellow, but that's only a part of it. There are the people you meet, the places you go where the races are held in France and Italy and so on. There's always a certain crowd, and somebody or other is always having a party. I suppose flying isn't much different in that respect. There are air shows and races being held everywhere nowadays. I think there's quite a lot of prize money to be had, especially on the continent.'

William wondered what it would be like to live that kind of life.

'You ought to think about taking it up, you know,' Christopher said.

'Me?'

'Why not? You've only been flying for a month or so but you're already a better pilot than I am.'

'Rubbish.'

'No, it's true,' Christopher insisted. 'Wentworth thinks so too. It's because you have a natural feel for it. Not just the controls, but the whole business of the design and what makes it work and so on. You know far more than I do. You're always thinking about how something can be improved. I knew it the very first time we met. Do you remember when you came to help me after I crashed that day? I was watching you as you poked about in the wreckage. Even then you were trying to see how it all went together, and I knew then that I was going to ask you to help me fix it up.'

William laughed. 'I don't believe you.'

'It's true. Anyway, for a chap who reads Homer and Virgil, surely flying aeroplanes would be far better than mending cars for a living.'

William smiled, though he was stung by Christopher's casual dismissal of the way he made his living.

The race was won by Kerridge in the end. He got ahead of the Peugot on the final curve and held his lead by half a length on the finishing straight. After lunch, William and Christopher went to the flying village as it was known, a collection of wooden buildings that housed the aviation firms that had grown out of Brooklands. They were told that Tommy Sopwith was no longer there. He'd formed the Sopwith Aviation Company the previous year and it was housed in a disused ice rink in Kingston Upon Thames. But there were others there who were happy to talk to them, and they spent the rest of the afternoon meeting people and discussing their ideas.

The thing they all had in common, William discovered, was a belief in the future of aviation. They all had different opinions about what were the best design characteristics of aeroplanes. Some favoured monoplanes as opposed to biplanes, most were in favour of pusher type layouts with the engine and propeller behind the pilot, though one man they met believed more could ultimately achieved with an engine in front of the plane driving a different shaped propeller, one that pulled the machine through the air. But whatever opinions they had, it was generally agreed that development was happening very quickly, and that it was being driven primarily by two things; one was that engines were being produced that were increasingly lighter and yet more powerful, and the other was that throughout Europe in particular, the military had become very interested in the possibilities that aviation offered.

'Tommy Sopwith is working pretty closely with the Admiralty to design a plane that can land and take off on the sea,' they were told by one man. 'Already Germany and France have both formed a military air service, and our own army is interested in using them for reconnaissance. Have you heard about the trials?'

'What trials?' William asked.

'The army are holding them at Farnborough in the autumn. Essentially the idea is to turn up with your machine, and whoever can convince the army brass that theirs is the best for the job will win a contract to supply.'

'Are you going to enter?'

The man smiled. 'Of course.'

13

On the day of the airshow the weather was perfect for flying. Scattered cumulus rose in billowing columns of pure white from three to ten thousand feet and there was a light easterly breeze. A combination of warm temperatures and the novelty of the event had brought a huge crowd to Sywell. Men, women and children of all backgrounds arrived by motor car or by public motor-buses from all over the county. Stalls selling food and refreshments added to the festive air. For the better-off a table could even be had in a marquee where a five course lunch was served by waitresses in uniform.

The aeroplanes were lined up along one side of the field, separated from the public by a rope barrier to prevent either the risk of injury to the overly curious or damage to the machines. A reporter from the Northampton Gazette had come to cover the event, and with him was a photographer who was preparing to take a photograph of Christopher standing beside his plane. Sir James and Lady Horsham had been driven up from London for the show in their Rolls Royce and were mingling with their guests, who were being served canapés and champagne by a pair of maids who circulated among them.

'You come from near Brixworth, I understand, Mister Reynolds,' Elizabeth's mother said after William had been introduced. 'Do you know the Mannings? They live at Brixworth.'

'I'm afraid I don't.'

'Mother, don't cross-examine him,' Elizabeth chided.

'I'm sure I was doing no such thing,' she said.

Elizabeth's father rescued him by asking about Christopher's plane. 'I understand you played a large part in rebuilding it, Mister Reynolds. Are you an aviator yourself?'

They discussed the future of aeroplanes, which Mister Gordon believed was limited. Already the novelty of races and air-shows was wearing off. He said that if this was Bournemouth, where a number of shows had been held in recent years, he doubted a quarter of the people here would have come.

'But Elizabeth tells us that you own a motor garage,' Mister Gordon said. 'Now there is a business with a future.'

'Actually I've decided to sell my garage,' William said, at which Elizabeth looked surprised.

'I didn't know that.'

'I was going to tell you. It was only settled a few days ago.'

'You mean you've sold it already?'

'More or less. Arthur's agreed to buy it.'

'The man who works for you?'

'Yes.'

William looked around for Arthur, wondering where he was. Though he couldn't see him, Sophie was standing alone nearby, holding a glass of champagne and watching the people around her. He noticed that Sophie was herself observed as much as she observed others, though she gave no sign of being aware of it. She wore a pale blue jacket and skirt of a style and quality that ensured she was in no way out of place, but it was her looks that made her stand out. It was hard to define exactly what made her beautiful, but William thought it was something people were instinctively drawn to; a perfect symmetry in her features, her startlingly large, almond shaped eyes.

'She's quite lovely, don't you think?' Elizabeth said beside him.

'Yes, I suppose she is.'

'Who is she?'

'Her name's Sophie Yates. She came with Arthur.'

'Really? Are they involved together? Romantically I mean?'

'I don't know, to be honest. I know Arthur likes her. In fact I suspect she's part of the reason he wanted to buy the garage. He wants Sophie to see him as somebody with future prospects.'

Elizabeth studied Sophie. 'I hope that wasn't his only reason.'

'What do you mean?'

'I'm afraid I can't imagine her with your Mister Hawkins, that's all. I imagine she has her sights set on bigger things.'

William wondered if Elizabeth was right, and was forced to admit that he found it difficult to picture them together too.

'Have I said the wrong thing?' Elizabeth said, seeing him frown.

'No, it's just that I hope I haven't pushed Arthur into more than he can manage, that's all. I wouldn't like to think he's taken on the garage for the wrong reasons.'

'Don't you think he's capable of running a business?'

'Yes I do. I wouldn't have agreed to lend him half the money he needed otherwise.'

'That was very generous of you,' Elizabeth said. 'Can you afford it?'

'It was the only way the bank would agree to lend him the other half. It's their way of making sure I still have a vested interest in the business, I suppose. Anyway, the arrangement is that Arthur will repay me in instalments. So as long as he doesn't somehow make a mess of it there isn't any risk really.'

'I'm sure he won't let you down,' Elizabeth said. 'And if he makes a success of himself, perhaps he'll prove me wrong where Miss Yates is concerned. She may be exactly the incentive he needs.'

Their conversation was interrupted by the photographer who was attempting to take Christopher's picture.

'I wonder if you'd mind putting your left hand on your hip, Mister Horsham.' He demonstrated by standing with his shoulders back, turned slightly in profile in classic empire pose; the Englishman, master of all he surveys.

Doing his best to oblige, Christopher gazed off into the middle distance, his chin held high, one hand resting on his machine the other on his hip.

Elizabeth smothered a laugh. 'You look awfully serious. I do think you ought to smile a bit.'

The photographer threw her an irritated glance. 'If you wouldn't mind not distracting him, Miss, I'd be most grateful.'

'Actually, I do feel a bit stiff,' Christopher said adopting a more casual pose, with one hand in his pocket. He smiled towards the camera. 'Is that better, do you think, Liz?'

'Much. Every mother in the county will want you to meet their daughters. Poor thing, you'll be absolutely snowed under with invitations.'

'Good lord, I hope not. I couldn't think of anything worse. All those vapid young girls with nothing on their minds except finding a husband.'

'You ought to know by now that's all we women want.'

'Except you, Liz.'

She smiled and sipped her champagne.

William left them, and seeing that Sophie was still alone went over to speak to her. 'Hello, are you enjoying yourself?'

She smiled. 'Yes, thank you.'

'What's happened to Arthur?'

'He saw somebody he knew and went to speak to him.'

'I suppose he's told you that I'm selling the garage to him?'

'Yes. He's very pleased. He told me that you're going to build another aeroplane.'

'That's right. I've decided to enter a sort of competition that the army are holding.'

'It sounds very exciting, I must say. I've never seen an aeroplane before today,' Sophie said as she watched Christopher posing for another photograph.

'Do you want to have a closer look? Come on, I'll show you if you like.'

As they went over the photographer finished taking his pictures and began to pack up his equipment. William introduced Sophie to Christopher and Elizabeth.

'How do you do, Miss Yates?' Christopher said as he shook her hand.

'Sophie wanted to have a look at your plane.'

'I'd be delighted to show you,' he said with a smile that would have dazzled practically any young woman in the county. He began to lead her around, pointing out various things and explaining how they worked, and as he talked, Sophie's eyes never left his face.

'Would you like to sit in her?' he asked.

She looked doubtfully at the pilot's position surrounded by a maze of wires. 'I wouldn't want to break anything.'

'Oh you needn't worry about that,' Christopher assured her. 'Come on, I'll help you up.'

She took his hand and he helped her into the seat, then climbed up behind her to explain how the controls worked, encouraging her to press the pedal under her foot to operate the rudder.

'And the stick there in front of you works the ailerons and elevator,' he said. 'Like this you see.' He put his arms around her to take the stick and show her how it worked.

Just then William saw Arthur come back and look around for Sophie. When he saw her he began to go over to her, but then a look of uncertainty crossed his face as Sophie laughed at something Christopher said. They were very close together, Christopher's hand now resting on her shoulder in a familiar way.

'I'll tell you what, there's still a bit of time before the race, why don't you and I go and have a look around at the competition, what do you say?'

Christopher's voice carried clearly, and at that moment he looked every inch what he was; a dashing young aviator whose privileged upbringing was evident in his confident, upper class tones. Everything about him, from the clothes he wore to his good looks, set him apart from ordinary people.

'I'd love to,' Sophie replied, and as she climbed down she didn't even notice Arthur, or the effect her carelessness had on him. He looked as if he'd been dealt a physical blow.

'We'll see if we can get some lunch if you like,' Christopher said as he led her away. 'I heard somebody say earlier they've got champagne and oysters in the marquee.'

William felt sorry for Arthur. He was briefly resentful of both Christopher and Sophie, but reasoned that it wasn't their fault. 'I'd better go and see him,' he said to Elizabeth, thinking that she must have noticed. 'He looks a bit lost.'

But she didn't appear to hear him, her gaze fixed instead on Christopher and Sophie as they vanished among the crowd. From her expression, William imagined that she was hiding an old and familiar hurt.

'Yes, of course,' she said after a moment and smiled to cover her feelings.

*****

The race was scheduled to begin at half past two. At a quarter past, an official addressed the crowd with the aid of a megaphone. Some of them had bought tickets for the temporary stands, while most gathered on the grass. The official pointed out the helium balloons that marked the perimeter of the course and explained that the contestants had to pilot their machines around each one, and that the first to successfully complete ten laps would be declared the winner.

The planes were lined up in pairs on the field ready to start their engines and take off, while the pilots and their helpers did their final checks. Wentworth came over to shake Christopher's hand and wish him luck.

'If either of us wins, I think he ought to stand the loser dinner and champagne in town tonight.'

'What do you think, William?' Christopher said. 'Do you think we should agree?'

'I don't see why not.'

'Perhaps you might like to bring along that young lady I saw you with earlier, William,' Wentworth suggested. 'If I win, I'd be willing to cut you in for a share of the prize money in return for an introduction.'

'You're too late, old man, I've beaten you to it,' Christopher said with a smile.

'Oh, I should have known. Well, in that case at least I'm bound to win the race. Nobody can be that lucky in one day.'

Wentworth returned to his machine, and soon afterwards an official announced that the competitors should start their engines. William shook Christopher's hand and wished him luck, then went around to the propeller to prime the engine.

'Contact?'

Christopher flicked on the switch. 'Contact.'

With another pull on the propeller the engine burst into life, and then one by one the others followed suit and a haze of blue smoke drifted across the grass towards the crowd, carrying with it the strong smell of oil and petrol. Of the fifteen competitors only one engine refused to start, and no matter how many times the mechanic turned the prop it was no use. The officials allowed the frustrated aviator a few extra minutes while the other machines began to take off, but the fault couldn't be diagnosed and in the end the plane remained on the ground like a stubborn, ungainly bird that refuses to leave the nest.

Christopher's plane gathered speed and rose smoothly into the air to join the others waiting for the flare that would signal the start of the race. There were some whose designs were clearly outdated. One had scalloped wing edges like a bird's and an elevator protruding from the front, while another's engine could be clearly heard misfiring, and in fact was eventually forced to land a minute before the race began. However, many of the planes shared common characteristics, such as elevators and rudders at the tail end, which in conjunction with ailerons on the wings provided the pilot with control. Nearly all of them were biplanes, since it was almost universally agreed that two sets of wings were inherently stronger and more efficient than one.

The chief difference among them, William mused as he looked on from the field, was the type and position of the engine. There were still two schools of thought regarding this. One believed the 'pusher' type, with an engine behind the pilot, was better than having it at the front with a propeller designed to pull the machine through the air. As he watched the planes circling, William decided it was difficult to decide which of the two designs was superior, because there were other factors to consider. Christopher's was a pusher designed by de Havilland, and was clearly faster than one of only two monoplanes that had their engines in front. But how much of that was due to it being a biplane and how much to the engine itself? And then there was the engine itself to consider. Nearly every plane was fitted with a French engine, except for two with British Greens, but even then no two were alike. Christopher's was powered by a seventy horsepower Rhone, but there were Gnome's and

Hispanos of varying sizes, and some were radials while others were in-line types, and though most were water cooled there was at least one air cooled Renault.

Despite all these variations, William felt it was the engine that made the most difference to speed in the end, though it was the overall design that affected manoeuvrability. He was already thinking about the plane he would build to enter the army's competition.

*****

When the green flare was fired to signal the start of the race, Elizabeth was sitting next to her mother in the stands. She watched through her glasses as Christopher crossed the line at about the same time as three or four of the other planes. For a few seconds their wings seemed so close that involuntarily she held her breath.

'Goodness!' Elizabeth's mother placed her hand against her chest in alarm. 'I really don't know if I can watch. It looks terribly dangerous.'

'I shouldn't think it's any worse than hurtling around a race track in a motor-car at eighty miles an hour,' Elizabeth said, though her heart was also thudding.

'Really, Elizabeth, sometimes I think you'd like everyone to think you have no feelings at all where Christopher is concerned,' her mother said archly. 'Poor Eleanor, imagine how she must feel.'

Lady Horsham was watching the race from the back of the Rolls Royce. She looked tense, and was gripping her husband's arm very tightly.

'I imagine she will be quite glad when Christopher decides to get married and settle down. Is he still seeing Catherine Mountford? He seemed very keen on her.'

'I really have no idea,' Elizabeth said, at which her mother frowned.

'I wish you wouldn't be quite so blasé.'

'I don't know what you mean, mother.'

'Oh really! I don't understand why you insist on pretending that you don't have feelings for one another, when it's quite clear that you do.'

'I don't deny that Christopher and I have feelings for one another,' Elizabeth said. 'They're simply not the sort of feelings you would like us to have.'

Her mother gave her a sceptical look. 'I'm afraid I don't believe that.'

'Well I'm sorry, but it's true. Besides, I hardly think Christopher is considering marrying anybody. Catherine Mountford is hardly the first girl he's been interested in.'

'That may be so, but he certainly can't remain single for ever.'

'Perhaps you should be telling him that, rather than me.'

Her mother regarded her speculatively. 'Tell me truthfully, Elizabeth. Do you love Christopher?'

'Of course I love him. We've known each other practically all our lives. But I'm not *in* love with him.'

Mrs Gordon made an exasperated gesture. 'You speak of love and being in love as if there is a vast difference between the two. The truth is that if two people care for one another and they are otherwise suited, then they ought to consider themselves extremely fortunate. Many married couples get along quite happily with less.'

Elizabeth wondered if she detected a faint note of regret in her mother's voice.

'I happen to know that Eleanor would be very pleased if you and Christopher were to marry,' her mother continued. 'Your father's cousin is married to a Horsham you know.'

'I am a person, mother, not some sort of breed mare. When I marry, if I ever do, it will be because I'm in love with somebody, and it won't matter a jot what his background is, or who his family are.'

'Don't be ridiculous. Love is something that grows from mutual respect between two people of the same sort. It is not some romantic ideal.'

Elizabeth gave up, determined not to be drawn into yet another argument on this subject. She raised her glasses as the planes approached the start line for the second time. 'Look, here they come again. Goodness, Christopher and Nigel are in front by the look of it.'

*****

Christopher's machine shuddered. The sound of splintering wood could be heard over the noise of the engine, and all at once the controls became leaden and the plane unresponsive. To his horror, Christopher realised that as he and Wentworth had rounded the last mark their wing tips had touched and one of his spars had broken, allowing a wire to become entangled between the two planes. He signalled desperately to Wentworth, who quickly saw the problem, and fortunately didn't do anything rash to try and separate them. For a few moments both planes flew on in a straight line on a level trajectory away from the race course.

As he looked at the fields two hundred and fifty feet below, Christopher began to appreciate the trouble they were in. If they weren't careful they would rip their wings to pieces, and both planes would plunge to the ground with virtually no chance of either he or Wentworth surviving. Sweat broke out all over his body and his heartbeat leapt. He forced himself to think clearly. He knew the only chance they had was to somehow time their descent and try to land together. The chief problem with his plan was that, since they could only communicate by gesture, it was going to be almost impossible to match their speed and rate of descent. As if he needed proof of that, the control stick was suddenly wrenched from his hand as Wentworth's plane altered course by a few degrees. Christopher's entire machine shook violently, and once again he heard the sound of splintering wood. Desperately, he signalled to Wentworth, gesturing frantically towards the ground. Wentworth, his face visibly pale, nodded his understanding.

With a motion of his hand Christopher indicated that he was going to slow his engine. He reached for the throttle and eased it off just a little so that Wentworth would understand, and when Wentworth followed suit Christopher gestured again and eased his stick forward a few degrees. Once again Wentworth matched him, and though the planes were shaking and straining against one another, Christopher began to think that perhaps they might actually manage it and live to tell the tale. They were already down to a hundred feet, and ahead of them was a large open field. Then without warning, there was an ominous crack and a sudden, shocking gash appeared like a wound in one of the main struts between the port wings of his plane, and Christopher knew his plan wasn't going to work. For a doomed instant he and Wentworth looked at one another helplessly, before suddenly the strut broke and both machines plummeted towards the ground.

*****

As soon as the planes rounded the mark William saw them touch, and when they didn't separate again he guessed it was because they couldn't. He began to run, following the course they were taking, and when the two planes began to lose height he understood what they were trying to do, though only moments later it was clear that they were going to crash.

He reached the field where they went down well ahead of the officials and spectators, who eventually began to follow him, and scrambling through a thicket of blackberry he saw the wrecks were lying a hundred and fifty yards apart. Christopher's was the closer of the two and had come to rest with the nose in the air, both wings broken off and the fuselage snapped in two. When William reached it, Christopher was slumped in his seat with his face covered in blood. The smell of petrol was very strong, and as William wrestled with the harness buckle he was afraid that at any moment a leak might ignite. As soon as the harness was undone he grabbed Christopher by his shoulders and unceremoniously pulled him free. When he hit the ground Christopher groaned and his eyes flickered open, glazed with pain and incomprehension, but William continued to drag him away from the wreckage.

When they were far enough away, William collapsed, gasping for breath. He turned towards Wentworth's plane and saw that the propeller was lazily turning from its own momentum, and since the magneto was connected directly to the shaft he knew it would still be sparking. Stumbling to his feet he began to run as fast as he could.

When William was only a little more than a hundred yards away, Wentworth saw that help was coming. He struggled for a few moments, but he was trapped in his seat by the wreckage. Behind him, a thin plume of smoke rose into the air. For several seconds Wentworth was unaware of the danger he was in, but even from fifty yards away William heard the soft whooshing sound of leaking petrol catching fire. Wentworth twisted in his seat and when he saw the flames behind him his expression contorted in terror, and he began to redouble his efforts to free himself. When that failed he tried to beat at the rapidly spreading flames with his hands.

Though William ran as fast as he could, the fire took hold with shocking speed. A veil of smoke spread quickly, and in the space of no more than a second or two it darkened and thickened into a rolling cloud with a greedy furnace of orange and red at its heart. Moments later the petrol tank exploded, spilling a liquid sheet of flame directly over Wentworth's head and setting the entire wreckage ablaze.

Doped canvas, ash and willow burned like tinder, and in the middle of it all Wentworth's clothes ignited. He screamed, his head a halo of fire as he writhed and twisted in agony. His terrible shrieks caused people running from the aerodrome to stop in their tracks, appalled at the sound.

By the time William reached the wreckage, Wentworth was still alive, but though William tried to reach him, he was driven back by the intense heat. He staggered and prepared to try again, the air filled with the roar of the flames and Wentworth's screams, but again the heat defeated him, causing his clothes to smoulder and his eyebrows and hair to crackle and smoke. He collapsed on the ground, choking on the thick smoke. Mercifully, Wentworth's screaming stopped.

After that there was nothing William could do. The fire quickly burned out, leaving the flimsy material of the aeroplane's construction reduced to ash. Only the engine and a few wires and Wentworth's contorted, smoking corpse remained. As more people arrived, the stench of roasted flesh caused many of them to turn away, some of them retching into the grass. Only then did William realise that Christopher had followed him and was standing a little way off, clutching an injured arm. His expression was dulled with pain and the shock of witnessing Wentworth's death. He met William's eye, and then looked back at his own machine. It too, had caught fire and was reduced to ash, and had it not been for William, Christopher would have burned with it as poor Wentworth had.

14

Five days after he had been killed, Wentworth was buried in the churchyard of St John's in Boughton, close to the house where he grew up. The church was full for the service, and afterwards Christopher was one of the bearers who carried the coffin outside. The crowd followed silently and gathered around the grave. As the coffin was lowered into the ground, William couldn't help but think of Wentworth's terrible death. Opposite him, Christopher stood with his hands clasped in front of him, his head bowed. When he looked up his eyes were haunted, his face unnaturally pale.

When the service was over, Elizabeth and William walked to the gate to wait for Christopher. Cloud scudded overhead, the leaves stirred by a fresh breeze.

'I'm worried about Christopher,' Elizabeth commented. 'He looks terrible.'

'He told me he hasn't been sleeping,' William said. 'He has dreams… nightmares I suppose.'

'Poor Christopher, it must be awful for him. He and Nigel were at school together, you know. But what about you? You were closer than anybody. He was alive when you tried to help him.'

'I try not to think about it.' For an instant William remembered the screams, the thrashing agonised figure in the flames.

'I'm sorry, I shouldn't have reminded you,' Elizabeth said, placing her hand on his arm.

'It's alright.'

When Christopher joined them they drove to a pub nearby and ordered three large whiskies. There was a garden outside. Sunlight filtered through the leaves of a birch to dance on the grass in flickering patterns of silver. Christopher lit a cigarette and emptied half his glass in a single swallow.

'I'm sorry about the prize money, by the way,' he said to William.

'It doesn't matter.'

'It's good of you to say so, but I expect it would have been useful to you. Will you still sell the garage?'

'Yes. Actually, I've already signed the papers.'

'Are you still planning to build this plane you were talking about?'

'I think so, yes. Do you remember that chap at Brooklands who told us about the army trials?'

'Yes. What was his firm called? British Colonial wasn't it?'

'That's right. Anyway, I've been in touch with him, and he was kind enough to send me some information. Apparently the army want a machine that can carry a pilot and an observer, with a wireless set to transmit information about enemy movements back to the ground. A sort of airborne cavalry unit.'

'Do you think you can do it?' Christopher asked.

'I don't see why not. I've already made some drawings of the sort of thing I've got in mind. I just have to speak to the landlord at the pub about continuing to rent the barn.'

'But where will you live?' Elizabeth asked.

'I can set aside somewhere to sleep in the barn. I'm used to making do.'

Christopher thought for a moment. 'I must say, I've complete confidence that if anybody can manage it, you can William, but surely building a new plane from scratch is going to be an expensive business. I hope you don't mind me asking you this, but can you afford it?'

'To be honest with you, I'm not sure,' William admitted. 'Unfortunately the most expensive part of a plane is the engine, and I need that first. Everything else depends on it, and I want the very latest thing. I've already written to Rhone and the other French manufacturers.'

'I'd be happy to lend you what you need,' Christopher offered.

'Thanks, I appreciate the offer, but I'd rather not.'

'I thought you'd say that. Look, how would you feel about taking on a partner in this venture of yours?'

'Do you mean you'd be interested?'

'Absolutely. As a matter of fact, you ought to come and live at Pitsford. We can build your plane there. It's not as though we haven't the room.'

William hesitated, torn between taking Christopher up on his offer, and the feeling that by doing so he would be giving up a degree of the thing he valued most, which was his independence. However, he made up his mind that the benefits outweighed the disadvantages. 'Alright, if you're serious, I agree,' he said. 'So long as it's understood that we would be equal partners. I insist on paying my full share of everything.'

'Then that's settled. How soon do you want to get started?'

'The sooner the better. The trials are only three months away.'

'In that case you might as well pack your things and come over tomorrow. I'll send some men over to clear out the barn.'

As they shook hands, William reflected that these things were much easier to arrange if you happened to have an army of estate workers at your disposal.

'I think we ought to have another drink to celebrate,' Christopher said, and went off to the bar leaving William and Elizabeth alone.

'Is anything wrong?' William asked, thinking that she was very subdued.

'I expect it's the funeral. Don't take any notice of me.'

'I imagine it must seem very callous to you, making plans like this. I hadn't thought of it until now.'

'No, it isn't that. I was just thinking that life continues no matter what, doesn't it? A week ago Nigel was alive, and now he doesn't exist except in our memories.' She faltered, struggling to express herself. 'I don't know what I'm trying to say.'

'It's alright, I think I know what you mean.'

She made an effort to smile. 'Anyway, I'm glad you'll be living at Pitsford. It means we'll continue to see each other.'

'Yes,' William agreed. He had thought of that too.

*****

It was the first week of July and the days were still and hot. The villages throughout the county lay quietly sleeping in the heat. On the farms, the wheat was ripening, painting the slopes of Brampton valley with pale gold.

A stone wall along the edge of a lane marked the boundary of the Horsham family estate. Driving from Sywell, there was a point on the hill before the road dipped into the valley, where Pitsford House could be glimpsed surrounded by oak-studded parkland. It was an imposing, Victorian, country mansion with chimneys bristling from the rooftops. Beyond a pair of iron gates, a drive flanked by chestnut trees meandered for three quarters of a mile through the park. When the house came properly into view it was even bigger than William imagined, and he began to appreciate that he was entering a very different world from the one he was used to.

When he arrived, a formal, slightly intimidating butler showed him into a drawing room while somebody was sent to find Christopher. The room was vast, with a high ceiling and two fireplaces. Windows at one end overlooked a terrace leading to neatly kept lawn and gardens. The house was quiet, but there was a sense of hidden machinery that kept it all working smoothly; a small army of servants.

Christopher appeared wearing a shirt open at the neck with the sleeves rolled back. 'Sorry I wasn't here to meet you, old man. I've made a start clearing out one of the garages for us to use. Has somebody taken care of your things?'

'Yes, I think so. Your butler said he'd have them fetched from the car.'

'Jolly good.' Christopher looked at his watch. 'Lunch will be at one. Can you wait until then or would you like something now? A drink perhaps.'

'I'm alright at the moment.'

'Come on then, I'll show you around. You'll see my mother at dinner, by the way, I think she's out at the moment. Henry's about somewhere though.'

'Is that your brother?'

'Yes. He's home from Eton. There'll only be the four of us. My father's in London. He spends most of his time there actually, though he usually comes up for a few weeks during the summer.'

'Where are your sisters?' William asked. He recalled Christopher mentioning them, though he couldn't remember their names.

'They're in Italy for the summer with David's family... he's Mary's fiancé, the eldest of the two.'

William tried to imagine four people sharing a house of this size. It was quite conceivable that they might never run into one another. He was given a quick tour of the downstairs rooms. There was a library and a smaller drawing room than the one they'd come from, a games room and a study that was used by Christopher's father, and also a ballroom that wasn't used very often at all.

'You must make yourself completely at home,' Christopher told him. 'Everything's quite informal. Breakfast is laid out from about half past seven, but feel free to come down anytime. Lunch is pretty casual. I suppose the only time we make an effort is in the evenings. Dinner's at eight, but we usually meet for drinks around half past six.'

'I wanted to ask you about that,' William said a bit awkwardly. 'I've only the one suit, I'm afraid.'

'Oh don't worry. We're about the same size. I can lend you something. We'll sort it out later when I take you to your room.'

They continued towards the back, past a door that led to the kitchens and servants areas. 'You won't need to go there, of course. If you want anything, just ring from one of the rooms.'

Behind the house there was a yard and stables, as well as buildings where the carriages had once been kept, though now they'd been converted to garages where a Rolls Royce and a Daimler were parked next to Christopher's Fiat. Furthest from the house was a large, empty building, with two sets of double doors at the front which could be pulled right back if needed.

'I thought we'd work here,' Christopher said. 'It's where I used to keep my plane. I had these doors installed so that I could get her in and out easily, and there's plenty of room behind for taking off and landing.' He flicked on an electric light switch. 'We should have everything we'll need here I think.'

Just then, a youth of about seventeen appeared from around the corner pushing a motorbike.

'Hello, there's Henry,' Christopher said. 'I wonder what's happened to him.'

Christopher and his brother were almost exact opposites in terms of their physical appearance. Henry was shorter, with a stocky frame, his pale skin and fair hair a direct contrast to Christopher's.

'This is the chap I told you about, Henry,' Christopher said, making the introductions.

'I'm very pleased to meet you, Mister Reynolds,' Henry said as they shook hands. 'I hear that you and my brother are going to be building an aeroplane?'

'Henry's keen on becoming an aviator himself,' Christopher remarked. 'Though I told him that if he'd been here to see what happened to poor old Wentworth he might not be so keen.'

'Oh, that'll never happen to me,' Henry proclaimed, with the arrogance of youth. 'Anyway, you managed to come out of it alright didn't you.'

'Yes, but only thanks to William here. Anyway, what's the matter with your bike?'

Henry frowned with displeasure. 'I don't know. I told that damn Hedges to make sure it was running properly, but I only got as far as the gate when the thing conked out. I'm just about to go and look for him and give him a piece of my mind.'

'I'm sure it isn't Hedges' fault, Henry,' Christopher admonished mildly.

'Well if it isn't I don't know whose fault it can be,' Henry said irritably. 'After all, it's meant to be his job isn't it? If you ask me the man is simply idle. If it was up to me, I'd have sacked him long ago.'

'Hedges is our chauffeur,' Christopher explained. 'Despite Henry's opinion of him he manages to keep the Rolls and the Daimler running pretty well. But then I suppose nothing much goes wrong with them.'

'I could have a look at your bike for you,' William offered at which Henry brightened.

'Could you? I'd be jolly grateful. I don't suppose Hedges would know what's wrong anyway.'

'I'll have a look now if you like.'

The problem turned out to be nothing more than a dirty sparkplug, and as soon as it was removed and cleaned the bike started easily and ran smoothly.

'I say, thanks awfully,' Henry said, as he sat astride the machine again and pulled on his goggles. 'By the way, when your plane's finished, I wondered if you'd teach me to fly?'

'You ought to ask your brother. After all, it was Christopher who taught me.'

Henry looked at Christopher. 'Well, will you?'

'We'll see,' he said. 'We haven't even started yet. By the time it's ready you might have gone back to Eton.'

'Oh well, perhaps I'll see if there's anybody at Sywell who'll teach me.' Henry revved his machine and put it into gear. As he roared off, Christopher gave William a wry look.

'It's lucky for Hedges that you were here. I'm afraid Henry can be a bit heavy handed with the servants sometimes. I can't help feeling sorry for whatever poor chap is fagging for him at school.'

Later, Christopher took William to his room, which was on the first floor, with two windows overlooking the view at the front of the house. After Christopher had left him to unpack his things, William took stock of his new home. The room was large and airy, with a desk where he could work on his drawings and a pair of chairs beside the window where he could relax to read a book, or simply gaze at the view of the countryside. He'd even been provided with a decanter of whisky and some glasses.

He thought back to when he'd first arrived in Northampton a little over four years ago, comparing his current surroundings with his room at Mrs Hall's and then later the room he'd shared when he worked at Ballantynes. It all seemed so long ago, made unreal by where he sat now. He was happy, he thought, perhaps happier than he'd ever been, and it was because of his friendship with Christopher, and of course Elizabeth. It struck him as ironic that he was only there because he'd gone to Oundle, and yet his school years had been miserable and lonely.

He looked around at the comfortable furnishings, the

thick carpet and the paintings on the walls. He admitted he liked the comforts that money could bring, and yet he felt a little like an imposter being there, as if he didn't really belong and that if he was found out he would be ejected. He didn't know why he'd never told Christopher or Elizabeth the truth about himself. He didn't see what difference it would make to them. They knew he had no money, and he'd never pretended to be something that he wasn't. He was afraid the real reason for his secrecy, or his mysteriousness as Elizabeth liked to call it, was that he was ashamed of his background.

That evening, before dinner, William met Lady Horsham again. She was pleased that he had come to stay with them. He was to her, apart from anything else, the young man who had saved her son's life. She was an intelligent woman, who managed to give the impression of being utterly informal and down to earth without really being either.

'Anyway, I trust you'll be quite at home here, William, and if there's anything you need you must ask Morton and he will see to it for you, won't you Morton?'

The butler to whom she was referring brought her a glass of sherry on a silver tray. 'Yes, Lady Horsham,' he said.

'Everything that takes place in this house does so under Morton's watchful eye,' she said. 'Without him there would be chaos. Incidentally, Morton, did you see the painting I brought home today?'

'I did indeed, My Lady.'

'What did you think of it? I wondered if it might go quite well in the library.'

'I believe it would look very well there.'

'Good. I wanted to be sure you approve. Perhaps tomorrow you could arrange for somebody to hang it?'

'Of course.'

When Henry appeared, Lady Horsham asked what he'd

been doing.

'I took my bike for a spin out to Sywell to see about flying lessons.'

His mother was distressed to hear this, and would have forbidden it if Henry hadn't told her that there was nobody there giving lessons anyway. It had evidently put him in a bad mood.

'By the way, where the devil is that fool, Hedges? My bike packed in today, but I couldn't find him anywhere.'

Lady Horsham behaved as if she hadn't heard him and turned instead to Morton. 'I meant to ask you, I wonder if there is a bottle of something special in the cellar to mark Mister Reynolds' first evening as our guest?'

'I'm sure I can find something, My Lady.'

'Thank you, Morton. I knew I could rely on you.' When he'd left the room she gave her youngest son a withering look. 'Please do not speak like that about the servants in front of Morton, Henry. If you have a complaint you must speak to me first in private, and if necessary I will take the matter up with Morton and he will deal with it.'

'Yes, mother, I'm sorry,' Henry said, but added sulkily, 'though I really don't know why you tolerate that fellow, Hedges.'

There was a rigid hierarchy in the house, William discovered, both above and below stairs, and everybody was expected to know their place and keep to it, though it was maintained on an understanding of mutual respect that Henry evidently hadn't mastered.

At first William found it unsettling to live in a house where everything was done for him, and where the servants outnumbered the Horshams and himself many times over. Wherever he went he seemed to encounter maids or footmen busily dusting and polishing and cleaning. They served him breakfast and dinner, laid out his clothes and laundered them, polished his shoes and even turned down his bed in the evening. Outside the house, there were gardeners and stable hands and Hedges the chauffeur, and throughout the day a constant parade of tradesman delivered supplies of all kinds. William was amazed that it took so much effort by so many to keep a handful of people in comfort, and yet as time went on he got used to it.

During the day, he and Christopher would work on their plane. They had decided to start by building the frame for the fuselage and wings while they waited to hear from the French engine manufacturers. In the evenings after dinner they would sit and talk and listen to music, just as they had before the airshow, though now they dressed for dinner and afterwards drank brandy from French crystal. Sometimes William missed the mixed smells of sawdust and the dope they used to stiffen the canvas, and also the quiet fields in the purple twilight. The thing he missed most of all though, was Elizabeth. He half expected her to turn up at the end of each day, but for two weeks he hadn't see her.

One evening after dinner they played a game of snooker, even though it was a game Christopher didn't like very much, and when Henry invited himself along Christopher told him plainly he wasn't wanted.

'I was thinking we ought to go for a picnic at the weekend,' Christopher remarked casually as he set up the balls. 'I'm sure Liz would be keen if you wanted to ask her.'

There was something speculative in his tone, William thought, as if he was curious to see how William responded. 'You mean the three of us?'

'Actually I was thinking of asking somebody else to join us.'

William took his shot. There had been several occasions when Christopher had disappeared in the evenings lately on some pretext or other. William hadn't thought much of it. He'd been happy to use the time to read or work on his design plans, but now he thought about it, he wondered if Christopher was seeing somebody.

'You like Liz, don't you?' Christopher asked.

'Yes, of course I do.'

'No, I don't mean that. I mean you've fallen for her. I could see it in your face when I mentioned her just now.' Christopher shook his head and smiled. 'I don't know why I haven't noticed before. Have you said anything to her?'

'No.'

'Perhaps you should. Anyway, I'm glad, because now I know you'll understand how I feel.'

'How you feel about what?' William asked, completely lost.

'About Sophie.'

For a moment William had no idea who he meant, and then he realised. 'Do you mean Sophie Yates?'

'Yes. We've seen one another a few times lately. I would've said something to you earlier, but I wasn't sure how you'd feel about it.'

'I don't know what you mean.'

'Because of that Hawkins chap, I mean. You know he rather likes Sophie, don't you?'

'Yes, but I wasn't sure his feelings were reciprocated.'

'Apparently they weren't. Not in that sense. Sophie says she only thought of him as a friend. I gather he had other ideas, but I'm afraid they were all very one-sided.'

'I see,' William said. 'To be honest I'm not surprised.'

'You don't mind then? After all, you're quite friendly with Hawkins aren't you?'

'Yes, I suppose I am, but it's none of my business if Sophie doesn't return his feelings.'

Christopher looked relieved. 'Good, I'm glad to hear you say that, because the truth is I think she's a wonderful girl. I thought so the moment I saw her, but as I've got to know her better I'm even more convinced. Of course she's a stunning looker, and I don't deny that's what attracted me at first, but she's very sweet too and damn plucky. She's done marvellously well to achieve what she has, given her background.'

'Does Elizabeth know?' William asked.

'Not yet. That's why I thought it would be good if we all went for a picnic somewhere. It would be a chance for them to get to know one another.'

'Yes, I see. Alright then,' William agreed, though he wasn't certain how Elizabeth would feel about it. He recalled her expression at the airshow when she had seen Christopher and Sophie together. Whatever Elizabeth claimed about her relationship with Christopher, sometimes William wondered if Elizabeth truly understood her own feelings.

On Sunday morning the household attended services at the church in Pitsford, where the Horsham family had their own pew. The vicar read a passage from Corinthians, his sonorous tones filling the space to the high, arched roof. It was cool in the church, though outside it was already hot. Elizabeth had driven over early that morning and she and William shared a hymn book as the congregation stood to sing Come All Ye Faithful, to the wheezing breath of the organ. Now and then their eyes met, and she smiled.

When the service ended they waited outside while Christopher and his mother chatted with the vicar and one or two other prominent local landowners.

'Are you enjoying your stay at Pitsford?' Elizabeth asked.

'Yes. Though to be honest I miss the evenings we all used to spend together.'

'They were rather fun, weren't they,' she agreed neutrally.

He thought of the time they'd gone for a walk together, when he'd almost kissed her. He'd felt that she wanted him to, but since then they had hardly ever been alone together, and he wondered if that was by design or merely chance.

'I thought you might have come over to see us,' William said.

'I would have. It's just that things have been rather

hectic lately. How are you getting on with Henry?' she said, changing the subject. 'He's quite different from Christopher don't you think?'

'Yes he is.'

She looked at him questioningly. 'You say that as if you don't like him.'

In fact, Henry reminded William too much of some of the boys at Oundle. Perhaps it was Henry's age, but he had an air of supercilious arrogance that William disliked. 'As you said, he's not like Christopher.'

'I think it must be difficult for him having an elder brother like Christopher. It doesn't seem fair really. Christopher will inherit everything of course, but not only that, he got more than his fair share of good looks. Henry thinks very well of you anyway. I was talking to him earlier.'

'Does he?'

'You sound surprised.'

'I am,' William admitted. He'd assumed Henry looked down on him a little, though there was no real reason for him to think so. Another hangover from Oundle.

'You saved Christopher's life,' Elizabeth said. 'I imagine Henry and his mother wouldn't mind if you wanted to stay at Pitsford for ever.'

She meant it as a joke, William knew, and yet somehow it made him uncomfortable. 'I'm not a charity case,' he said lightly, though it came out more sharply than he'd intended.

Elizabeth was taken aback. 'Of course you're not. That isn't what I meant at all.'

A few moments later Christopher joined them. He'd suggested earlier that they should go to the reservoir at Ravensthorpe as it was such a nice day, but when they set off in his car he turned onto the main Northampton road.

'Where are we going?' Elizabeth asked.

'Didn't William tell you? We're picking Sophie up

first,' he replied casually.

'Sophie?' She looked at William questioningly.

'Sophie Yates,' Christopher said. 'You remember her, she was at the airshow with that chap who bought William's garage.'

'Oh, yes of course. I didn't know that you knew each other so well, William.'

'I don't,' he said. 'It was Christopher who invited her.'

Elizabeth looked surprised, though she didn't say anything.

Sophie was waiting for them by the side of the road near the last tram stop on the edge of town. She seemed nervous until Christopher jumped out of the car and kissed her.

'Hello, Sophie, you look absolutely wonderful. We're not late are we? You've met Liz haven't you? And of course you know William.'

They all said hello, and then Sophie sat in the back next to Elizabeth as they set off. William had wondered if they would get on together, but they were soon chatting easily and complimenting one another on their outfits. A few minutes along the road they passed the garage that was now owned by Arthur. His name was on the sign at the front, but otherwise nothing much appeared to have changed. It was closed and there appeared to be nobody about.

When they arrived at the reservoir, Christopher turned down a narrow road that led to a wooden building that housed the sailing club.

'Have you done any sailing, old man?' he asked William.

'I'm afraid not.'

'Never mind, Liz has. I've arranged for us to borrow a couple of dinghies.'

The door of the boatshed was open but there was nobody around. The surface of the reservoir rippled in the breeze and glittered in the sun like shards of glass. At the far end there was a public area and a kind of beach where people came to swim and picnic. They could hear the shouts of children playing. Half a dozen boats could be seen out on the water, their white sails dipping as they tacked to and fro.

'We ought go across to those trees I think,' Christopher said pointing to a line of willows on the distant shore. William helped drag a pair of wooden dinghies down to the jetty on trolleys, and then Elizabeth set about rigging one of them with a single mainsail while Christopher did the other.

'We ought to have a race,' he said. 'Sophie and I against you two.'

When the boats were ready Elizabeth showed William where to sit, and then she tightened the sheet so that the sail caught the wind, and with a smooth motion they began to move away from the shore. A few moments later Christopher followed, and Elizabeth allowed the sail to flap so that he could catch up.

'Are you ready?' he called out.

'Whenever you are.'

At once they tightened their sails and both boats caught the wind and quickly gathered pace. William was content to sit where he was told and watch Elizabeth work the tiller with one hand and the sheet controlling the sail with the other. She had taken off her hat and the sun was on her face, her eyes constantly going from the sail to the water as she judged the breeze. Occasionally they had to tack to change course, which meant that they had to duck under the swinging boom and move from one side of the boat to the other. Each time, Elizabeth managed it smoothly and quickly so that the dinghy barely lost any speed, and they began to edge ahead of the other two.

'When did you learn to sail?' William asked.

'We used to race like this when we were young.' She glanced back at the other boat and William caught a sudden wistful look in her expression, and wondered what she was thinking. He pictured her as a girl of twelve or thirteen, sailing here with Christopher, her arms and face brown from the sun, free of the emotional eddies and currents of adulthood.

They heard Sophie shriek, and looking back saw that as Christopher tacked, their dinghy had tipped violently as if it might capsize.

'He's doing that on purpose,' Elizabeth said. 'He isn't trying to win.'

It was true, William thought. Christopher was far more intent on playing the clown and he and Sophie slipped further and further behind, their laughter carried away on the breeze.

For a little while Elizabeth concentrated on sailing the boat, until it was clear that the others couldn't catch up even if they wanted to. Neither of them spoke and William was happy to watch her. She caught his eye. 'How long have they been seeing each other?'

He knew who she was referring to. 'Since the airshow, I gather. Though I think they've only met a few times. Christopher only mentioned her to me the other day.'

'He seems to like her.'

'Yes, I think he does.'

'What happened to your friend, Mister Hawkins?'

'I don't think he and Sophie were really seeing each other in that sense.'

A few minutes later, as they approached the shore, Elizabeth dropped the sail and William rolled up his trousers and climbed out into the cold water to pull the dinghy up to the bank. Christopher and Sophie were still some way off, in no hurry at all.

William carried a blanket and the picnic basket onto the grass. Elizabeth poured them both a glass of wine, while William took several bottles to the shallows, where they would keep cool.

'I've never been here before,' he commented. 'It's really quite beautiful.' It was the combination of the water and the shady fringe of willows, the sound of a cuckoo in the woods nearby. But perhaps in the end these things only created a mood, or helped to. It was because he was there with Elizabeth that he felt the way he did. But when he looked at her she was lost in her own thoughts, and he followed her gaze out onto the water where Christopher was standing up now, acting the fool as he dropped the sail. The boat rocked precariously, and Sophie laughed as she gripped the sides, and then abruptly Christopher lost his footing and fell into the water. For an instant he vanished, and then reappeared in a burst of spray.

When they finally reached the shore, Christopher had to change into his swimming costume and hang his clothes on the trees to dry. His body was pale and slim.

'Do you know, we ought to have brought a gramophone with us,' he said. He was lying on his back with his head on Sophie's lap. Twisting himself around, he looked up at her. 'What kind of music do you like, Sophie?'

'Something with a bit of life,' she said. 'A foxtrot, or that American ragtime. I don't like anything dull.'

'We should go out one evening,' he suggested. 'The four of us. There's always one hotel or another where there's a band. What do you think?'

'Yes, lets!' Sophie replied eagerly. 'I love dancing.'

'We'll go next week then. What do you say you two?'

Elizabeth smiled. 'Yes, alright,' she said though William thought she didn't sound very enthusiastic.

Christopher didn't notice though and began making plans. He said he'd find out from some people he knew where the liveliest places are. 'Harry Thwaites will know.'

As the sun reached its zenith the breeze died away, but in the shade of the trees, with the sapphire reservoir beyond, William thought there was no more perfect place to be. They ate the picnic prepared for them by the cook at Pitsford House, and drank the wine that William had put in the water to chill. After they'd finished it was too hot to be bothered speaking about much. The heat and wine made them heavy limbed and drowsy. Christopher resumed his supine position with his head in Sophie's lap, and dozed while she gazed lovingly at his smoothly aristocratic features. They made no attempt to disguise their new intimacy. William was surprised at how close they were, as if they'd known each other for months. Elizabeth was reading a book of poetry, though he noticed she rarely turned a page. She seemed distant.

Eventually, William decided he would go for a swim. He walked along the bank underneath the hanging branches of the willows, and when he was out of sight he got changed and waded into the water. It was freezing cold, but it cleared his head, and once he was over the initial shock he swam fifty yards out and then turned and came back again. When he was close to the shore he saw Elizabeth sitting beneath the trees where he'd left his clothes, watching him.

'Is it cold?' she asked.

'Yes.' He came ashore and began to towel himself dry.

'I'm worried,' Elizabeth said.

'Worried? What about?'

'Sophie.'

'Why are you worried about her?'

'Because I'm afraid Christopher will hurt her. Not intentionally perhaps, but he will nevertheless. Christopher doesn't take things seriously. He races his cars and flies aeroplanes and goes to parties.'

'Perhaps Sophie doesn't take things seriously either.'

'She does though, can't you tell? There was a girl he was seeing two years ago. I won't say her name because her family is well known. She was in love with Christopher, and she thought he was in love with her. He didn't mean to deceive her. When she realised he wouldn't marry her she tried to kill herself. And then there was that business with that girl last year after she saw his picture in the paper, the one you saw in town that day.'

'I thought you said it was her own fault.'

'It was. But the point I'm making is that the same thing is going to happen to Sophie…' Elizabeth broke off, aware at last of his expression. 'Why are you looking at me like that?'

'Are you in love with Christopher yourself, Elizabeth? Is that what this is about?'

She was taken aback. 'What on earth are you talking about? Of course I'm not.'

But William didn't believe her. 'I've seen the way you look at him.'

'You're being ridiculous!' She said angrily. She stood up and began to walk away, but then stopped and turned back to him. 'How on earth can you presume to know what I feel?'

'Perhaps because I'm in love with you.'

Her eyes widened. 'I wish you weren't,' she said, then turned and went back through the trees.

He wondered why he had told her how he felt when he hadn't planned to. He wasn't even sure he was in love with her until the declaration spilled from his mouth, but now that it was out in the open he realised it was true.

Late in the afternoon they loaded everything into the boats and sailed back across the water. Elizabeth barely spoke the whole time and avoided looking at William.

When they reached Pitsford, Christopher pulled over and asked if they minded walking the rest of the way so he could drive Sophie home. Sophie waved as they drove off.

'Bye, see you soon,' she called out.

The sound of the engine faded, leaving William and Elizabeth to walk in awkward silence. The lane shimmered with light streaming through the leaves of the trees, and as they walked a thin layer of dust covered their feet. They reached a bend from where Pitsford was visible, standing magnificently alone in emerald parkland, and William paused to admire it. After a moment, Elizabeth realised he'd stopped and turned back to him. For a few moments they regarded one another.

'I'm sorry,' she said at last, and then she turned and walked on and left him wondering what exactly she was sorry about. When he caught up with her she gave him a wan smile, and though they continued in silence it felt a little easier than before.

15

A few days after the picnic at the reservoir, William had to go to Northampton to see about some parts he wanted engineered, and on the way back he stopped at the garage to see Arthur, who told him there were some letters for him.

'I've been meanin' to send them on,' he said.

They were from the French engine manufacturers that William had written to, and he was irritated that they had been sitting unopened for a week, though his irritation became dismay when he saw the disorganised mess of paperwork cluttering Arthur's desk. There were letters addressed to the garage that were also unopened, and incomplete work sheets that ought to have been used to make up invoices. Some of them were from a fortnight ago.

Arthur made a vague gesture. 'I'm a bit behind. It's just we've been so busy I 'aven't 'ad the time.'

'You can't afford to let it pile up like this,' William told him. 'If you don't get your invoices out people won't pay you on time and then you won't have the money to pay your bills.'

Arthur regarded the confusion of paperwork with a dispirited look. 'I never were much good at writin' and figures and all that. I thought Sophie would help me, but I 'aven't seen her lately. Not since the airshow.'

For a moment William thought of Sophie sitting by the reservoir with Christopher's head in her lap. It annoyed him to see things in such a state at the garage, but he supposed he felt a kindred sympathy with Arthur since they were both in love with people who didn't return their feelings. But at the same time there was no use in Arthur allowing his disappointment to destroy him.

William looked about his old living quarters. Without his few possessions; his books and a picture or two to make it feel more homely, the place had a mean, wretched air. The bed was unmade, and the remains of a meagre meal of bread and cheese had been left out. At least the garage appeared to be busy. There were cars outside, and the mechanic Arthur had taken on was busy hammering away at something or other underneath a Ford in the workshop.

'If you don't think you can manage the paperwork you ought to hire somebody to help you,' William suggested. 'A few hours a day would do it. What about the landlord's wife at the pub? You could ask her.'

'You're right, Will. I'll do what you say. Anyway, things aren't as bad as they look, I've got your money 'ere, see.'

He went to a drawer and took out some notes and counted out the first month's instalment of the money he owed William. Though William was glad of the money he worried that Arthur couldn't afford it.

'Are you sure this leaves you enough to keep up with your bank payments?'

'I already paid the bank,' Arthur assured him.

'Alright, thanks.' William put the money away and then gestured to the paperwork. 'Look, I'll sort out this lot and then you can have a fresh start. So long as you promise me you'll get someone to help you.'

'You're good to me, Will, an' I appreciate it. I'll see the landlord's wife later.'

Having sent Arthur off to his work, William settled down at the desk to wade through the backlog of invoicing and bills. Though it took him most of the rest of the day to get things up to date, at least by the end he was reassured that the garage was still getting plenty of work.

Nevertheless, before he left, he sat Arthur down and did his best to impress upon him again that it was no good getting the work if he didn't manage the financial side of the business.

'You could have a hundred cars out there, but it won't make any difference if you don't get paid. You have to keep the money coming in so that you can pay your bills, otherwise you'll go under before you know it.'

Once more Arthur made him a faithful promise that he wouldn't allow things to fall behind again, and reassured that Arthur would keep to his word, William promised to look in again when he had a chance.

It was late in the afternoon by the time William arrived back at Pitsford House. After he'd taken a bath and changed he went downstairs and found Christopher in the drawing room.

'There you are, old man,' Christopher said as he poured a drink. 'I wondered what had happened to you. Whisky?'

'Yes, thanks. I'm sorry I was away so long. I dropped in at the garage on the way back from the engineers.' He related what he'd found and that he'd spent most of the day sorting out the accounts.

'I must say he didn't strike me as the sort who could manage a business very well. Presumably he'll take your advice and hire somebody to help him now?'

'Yes, I think so. Anyway, there were some letters waiting for me from the French engine manufacturers I wrote to. We ought to talk about what they had to say.'

'I'm all ears,' Christopher said as he lit a cigarette. 'Is it good news?'

'In a way.' William had written to four firms, all of whom had replied offering him their latest engines and had included specifications, delivery times and pricing. 'My pick would be the Rhone,' he said once he'd outlined the salient points.

'That's a radial type, didn't you say?'

'Yes. It has seven cylinders and produces eighty horse-power, which is slightly more than the Clerget. But what I like most about it is that the previous models have been quite reliable, which is pretty important of course. Apparently a lot of the French Air Service machines have them.'

'What about availability?'

'They say they can have one here in about six weeks.'

'That doesn't give us very long does it?' Christopher said doubtfully.

'No, that's true, but we've got all the specifications. We can go ahead and build the rest of the plane, so that when the engine does arrive all we have to do is fit it.'

'Unless it's late for some reason, and then we risk missing the trials.'

'Yes, I know. It's tighter than I'd like,' William admitted. 'And there's another thing, the Rhone is the most expensive option.'

'You know that needn't be an issue,' Christopher said.

'It is for me. We agreed we would be equal partners and I want to keep it that way.'

'I only meant that I can loan you some of your share if you need it.'

'I appreciate the offer,' William said. 'But I'd rather not. It's nothing personal, it's just a matter of pride I suppose. Besides, I think I can afford it so long as nothing untoward happens.'

'In that case, I agree with you. We should plump for the Rhone. We can send them a telegram in the morning.' Christopher emptied his glass and began to pour another. 'Now that's settled, there's something I want to ask you.'

'What is it?'

'It's about Sophie. Would you mind not mentioning her to mother or Henry? The thing is… my mother is very keen for me to find myself a wife. She thinks it's time I settled down to my responsibilities as the eldest son and all that rot, and I'd rather avoid a lot of unnecessary questions at the moment.'

'Yes, of course.'

'Thanks, I knew I could rely on you. Oh, and by the way, I spoke to my chum Harry Thwaites earlier. Apparently there's a dance at the Royal Hotel on the Bedford Road this Friday. I thought we might all go, what do you say?'

William thought of Elizabeth and how they'd parted. He was torn. He wanted to see her again, but he didn't know if she would agree to come. 'Have you asked Elizabeth already?' he said.

'No, I only spoke to Harry this afternoon. Besides, I thought you'd like to ask her yourself. How did the pair of you get on the other day? I thought you were both a bit quiet actually. Everything's alright isn't it?'

'Yes, fine,' William answered vaguely. Christopher seemed oblivious to the way Elizabeth felt about him, he thought. He wondered if it had always been like that. Had Elizabeth always been waiting in the wings while he went out with different girls, always hoping that one day he would see her, not as his childhood friend, but a young woman in her own right?

'There's a telephone at her house. I'll give you the number,' Christopher offered.

'Yes, alright.'

William waited until after dinner before he telephoned and asked the operator to put him through. The man who answered said that he would see if Miss Gordon was available.

'Who may I say is calling, sir?'

'William Reynolds.' He waited while his message was delivered. His heart was beating faster than normal and he felt nervous. He decided that being in love could be unpleasant.

'Hello? William is that you?' Elizabeth asked when

she finally answered.

'Yes, it's me. How are you?'

'I'm fine, thanks. What have you been doing?'

'Oh nothing much, other than working on the plane,' he said. They spoke for a few minutes like that, exchanging meaningless chat while he tried to discern from the sound of her voice if she was pleased to hear from him. In the end he gave up and simply told her about the dance. 'Christopher thought we might all go together.'

She hesitated briefly before she replied. 'Yes, of course, that sounds wonderful.'

'Good. We'll see you on Friday then.'

'Yes, goodbye.'

He replaced the receiver. She had been friendly enough, he thought, but there was a distinct awkwardness between them now and he wished he'd never blurted out his feelings to her the way he had.

On Friday they went in Christopher's car, driving along the lanes and roads in the fading copper light of evening. William had borrowed evening clothes from Christopher, while Sophie was stunning in an elegant dress of mauve silk that, with her dark hair and olive complexion, lent her beauty a kind of arresting and exotic touch. By contrast, Elizabeth wore a simple pale dress with a pattern of black panels set off by a string of pearls around her neck. It was as if she had deliberately chosen not to attempt to compete with Sophie, and yet to William, Elizabeth was the more striking of the two. Sophie made him think of the lushness of the tropics, of brightly hued orchids, while he likened Elizabeth to a single pale rose or perhaps a lily.

When they arrived at the hotel there were motors parked on both sides of the road outside. Every window was lit and the jangling notes of a rag-time tune tumbled into the evening air. People were standing outside, chatting and smoking cigarettes. Inside, the place was packed. It was a young crowd, everybody drinking and dancing to the band.

'Harry Thwaites is around somewhere,' Christopher said, speaking over the sound of voices and the music. 'Hang on here a minute while I go and find him.' When he returned he led them to a table where half a dozen people were already sitting.

'Come and meet Harry,' he said to Sophie and introduced her to a short, slightly overweight man with a thick head of softly curling glossy black hair like a cocker spaniel's.

Harry Thwaites got up from his seat. His face was flushed and his eyes glassy from drink. 'I say, I'm jolly pleased to meet you. Christopher told me you were a beauty, but I think he did you an injustice. Here, I insist you sit beside me.'

'Don't mind him,' Christopher said, though he was smiling.

'Do you like to dance?' Harry asked her.

'I love dancing,' Sophie said.

'In that case I bags the first one.' He poured her a glass of champagne. 'I hope you like champagne too.'

'Of course, who doesn't like champagne?'

He laughed. 'Oh yes, Sophie, I can see we're going to get on famously, my dear.'

Elizabeth already knew everyone at the table, and she introduced William to them, though he couldn't remember all of their names. A couple at the end were called Marian and Edward, and were over from Shropshire for the weekend, while the young woman he sat next to was called Emily something or other. She took out a cigarette, and when William lit it for her she asked if he had known Elizabeth for long.

'No, not long at all actually.'

'William helped Christopher fix his plane after he crashed it,' Elizabeth said.

'Are you an aviator too then, Mister Reynolds?'

'Yes, I suppose so.'

'You must have been at Sywell when that frightful accident happened. Gosh, wasn't it absolutely awful? Poor Nigel.' She shivered at the memory, and took a large drink from her glass, and then turned to the man next to her. 'Did you hear that, Hugh? Mr Reynolds is an aviator.'

'I say, are you really? I've been thinking I ought to have a go at flying myself actually,' the man said.

'Oh, I hope you don't!' Emily said. 'We've already lost Nigel. In fact it's lucky that Christopher wasn't killed too. '

'It was William who pulled Christopher out of his machine,' Elizabeth said.

The young woman's eyes opened even wider. 'How exciting! Hugh, this is the chap who saved Christopher's life!'

Though William protested, the young woman paid no attention, and now everybody at the table was listening and he found himself the centre of attention.

'Do you live in Northampton?' Emily asked.

'Actually I'm staying with Christopher at the moment,' he said.

'But you come from Northampton don't you? You're not related to Caroline Reynolds by any chance?'

'I'm afraid not.'

'There's no use asking William anything,' Elizabeth said. 'He won't tell you. He rather enjoys being mysterious, I think.'

'The truth is I'm embarrassed that there's so little to tell,' he said. He was relieved when the band took their positions again and began to play another tune. He noticed Sophie looking at him, something indecipherable in her expression, and then she emptied her champagne and took Harry Thwaites by the hand.

'I love this one. Come on Harry, you can dance with me now.'

As she dragged him off, Harry went willingly enough,

though he looked back at the others with a comical, helpless expression, his eyes like an owls' behind his round spectacles. They soon attracted the attention of half the room, or at least Sophie did. The combination of champagne and the heat brought a flush to her face, and when Harry said something to her she threw back her head and laughed.

There was something about her that was raw and visceral, and at the same time innately sensuous. William glanced at Christopher who was watching her proudly, one arm languidly draped over the back of his chair. Now and then Sophie would look over and they would smile at one another, and throughout the evening William noticed that no matter who Sophie danced with she did this. He saw there was a bond between them that surprised him, because it had developed so quickly. He thought of Elizabeth's warning that Christopher didn't take things seriously, and wondered if in Sophie's case, what Elizabeth was truly afraid of was the exact opposite.

At one point, when Christopher and Sophie were dancing together, William overheard a thin, rather cool looking woman ask Elizabeth who Sophie was.

'She works in a solicitor's office in town, I think.'

The woman raised a disdainful eyebrow. 'I didn't think she could be one of us.'

'Oh, don't be such a dreadful snob, Hilary,' Harry Thwaites said. 'She's a marvellous dancer, not to mention an absolute cracker.'

'What do you think, Mister Reynolds?' the woman asked.

'I doubt that you'd be interested in what I think,' William said, and with a tight smile he excused himself and got up from the table. As he crossed the floor, the music ended and somebody grabbed his arm.

'You haven't asked me to dance,' Sophie said.

'I haven't had a chance, everybody keeps getting to you before me.'

'Well, you can take my place,' Christopher said. 'I could do with a drink.'

'But only if you want to,' Sophie added.

'Of course, I'd love to.'

The band started to play another tune and William put his hand on her waist. 'I'm not much of a dancer, I'm afraid.' He was conscious of his old injury, and Sophie seemed to sense it because she looked down at his feet.

'Have you hurt yourself?'

'No. I was injured when I was young, and sometimes it bothers me, but I think it's really up here.' He tapped a finger to his temple.

'You're sure it isn't because you don't want to dance with me?'

'Why would you think that?'

Sophie smiled, but didn't answer him. 'You have to listen to the music and relax. That's better.'

They danced in silence for a little while. William wondered if the thin woman was watching them and asking who he was now. He glanced towards the table, but she wasn't there anymore.

'Have you seen Arthur lately?' Sophie asked, unexpectedly.

'I went to the garage the other day, actually,' he said guessing that Christopher must have said something to her.

'How is he?'

'He seems alright. The garage was busy. Although he's been neglecting the books a bit.'

'Hasn't he got somebody to help him yet? I told him he should.'

'Did you?' he asked in surprise.

'Yes. Why do you look at me like that?'

'I don't know. It's just that Arthur mentioned something about you helping him, that's all.'

'I might've said I would to begin with, but I decided not to. I told him after the airshow. It would only have given him the wrong idea and I didn't want to encourage him.'

William wondered if Sophie's attitude would be different if she hadn't met Christopher, but he knew he was being unfair. He caught her watching him, and had the uncomfortable feeling that she knew what he was thinking. He was relieved when the tune ended and Christopher cut in on him again. He went outside for some air and lingered on the edge of a group of people who had the same idea.

'It's terribly hot in there, isn't it?'

He turned around to find that Elizabeth had followed him outside. 'Yes, it is.'

A man said hello to her and she spoke to him briefly, and when he went back inside she asked William if he wanted to go for a walk.

'Emily was quite taken with you after she discovered you're an aviator,' Elizabeth said. 'She thinks you're terribly dishy. She wanted to know all about you.'

'What did you tell her?'

'I told her that you're the enigmatic type. Of course that only made her even more curious.'

'Like your other friend who wanted to know about Sophie.'

'You mean Hilary? She's not a friend of mine. You shouldn't worry about her.'

They walked on in silence for a few moments until they came to a gate. The moon was in its first phase. The air was fragrant with the scent of burdock and rosehip growing in the hedgerow.

'Is it really true what you said the other day about being in love with me?' Elizabeth asked suddenly, facing him.

'Yes, I'm afraid I am.'

'Why are you afraid?'

'Because I know you don't feel the same way.'

'I didn't say that.'

She had spoken so quietly, turning her face away from

him that he wasn't sure he'd heard her properly. It was almost as if she was speaking to herself.

'What I actually said was, that I wish you weren't in love with me.'

'Isn't that the same thing?'

'Not necessarily. You also accused me of being in love with Christopher.'

'Are you?'

'I want to try and explain something to you about us,' Elizabeth said. 'You know that Christopher and I have known each other since we were quite young. I was especially young. I had a crush on him then. Of course it was inevitable. A young and impressionable girl, the dashing older boy. But of course eventually Christopher wasn't a boy anymore, and he started going around with a girl of his own age, and I was heartbroken. I cried my heart out. I was convinced I couldn't live any longer.' She laughed wryly. 'Just the sort of dramatic, highly emotional rubbish you'd expect really. I thought I was in love, you see. Have you ever felt like that?'

'Not quite like that.' William thought of Emmaline.

'But there was someone when you were young?'

'Yes.'

'I'd like you to tell me about her one day. But for now, just tell me this: if she were here now, if she just appeared out of the hotel and came towards us, how do you think you would feel?'

'I don't know,' he said, though he could see what Elizabeth was getting at.

'But you'd feel something?'

'Something, yes. Are you telling me that's how you feel about Christopher?'

'I'm telling you that Christopher has never been out of my life, and we were friends long before any complicated adult feelings cropped up. It's just that I find it difficult to separate my feelings. I've always found it difficult, especially when I see him with some other girl. But this time it's much worse.'

'Why? Is Sophie so different from the others?'

'Yes, I think she is, actually. You only have to see the way men look at her to know that. But that isn't what I mean. It's worse because of you.'

'I don't understand.'

'I said that I wish you weren't in love with me,' Elizabeth explained. 'But what I really meant is that I wish you hadn't told me, because it made me confront the things I've been trying to ignore. Things I wasn't sure I wanted to feel. About you - not Christopher.'

'Are you saying you...' he hesitated, not sure what word to use.

'I'm saying I care for you more than anybody I've ever met, except for Christopher. And what I feel for you is different from the way I feel about him. I've never experienced anything like this before. Perhaps a part of me has always felt that I was in love with Christopher, but this has made me realise that feeling was only a kind of leftover from when I was younger. Do you understand what I'm trying to say?'

'I think so.'

'It's just that letting go of things that you've always believed isn't easy. I know it might sound silly, but the only analogy I can think of is when a child first discovers there really isn't any such person as Father Christmas. At first, you don't want to accept it.'

Elizabeth looked at William, her eyes swimming in confusion, and he didn't know what to say or what she wanted him to say. He only knew that half an hour earlier he wouldn't have dared dream any of this.

He knew that if he kissed her she would let him, that she wanted him to. She both did and didn't. He bent towards her and she turned her face up to him, her eyes closed.

*****

It was three in the morning before the band played their final number, and then as people began to leave, Christopher took William aside and gave him the key to his car.

'Listen old man, would you mind awfully driving Liz home?' he asked.

'No of course not. But what about you and Sophie?'

'Actually, I've arranged a room for us here for the night.'

William was surprised, though he didn't know why he should be. They went back to the table and Christopher told Elizabeth about the arrangement. For just an instant she was taken aback, but then she recovered and kissed Sophie's cheek.

'Well, goodnight then.'

'Goodnight.'

As they were leaving, William remembered the bill. He had been dreading it all night. Their table had consumed more than half a dozen bottles of champagne not to mention the late supper they'd been served.

'What do I owe you?' he said taking out his wallet but Christopher made a casual gesture.

'Oh, don't worry about that. Harry and I sorted it out earlier.'

'I'd prefer to pay my share.'

Christopher hesitated. 'Yes, alright then. A couple of pounds ought to do.'

As William gave him the money he realised that he should have considered the cost earlier. Two pounds was, to him, a vastly extravagant amount to spend on an evening out. 'How will you get back tomorrow?' he asked. 'Do you want me to pick you up?'

'No need to do that. Get Hedges to drive over. And if anyone asks where I am just say I went on somewhere with

Harry.'

'Yes, alright.'

When he went outside, William started the car and waited for Elizabeth, who had gone to fetch her coat from the cloakroom. When she appeared she climbed in beside him and they set off, following the lights of other cars going the same way. William glanced at Elizabeth, wondering if she was thinking about Christopher and Sophie.

'Can I ask you something?' she said.

'Of course.'

'Have you been to bed with very many girls?'

He was taken aback by such a direct question. 'Only one.'

'Was it the girl you thought you were in love with?'

'No, that was a long time ago, when I was at Oundle.'

'Who was she then, this other girl?'

'Just somebody I knew.'

'Were you in love with her?'

'No.'

'I'm sorry, I expect you think I'm being nosy. You don't have to tell me.'

'It's alright. It was several years ago. Before I had the garage. I don't think about it anymore.'

'Your secret past,' she murmured.

William was tempted to tell her that there was nothing mysterious about it.

'I've never slept with a man,' Elizabeth said candidly. 'I don't suppose I know much about that sort of thing. Do you mind?'

'Why should I mind?'

'I don't know. Men are confusing. They all want to sleep with you, but they want the girl they marry to be a virgin, don't they? Do you want the girl you marry to be a virgin?'

'I've never thought about it before. But I don't think it matters.'

'What if I told you I'd had lots of lovers. Well, perhaps not lots, let's say two or three. Would you still love me do you think?'

'Yes.'

'You wouldn't mind about the other men I'd slept with? I'm not sure I believe that.'

'I would mind. But only because I'd be jealous.'

She thought about that. 'I think I might be a little bit jealous of the girl you slept with. Did you like sleeping with her? I'm sorry, you needn't answer that. I'm curious you see. Anyway, as I said, I haven't slept with anyone.'

She fell silent until they reached the turnoff towards Earls Barton where she lived, and then she suddenly asked him to keep going.

'Where am I going?'

'It isn't far.'

When they'd gone another few hundred yards she pointed out a track through a gap in the hedge, but when he turned onto it the ground was too rutted for the car.

'It's alright, we can walk from here, anyway,' Elizabeth said as she climbed out.

'Where are we going?'

'I'll show you.'

He let her lead the way, and within a few minutes they reached a barn. Inside, the air smelt sweetly of fresh hay. It was dark without the moon and the stars, but after a little while their eyes became accustomed to it.

'Do you think I'm brazen to bring you here?' Elizabeth said quietly.

William kissed her. His heart was thudding so hard he thought it would burst from his chest. At first she was hesitant, uncertain, but then her lips parted and she held him tightly.

'What do we do now?' she breathed when they parted.

He led her to the hay and they lay down, and he kissed her again. He undid the first few buttons of her dress, exposing her throat, and then he kissed her there and felt her sharp intake of breath at the touch of his lips. She made a sound, a soft exclamation of pleasure, and then he felt her fingers between them unfastening the rest of her clothes. In a fumbled rush they undressed. Her body was pale in the darkness, patches of shadow and darkness that excited him. He kissed her breasts and felt her nipples harden, and then she held him against her, arching her hips against his erection and he felt her hands seeking him.

'I want to touch you,' she said, her voice a husky whisper.

He groaned, and they kissed deeply again. He slid his hands over her body. He loved the feel of her skin. He loved the softness of her breasts and the firmness of her narrow hips, the hard slope of her belly. Her pubic hair was fair and sparse, and when he lowered himself to kiss her there she moaned and held his head in her hands.

'William....' she said, urging him away, embarrassed by what he was doing. But he put his hands underneath her and she surrendered to his touch, and when he kissed her again she gasped. When he entered her, she pushed herself against him and there was a delicious sensation of slippery warmth and tightness, and then they were moving together.

He told her he loved her and kissed her again, and she looked into his eyes.

'I love you, William,' she said. 'With all my heart I love you.'

16

Throughout the summer the plane gradually took shape, and though sometimes William altered aspects of the design after he'd read of some new innovation, or because of a theory of his own, it seemed certain they would finish in plenty of time for the army trials. They even received good news from the Gnome factory in France when a letter arrived to say that a cancelled order meant that their engine would arrive earlier than expected.

Quite often William and Christopher would have their dinner brought out to them so that they could keep working and make the most of the light and the warm evenings. Several times during the week, however, Christopher would drive into town to meet Sophie and wouldn't return until the early hours of the following morning. He would take a room at the Grand Hotel, and when Sophie finished her work he'd take her for dinner somewhere, and perhaps dancing if there was a band playing, and afterwards the two of them would spend most of the night together. Lady Horsham occasionally made dry observations regarding Christopher's nocturnal habits, but he always claimed that he'd merely been out with Harry Thwaites or some other fellow he knew. It was clear that she didn't believe him for a moment.

On these occasions William would drive over to Earls Barton to pick up Elizabeth, and they would go somewhere local for a meal or a drink. Afterwards they would return to the barn where they'd first made love to spend a few hours together before he took her home again. Though William made their assignations a little more comfortable with the aid of some rugs and other comforts that he kept in his car, he worried that Elizabeth thought he was being cheap, but whenever he offered to take a room somewhere, she wouldn't hear of it.

'I think it's terribly romantic here,' she told him one evening when they were lying together beneath a rug. 'Besides, if we went to a hotel or somewhere I'd hate the idea of people looking at us and knowing why we were there. This way it's just you and I.'

He sometimes wondered what Elizabeth's parents thought about their relationship. When he'd met them at the airshow he'd found them to be pleasant and friendly enough, but the first time he arrived to pick Elizabeth up their manner was quite different. He was invited into their substantial manor house in Earls Barton and offered a drink before being subjected to a subtle interrogation about his background. The fact that he'd gone to Oundle stood him in good stead, but as usual he was vague about his parents other than to say that they were dead.

Later, he told Elizabeth that he thought her mother disapproved of him, but she brushed his concerns off.

'When she gets to know you better she'll love you as much as I do.'

'I don't think I'll ever tire of hearing you say that, you know,' he told her.

'What, that I love you? I'm glad because I intend to keep on telling you for a very long time.'

He kissed her and held her close, inhaling her scent. 'What about your father, will he grow to like me too do you think? I'm sure he imagines I'm after your money,' he said when he released her.

'Actually I don't think he does,' she said. 'I'm afraid I might have given them the impression that you've got your own money. You don't mind do you?'

'I suppose not,' he said, though he couldn't deny that

he wished that she hadn't. 'What exactly did you tell them?'

'Only that you and Christopher have gone into partnership, that's all. Though I think when I told them you're planning to build aeroplanes for the army, they sort of assumed that meant you must be well-off. Anyway, I expect you're going to be tremendously successful and rich one day, so it won't matter will it?'

He took heart from the inference that she thought of a future in which he was still a factor.

In August, Lady Horsham and Henry left to spend a few weeks in London before leaving for a month in Italy and France. The day afterwards, Christopher suggested that William invite Elizabeth over to stay for the weekend.

'I'll ask Sophie to come. We'll have a marvellous time, just the four of us, what do you say?'

'It sounds wonderful.' William agreed.

On Friday afternoon Elizabeth arrived early. William was working when he heard her car come into the yard behind the house and he went outside to meet her.

'Hello,' she said. After he'd kissed her she peered beyond him into the dim interior of the garage. 'Are you going to show me your plane?'

'Alright.' He pulled the doors fully open and led her inside.

'Gosh, what's that awful smell?' she said, covering her nose with her hand.

'It's what we use on the canvas to stiffen it,' William explained. 'I was doing some earlier. Anyway, here she is. What do you think?' He gestured with a flourish to the biplane standing before them.

Compared to Christopher's old pusher, the new plane was very streamlined in appearance, and because the fuselage was entirely covered rather than consisting of primarily an exposed skeleton, it had a far more solid look.

'I didn't realise you'd done so much,' Elizabeth said, clearly surprised. 'Is it finished?'

'Not yet. We have to fit the engine and propeller, though with any luck the engine will be here next week. It shouldn't take long after that. Of course we'll have to do a few test flights, and I expect there will be adjustments to make, but on the whole I think we've done pretty well.'

He showed her the two cockpits, explaining that the pilot sat behind with the observer in the front, and then helped her up so that she could sit inside and see how it felt.

'You ought to let me take you up in her one day.'

Elizabeth looked horrified by the idea. 'I told you, I'm not very good with heights.' She climbed down and kissed him. 'But I do love your aeroplane and I think you're very clever.'

'Thanks.'

'And now you might like to offer me a drink.'

'Alright, let's get your things.'

After they'd fetched her suitcase they went inside, and on their way through the house they met the butler in the hall.

'Good afternoon, Miss Gordon,' he said, obviously pleased to see her.

'Hello Morton, how are you?'

'I'm very well, thank you, Miss. Shall I fetch Edward to take your things to your room?' He looked at the case William was carrying.

'It's alright,' William said. 'I'm going up anyway.'

'Very well, sir,' Morton said, managing to sound faintly reproachful.

'Do you know I find him a bit intimidating,' William joked as they went upstairs. 'I always feel as if I'm going to do something he disapproves of.'

'You just did when you wouldn't let him fetch a footman to take my case,' Elizabeth laughed.

'But what was the point? We were coming up anyway.'

'Yes, but that isn't the issue. Morton is old school.

He's an absolute stickler for the way things ought to be done. Anyway, never mind him, which is my room?'

'This one.' William opened the door. 'Mine's next door. Christopher thought we all ought to have separate rooms for appearance sake.'

'Goodness, yes. Morton would certainly disapprove otherwise. Where is Christopher anyway?'

'Oh, he went into town to fetch Sophie. They shouldn't be long.' He put Elizabeth's case down and turned to find her sitting on the bed eyeing him with a slow smile. 'I suppose we've got a bit of time to ourselves then haven't we?'

'I suppose we have.'

'Good.' She reached behind her head to let down her hair, and then began to unbutton her blouse while he leaned nonchalantly against a chest of drawers watching her. 'Are you intending to simply stand there and stare like that?'

'As a matter of fact I am,' he said. 'For a little while anyway.'

'I see,' she said and then stood up and proceeded to strip in front of him without any hurry at all until she was completely naked. But when he stepped towards her she put her hand against his chest. 'Oh, no you don't. Now it's your turn.'

William laughed, slightly embarrassed. As always he was both surprised and delighted by her lack of inhibition. She was far less self-conscious than he was. As he took off his clothes he was conscious of the scars on his leg. Elizabeth, however, was quite comfortable with her body. She lay on the bed and leaned on her elbow, delighting in the effect her nakedness was having on him.

'My, my,' she said, holding out her hand to him.

*****

That evening, when William was ready to go

downstairs, he knocked on Elizabeth's door.

'Are you decent?'

'No,' she said, opening the door to him wearing her under-things. 'I'm not ready yet, and it's your fault for refusing to let me get out of bed.'

'I don't remember you needing much persuasion,' he said taking a step towards her. However she held him firmly back.

'You can't come in otherwise I'll never be ready in time. Go downstairs and pour me a drink.'

'Alright, if I must.'

'You must.' She kissed him quickly. 'Have the others arrived yet?'

'Yes, I heard Christopher's car earlier, though I haven't see them yet. I expect he was eager to show Sophie her room.'

For an instant something flashed in Elizabeth's expression, but just as quickly it was gone. 'You men are all the same,' she said, pulling a face of mock disgust. 'Now go downstairs and let me get dressed.'

As William went down to the drawing room he thought about her reaction to his joke. It was as if she had flinched from a sudden image of Christopher making love to Sophie? And yet what of it? She'd told him that her feelings where Christopher was concerned, had always been confused. He reminded himself that not more than an hour ago she had been naked in his arms, breathing her love for him in his ear while demonstrating her feelings in the most intimate manner possible.

There was nobody about downstairs, so William poured himself a drink and lit a cigarette. At one end of the room there were doors leading onto a terrace, and since it was a warm evening he went outside to smoke and watch the light soften. After a few minutes he heard voices, and went back inside to find Christopher and Sophie had arrived.

'Hello, there,' he said.

'Hello, old man. Have you been down long?'

'Only a few minutes. Elizabeth is still getting ready. Hello Sophie, it's nice to see you again. You look stunning.'

'Thank you,' she said.

'Doesn't she just,' Christopher agreed as he handed her a drink and put his arm around her waist.

Sophie was wearing a dark blue evening dress, and she did indeed look stunning. But then she always did, William thought.

'I'd better just go and find Morton and make sure everything's alright downstairs,' Christopher said. 'I gather the cook was making a fuss about something or other earlier.' He kissed Sophie's cheek, his hand lingering against her waist as if he was reluctant to leave her even for a moment. 'I won't be long, darling. William will look after you.'

'Alright.'

As he watched them, William was suddenly struck by the realisation that Christopher and Sophie were in love. He didn't know why he hadn't seen it before when it was so patently obvious. When Christopher had gone, Sophie looked about the room, her eyes lingering on the portraits of Christopher's ancestors on the walls. For once her usual confident manner was a little subdued.

'It takes a bit of getting used to, doesn't it?' William remarked.

'Yes,' Sophie smiled, perhaps relieved that he thought so too.

'Would you like to go out onto the terrace?'

'Yes, alright.'

He offered her a cigarette, and told her how he'd felt when he first arrived at the house. 'The sheer size of it is sort of overwhelming. It's one thing to see it from a distance, but quite another to actually live in a place like this. I suppose unless you've been brought up in these sorts of surroundings you never really accept it as quite normal. I couldn't get used to the number of servants there are. It was a bit strange having all these people looking after me when I first came here. Have you met Morton yet?'

'Is he the butler?'

'Yes. Bit of a stiff sort. Quite intimidating in a way.'

'I saw him when we arrived. I know what you mean, though he was very polite and nice to me.'

'Oh yes, he would be.'

'It's funny, but when Christopher asked me to come for the weekend I'd never thought about where he lived. I knew he was a viscount, and that he was rich of course, but I never imagined anything like this.' She looked at him curiously. 'Do you really find it strange living here?'

'Yes,' he said, surprised at her question. 'Why do you ask?'

'It's just that you look as if you belong somewhere like this,' she said. 'It's the way you dress and how you speak I suppose.'

'This suit belongs to Christopher, actually,' William told her.

'It's more than that though isn't it? I remember that day I met you when you were with Arthur. I thought you must be rich, and then when I heard Arthur call you by your first name I thought it was a bit funny.'

'Well, I'm not rich, as you know. I just went to a good school.'

'Was your family rich then?'

'No,' he said.

Sophie looked around again. 'Does Elizabeth live in a house like this?'

'Not like this, no. To be honest, the first time I went to pick her up I was relieved to find it was just your regular ten bedroom manor, or whatever it is.'

Sophie smiled. 'You must have met her parents then have you?'

'A few times, yes. They gave me a bit of a grilling the

first time, actually. Especially her mother.'

'That's what I was scared of when Christopher asked me to come here. I didn't realise it would only be us four.'

'I see.'

'I think I'll feel much better about it now I've been here and I've got an idea of what to expect.' She made a rueful face. 'Well, a bit better anyway. Besides, I can get some tips from you can't I? How do you speak to his mother anyway, do you call her Lady Horsham all the time?'

'Yes, I suppose if you're addressing her directly,' William replied. He realised that Sophie wasn't aware that Lady Horsham had no idea of her existence.

A few moments later Christopher returned and they went back inside. He had found Morton and sorted out the trouble with the cook, who it turned out was worried about the quality of the venison she had planned to prepare for their dinner.

'So whatever you do, you have to pretend that it's delicious even if it isn't,' he said. 'She can be very sensitive about her cooking.'

When Elizabeth arrived they all had another drink. She asked if Christopher had shown Sophie around yet.

'Well, no, there hasn't been time really,' Christopher said. 'I'll give you a bit of a tour in the morning though if you like,' he told Sophie.

'Oh it's no good leaving it to you.' Elizabeth took Sophie's arm. 'You'll only whisk her around in five minutes flat. Come on Sophie, I'll show you around now.'

'Alright, but don't take all night about it. If we're late for dinner Mrs Peters will be furious.' When they had gone, Christopher turned to William. 'I expect she'll tell Sophie all the family gossip. That's what really interests them isn't it? You know, which of my ancestors was in love with his manager's wife and all that sort of thing.'

'Was one of them in love with his manager's wife?'

'Yes, actually. It was my great grandfather. His

manager was a fellow called Fuller, and when he found out that my grandfather was sniffing around he was absolutely furious. The lady's name was Eleanor, very beautiful actually. Apparently the old goat was in the habit of sneaking around in the dead of night to peer into her windows, so Fuller set a steel trap in the garden to catch him out. Almost severed my grandfather's foot.'

'Good lord. What happened?'

'Nothing much, actually. My grandfather wouldn't sack the fellow because if he did he knew he'd never see Eleanor again. I don't know why Fuller stayed on under the circumstances, but he did. The rumour is that his wife actually fell for my grandfather in the end, though she refused to leave her husband, and so they managed to get along in some kind of ménage-a-trois. So the story goes anyway. My mother's the one to ask, she relishes all that sort of thing.'

'Speaking of your mother, when I was talking to Sophie earlier she gave me the impression that she was expecting to meet your mother at some stage.'

'Oh? What did you say?'

'I wasn't sure what to say, to be honest. Lady Horsham doesn't know about Sophie, does she?'

'No, of course she doesn't, and obviously I can't introduce them.' Christopher frowned. 'It's a bit tricky actually. How do I explain it to Sophie without hurting her feelings? I mean it's terribly snobbish I suppose, but there it is, there's not much I can do about it.'

'But surely your mother will find out about Sophie eventually.'

Christopher looked surprised. 'Well, of course she will. She may already be aware, for all I know. But that doesn't mean to say I can introduce them does it?'

'I don't see why not,' William said.

Christopher looked at him oddly. 'It's simply out of the question. Don't misunderstand me; I think Sophie is absolutely wonderful. In fact, between you and me, old man, I think I might be in love with her. I might as well tell you I've been looking at a flat in Northampton.'

'A flat? Do you mean you're going to live there?'

'Not me, Sophie. Of course I'd spend some of my time there. It would be much more pleasant than creeping around all these hotels as we do now. And it would be more like having our own place together, you know. Somewhere homely, where we can relax.'

What he meant, William realised, was that he intended to keep Sophie as his mistress. 'Does Sophie know about this?' he asked.

'About the flat? Yes of course. She's tremendously excited.'

'That isn't what I meant,' William said, unable to keep a note of censure from his tone.

'There's no need to sound like that, old man,' Christopher said. 'Once I've explained everything to Sophie properly, she'll understand.'

'Hadn't you better tell Elizabeth then?' William said. 'Otherwise she might say something inadvertently.'

'Liz? Goodness, I don't need to worry about that. Liz understands how these things are.'

'Yes, I expect she does,' William realised.

Over dinner, and later when they danced and drank until the early hours, Sophie and Christopher behaved lovingly towards one another, and as William observed them he wondered how Christopher could feel as he claimed to, and yet contemplate living the kind of double life he was entertaining. That night, when they finally went to bed, William asked Elizabeth if Sophie had said anything about the flat Christopher had mentioned. They were lying together in the darkness, their bodies still hot and slick from their lovemaking, in a languid state of deep contentment. He felt her stiffen.

'What flat?' she said.

He realised she didn't know about Christopher's plans, though he couldn't see any harm in telling her now. He repeated what Christopher had told him, including that he'd said he thought he was in love with Sophie. 'I thought he must have told you. Do you mind?'

'No of course not,' she said and kissed him. 'It was just a surprise that's all.'

Though William believed, her he wished he could see her face in the dark. He wondered if he would always be like this; doubting her, harbouring vague suspicions concerning her true feelings for Christopher. It was only jealousy on his part, he thought, though he knew there was nothing for him to be jealous about in reality. As if to affirm it to himself, he pulled her closer and she laid her head against his chest.

'I feel sorry for Sophie, don't you?' William said eventually.

'Why?' Elizabeth sounded genuinely puzzled.

'Because I think she's in love with Christopher. She doesn't realise that he wants her to be his mistress.'

'But what else does she expect?'

'I don't know. Would you be happy if I asked you to be my mistress?'

Elizabeth was astonished. 'William, it simply isn't the same thing. You're not a viscount for one thing, and I'm not Sophie. If you and I wanted to marry there would be nothing to stop us.'

He was tempted to argue the point with her, tell her that there was no law preventing Christopher from marrying Sophie either if it was what he wanted. And yet he knew that in a way it was naïve, and he didn't want an argument. They had never spent the night together and he didn't want to spoil it.

He listened to her breathing grow deeper and more even, thinking about what she'd said, that there was nothing to stop them marrying if they wanted to. He tried to imagine what that would be like. If he and Christopher were to win a contract to build aeroplanes for the army they would have to set up a factory somewhere. He would design new aeroplanes, each with a different purpose. A sports machine for the wealthy landowner who wanted to travel to his estates quickly, a plane designed to carry passengers between major cities. Even countries. And not only passengers, but freight and perhaps mail. He imagined the firm becoming ever more successful, perhaps even leading the development of aviation in Britain. He and Elizabeth would be together from the beginning. They might rent a small house somewhere to begin with, and then as they could afford it, perhaps buy something larger, big enough for a family. He found he could quite easily picture himself playing with his children on the lawn while Elizabeth looked on. He supposed it was an idealist sort of vision. No doubt there would be difficulties and life wouldn't always go smoothly, but what did it matter so long as they loved one another and were happy together?

Perhaps because his mind was so active with his plans for the future he couldn't sleep. In the end he got up, and because he didn't want to wake Elizabeth he thought he'd go downstairs. He closed the bedroom door quietly behind him, and as he went along the corridor he thought he heard something from the direction of Christopher's room. He stopped and listened, and then he heard it again. It was Christopher. He uttered a sound like a stifled cry. For a moment he thought he'd inadvertently overhead an expression of passionate intimacy, but then he realised that what he'd heard was not passion but anguish. Perhaps even fear.

He went to Christopher's room and knocked. 'Christopher? Are you alright?'

He heard Sophie's voice, and then a moment later she opened the door. She was wearing one of Christopher's dressing gowns, which she held together with one hand, though underneath she appeared to be naked.

'Is everything alright? I thought I heard something.'

'Yes, it's only a dream.' She went back to the bed where she sat on the edge and stroked Christopher's brow. The bedclothes were tangled and he was lying on his back, his body jerking now and then.

'It's alright, I'm here. It's just a dream. Shhhh.' Sophie continued to smooth his brow and gradually Christopher relaxed. He murmured something and his breathing became easier.

'He'll be alright, now,' Sophie said, and went with William to the door again. 'He's often like this.'

'I had no idea.' He looked back at Christopher, who was now sleeping peacefully.

'I think it started after that man was killed at the airshow. In the morning he never remembers. Or he pretends not to.'

'Is there anything I can do?'

'No, he'll be alright now, really. He'll sleep until morning.'

'Well, goodnight then.'

'Goodnight. And thanks.'

She closed the door and William went downstairs. In the drawing room he poured a drink. He was struck by the way Sophie had soothed Christopher from his nightmare. How gentle and loving she was. Her voice and her touch seemed to banish his demons.

When he went back to his room, Elizabeth murmured in her sleep and cuddled up to him and within minutes he fell asleep.

In the morning Christopher made no mention of the night before and William assumed Sophie hadn't said anything, so he didn't either. After breakfast Christopher suggested they ought to take a picnic and go fishing on the estate, though William said that first he needed to drive over to the garage and see Arthur. Since Arthur's initial difficulties everything seemed to have been sorted out. He'd taken on the wife of the landlord at the pub for a few hours each day to look after his books, and for a while William had received regular cheques in the post. But now Arthur was overdue with his payments again, and William wanted to make sure that everything was alright.

'You haven't heard from him have you, Sophie?' he asked, but she shook her head and said she hadn't. 'Alright, I'll be back in an hour.'

Elizabeth went with him, but when they arrived at the garage they found it closed.

'That's odd,' William said. 'He should be open today. Saturday's are always busy with cars stopping for petrol. And you can guarantee there'll be a few breakdowns.'

'Perhaps he's ill,' Elizabeth suggested.

'It's possible I suppose, but he took on a man to help him, so somebody ought to be here.' He knocked on the locked doors, but there was no sound from within. 'I'll just try the pub. Perhaps they might know something.'

But it was too early for the pub to be open and when William knocked on the door there was no reply, so he had no choice but to leave and try again another day. As they drove back to Pitsford, he worried that something was wrong.

'Are you really that concerned?' Elizabeth asked.

'Yes. Apart from anything else, I'm relying on Arthur to pay what he owes me.'

'Don't worry, I'm sure it'll be alright.'

'I suppose you're right,' he agreed, though for the rest of the weekend it was on his mind.

On Sunday evening, when Christopher came back after taking Sophie home, he gave William an envelope. 'I thought I'd drop in on the garage and see if your friend Hawkins was there. He gave me this.'

'You saw him then?' William tore open the envelope to find a cheque inside and also a hastily scribbled note apologising because it was late. 'How did he seem to you?'

'Alright, I think. He said he'd had a bad cold for the past few days, which is why he wasn't open when you went there yesterday. Apparently he heard you, but by the time he got himself out of his sick bed you'd already gone.'

William was relieved that there was nothing seriously wrong, and the cheque reassured him, but he decided that when he got a chance he'd drive over and see Arthur anyway.

'He's an odd sort though, isn't he?' Christopher remarked. 'Bit of a surly devil if you ask me.'

'He's a socialist,' William said.

'Ah, that would explain it then.'

But as it turned out William didn't get a chance to visit Arthur that week, because a few days later the engine arrived from the Gnome factory and they were kept busy getting it fitted and finishing off the rest of the plane.

17

By mid-August the new Gnome engine had been fitted, and during the second half of the month William flew several test flights. After each one he made alterations to the design and by the beginning of September, two weeks before the army trials were due to begin, the biplane was finished.

For the final test flight they chose a clear morning when the end of summer could be felt in the cooler air, a day reminiscent of apples ripened in orchards almost ready to be picked.

'We should both go up today,' William said as he and Christopher pushed the plane out onto the grass. The army had published a list of criteria covering rate of climb, speed, range and a host of other factors they intended to use as a measure of a machine's suitability. William's plan was that while one of them flew the plane the other should sit in the observer's cockpit and record the results. 'You can fly her if you like,' he suggested. 'After all, I've already done the test flights.'

'Alright,' Christopher agreed. 'I'll just fetch my goggles.'

William climbed up to the front cockpit, and as he did he saw that Christopher's goggles were in fact on the seat. He turned to call him back just as Christopher took something from his pocket and went into the garage. For an instant William saw the flash of sunlight on silver.

When Christopher returned, William could smell the

whisky on his breath. He handed him his goggles. 'They were on the seat.'

'Thanks. I thought I'd left them inside.'

With a jolt, William realised that Christopher was nervous. It occurred to him that this would be the first time Christopher had flown since Wentworth had been killed, and he recalled the night he'd heard Christopher dreaming. He wondered if he should say something. Christopher's manner was more than usually breezy, but William guessed it was a front. He supposed he could invent some reason to postpone the flight, perhaps a mechanical defect. He was sure Christopher would go along with it, but then what? It needed both of them to do the final test flight properly, and perhaps it was exactly what Christopher needed. He decided they should go ahead.

'Ready?' he said when Christopher was in his seat.

'Absolutely.'

William went around to the front and gave the propeller a half turn. 'Contact?'

'Contact,' Christopher responded as he switched on.

William gave the prop another turn, and at once there was a sudden, small explosion, and the engine roared into life. Hurriedly, he climbed up to his seat, and then they began to move across the grass, quickly gathering pace until all at once they were in the air and climbing. He turned around and gave Christopher the thumbs up sign, which Christopher returned. Reassured, William pressed the button to start his stopwatch and then turned his attention to the set of instruments they had fitted to record the performance of their machine.

*****

Two days after they had carried out their successful test flight, William was tinkering with the biplane when a car stopped outside. For a moment he thought it was

Elizabeth, but when he went outside he was surprised to see that it was Arthur.

'How have you been?' William asked as they shook hands, though in fact Arthur looked terrible. He hadn't shaved for several days and his eyes were bloodshot.

'Not so bad. I thought I'd come and see how you're getting on.' Arthur looked about in a slightly furtive way. 'Is your friend 'ere then?'

'You mean Christopher? No, he's in town. Actually I'm glad you've come. I've been meaning to look in at the garage, but I haven't had time lately. How are things?'

'I 'ad to let Mathew go,' Arthur said, referring to the mechanic he had taken on.

'Why?' William said in alarm.

'I couldn't afford his wages. I might as well tell you I can't pay what I owe you either, Will. Not at the moment. But things'll pick up I 'spect.'

'What's happened?' William asked anxiously. 'I thought things were going well.' The fact that Arthur had fallen behind with his repayments again was bad enough, but what was more worrying was that more than three quarters of the total debt was still outstanding, and William was already overdrawn at the bank.

Arthur was annoyingly vague with his answers. 'I've 'ad to turn customers away,' he admitted in the end when William continued to press him. 'I couldn't get the parts anymore.'

'You mean you couldn't get credit?' William guessed, knowing there could only be one reason for that. With a sinking feeling he saw how bad things must be. 'Do you owe them money?'

'I got behind,' Arthur said refusing to meet his eye.

'Damn it, Arthur, I warned you about this,' William said angrily. 'What about the bank? Have you kept up your payments?'

Arthur stared at the ground, the answer obvious, but

when he looked up again there was an odd look in his eyes. 'How's Sophie, Will?' he asked as if the question of the bank and his business troubles had entirely slipped from his mind.

'She's well, as far as I know,' William said, immediately cautious.

'I've seen 'er in town sometimes, but she won't talk to me anymore.'

'What do you mean?'

'She told me not to bother 'er. Said she'd get the police on me if I kept on.'

'When was this?' William asked, wondering what had provoked Sophie to such a response.

'A while back.'

'Have you been bothering her?'

'I only wanted to talk to 'er! I'd just wait outside where she works, that's all. But she didn't want to see me after she started goin' about with that friend of yours.'

How long had this been going on, William wondered. He suspected Sophie was the reason Arthur had neglected his business.

'I'm worried about 'er, Will,' Arthur went on. 'She'll lose 'er position if she's not careful.'

'What do you mean? Why will she lose her position?'

'She's late for work sometimes after she's been out late at those hotels. It's that friend of yours who's to blame. I shouldn't say it 'cause I know 'ow you're staying here and all, but it's not right Sophie livin' in that flat of his.'

'How do you know about that? Have you been following her?'

'No, 'course not,' Arthur protested, but William didn't believe him.

'You have to stop this. You have to realise that Sophie has a life of her own,' William warned.

'I thought if you talk to 'er, Will, she might listen to you,' Arthur said as if he hadn't heard.

213

'Arthur! Listen to me! Did you hear what I said? You have to forget about Sophie!'

Arthur stared at him, and then his manner changed. A dull, sullen look of resentment crept into his eyes. 'I thought you'd understand, Will. But I was wrong about you. You're different now you're living 'ere.' He gestured contemptuously towards the house. 'I shouldn't 'ave come.' He turned and went back towards his car.

'Wait!' William said going after him. He thought there must be something wrong with Arthur. Perhaps it was the strain of the business. He had to persuade him to see somebody, perhaps a doctor who could give him something to calm him down. 'Wait here a minute while I get my jacket and I'll come with you. We'll go back to the garage and talk this through. I'm sure we can sort everything out. You'll see things differently then.'

Arthur stared at him wordlessly. As William went back inside he thought this was partly his fault. If he'd kept a better eye on the garage this wouldn't have happened. He'd become so tied up with his own life that he had just left Arthur to get on with it, even though there had been signs right from the beginning that things weren't going well. Just then he heard Arthur's car start, and when William went outside Arthur was already driving off. He called out to him, but Arthur ignored him. Deeply concerned, William got in his own car and drove to the garage, but he found it locked up, an air of abandonment and neglect about the place.

A few days later, William and Elizabeth drove into Northampton one evening, to the flat where Sophie was now living. The four of them were going to a dance at a hotel on the Wellingborough road. When they arrived, Christopher was already there. Sophie showed them around, clearly very proud and happy, though William thought she seemed distracted. He put it down to nerves. They were the first visitors she'd had to her new home.

The flat was very spacious, with two large bedrooms

and a smaller one for a maid.

'I've managed to find a cook who'll come in to do dinner,' Sophie said as they returned to the spacious living room where Christopher had made them all a drink. A little later, when Sophie went to the kitchen, William saw a chance to speak to her alone.

'Hello,' she said when she saw him. 'Do you need something?'

'I just wanted a glass of water,' he said. As he filled a glass he mentioned that he'd seen Arthur a few days earlier. Sophie frowned but didn't say anything. 'He's got himself into trouble with the garage. By the sound of it he's going to lose the business.'

'I'm sorry about that. For Arthur's sake.' She sighed heavily. 'I told him he had to concentrate on his work instead of bothering me all the time.'

'Has he been bothering you?'

She nodded. 'He won't leave me alone. In the end I had to threaten to put the police onto him.'

'He knows you're living here,' William said.

'I know, but I didn't tell him. He must have followed me.'

'Does Christopher know about any of this?'

'No, I didn't want to say anything. I was frightened of what Arthur might do if Christopher went to see him. Arthur keeps going on about him, saying it's wrong for Christopher to make me live here. I keep telling him that I want to be here and that Christopher and I love each other, but Arthur won't listen. He's got this idea in his head that he loves me, and if only I could see that we should be together, everything would be alright.' She looked despairingly at William. 'What do you think I should do?'

'I think if you see him again you ought to tell Christopher. I don't think Arthur's dangerous.'

'I hope you're right,' she said.

'We better get back to the others or they'll wonder

what's going on.'

Sophie offered a wan smile.

'You are alright, aren't you?' he asked. 'You're not worried?'

'No, not really.'

'It's just that you're not your usual self.' For a moment he had the feeling she wanted to tell him something, but then she evidently changed her mind.

'I'm fine. Really.'

Later that evening, as William danced with Elizabeth, she was unusually quiet. 'What are you thinking about?' he asked, though he had already guessed what was on her mind.

She glanced toward their table, where Sophie and Christopher were sitting. 'They look very happy, don't they? I thought that earlier when we went to the flat.'

'Does it bother you?'

She looked into his eyes. 'No, of course it doesn't. It's just that everything is changing and it takes time to get used to the idea.'

'Are you sorry that things are changing?'

'No,' she said. 'A bit sad in one way perhaps, but I'm very happy in another way. Be patient with me. Can you do that?'

'Of course.'

She touched her fingers to his lips. 'I love you.'

When the dance ended, Elizabeth went to the powder room and William took the opportunity to get some air. He went outside and walked along the road a little way. When he looked back the windows were all lit up and music drifted on the evening air. A group of people stood in the light by the entrance. One of them laughed and a man lit a cigarette for a woman who put it into the end of a long holder. William watched from the obscurity of the darkness. He felt separate from them, and he thought that in a way he had always felt like that, that he was something of an outsider. Elizabeth came outside, and William knew she was looking for him. When he was with her he felt differently. She made him feel that he wasn't alone. He decided then that he was going to ask her to marry him.

He began to go back, and as he did he threw away his cigarette. A movement in the darkness caught his eye. A figure stood a little further along the road concealed beside a tree. It was Arthur. For an instant they looked at one another, and then before William could say anything, Arthur turned and vanished. His footsteps became faint, and then a car started and drove away with its lights off.

When he went back to the hotel Elizabeth saw him and smiled. 'Is that you? What are you doing?'

'Just getting some air.'

'I wondered where you were. Come on, I want you to dance with me.'

She took his arm and they went inside.

*****

In the morning, William opened the curtains to his room. A scattering of pale, golden leaves fluttered on the grass beneath the oaks. Elizabeth had come back with him the night before, having made up some story or other for her parents' benefit, which she was sure they didn't believe. She was still sleeping, but as he got dressed she stirred.

'Come back to bed,' she said.

'I've got a surprise. Get dressed and I'll see you downstairs.'

'What sort of surprise?'

'You'll see. Hurry up.'

An hour later he led her outside, and when Elizabeth saw the biplane parked on the grass she stopped in her tracks.

'Oh no, William! You're not suggesting what I think you are?'

He handed her a pair of goggles and a leather helmet.

'You'll need to wear these. Not very glamorous I'm afraid, but necessary.'

She took them reluctantly. 'You're serious, aren't you?'

'You needn't worry. I've flown her half a dozen times already.' He took her hands. 'There's a purpose to this, beyond just getting you up in a plane at last. Trust me Elizabeth. Will you do that?'

She hesitated, but then nodded. 'Alright. I will.'

He grinned, then helped her to climb up into the front cockpit and showed her how to buckle her harness.

'Are you sure it's safe?' she asked, looking doubtfully at the maze of wires and struts between the wings.

'Perfectly. And with any luck she's going to make my fortune.'

She laughed. 'I've never heard you sound so confident before. Do you really think it will?

'Well, I expect it will set me along the path anyway. And then your parents will approve of me.'

He kissed her before she had time to think about what he meant, and then he jumped down and gave the prop a turn to prime the engine.

'Ready?'

Elizabeth nodded gamely, and he went back to switch on then, gave the prop another turn and the engine caught and fired. The plane was already moving as he climbed into his seat and opened the throttle. Elizabeth held on tightly to the sides of her cockpit as the noise of the engine grew louder. They bumped quickly across the field, and then as William pulled back on the control stick they rose smoothly into the air.

The plane climbed quickly, and within a few minutes they were flying at three thousand feet. Far below them, the woods and fields were spread out in a collage of greens and browns and gold, and threaded through it all were silvery threads of rivers and streams. As they passed over a small village Elizabeth found the courage to look down. Once she got over her initial terror, she stopped holding on so tightly, mesmerised instead by this new perspective of the world. William flew them above Pistford House so that she could see something she knew well, and from there he flew to Earls Barton and her own house. He made a pass over the roof at a hundred feet and then came back a second time. Elizabeth's mother and one of her sisters had come out into the garden and were looking up at them and Elizabeth waved and then turned to him, grinning in delight. He pushed the stick from side to side to waggle the wings and turning east he began to climb again.

At ten thousand feet the clouds looked solid enough to walk on. Elizabeth gazed all around at the landscape of billowing, cotton-like mountains. Towering cumulus rose far above them, and beyond was the never ending cerulean blue. The slanting rays of the sun cast shadows that raced like vast armies across the earth far below.

They began to descend, and the shadow of the plane crossed the fields like a cross carried before crusaders of old. And then they were following the course of the river Nene along the valley floor, past the mill at Barnwell. William turned to take them over Oundle. He looked down on the buildings of the school where he had spent so much of his childhood, and the market square where he first saw Emmaline, and the churchyard where he had sat with her. Leaving the town behind he followed the path that crossed the water meadow and ran beside the river, until he saw Fotheringhay Castle, no more than a mound of earth where once he'd seen a ghostly figure in the mist. He remembered the air of melancholy that enveloped the place and the aura of loneliness he'd identified with. Eventually he changed direction again.

When they reached Scaldwell, he flew over the village and landed the plane in a grassy field. As they came to a stop he switched off the engine, and the sudden quiet after the constant roar of the engine was almost startling. He climbed out of his cockpit and helped Elizabeth down. She took off her helmet and goggles and shook her hair free.

'Why did you wait so long before you took me flying? I've never experienced anything like it.' She laughed in delight and then she threw her arms about him and kissed him.

William thought she was beautiful, with her long hair swept back and her smiling face upturned to the sun, her sea green eyes.

'Where are we?' she asked looking around. 'I know that was Oundle we flew over before, but what was the other place?'

'It's all that's left of Fotheringhay Castle. When I was at school I used to run there to make my leg strong again.'

She heard something in his voice and then she looked around again. 'This is where you grew up, isn't it?'

He took her hand. 'I'll show you.'

The cottage was exactly as he remembered it, though the forge was empty. He told Elizabeth everything about himself, beginning with how his parents met and ran away. He told her about his mother dying, and about the accident in the wheat field that almost cost him a leg, and as they walked into the village he tried to explain what it had been like for him when he was sent to Oundle. When they reached the church he showed her where his parents were buried.

'At my father's funeral I stood here surrounded by people I had grown up with, and I realised I didn't belong here anymore.'

'Is that when you went to Northampton?'

'Yes.' He told her how he'd run out of money and ended up wandering the streets until eventually he went to work at Ballantynes. She listened in silence to his description of his life there, and he could see in her eyes that it was so far removed from her experience that she could barely comprehend it.

'Do you think it matters to me where you came from? Is that why you brought me here?' she asked at last.

'I wanted you to know who I am.'

He'd planned to ask her to marry him at that point, but suddenly he changed his mind and he decided he would wait until they got back to Pitsford. Scaldwell was his past, whereas his future lay elsewhere.

*****

As they flew over Pitsford House, William saw Christopher's car in the yard, and as soon as they landed, Christopher strode towards them.

'Where the hell have you been all this time?' he said, sounding agitated. 'We've been waiting here for absolutely ages.' He glanced at Elizabeth with a sort of mute appeal. 'Sophie's inside. She's rather upset.'

'What is it? Is something wrong?' Elizabeth asked.

'Yes. Christ, it's such a bloody mess. Liz, will you talk to her for me? Please. She'll listen to another woman.'

Elizabeth glanced worriedly at William. 'I'd better go and see her.'

As she went off towards the garage, William turned to Christopher. 'What's going on?'

'I'm sorry about this, old man. I suppose I'm a bit on edge to tell the truth. I was looking for Liz, you see, and when I telephoned her house I heard she was with you. Where have you been anyway?'

'I took her up for a bit a joyride.'

'Oh, I see.' Christopher took out his cigarette case and offered one to William. 'You did well getting her to go up with you. I could never persuade her.'

'Why did you want to see her in such a hurry anyway?'

'Because I couldn't think what else to do. It's Sophie. She's going to have a child.'

William was too taken aback to say anything. Christopher walked off a little way and stood smoking his cigarette.

'What will you do?' William asked eventually.

'I really don't know. What do you think I ought to do?'

'I'm not sure I feel qualified to offer advice. I've no experience in these things.'

'I hope you don't think that I have,' Christopher said defensively.

'No, of course not. That isn't what I meant.'

'I'm sorry, it's shock that's making me like this.'

'It's alright.'

'You are a good fellow, you know.' Christopher managed a brief smile, a flicker of his old self. 'To make matters worse, I telephoned the place where she works,' he went on. 'Obviously she wasn't in a state to go in, so I told them she wasn't feeling well. The woman I spoke to took quite a sniffy line with me. Put me on to the chap who runs the place. Walker, I think. The solicitor. Anyway, the bloody fellow made it clear that I could tell Sophie that she would no longer be required. I tell you, if I could have, I think I would have hit him.'

'Did you tell Sophie?'

'Yes. I told her that she needn't worry of course. I was going to ask her to leave anyway. I said she'd be too busy looking after me, or something like that. She brightened up a bit then. The trouble is she misunderstood. She thought I meant we'd get married.'

'You never got around to explaining things to her then?' William guessed.

'No, not exactly. Anyway, I thought she understood. She seemed happy when I bought the flat. I mean, why else would I have bought the bloody thing? I've tried to explain to her that marriage isn't possible, but she became hysterical. I'm afraid I've made an absolute hash of everything. Perhaps I should go and see how she is. She was very upset.'

'What will you say to her?'

'I've no idea.'

'Can I ask you something?' William said.

'Of course.'

'Has this changed the way you feel about her? I mean, do you still love her?'

'Yes, of course I do. What sort of chap do you think I am?'

'I'm sorry, I just feel that if you love Sophie I don't really see why you can't marry her. Is it really out of the question?'

Christopher was astonished at the suggestion. 'You have to understand my position, William. My personal feelings don't enter into this at all. Unfortunately, being born into a family like mine means I have certain obligations. In many ways my life isn't my own. It's one of the things I envy about you.'

'About me?'

'Yes. You have your plans and your ambition, but my life is rather preordained by comparison.' He made a gesture, encompassing their surroundings. 'All of this will be my responsibility one day. I have a duty to my family, to generations past and future. I know it might all sound a bit old hat to some people these days, but I take the expectations placed upon me very seriously. And those expectations include having the right sort of wife. I can't simply marry anyone I choose. It's a tremendous burden really, but it's simply the way things are. I tried to explain this to Sophie. Do you know what she said? She told me that she had read of Dukes and Earls who had married girls from the Gaiety Theatre. Can you imagine? I suppose it's quite true actually. But it's hardly the point.'

'But surely if you love each other, none of it matters,' William insisted.

'Of course it matters,' Christopher replied with the

faint air of somebody explaining what ought to be perfectly apparent. 'If I married Sophie, in all likelihood I would be disinherited. It isn't the money, you understand, I would always have an allowance of some sort. It's everything else. The tradition. Responsibility. It's who I am, William. I suppose it's not as obvious to somebody like yourself, but to me it's an impossible thing to ask.'

'As you say, I expect it isn't obvious to somebody like me,' William said with a faintly scathing tone, though if Christopher heard him he didn't register it. Instead his attention was diverted when Elizabeth emerged from the garage bringing Sophie with her. Sophie looked awful. Her eyes were swollen from crying, and her whole posture sagged in despair.

'I'm going to take Sophie home,' Elizabeth said. 'We've arranged that in the morning I'll call for her, and then we'll decide what we're going to do. I'll telephone you later, once I've seen that Sophie is alright.'

'Yes, alright,' Christopher agreed, clearly relieved that she was taking charge, and he gave her the keys to his car before kissing Sophie on her cheek. 'I'm sorry, darling. I know I've been hopeless. Everything will be alright though, I promise.'

She seemed heartened by his assurance and allowed herself to be led away.

'I think I need a drink,' Christopher said and started towards the house. 'Are you coming?'

But William didn't feel like a drink. 'I don't think I will.' Christopher hesitated, hearing the note of censure in William's tone. William gestured to the plane. 'I want to check something,' he said, though it was obvious he was making an excuse.

They looked at one another, as if both of them saw something unexpected that they had somehow missed before. Then Christopher nodded and turned away.

'Alright. I'll see you later then.'

18

Dinner that evening was a strained affair. It seemed to William that any attempt at conversation would be a pointless pretence and a denial of the subject uppermost in their minds, which Christopher was unwilling to broach. Christopher barely touched his food, but drank steadily instead, often staring for long periods into his glass, absorbed in his thoughts.

A few minutes after they were served a main course of beef, which neither of them had touched, Morton came into the room to tell Christopher that there was a telephone call from Miss Gordon.

'Thank you, Morton.' Christopher glanced at William as he got up, his expression managing to convey a whole raft of anxieties, and yet revealing nothing at all. He was gone for about ten minutes, and when he returned he said, 'Liz is going to come over tomorrow.'

'Is Sophie alright?'

'Yes.'

After that nothing more was said, and a few minutes later William excused himself and went to his room, leaving Christopher to brood alone.

The following day Elizabeth arrived early in the afternoon. William was busy making last minute adjustments to the biplane that weren't really necessary, but which gave him something to do. He hadn't spoken to Christopher at all that day, though he'd seen him earlier, out walking alone with the look of somebody preoccupied with the weight of his troubles. At the sound of a car William went outside, and was in time to see Elizabeth going to the house. He almost called out to her, but in the end he thought it was better if he left them to it.

It was almost six o clock by the time he went inside. As he passed the open door to Sir James's study, Elizabeth called out to him. Christopher sat at the desk with a glass of whisky in his hand. He looked dejected and tired.

'I was going to come and find you in a minute,' Elizabeth said. 'Would you like a drink?'

'Yes, alright, thanks.'

Elizabeth gave him a whisky and gestured to some legal looking documents on the desk. 'We've been sorting out what to do about Sophie.'

'How is she?' William asked, putting aside the implication that Sophie was a problem to be dealt with, rather than their friend and Christopher's lover.

'We had a long talk yesterday. She calmed down in the end.'

Christopher got up and went to the window, where he gazed outside as if their conversation wasn't his concern.

'I'm going to go and see her again in the morning,' Elizabeth went on. 'To explain everything.'

There was a brief silence. William wondered what exactly needed to be explained, though he guessed it had to do with the documents on the desk. Elizabeth glanced towards Christopher as if seeking his support, but he had clearly decided to leave this to her.

'We think the best thing would be for Sophie to go away somewhere to have her baby,' she said finally. 'I thought perhaps the south coast, though Sophie could choose somewhere herself, of course.'

'So long as it's far enough away, I suppose,' William commented acidly.

'Why do you say it like that?'

'You want to get rid of her now that she's become an

embarrassment, isn't that what you're saying?'

'That isn't it at all!' Elizabeth protested. 'Surely it would be better for everyone, especially Sophie, if she goes far enough way that she can start a completely new life without having people spreading gossip. People here know that she and Christopher have been seeing each other. They're bound to draw the obvious conclusion when it becomes known that she's pregnant, and then it will follow them both around for ever. At least this way, Sophie can tell people that she's a widow or something, and nobody will ever know it isn't true. It won't stop her from marrying in the future.'

William turned angrily to Christopher. 'You said you were in love with Sophie! However you try to justify it, the fact is you simply want to bundle her off somewhere out of sight because suddenly she's become inconvenient.'

'That isn't fair, William!' Elizabeth said before Christopher could respond. 'We're simply trying to do what's best.'

'Best for who? Have you asked Sophie her opinion about any of this?'

'For goodness sake, what else can he do?'

'If he loves her, he could stand by her,' William said.

'You mean marry her? That simply isn't realistic, William. Surely you can see that. And if Sophie stays here neither of them will be able to get on with their lives properly. It isn't as if Sophie won't be looked after financially. She'll receive enough money to buy herself a modest house, and she'll have an allowance so that she won't ever have to work again, and her child will be provided for. I should have thought that all things considered, that isn't such a terrible outcome.'

'It's their child,' William pointed out, but Elizabeth regarded him blankly, missing his meaning. 'You said Sophie's child will be provided for, but it's Christopher's child too, or had you forgotten that?'

'Of course I haven't.'

But William saw that in a way Elizabeth had forgotten, or more accurately she had chosen to. In the same way she was choosing to ignore Sophie's feelings, even insinuating that so long as Sophie was given enough money to allow her to live comfortably nothing else would matter to her. He suddenly understood that this was all Elizabeth's idea. 'Why are you doing this?' he asked her.

'What do you mean? I'm trying to help.'

'Are you? It seems that you're the one making all the decisions. Christopher hasn't even said a word.'

She stared at him, and though she denied it, he saw in her eyes that he was right. 'I resent what you're implying. Christopher asked me to help as a friend and that's what I'm doing.'

Christopher turned away from the window. 'Liz is right, old man,' he said, speaking at last. 'She's only doing this because I asked her to. She's always been dependable. I know this is all terrible, but whether you believe it or not I care very deeply about Sophie. In a way that's why it really would be better for her to move away somewhere. Apart from anything else, if she stays here I won't be able to stop myself from seeing her. I know I won't. And that's not really fair on Sophie is it? That's why I've decided to leave Northampton for a little while. Give her time to find somewhere to live.'

Christopher glanced at Elizabeth, and William realised from the look they exchanged that they hadn't intended to tell him this yet.

'I thought I might go and spend a bit of time in the South of France. There's a motor race there I might enter, actually. It would give me something else to think of.'

'You mean you're going to turn your back on her?' William said tightly. He could barely control his anger. It was clear that Elizabeth knew of Christopher's plan. Perhaps she'd even suggested it herself. She looked away, avoiding him. Suddenly William felt that he didn't know them at all, either of them. He could hardly believe they were capable of any of this, and yet they spoke as if he was the one being unreasonable. It was all about one's position and appearance.

'When will you leave?' he asked coldly.

'In a day or two. It's probably for the best.'

'What about the army trials?'

'I know it's a bit of a blow, but you'll be able to find somebody from Sywell to go with you. You only need somebody to take the observer's seat after all. It's not as if I'd actually be doing anything.'

Though what he said was true, William still couldn't comprehend that Christopher would simply abandon the trials after all their work. 'Don't you care what happens?'

'Yes of course I do. But let's face it, old man, it's really your baby isn't it?' Christopher stopped, realising that he'd chosen an unfortunate turn of phrase. 'What I mean is, you've always been the real force behind building this plane. I'm sure you'll do well without me there. You can come down to France afterwards and tell us all about it.'

'Us?' Struck by the plural term William looked at Elizabeth.

'Yes, I thought I'd go along too,' she said with forced lightness. 'It might be best if somebody keeps an eye on him at a time like this.'

In a moment of revelation, William saw the truth. All of his doubts and uncertainties regarding Elizabeth and her feelings for him crystallised into the sudden certainty that, in the end, her loyalty lay with Christopher. This wasn't about the ingrained allegiances of position and background, but rather, for Elizabeth, it was an opportunity she couldn't let pass.

'Why are you looking at me that way?' Elizabeth demanded, but before William had a chance to respond she turned her back on him in a show of exasperation. 'I knew you would react like this. That's why I didn't want to say anything yet.' She shot a reproachful look at Christopher, who drained his glass and apologised.

'I didn't mean to put my foot in it,' he said. 'I think I ought to leave you two alone.' He left the room, avoiding William's eye.

Eventually, Elizabeth turned to face him again. 'You have to understand, Christopher shouldn't be alone at the moment,' she began. 'He'll only brood and drink too much and then he might do something impulsive.'

'You mean he might realise what he's done and come back to Sophie?' William questioned, knowing he sounded angry and bitter.

'I know you think that would be a good thing, but you're wrong,' she said.

'And is that why you're going with him? To stop him doing something 'impulsive'?'

'Don't,' Elizabeth said tightly.

'Tell me you're not in love with him, then.'

'For goodness sake! You've never believed me, have you, William? You've always thought that, despite everything.'

'If I'm wrong, tell me.'

'I shouldn't have to,' she said.

'Perhaps not, but I think if I am wrong, you would tell me.'

They stared at one another, both angry and neither prepared to yield. A heaviness fell over William, and with it the pain of intense disappointment. He would have done anything if Elizabeth had come to him and told him she loved him. He would even have forgiven her for what she and Christopher were doing to Sophie, but he knew from her expression that there was nothing more to say.

As he turned to leave, she spoke his name, but he heard the uncertainty in her tone, as if she wasn't sure herself what she wanted to happen. He kept going without looking around.

*****

From the street, William saw lights in the windows of the flat. He rang and Sophie let him in. When he reached her door she was waiting. He expected her to look wan or dishevelled from despair, but he found that she was composed and quite normal, though there wasn't a hint of friendliness in her expression.

'I expect you've come to make sure I won't make any trouble,' she said scornfully.

'I came to see if you're alright.'

She made a derisive sound. 'Who sent you?'

'Nobody sent me. I've been wandering around for hours.'

Perhaps it was his tone that made her look more closely at him. 'Have you been drinking?'

'Yes, though I'm not drunk. It's funny, I've had quite a lot, but it doesn't seem to have affected me.'

His sardonic tone made her curious. 'Why have you come here?'

'I told you, I wanted to see if you're alright.'

She remained suspicious of him, but stood aside. 'You'd better come in then.'

He followed her into the living room and she offered him a drink. 'Thanks. I might as well have a whisky if you've got it.'

She fetched him a glass and poured herself one too from a decanter on a drinks trolley, and then sat down opposite him and lit a cigarette. He wondered if it was good for her to drink and smoke in her condition, though he didn't say anything.

She saw him looking at some documents on the table. 'I suppose you know what those are.'

'I think so. Who brought them?'

'Who do you think?' she said contemptuously. 'Your precious Elizabeth. I'll tell you the same as I told her. I won't sign them!'

'I didn't have anything to do with it, Sophie,' William said, realising she thought he'd come to pressure her. 'I only found out what was going on this afternoon. I told them what I thought of it and walked out.'

She studied him as if she was trying to make up her mind whether to believe him or not. 'She'd like me to disappear and never come back,' she said bitterly.

He didn't need to ask to know that she meant Elizabeth.

'You know she's in love with Christopher, don't you?'

'Yes,' he said heavily. 'Have you always known?'

'I knew it the first time I saw her.'

'Is Christopher in love with her?'

'No. That's the stupid thing about all of this. Christopher loves me. I know he does. He wouldn't do this if it wasn't for her.'

'I'm not defending her, Sophie, but Christopher isn't being forced into anything.'

'No, but she's making it easy for him. If he had to come here and tell me himself, he wouldn't do it. I know him.' Sophie shook her head miserably. 'We're in the same boat you and me, aren't we?'

'I suppose we are.'

'You don't think it's my own fault do you?' she asked him. 'That I meant to get pregnant?'

'No, of course not.'

'I was afraid Christopher would think I did. They haven't said anything?'

'Not to me.'

'I'm glad you don't think that. I thought you might.'

'Why?'

'I always thought you looked down on me a bit. Like you thought I was after Christopher because he's rich.'

Though he didn't admit it to her, William thought there was a part of him, a small part, that suspected Sophie of being an opportunist.

'I always thought it was funny really,' she mused.

'In what way?'

'Because we're the same you and me, really. Do you remember that day at the airshow? I met somebody there I knew. She saw you talking to me and said she knew you when you worked at Ballantynes as a stock-boy.'

'You never mentioned it,' he said.

'It wasn't my business.'

William realised that Sophie had probably thought he was the opportunistic social climber and the irony made him smile.

'What will you do about Elizabeth,' she asked.

He shook his head. 'Nothing. You can't make somebody love you.'

'I think she does love you,' Sophie said, which surprised him.

'You told me a moment ago that she's in love with Christopher.'

'People don't always know what they want. And anyway, Christopher doesn't love her. I've seen the way she looks at you. Perhaps you should fight for her.'

But William knew she was wrong, that Sophie only wanted him to get Elizabeth away from Christopher because she thought then, Christopher wouldn't try to send her away.

'I don't agree with what they're trying to do,' he said. 'I've told you that. But perhaps you should take their offer. Christopher will never marry you. The truth is... when he does marry it will be to somebody like Elizabeth. Perhaps it will be her, I don't know. At least if you do what they want you'll have a home and enough money to live on. You won't have to work.'

But Sophie shook her head determinedly. 'If I stay here I'll make things how they were again, and then he'll come back.'

'What do you mean?'

'I just mean we were happy before. He'll come and see me, I know he will. It'll be different then.'

William realised that she didn't know about Christopher's plan to go away. 'They're leaving,' he said, hating having to break the news. 'Both of them. They're going to France in a few days.'

She stared at him. 'How do you know?'

'They told me. That's when I left.'

He could see she was shocked, and he offered to stay with her, but she shook her head.

'I'll be alright.'

'I'll come and see you before I go to the trials. Think about what I said.'

She promised she would, but he thought her mind was elsewhere. After he had left the flat he threw his cigarette down and ground it viciously beneath his heel. He thought if he could stop himself from being in love by an act of willpower he would do it. To love somebody meant entrusting a part of your very soul to them. You became as vulnerable and exposed as an infant. But it seemed to William that the only reward anybody could expect was a kind of torture. He found himself going over every memory he had of the time he'd spent with Elizabeth. He'd been a fool. She had used him and told him she loved him, but it wasn't true. He felt as if his insides were being torn from his body. The sense of loss and betrayal he experienced was a visceral, physical pain far worse than anything he could imagine. What was the point of loving anybody when it ended like this? Love was a tangled web of emotions that brought misery instead of happiness. Look at what love had done to Sophie.

He clenched his fist tightly. There was a brick wall beside him and he would have hit it, preferring the agony of broken, bloodied knuckles to what he felt. But he glimpsed a figure standing in the shadows and was shocked to see that it was Arthur. His eyes were dark and wild, his appearance dishevelled. William crossed the street towards him, but Arthur turned and began to walk quickly away.

'Wait! Come back!' William called out, but it was no good. He supposed he could have chased him and caught up, but what was the point? Arthur was another one for whom love had brought only misery.

19

Two days after he saw Sophie, William returned to Pitsford House. Christopher was getting ready to leave for the station, though to William's relief Elizabeth was nowhere in sight.

'Look, old man, this has all turned out badly and I feel terrible about it,' Christopher said. 'I wish you'd reconsider about coming down to France after the trials.'

'I'm afraid I can't do that,' William said tightly, hardly able to believe that Christopher would suggest it.

'If it's because of Liz, you've got the wrong end of the stick there, you know.'

'Have I?'

'Liz and I are friends. We've been friends for a long time.'

He believes it, William thought, though even if for Christopher it was true, he must realise that Elizabeth's feelings were not so straight forward.

'Well, I ought to be off,' Christopher said. He offered his hand. 'Good luck with the trials, and I hope that we can be friends again one day.'

William ignored his outstretched hand. 'I'll let you know about the trials.'

'Yes, alright.' Christopher said, appearing saddened that the olive branch he was extending had been rejected. 'Morton's got the address where we'll be staying.'

'If we win the contract we'll need to sort out what we're going to do.'

'Of course. I'll be happy to go along with whatever you suggest.' As he climbed into his car, Christopher hesitated. 'If you see Sophie, will you tell her something for me? Tell her that… tell her that I'm truly sorry.'

It was, William thought, the only thing he'd said that sounded completely sincere, but as far as he was concerned it made Christopher's actions all the more incomprehensible.

After Christopher had gone, William went to find Morton to tell him that if it was alright he would stay a final night in the house and leave in the morning. He planned to take the plane to Farnborough and find a cheap room to rent until the trials began the following week.

'Very good, sir,' Morton said. 'Though Mister Horsham left instructions that I should tell you that you are welcome to stay as long as you like.'

'Thanks. But it'll just be the one night.'

That evening William ate alone in the dining room, waited on by a footman who was overseen by Morton. William wore one of Christopher's suits for the occasion, and asked for a decent bottle of wine from the cellar, which Morton brought without a murmur. William didn't know why he hadn't simply asked for something on a tray to be brought to the drawing room, but he supposed it was an ironic gesture. He'd thought that one day he wanted all of this; a house like Pitsford with its estates and servants, but he realised now that if he became successful he would prefer to live in far more modest surrounds. It was perhaps a farewell gesture as much as anything, he thought. A farewell to dreams of an England that he didn't belong to.

After dinner he got slightly drunk, and when he went to bed he collapsed without getting undressed.

He was woken by urgent knocking at his door, and was confused to find that it was still dark. When he opened it he found Morton there looking as if he'd just climbed from his bed. 'What is it?'

'A young lady is on the telephone, sir. She insists on

speaking to you, though I told her you had retired.'

'A young lady?' He thought it must be Elizabeth, and despite everything, foolish hope sprung in his heart, but as he went downstairs he realised that it couldn't be her because Morton knew her and would have told him.

'Hello?' he said when he picked up the phone.

'William, I need you to come.'

He recognised Sophie's voice immediately though she sounded very faint and her words were slurred as if she was drunk or half asleep. 'Sophie, are you alright?'

'Please. I need help.'

'Sophie?' her voice sounded even fainter and he became alarmed. 'Tell me what's wrong! Has something happened?'

She said something he didn't catch, and then he heard a sound as if the phone had been dropped and the line went dead. He tapped for the operator and asked her to try the number again, but she told him she couldn't get through. Within a few minutes he was driving as fast as he could towards Northampton.

When he arrived outside the flat there was a light on in the living room window. He went to the front door and rang the bell for the flat, but there was no reply. He tried the handle and found it unlocked. He ran up the stairs to find the flat door slightly ajar. Inside, the hallway was dark though he could see a light coming from the living room along the corridor.

'Sophie?' He stepped inside, and as he did he heard something from further within the flat. It was just a rustle of movement or perhaps a footstep. 'Sophie, is that you?' He listened but there was no response and as he advanced slowly along the corridor his heart was pounding. After Sophie's strange call asking for help he was sure something had happened to her. He felt along the wall and found a light switch. The phone was lying on the floor beside a table, and as he bent to pick it up he noticed a rusty smudge on the wallpaper. When he touched it he found it was damp and the tip of his finger was stained red with blood.

There was more blood against the wall leading down the corridor and he pictured Sophie coming to the phone with one bloody hand out to support herself. Quickly he strode towards the living room door, already afraid of what he would find, but as he passed the corridor leading to the bedrooms he stopped. A light showed from one of the rooms and he thought he heard something. The living room was just in front of him and he went in and picked up a heavy silver candle holder from a table, before going back towards the bedrooms. There were more bloody marks on the walls and on the carpet too.

At the door to the main bedroom he froze at the sight before him. Sophie lay on the bed wearing a nightgown drenched with blood. More blood streaked her legs and arms and her hands were completely red, as were the covers on the bed. She was very pale and perfectly still. Her eyes were closed and her arms were crossed across her breast. Beside her, Arthur was kneeling on the floor. He turned to look at William with bloodshot eyes, his face streaked with tears. His hands were covered in Sophie's blood.

'My God,' William breathed. He stepped forward, lowering the candle holder. 'What have you done?' He reached for Sophie's wrist to check for her pulse, but as he did Arthur grabbed his arm in a vice-like grip.

'Don't touch 'er!'

His eyes blazed madly. For a moment William thought he would be attacked, but then Arthur looked back at Sophie's lifeless body and tears rolled down his face. His shoulders shook with grief.

'Arthur,' William said after a few moments, this time more gently. 'Tell me what happened? What did you do?'

But Arthur shook his head. 'I didn't do it. I loved 'er. I would never hurt 'er.'

'Are you saying you found her like this? How did you

get in?'

'She let me in. I saw 'er come back and I knew something was wrong, so I went to the door and she let me in. I found 'er in the hall.' He turned to look at William accusingly. 'It were your friend who did this.'

'What do you mean? Are you talking about Christopher? That's ridiculous, he wouldn't do something like this.'

'He put 'is bastard in 'er and then he left 'er! That's why she tried to get rid of it. He might as well have cut 'er open himself.'

William looked at Sophie's body again, at the mass of blood that soaked through her nightgown around her groin. Horrified, he realised what Arthur meant.

'You should have helped 'er,' Arthur said accusingly.

'I came as quickly as I could. As soon as she phoned.'

'You shouldn't have let him leave 'er like that, Will. Why did you do it to 'er? My poor Sophie. My lovely Sophie.'

Arthur began murmuring her name and rocking back and forth on his heels. Tears poured from his eyes as he took one of her bloody hands and raised it to his lips to kiss her.

William realised that Arthur had lost his mind. The shock of finding Sophie bleeding and dying must have snapped whatever remained of his reason. At least he had been there when she died, William thought. She would have died knowing that she was with somebody who truly loved her and William was glad for that.

'I'd better telephone the police,' he said, though he didn't think Arthur heard him. As he went back to the hall he saw that he'd managed to get blood on his hands and he went to the bathroom to wash it off. As he turned on the tap he looked at his reflection in the mirror and then at his bloody palms. Arthur had said he should have helped Sophie, as if he was partly to blame, and William wondered if it was true. He recalled what Sophie had said about making things the way they were again, and he guessed she'd been planning this when he saw her. Discovering that Christopher was leaving for France must have finally made up her mind.

After he'd washed his hands, William picked up the phone and asked the operator to put him through to the police. When he was connected, he told the officer he spoke to that there had been a death and gave the address. Afterwards he went back to Sophie's room to try to get Arthur to come away. He thought the police would want to ask him questions, and he wanted to make sure they didn't jump to the wrong conclusion as he had, but Arthur was nowhere to be seen. He went down to the street but there was no sign of him there either.

*****

Sophie was buried three days later. Though William had sent a telegram to the address in France that Christopher had given to Morton, no word had been received back, but still he thought he might turn up at the last moment. It was possible that they hadn't arrived there yet, William thought. He couldn't believe Christopher wouldn't have been in touch otherwise.

William used up the last of his money to pay for Sophie's funeral, and he did all he could to make sure everyone who knew her was informed. Her mother came, and one of her sisters, though they seemed more curious than anything else. He gathered from them that Sophie had had little to do with them for several years. There was a wreath and card from the solicitor's office where Sophie had worked, but nobody came to the service. Arthur Hawkins appeared however, though he stood apart from the other mourners. William looked over once or twice and found Arthur staring at him, his expression indecipherable.

When it was over, William looked for Arthur again. He

wanted to see if he was alright, and perhaps try to persuade him to see a doctor, but he had again slipped away and was nowhere to be found. That night William went to a hotel in the town and tried to get drunk, but the liquor didn't seem to have any effect on him except that he became ever more morose. When he finally drove back to Pitsford House it was after midnight. He saw the orange glow in the night sky long before he realised what it was. By the time he got there men were running everywhere trying to douse the flames with buckets of water, their faces lit by the flames. He did what he could to help and eventually the fire wagon arrived, but by then it was far too late. The garage behind the house had been completely destroyed along with the biplane inside.

When everyone had finally gone, William sat alone waiting for the dawn. One of the gardeners had told him he saw somebody creeping around just before the fire was noticed. William wondered if it was Arthur who'd set the barn alight. As the light crept over the fields he noticed something in an oak tree not far from the house, and when he went to see what it was he found Arthur hanging from a branch, his face swollen and black.

With a leaden heart, William climbed up and cut him down then laid his body out on the damp grass.

PART TWO

20

FRANCE APRIL 1917

A line of poplars along the banks of the river Lys marked the edge of the aerodrome where No. 28 squadron of the Royal Flying Corps was based. The officers were housed in a farmhouse and its surrounding outbuildings, while the other ranks lived in tents near the canvas hangars.

On a cold afternoon, Lieutenant William Reynolds climbed into the cockpit of an RE8 reconnaissance plane in front of Smale, his observer. A mechanic grasped the propeller and gave it a half turn to prime the carburettor.

'Contact?'

'Contact.' William flicked the switch on and the engine fired and then exploded into life in a brief cloud of smoke. In another identical two-seater to his left, piloted by Pervis, with Thorne as the observer, the same procedure was followed. William opened the throttle and his plane bumped across the grass and lifted into the air.

There was very little wind. At five thousand feet, a grey mass of cloud threatening rain covered the landscape. The bombardment on the ground signalled that the offensive at Arras would begin shortly. The sound of the guns was continuous. Geysers of mud and dirt erupted around the German positions as the artillery shelled the enemy in preparation for the attack, though most of the shells were falling beyond the intended target.

When William was in position at two thousand feet, his

observer, Smale, began to tap out instructions in Morse code, which were sent by wireless to the artillery. The artillery shortened their range, and on the ground the explosions crept closer to the German positions. At the same time the German anti-aircraft guns opened fire, and black clouds of smoke began to unfurl in the air. At first the gunners struggled to find the correct range, but gradually the explosions became closer and the plane was buffeted and rocked by turbulence.

As Smale continued to do his work, William scanned the sky all around. There were a dozen or more two-seaters working nearby. Pervis and Thorne were less than a quarter of a mile away and a lone DeHavilland scout was patrolling above, keeping a lookout for enemy machines, though his presence gave William little comfort. Apart from the DeHavilland being a hopelessly outdated design, the German scouts hardly every flew alone.

An explosion rocked the plane violently and shrapnel whizzed through the air. William took the plane down a few hundred feet and changed direction to put the gunners off. A hole had appeared in the starboard wings, and looking down he saw a group of German troops had come out of their dugouts where they'd been sheltering from the British barrage. One of them was aiming his rifle into the air to take another shot, though the plane was not their principle target. A reconnaissance party from the British lines were pinned down in no-mans land, and the Germans were setting up a pair of machine guns to catch them in a cross fire.

Turning in his seat, William gestured to Smale, who saw what was happening, and understanding William's intention he put his radio set away and swivelled the Lewis gun on its mount so that he could aim it over the side of the plane. As William brought the plane around for a run along the enemy positions, the British soldiers looked up at them. There were five or six of them left alive, huddled in a shell hole. They must have crawled across no-mans land during the night to reconnoitre the enemy positions, but somehow had become trapped before they could get back. At least half of them had been killed already. All at once the German machine gun crew opened fire from their mound, and immediately one of the British soldiers threw up his arms and fell backwards into the crater. His companions slithered down with him until only their heads were above the water while the ground around them was torn to pieces by bullets.

With the throttle wide open, William pushed the two-seater into a shallow dive, and then levelled out to make a pass in front of the German lines. Smale took aim and the Lewis gun kicked and barked. As they climbed again William looked back. Smale had killed the machine gun crew, but almost immediately others came to take their place. Almost immediately, they too were suddenly spinning and falling and looking around, William saw that Pervis had followed his lead and was also attacking. The British soldiers took their chance and began to squirm and slide on their bellies from the shell hole back towards their own lines, though their progress was painfully slow.

Once again William turned to make another pass. When he had first seen the trapped men, he'd wanted to try to help them, even though he knew the odds were long. Now he desperately wanted them to survive. He had witnessed enough of the conditions on the ground to know they must have imagined their fate was sealed. Trapped in the open, their only choices were to either cower in the freezing mud and water until the Germans directed artillery fire to tear them to shreds, or else to climb out and be killed by the machine guns. Suddenly, they had been given a chance. On either side of them, millions of men were ranged with artillery and guns. When the offensive began, tens of thousands would perish, all for the gain of a few feet of mud that would probably be lost again the following week. There was nothing that William could do to prevent the senseless carnage, but the lives of the handful of men below were somehow all the more important because of it.

A pair of German soldiers ran to the machine gun to replace their fallen comrades and Smale opened fire with the Lewis again. More German troops appeared from their dugouts, and began firing rifles from the trenches both at the British soldiers and the plane. Several bullet holes appeared in the fabric of the wings, and a sharp crack sounded as the edge of a strut was hit. A splinter of wood hit William's cheek, but his face was numb from the cold and he barely felt it. He held his course and Smale fired again. A German soldier toppled, his rifle spinning from his grasp. For an instant William saw his upturned face. He was young, his mouth opened as he cried out in pain or surprise as the bullet struck his chest and then William could no longer see him as he pulled back on the stick for height.

Pervis followed them again, and the air was full of the crack of bullets as the planes became the Germans' target. William thought it would be a miracle if they managed to get away. On the ground the British soldiers took advantage of the situation and ran at a crouch for their lines, dodging this way and that. One of them fell, but the others made it, and the last William saw of them was a hand raised in acknowledgment or thanks. He continued to climb away from the hail of fire, afraid that a bullet would hit the engine, and when he glanced back he saw Pervis still following.

Within a few minutes they were at three thousand feet again. During the climb they had drifted back over the German rear positions. The fuel gauge indicated half a tank and William deliberated whether or not to continue their observation work. As he automatically scanned the sky all around for danger, he saw four machines fly out of the clouds two thousand feet above. He recognized the shape of the German Albatross's at once and gestured frantically to Smale, who froze for a split second before he hurriedly started reloading the Lewis gun.

Pervis had seen the danger too, and though both planes

turned and dived for speed, William knew they were too late. He looked over his shoulder as the Albatross's split into pairs. There was nothing he could do but race for the lines and hope that Smale could fend them off, though a single Lewis gun against the Spandaus of an Albatross meant they were hopelessly outgunned, as well as being slower and far less agile than the German fighters. Within moments Smale opened up with the Lewis gun, which was immediately met with the heavy thump of the Spandaus. Lines of tracer cut the air on either side of the plane. William banked hard and turned to try to put the German pilots off their aim, but the RE8 was a lumbering, unresponsive machine and straight away his port wings were filled with holes. The engine took a hit and coughed a slick of oil, and then an Albatross went past on either side, each of them banking and climbing to attack again. The Lewis was silent as Smale desperately worked to change the drum.

William put the plane into the steepest possible dive he dared to in a last ditch effort to gain speed. He knew of he could reach no-mans land they had a chance. Looking over his shoulder he saw the Albatrosses turning to give chase. The RE8 was rattling and shaking as if it was going to fall to pieces. The engine leaked a steady stream of oil. Underneath them the ground rushed up to meet them and William pulled back on the stick with all his might. He thought he had left it too late even as the nose began to inch upwards. All he could hear was the roar of the exhaust and any moment he expected to feel German bullets rip them apart.

Then suddenly the machine responded to the controls and began to level out and they roared above the lines at less than fifty feet. In the trenches men cheered and William glanced behind. The Albatross's had broken off their attack. Either they were low on fuel or else unwilling to risk crossing the lines. There was something arrogant, almost disdainful about the way they chose not to finish them off. It was the same arrogance that made them paint their machines in garish colours to identify their jastas; red for Richthofen's, green or purple or some other combination for the others. It was an expression of their utter confidence in the superiority of their machines. Or perhaps, William thought, the German pilots had a more prosaic reason for turning back. Perhaps they thought they had already done their job.

The engine spluttered and emitted another slick of oil. He could feel the loss of power. It began to miss, and he wondered if he would make it to the aerodrome. Nearby, Pervis was also in trouble, his machine trailing a thin stream of smoke. He was flying erratically and it looked as if Thorne in the back was slumped across his gun.

Ten minutes later William was descending towards the poplars alongside the river. The engine note rose and fell, and it was difficult to keep the speed up, but as the grass rushed up to meet the wheels, William kept the throttle open and found another surge of power in the nick of time. As soon as the plane came to a stop, he and Smale jumped out to watch Pervis come in to land. A few of the riggers and mechanics came out of the hangars, and William shouted at them to fetch water. There was now thick smoke pouring from the front of Pervis's machine.

'He's going too fast,' Smale muttered.

The plane was weaving drunkenly, and losing height but not speed. Everybody stood in silence, powerless to do anything but watch and hope. When it landed, the plane bounced twenty feet, and then almost in slow motion tipped on one side. When it came down the starboard wings were sheared off in a mass of splintered wood and trailing wire, and the engine was pushed back into the fuel tank which immediately ruptured. Within moments a sheet of flames engulfed both cockpits.

The men who rushed to help with buckets of sand and water were driven back by the heat. In the back seat, Thorne remained still and William thought that he must already be dead, but in the front Pervis managed to climb onto his seat, where he paused for an instant as if to jump. His clothes were on fire. Flames danced greedily about his head. The air was thick with the smell of petrol and roasting flesh. He began to scream, his arms beating at the flames, but the fire was feeding on the fats in his body. He threw back his head, and amidst the yellow and orange was a dark ragged hole from which came a final anguished cry before his vocal chords melted, and Pervis slowly collapsed with his arms outstretched.

It took several minutes for the flames to begin to die down. The grotesque remains of Pervis and Thorne fell free as what held them was reduced to charred ash. A streak of white revealed bone laid bare.

*****

By the time William left the hangar and made his way across the field, the rain had stopped, though it was cold. He thought of the poor devils in the trenches living in their muddy burrows. It must be especially miserable in the winter, forever cold and never entirely dry, and often under fire from shells or snipers. By comparison, his own existence was comfortable. The aerodrome was well behind the lines, out of reach of the enemy guns. Occasionally they had to put up with a German plane sneaking over to try and drop bombs on them, but the anti-aircraft gunners usually saw them off.

Light from the windows of the farmhouse beckoned with a warm glow. He could hear a gramophone record playing, a ragtime tune played on the piano. Somebody laughed, an unnatural sound, and it was followed by a chorus of voices. His fellow officers were playing some sort of drinking game, drowning their morbid thoughts in whisky and wine. He continued on to the barn, which had been roughly partitioned so that each officer had his own private area big enough for a bed and somewhere to keep clothes and personal effects. After he'd washed and changed he joined the others in the room that served as the officer's mess. The table was laid for dinner.

Major Thompson, the squadron CO, threw William a curt glance and looked pointedly at his watch. 'There you are, Reynolds. I was about to send somebody to find you.'

'I'm sorry I'm late, sir,' William murmured.

'Dinner is served at eight I clock. I expect my officers to be in the mess promptly by half past seven.'

A mess steward approached and William asked for a whisky.

'These things matter,' Thompson continued. 'The moment you allow standards to slip, discipline breaks down, and without proper discipline the army cannot function. Where have you been anyway?'

'I was over at the hangars. My machine was shot up today.'

'You could have let the men sort that out. That's what they're for.'

'I prefer to look after my own machine, sir.'

'Yes, well I'm not at all sure I approve of that. You're an officer, Reynolds, not a damned mechanic.'

The arrival of the steward with William's whisky saved him from having to reply. As the officers took their places at the long table, Captain Wright took the opportunity to speak quietly to William.

'I hope you're not intending to antagonise him this evening, Reynolds.' Wright was very tall and thin, and had extraordinarily long fingers. His hands were almost feminine. He was known to be a very good classical pianist. 'Try to keep in mind that we've lost two good men today.'

'Perhaps you ought to remind Thompson of that,' William replied acidly. 'He seems to be more concerned about me being late for dinner.'

Wright stiffened. 'You shouldn't speak about him like that. He's your commanding officer.'

'He's a fool.'

Wright glared at him and turned away. At dinner they sat opposite one another and to either side of Thompson at the head of the table. As the officers took their places, the two chairs which only the evening before had been occupied by Pervis and Thorne, were conspicuously empty. Thompson waited for the men's attention and the talk and laughter, fuelled by several hours drinking, died away to an uneasy quiet.

'Gentlemen, as you are all aware the squadron has suffered the loss of two very brave men today. Of course it is always difficult to accept that men we have all lived and fought with are no longer with us, however we must remember that it is the willing sacrifice made by chaps like Pervis and Thorne that will inevitably ensure our victory against the Hun.'

Thompson raised his glass and the officers all stood. 'Gentlemen, I give you Lieutenants Pervis and Thorne. May God rest their souls.'

The officers solemnly echoed the names of the dead men, and as they took their places again the stewards brought out the first course.

Thompson unfolded his napkin. 'Ah, here's the soup. Jolly good. What is it Dawkins?' He lowered his nose to appreciate the aroma coming from his plate.

'Cream of chicken, sir.'

He frowned and examined the label on the wine. 'I'm not sure a Cote de Rhone is appropriate with chicken soup. See if there's a Bergundy or something will you?'

'Yes, sir.'

William looked at the faces of the men around the table. He didn't know any of them well. Many had only been at the squadron a short time, having arrived as replacements for men who'd been lost over the winter. Pervis and Thorne, like himself and Wright, had been old timers. Not that he could claim to have known them well either, or Wright for that matter. The squadron had flown BE2's before the new RE8's arrived, which had proved so disappointing. They had all hoped for a machine capable of taking on the Albatross, but the cumbersome RE8 proved that the brass's thinking was still a long way behind the Germans'. Now two more men were dead.

'What is it, Reynolds? Don't you like chicken soup?'

Thompson's question jolted William from his reverie. 'For some reason I haven't much appetite this evening,' he said. 'I can still smell roasting flesh, though I suppose I ought to be used to it by now.'

Thompson and the other officers who were close enough to overhear, stopped eating and stared in shocked silence.

'Good God man!' Thompson said in disgust. 'Is that some sort of depraved attempt at humour?'

'I can assure you, sir, I don't find anything amusing about watching men burn to death. Especially when it is unnecessary.'

'Death is an unfortunate but inevitable fact of war,' Thompson said with patronising banality.

William caught the warning look that Wright flashed him, but he ignored it. 'It is when the brass who sit safely behind their desks refuse to acknowledge what even a fool can see.'

'If that comment is directed towards me personally, Reynolds, you would do well to remember your place,' Thompson warned icily.

'I'm referring to the idiots at HQ who insist on sending us out in outdated machines,' William said, though he thought Thompson was no better than they were. 'They give us planes designed for reconnaissance when the Germans are equipping entire squadrons with fighters whose only purpose is to shoot us from the air.'

'Lieutenant Reynolds!' Thompson banged the table with his fist, his face almost purple with rage. For a few moments the room was utterly silent, and then Thompson turned to the stewards lingering uncertainly near the door. 'Get out!' he barked. When they were gone he turned to William again. 'You will not criticise the decisions made by senior officers, do you hear me? It is your duty and your place to follow your orders, and that is what you will do, or by God I will have you on a charge. You are an officer, man! How the hell do you expect to maintain discipline among the men if they hear an officer speaking as you did?' He glared furiously. 'Is that understood?'

Across the table, Wright flashed William another look that was both disapproving, and a silent plea to back down and William knew that it was futile to argue.

'Yes, sir,' he said. 'It's understood.'

'Very well.' Thompson picked up his spoon again to resume eating his soup, but then put it down and pushed his plate away. 'Somebody tell the stewards to take this bloody soup away,' he said.

A new subaltern called Stringer got up and went to the door, and a few moments later the stewards returned to clear their plates.

'Since you're so concerned about the damned Albatross jastas, Reynolds,' Thompson said. 'I expect you'll be pleased to hear that I want you and Wright to go to St Omer in the morning. You can pick up a pair of scouts we've been given to act as escorts for our patrols.'

'I say, that's good news, sir,' Wright said. 'May I ask what type they are?'

'Nieuports I believe.' Thompson smiled thinly towards William. 'You see, Reynolds, it appears that HQ concur with you on this occasion. I'm sure everybody will be greatly relieved to know that in future they'll have you to protect them from the Germans.'

He looked around at the other men, who all obediently smiled at his gossamer veiled sarcasm.

When dinner was over, William left the mess and went

outside. Somebody put on the gramophone again and the hum of voices resumed. As he lit a cigarette the door opened behind him and Wright came out.

'That was bloody stupid of you,' Wright said. 'It doesn't accomplish anything you know.'

'You know that what I said is true. Even Thompson knows it.'

'That isn't the point.'

'No of course,' William murmured. 'One mustn't rock the boat must one.'

Wright looked at him with a puzzled air. 'Do you know, I really don't understand you, Reynolds. You behave as if you detest us all.' William didn't answer and Wright took his silence as encouragement. 'You can't live your life completely alone, you know. None of us can. Especially here.'

The sound of drinking and singing came from the mess. It was the same in all the squadrons; the pilots drank to forget that the fates of men like Pervis, could easily be their own. Most had a terror of burning. William wondered if it was better to be like the others and drown his fears in whisky? He threw his cigarette into the darkness where it landed in a shower of sparks.

'I think I'll turn in. I'll see you in the morning.'

'Goodnight,' Wright said stiffly, offended at the rebuff.

Alone on his bed William tried to read, but even Homer couldn't hold his attention. He could still hear the faint sound of music from the mess. The table would be littered with empty bottles. By the time some of the officers finally get to bed they would have had no more than a few hours sleep before they had to get up for the early patrol.

Much later, as he lay awake in the dark, he heard somebody moan in his sleep. They were all afraid, though none of them would admit it. They drank so that they could sleep, and in the morning put a brave face on it, their reactions blurred by hangovers. Wright was wrong. In the end, William thought, every man was alone.

*****

When they arrived at St Omer in the morning a clerk told them that the Nieuports they'd been sent to collect wouldn't be ready until the afternoon, and faced with the prospect of spending half the day together Wright decided to drive to a nearby squadron to see somebody he knew.

'You're welcome to come with me if you like,' he offered, but William declined, which he thought Wright was pleased about anyway.

He spent the time instead in the hangars, where there were several French Spads waiting to go out to Squadrons in the north. Some of the men were talking about a new squadron that had been formed and equipped with a new fighter called the SE5. There was talk that this squadron would form the vanguard of many more that would break the dominance of the German jastas. It was even said they'd been given the task of killing the German ace, Richthofen, as a way of proving their capability and lifting morale. Perhaps the brass really had finally realised the futility of clinging to the old notion of planes designed purely for reconnaissance, William mused.

In the afternoon he met up with Wright again, who hadn't been able to see his friend as he was flying a patrol. They went to the clerk's office and were told there had been a delay and now their Nieuports wouldn't be ready until the morning. Wright telephoned the squadron to let them know what was going on and the adjutant told him they may as well stay the night.

The clerk gave them the name of a hotel where they could probably get rooms, and that evening they ate dinner together in the hotel's restaurant, which was full of army officers on leave from the front.

'I'm due for a spot of leave myself,' Wright

commented as he looked around. 'It would be nice to go home for a few days, but I don't suppose that's very likely at the moment.'

'No, I suppose it isn't,' William agreed.

'I'm from Norwich, you know,' he added and took a picture from his wallet which he showed to William. 'That's my wife, Marjorie. We weren't planning on getting married yet, but last time I was home we decided we ought to. Well, Marjorie did, actually. I wasn't sure it was fair on her really, but she insisted we had to think positively about the future. She's a wonderful girl.'

The picture showed a rather plain looking young woman with a round face wearing a shy smile, but William found he could imagine her and Wright together. He made some polite comment and gave it back.

'Are you married, Reynolds?'

'No.' A memory insinuated itself, an image of Elizabeth. For a long time he hadn't been able to get her out of his thoughts. He'd been plagued with feelings that alternated between a sort of profound loss, and anger that arose from what had happened to Sophie. Then for perhaps a year he had barely thought of her at all, and he'd begun to think he'd put all that behind him. Now he remembered her at odd moments, sparked by a question or something that he associated with that time in his life. He was surprised at the intensity of his feelings after all this time.

After dinner, William felt like going for a walk. The night sky was lit with the flashes of the barrage at the front. He thought it couldn't be long now before the offensive began, and he remembered the soldiers he'd helped get back to their own trenches the day before. Saving them had probably cost Pervis and Thorne their lives. He wondered if that made their deaths worthwhile, especially when the soldiers would probably be killed in the offensive, but he knew there was no point in trying to balance the scales like that. None of it made any sense.

As he walked through the streets a young woman approached him and asked in faltering English if he wanted to go with her to her room. He was about to refuse, but then he changed his mind. She was attractive, with long fair hair and her eyes were green.

'Is it far?' he asked.

'Non, it is only a small distance, monsieur.'

She gestured along a narrow street. He wondered why she wasn't working in one of the regular places if she was a prostitute, but looking at her more closely he decided this was something new to her. She was older than him, perhaps thirty. Her expression was set in determined lines, and she didn't look at him until they reached her door. For a moment he had the impression that she would change her mind, but then she opened the door and led him inside.

A dark, narrow staircase led to her room. He paid her, and as she undressed with her back to him he unbuttoned his tunic and shirt. The room looked very ordinary, and was devoid of personal effects like photographs. He imagined she preferred it that way. He noticed a mark on her finger where she must have worn a ring.

'Are you married?' he asked her.

She looked over her bare shoulder, surprised by his question. 'My husband is killed,' she said.

She continued undressing, but William suddenly wondered what he was doing there. 'Do you mind if we don't? You can keep the money.' She looked over her shoulder, and seemed puzzled. He supposed it was strange to ask if she minded. Why would she mind so long as he was paying her? He gestured to a chair by the window. 'Can we just sit?'

'Sit?'

'Yes.'

'Alright. If it is what you wish.'

'I do.' He sat down, and she came to sit in his lap thinking it was what he wanted, but he didn't and he asked her to sit on the bed. She did as he asked, her hands folded on her lap, still wearing her slip. She seemed confused, as if she was waiting for him to tell her what to do.

'I just want to be quiet like this,' he said and they sat in the darkness. He watched her, and at first she was uncomfortable under his gaze, but after a little while she relaxed.

'Do you have a sweetheart?' she asked him.

'No,' he said. He reached over and touched her hair. He started to tell her that she reminded him of somebody, but changed his mind. After that they didn't speak, but let the quiet of the room envelop them. After an hour had passed he gave her some more money and left.

In the morning, William and Wright returned to the aerodrome to find their Nieuports waiting. William was disappointed to see that they were old models, with a single Lewis gun fixed on the top wing and eighty horsepower engines. They were no match for an Albatross, and they had only two of them to protect an entire squadron.

21

The rain drummed on the canvas roof of no. 2 hangar, so loud that it drowned out the constant thunder of the guns at the front. In the dim glow cast by a hurricane lamp a group of men were sitting around a stove playing cards, glad that they were not in the trenches. One of them made a brew.

'D'you call this tea, Smithy?' a rigger protested when he took a sip from his mug. 'Tastes like you boiled your socks in it.'

'Gives it flavour,' was the laconic response.

The others laughed. Sergeant Bell lost a shilling with two pairs and decided he wasn't feeling lucky. 'Count me out, lads,' he said.

He leaned back against a packing crate that contained a new engine for one of the two-seaters and rolled a cigarette. He thought this wasn't so bad really. He liked being with the other men, listening to them laugh while he smoked and drank his tea in the warm. He missed his wife at night though. You got used to lying in bed with someone warm beside you. It wasn't the other so much. Not like the younger men. You didn't worry about that sort of thing when you got to his age.

'What do you think then?' said Smithy.

Bell looked at him blankly. 'About what?'

'Should I take 'im a brew?'

Smithy nodded towards the front of the hangar where Lieutenant Reynolds was working on one of the new Nieuports. He was a funny one, was Reynolds, thought Bell.

Wouldn't let anyone work on any plane he flew. Did everything himself. Kept to himself too. Didn't have much to do with the other officers from what you could see. Shields reckoned they talked about him in the mess when he wasn't there. Said he was a cold fish and thought he was better than everyone else. Well, Shields must know, being a mess steward. It were true that Reynolds were cold, Bell supposed, but he didn't think Reynolds was stuck-up. Lieutenant Pervis, the poor bastard, he were more that sort. Treated the men like his bleedin' servants. Still, it were wrong to think badly of the dead. 'Specially when they went the way Pervis did. What was he? Twenty? Twenty one? Fucking hell. They were kids, most of 'em. Just kids.

'Fuck 'im. Let 'im get his own brew,' another man said.

Bell shook his head and wearily got to his feet. Some of the men didn't like it that Reynolds did his own work. They took it as an insult. 'Give us another mug,' he said to Smithy. 'I'll see if he wants it.'

*****

William was standing on the pilot's seat taking, off the Lewis gun fixed above the upper wing, when Bell approached.

'Thought you might like a cuppa, sir.'

William was surprised. Some of the men by the stove were watching to see what he would do, and the refusal that sprang to his lips died. 'Thank you, Sergeant.' He took the gun off its mounting. 'Take this would you, and I'll come down.'

The tea was hot and sweet with an odd aftertaste. William took out his cigarettes and offered one to Bell.

'Thanks very much, sir.'

The Nieuport had a Rhone engine, a nine cylinder eighty horsepower rotary. It was very small compared to the two-seaters, ten feet shorter, and the span slightly more than that. The top wing was much wider than the bottom, which added to the impression of its small size, but also gave it a raked back, fast appearance.

'What do you think of it, sir?' Bell asked.

'It's built for speed,' William said. 'And manoeuvrability so that it can turn and climb quickly in a fight. It's just a pity we've only been given two of them.'

'Who will fly that one, sir?' Bell wondered, indicating the other Nieuport.

'Captain Wright I expect.' William finished his tea and, thanking Bell again, gave him back the mug. 'I'd better get on. I want to strip the Lewis gun. That drum is going to be difficult to change mounted on the top like that. I want to make sure it won't jam.'

He looked up at the mount thoughtfully. The latest Nieuports had a bigger engine fitted with the new interrupter gear that allowed a Vickers to be mounted on the cowling in front of the pilot and fired through the propeller arc. Still, a Lewis gun was better than no gun at all.

'Are you flying in the morning, sir?' Bell asked.

'Yes, there's a long patrol to St Quentin to photograph the rail yards. The Nieuports are going as escorts.'

'Haven't the Huns got an aerodrome near there?'

'At Douai, yes.'

As William began to strip the Lewis, Bell looked at the other Nieuport, then he went back to the men playing cards.

'Right, you lot, I want the Lewis on that other Nieuport stripped and checked. And then run the engine up too. Check every bloody thing.'

*****

Before dawn the planes were pushed out of the hangers onto the grass. The aerodrome was white with a heavy frost. By the time Wright arrived, William had finished his final check and he watched Wright walk around his own machine checking the wires.

As the two-seater crews began to arrive, pulling on their helmets and goggles, William went to speak to Wright.

'When we get up I think we ought to stay above the two-seaters. That way we can keep a lookout for enemy scouts.'

'The CO wants us to stay with the group.'

'Thompson hasn't flown anything other than a desk for two years,' William reasoned. 'If we meet up with Albatrosses they're going to be up high. I doubt that the Nieuports can match them, but at least we'll have a chance to intercept them if the others are attacked.'

Wright hesitated, his face pale. He had the hollow eyed look they all developed after a while.

'They'll know we're coming,' William said, gesturing to the clear sky. 'When we cross the lines the Germans will telephone Douai to let them know. If the Albatrosses are there they'll come after us.'

Wright nodded. 'Alright.'

A few minutes later, the Nieuports' engines were started, and while they warmed up the two-seaters took off in pairs. When the other planes were safely away, the Nieuports followed. They gained height quickly and were soon above the two seaters and heading for the lines.

The journey to St Quentin was uneventful. The ruined swathe of land that marked the trenches of the opposing armies, and no-mans land between them, fell behind and the countryside was again green and strangely unblemished. Puffs of smoke from anti-aircraft fire dogged the two-seaters for part of the way, but at ten thousand feet they were untroubled. There were six of them flying in formation, with William and Wright five thousand feet above them. Though William constantly scanned the skies in every direction, there was very little cloud and nowhere for enemy scouts to hide, so he knew that he would see them in plenty of time. At the same time he was acutely aware that their progress couldn't fail to be seen from the ground, and somewhere to the north he imagined a telephone ringing at a German aerodrome. He could only hope that the jastas were busy elsewhere that day.

He thought briefly of the year before the war, when he had flown over the valleys and woods of Northamptonshire. It seemed like a lifetime ago, almost as if it had happened to somebody else. He saw himself as a boy at Oundle, learning his Latin grammar while shafts of sunlight poured through the tall windows and chalk dust swirled in the air. How many of the boys who had sat in that room were dead now, he wondered?

When the patrol reached their target, the two seaters went down to photograph the railyards. William felt for them as he and Wright circled like hawks far above. The sky was pockmarked with dissolving smoke from the torrent of anti-aircraft shells thrown at them. The Germans were used to British patrols pushing into their territory and places like St Quentin were well defended. The two-seaters ranged back and forth in a slow, steady pattern as they did their work. It was an agony to watch. William kept an eye out for the enemy and willed the patrol to hurry up. With every second that passed he felt a premonition of disaster.

Finally the patrol finished their work and turned away for home. One of the planes lagged behind, and though his engine was trailing a bit of oily smoke he appeared to be alright. William decided that if the plane fell any further behind he would go back and keep watch over him. He began to think that they might be lucky. Another ten minutes would see them over their own lines.

He saw the scouts a few minutes later. They came from the north east at about seventeen thousand feet. He counted ten of them flying in an elongated V, and he saw the flash of red paint on their wings. They had already spotted the two-seaters and were picking up speed as they dived to intercept them, though it appeared they were unaware of the

Nieuports. Wright spotted them too, and together he and William changed their course.

At first the patrol flew on, oblivious to the danger that was rapidly closing on them. It was the straggler who saw the Albatrosses first and immediately put his nose down and dived for speed. At the same time two of the German planes broke off from the others and straight away it was clear they would catch him. There was nothing William or Wright could do for him.

The growl of the engines became a high pitched roar. The freezing wind tore at William's face, numbing his skin and singing in the wires like a banshee. He reached up to cock his gun. At the last moment the two-seaters saw the danger and began to dive and break formation. Further back, the straggler was attacked, and immediately smoke poured from the front and it went into a spin and plummeted earthwards.

Still the Nieuports hadn't been seen, and William dared to hope that with the advantage of surprise they might somehow pull off a miracle and drive the enemy planes off. Then the German leader opened fire. Tracer spat towards one the two-seaters and William saw the observer collapse. A second later the plane turned over onto its back, and with its nose pointed down, began to spin. Another German plane delivered the coup de grace and the hapless two-seater burst into flames. At the same time William fired off a burst from the Lewis gun. He heard Wright's gun too, and then the Germans realised they were being attacked and broke formation, zooming up as they searched for the threat.

After that there was only confusion. William banked hard and dived, turning as tightly as he could to try and get his gun onto one of the enemy. They seemed to be everywhere at once, and no matter where he looked there was an Albatross angling to get behind him. He twisted in his seat trying to keep track of them. He glimpsed Wright diving to avoid an Albatross that had latched onto his tail.

The heavy thud of Spandaus drowned out the bark of the Lewis guns. Engines screamed and smoke trailed from damaged machines. Lines of tracer stitched the sky. A two-seater went down and broke up two thousand feet over the earth.

Suddenly an Albatross flashed in front of him and William let off a burst from the Lewis. Almost immediately he threw his machine in the other direction and zoomed up, reaching to change the empty drum. Tracer zipped past his wings, bullets whizzing through the air. He felt his machine take repeated hits, and then a horrible metallic clunk came from the engine and it coughed black smoke. He banked and dived, and far below, the ruined scar of no-man's land rushed to meet him. He was losing power. The Spandaus barked again. Smoke poured from his engine. He twisted all the way down, smoke filling his cockpit, choking him. Looking back he saw an Albatross on his tail and applied hard rudder as the Spandaus opened up again. He felt his plane shake and vibrate as the bullets struck home. Below, he could see trees and fields and the contours of the land. His engine stuttered and something screamed, a grinding metallic protest as oil leaked back covering his goggles, making everything suddenly black. For an instant he was blind and gripped with panic. Frantically he wiped them clean, leaving an oily smear. The ground was close now, too close. He saw trees and pulled back hard on the stick, but he knew he was too late. He felt heat from the fire and thought briefly of Pervis. Fear took hold of him and he scrabbled for his revolver. He didn't want to burn. Then a blur of green obscured everything. He heard guns and the splintering of wood and canvas, the roar of the Albatross overhead. Fleetingly, William wondered if he would feel the impact.

22

Elizabeth paused before she entered the officer's ward. The hospital at Amiens was where the seriously wounded were eventually brought. Many of those who survived were eventually returned to England to convalesce, but Doctor Ramsay had already warned her that it was unlikely that the burned pilot would live.

She went inside. It was late, and most of the injured were asleep, though she felt some of them watching her as she passed between the rows of beds.

'Miss?'

The man who called out to her was propped up into a half-sitting position. His torso was heavily bandaged though his face was unmarked. In the dim light she could see he was very young. Not even twenty.

'Yes, is there something that you want?'

'I thought I was dreaming,' he said.

She took his hand, wondering who he'd thought she was. His mother? A sister? Or perhaps his sweetheart? 'What's your name?'

'Perkins. John Perkins.'

'Well, you'll soon be home John Perkins. Where do you come from?'

'Somerset.'

'That must be lovely.'

'My family has an orchard. We grow apples and pears.'

'You must get strong again then or you won't be able

to help with the picking. If you try to get to sleep I'll sit here with you for a little while.'

'Will you keep holding my hand?'

'If you like.'

He closed his eyes and his breathing became regular. It was all they wanted from her. The soft touch of a woman's hand, the sound of her voice. After a little while she got up, relinquishing the hand of the now sleeping soldier and continued along the ward.

The figure in the bed was sleeping. His body twitched in rhythm with morphine induced dreams. Elizabeth's heart was thudding. She was terrified. His face was covered with bandages except for holes for his mouth and nostrils. Not even his eyes were visible. This came as a shock to her. She had thought she would know him by his eyes, but she realised his eyes were gone, cut to pieces by his shattered goggles.

She did not try to stop her tears. She cried because of his terrible injuries, but also because she could not tell if he was William.

*****

In Cannes, three and a half years earlier, she'd found Christopher standing by the window looking out over the sea.

'Hello.'

He didn't reply, and she sensed that something was wrong. When she went to him he looked at her with deadened eyes.

'Sophie's dead.'

At first she couldn't believe it, but she knew he wouldn't say something like that unless it was true. A hundred questions jostled in her mind, but for some reason the most prosaic of all was the one she asked first. 'How do you know?'

He showed her a telegram. 'It's from William. Sophie tried to get rid of the child.'

'Oh God, no.' She put her hand on his arm, meaning to comfort him, but the way he looked at her made her take it away again. There was no life in his eyes. No light.

'I think I'd like to go for a walk,' he said.

'Would you like me to come?'

'I think I'd rather be alone.' At the door he turned back to her. 'There's a train this evening, by the way. I've booked our tickets.'

She knew then that it was over between them, though she'd known it during their first night on the ferry, when, after they'd made love, they lay together trying to pretend that everything was alright.

By the time they arrived home, William had gone. Nobody knew where to. The scorched remains of the aeroplane he and Christopher had built remained amid the burnt out wreckage of the barn. When Elizabeth saw what had happened she understood in a rush of insight how devastated he must have been. She felt as if everything was rushing from inside her, and she didn't know how she could have treated him so terribly.

A few days after their return, Christopher sent a note to say he was leaving. He didn't say where he was going. He said everything reminded him of Sophie and what he'd done. Including her, Elizabeth thought. He wanted her to know that he didn't blame her for any of it, but she knew he did whether he admitted it or not. She didn't pretend to herself that she wasn't at least partly responsible. But she hadn't known what would happen.

The following year Germany invaded Belgium and marched for Paris. England declared war, and in October Elizabeth took a train to Waterloo. She found a taxi and gave the driver an address in St. Johns Wood. The house was one of a Georgian terrace. It had a walled garden that opened into the park. A maid answered the door and showed her into an elegantly furnished sitting room.

The woman she had come to see was an old friend of her mother's, and though Elizabeth had met her several years before, she could only vaguely remember her. She went to one of the windows at the end of the room and looked out over the elms that flanked the quiet street outside. A woman wearing a nurse's uniform walked past pushing a baby carriage, and Elizabeth thought of Sophie, and was overwhelmed by sorrow and regret.

'The trees look very bare at this time of year, don't you think?'

The voice startled her, and Elizabeth turned around to find Catherine Beauchamp had come into the room. She was tall, her once fair hair now partially grey.

'I'm sorry I wasn't here when you arrived. I've been at the hospital.' She kissed Elizabeth's cheek. 'I haven't seen you since you were very young, you know. You have your mother's eyes. Shall we sit down? I've asked for some tea.'

They sat on either side of a fireplace. 'I hope there's nothing wrong?' Elizabeth said.

'Wrong? Oh you mean because of the hospital. No, not at all. I'm learning to be a sort of nurse actually.' Catherine looked away, her eyes shadowed. 'Their injuries are so terrible,' she murmured.

While they had their tea Catherine asked about Elizabeth's mother. She recounted anecdotes from their younger days. Eventually Catherine turned to the reason for Elizabeth's visit. 'Now, you must tell me how I can help you. In your letter you said you wanted to find somebody.'

'His name is William Reynolds,' Elizabeth said. 'I think he may have volunteered to fight in the war. I was hoping that your husband might be able to find out where he is.'

'It's possible. He has contacts within the war ministry through his work in the House. Of course the more information you can give him, the easier it will be for

Anthony to make enquiries.'

'What sort of information would he need?'

'I imagine anything at all would be helpful. Of course, if you know his regiment that would make things a lot easier, though I suppose if you knew that you wouldn't need Anthony's help.'

'Before the war he was an aviator. I expect he would have wanted to do something in that area if he could.'

'That would narrow things down considerably, I should imagine,' Catherine said.

Catherine didn't ask who William was, or why Elizabeth wanted to find him, and Elizabeth knew that if she preferred not to say anything further, she wouldn't be pressed. But she felt she must say something. Or perhaps she simply needed somebody to confide in. 'You must think this is a strange request,' she said.

'Why would I think that?'

'You must be wondering why William can't tell me himself where he is, unless he doesn't want me to know.'

'And does he?'

'I think if he knew I was looking for him, he wouldn't want me to find him.'

'In that case, are you sure that you are doing the right thing?'

'No,' Elizabeth admitted. 'I'm not sure at all. I haven't seen William for more than a year. I behaved very badly towards him.' She paused, struggling to articulate her motivation. 'I want to tell him that I'm sorry. If I don't find him now, I'm afraid that he might be killed and I will never have another chance.'

'It must be very important for you to go to so much trouble.'

'It is. But I worry that it's very selfish of me.'

'You must care for this young man a great deal.'

'I do. I didn't realise how much until it was too late.'

'Is that what you want to tell him?'

'Yes.'

'Then I think you're right to try and find him.'

A week later, Anthony Beauchamp came home one evening with news that he thought he'd discovered where William was. 'There's a training camp for pilots at a place called Shoreham on Sea. It's on the south coast very near to Brighton. A man by the name of William Reynolds was posted there recently, attached to the Royal Flying Corps.'

For a few moments Elizabeth did not know what to say. They were in the drawing room where Catherine and her husband always had a drink before dinner. He was older than her, in his fifties, with almost white hair and a pleasant, kind face. His position in the government gave him access to a great many people of importance and to the entire networks of clerks and administrative offices beneath them. Though Elizabeth knew all of this she could hardly believe her search had ended so easily. Before the war she had tried everything she could think of to find William, but all to no avail. She was sure he'd left Northampton, but other than that she had no clues as to where he might have gone. He might even have left the country for all she knew. She'd reached the point where she believed she would never see him again and then when war was declared, ironically it had given her new hope.

'Do you know anything more about him?' she asked.

'He's a subaltern and he's twenty three years old,' Anthony Beauchamp said. 'I'm quite sure he must be the young man you're looking for, my dear. In fact I've taken the liberty of booking you a ticket on the twelve o' clock train to Brighton tomorrow.'

She knew he must be right. There could not be another person with the same name and of an identical age who had joined the Flying Corps. She ought to have been happy. She had achieved what she'd come to London for, and far more quickly than she had imagined possible. But instead she was anxious. Over dinner she couldn't concentrate on the conversation or manage to do more than pick at her food.

Afterwards, Anthony Beauchamp had to go out again. The impact of the war kept him very busy. Elizabeth and Catherine sat in the drawing room together.

'You seem worried, Elizabeth,' Catherine said.

'I suppose now that I know where he is, I'm afraid he won't want to see me,' Elizabeth admitted.

In the morning she packed her things, and Catherine went with her to the station.

'If you want to come back to London you are welcome to stay with us again,' Catherine said.

'Thank you.'

'I hope everything works out alright for you, Elizabeth.'

Catherine kissed her cheek and saw her onto the platform, and waved when she climbed aboard the train. The journey to Brighton didn't take long, and once there Elizabeth changed to a branch line that went to Shoreham. During the trip she thought about how she would contact William. She supposed that she couldn't simply walk up to the camp where he was stationed and ask to see him. Even if she did she was not at all sure that he would agree. In the end she decided to write him a letter asking him to meet her.

Shoreham on Sea was very small, and at that time of year the summer visitors had long since left. Elizabeth found a small private hotel on the seafront where she took a room, telling the woman who ran it that she was not sure how long she would be staying. Straight away she wrote to William. Her letter was not very long. She told him that she had come because there were things that she must tell him, and though she understood that he must feel angry with her and perhaps didn't want to see her, she begged him to. When she was finished she put down her pen and read what she'd written. She thought it was confused and made little sense. Finally she took up her pen and wrote another line.

I know that you can't believe that I was telling the truth when I told you that I was in love with you, William. Perhaps I didn't know myself how very true it was. If this means anything to you, please come and listen to what I have to tell you.

There was nothing more she could do. She gave the name of her hotel and said she would wait for three days, and if she had heard nothing from him, she would take it that he did not want to see her. As soon as she sealed her letter, Elizabeth went to find the woman who ran the hotel and asked her to arrange for it to be delivered to the camp.

That evening she put on her coat and walked along the seafront. A cold breeze came off the grey water. She sat on a seat and looked out across the sea. The sky was heavy, the deepening clouds almost black. She heard the faint rumble of distant thunder. It was only when it continued that she understood that it was too regular to be thunder and realised what it was. She had read in the newspapers that the sound of the guns in France could be heard from the coast.

That night she ate alone. She was the only person in the dining room, the only guest, in fact, in the hotel. She kept hoping that William would come, and every time the waitress opened the door she looked up quickly, only to be disappointed. She stayed late, lingering over coffee until it was clear he wouldn't come that night. She thought it might not be easy to leave the camp, though she was sure he could send a message. A hundred reasons occurred to her to justify why he might not be able to come straight away, and a hundred more why he could if he wanted to.

When she went to her room she slept badly. It was agony to think that he was so close, and yet she couldn't go to him. She kept thinking of him reading her letter, imagining him touching the paper she had touched, reading the words she had written.

*****

275

Elizabeth had fallen asleep again beside the pilot's bed. When she opened her eyes she was disoriented. She had been dreaming about the summer when she met William. The sound of music faded in her mind. She recalled fractured images of Christopher dancing with Sophie, and of herself and William. She had felt such conflicting and often confusing emotions. She was jealous of Sophie to begin with. She wanted Christopher to dance with her, to hold her the way he held Sophie, and yet she liked the feeling of William's arms around her, his quiet, serious gaze.

It was still dark. She could smell the pungent aroma of the injured, of wounds that needed draining and an underlying chemical taint of ether. In the darkness she heard men breathing, muttering, scratching in their sleep. She sat up in her chair beside the pilot's bed. His stillness seemed unnatural. She looked at his chest, but couldn't see any movement, and her breath caught in her throat. She thought that this is what had woken her. While she slept he had died. His body had given up, and whatever spirit lived in that prison of flesh and bone had gone.

But then he stirred, and she realised he was not dead after all. Only sleeping. His bandaged limbs twitched convulsively. She wondered what he dreamt of. Was it the summer they spent together? Could they have dreamt of the same time and place, and did that mean they'd been together in some otherworldly landscape where time stood still? And if so, could she change what had happened?

Or did he dream of the rush of cold air, the sound of guns and the flames that wrapped around his head and body like the greedy, devouring jaws of some bright, fierce animal?

His twitching became more agitated. She began to speak in a low, soothing voice. She spoke his name and told him she was there. Gradually he became calmer and the convulsive movements ceased, and he breathed more easily again.

When she got up, stretching her stiffened limbs, Elizabeth realised that she wasn't alone. A figure stood watching her from the door. It was Doctor Ramsay. Together they went outside where he offered her a cigarette.

'Do you sit with him every night?' he asked.

'If I can, yes.'

When he drew on his cigarette his features were thrown into sharp relief. 'Sometimes I envy him.'

She wasn't sure that she heard him correctly. How could anybody envy a man so terribly injured? But then he looked at her frankly, and she understood what he meant. He was married with three young children. She didn't condemn what she saw in his face though, because it was yearning rather than lust. A yearning for love. They all felt it, surrounded as they were by misery and death.

'Sorry,' he said. 'I shouldn't have said that.'

'It's alright.'

They smoked in silence.

'It's been decided he should be moved back to England,' he said.

She was alarmed. 'Surely he won't survive the journey.'

'The truth is, he's already lived longer than anyone thought possible. If he has a long term chance, it isn't here.'

'When?'

'A week perhaps.' He paused. 'You were dreaming earlier. I was watching you.'

'Yes.'

'What was your dream about?'

She understood that he wanted to know about the pilot. 'I was remembering when I met William.'

'Elizabeth… You are aware that it might not be him, aren't you?'

'Yes.'

'Have you ever been to Exmouth?' he asked, unexpectedly changing the subject.

'No.'

The beach is quite long and there are one or two small hotels along the front. Whenever I think of it I can smell the air. It's the sharpness of the salt I suppose, and the grittiness of sand on the breeze. We used to go for holidays there.'

'I stayed in a place called Shoreham on Sea once,' she said. 'Just for a few days.'

'Were you on holiday?'

'No. It was in October, after the war began. The army teach people to fly there. I went there to find William.'

She began telling him about how they met and about Sophie and Christopher, and how, after the fire, William had vanished and she had thought she would never see him again. 'Then a friend of my mother's discovered he was at Shoreham.'

The morning after she had sent a letter to the camp, Elizabeth sat nervously through breakfast, half expecting William to appear, or at least send a message. When he didn't, she went for a walk, resisting the urge to return to the hotel until she had completed an entire length of the seafront in both directions. She stopped to watch the waves boiling where they broke on the shelf of the beach, and attempted to find a metaphor in the repetition, some lesson that was both simple and profound that would give her a sudden insight into life. But her thoughts were only a way of distracting herself.

When she returned, the hotel lounge was empty. Casually she enquired whether any message had been delivered for her.

'I'm afraid not,' the woman said.

Elizabeth hid her disappointment. There was no message that afternoon either, and nothing that evening. On the second day she walked up the hill and along the cliffs towards the camp. She wasn't sure what she intended. At a distance she could see the hangers, and on the grass outside were several aeroplanes. A group of men were clustered around one of the machines. It seemed that one of them held their attention, an instructor she assumed. He climbed into the pilot's seat.

She remembered the day William took her up in his plane. She'd been nervous. She'd never liked heights. She didn't want him to think she was afraid, though wherever she looked she saw taut wires and flimsy wooden struts and thought a sudden gust of wind from the wrong direction would cause the machine to fold in on itself. When the engine had started she jumped a little. The plane bounced across the grass and then lifted into the air. The wind rushed past and she held tightly to the edges of her seat. She closed her eyes tightly and wished they would land again. When she opened them, the fields below were a patchwork of burnt yellow and russet brown, and gradually her fear gave way to fascination with this new world.

On the aerodrome, the instructor climbed down from the machine he had been demonstrating. One by one the men took their turn climbing into his place. She supposed they were being taught how to operate the controls. She wondered if the instructor could be William. She had been studying him, trying to discern if there was anything familiar about his movements, but she was too far away to tell. Eventually the instructor climbed back into the machine with one other man. The wind was coming from the sea so she didn't hear the engine start, but she saw a puff of blue smoke that was swept away on the breeze in an instant. The other men moved out of the way and then the plane began to race across the grass. It lifted into the air, the wings wobbling slightly, gaining height as it came toward her. The engine sounded like the angry buzz of a bee, but it grew rapidly louder. As the plane passed overhead, Elizabeth tried to see if the instructor was looking down, and imagined herself from his point of view: A woman in a hat and long skirt in a sea of emerald green, her face upturned.

That night Elizabeth ate alone again in the dining

room. She looked up every time the door opened, but she'd begun to lose hope that William would come. An elderly couple arrived and sat by the window several tables away. They said good evening to her politely. The man ordered wine, and when it came he tasted it fussily. Throughout their meal the couple barely spoke to one another. In the end the atmosphere became too stifling and Elizabeth went outside.

As she walked along the seafront a piece of driftwood bobbed in the waves. If the tide was going out it would be carried away, and in the morning she would leave. If it was washed ashore she would go to the camp and ask to see him. She watched as it seemed first to come in a little way, and then go out again. In the end though, the tide carried it further and further from the beach until it was lost against the dark green slabs of the waves. The following morning Elizabeth paid her bill and went to the station to catch a train back to London. As a final gesture of hope she left Catherine Beauchamp's address in London with the woman who ran the hotel, and asked her to forward any message that might come for her.

Even at the last moment, as she stood on the platform beside the train, she hoped he would come. Not until the guard blew his whistle did she finally, reluctantly climb aboard. She sat alone in a carriage and looked out of the window as the sea receded into the distance.

When she had finished telling Doctor Ramsay her story, Elizabeth said, 'I decided then that I would try to forget about William.'

Ramsay lit another cigarette. 'And how did you come to be here?'

'I wanted to be useful.' She told him that Catherine Beauchamp had persuaded her to train to become a nurse. 'Several months after I left Shoreham on Sea, I received a letter forwarded by the woman at the hotel where I had stayed. Inside the envelope was my own letter to William, and a short note from somebody at the camp called Captain

Davies. He was an instructor. Perhaps the one I'd watched the day I sat on the cliff near the camp. He told me that my letter arrived a few days after William had been sent to a camp at Farnborough as an instructor. He'd meant to forward my letter straight away, but somehow he forgot. He discovered it by chance almost two months later, and though he sent it on to Farnborough it came back again, because by then William had left for France.'

'That's why you wanted to come over here?'

'Yes. At least partly. I hoped I would be able to find him. But as you know, the army didn't want women here to begin with and I had to complete my training. It was another year before I left England.'

Elizabeth felt tired suddenly. The sky had altered subtly from the blackness of night. Towards the east a faint greyness was leaching into its edge. A bitterly cold breeze had come up. Elizabeth hugged herself.

'You're shivering.' Ramsay took off his coat and put it around her shoulders.

'Thank you.' He was a good man. Quietly intelligent. Stoic. A rock in a sea of mud. But he was married, and anyway she could never love anyone, however fleetingly, while there was hope for William.

Ramsay put out his cigarette. He smokes too many of them, Elizabeth thought. He told her she should get some sleep. 'When he's sent back I'd like to go with him,' she said.

He nodded, though she could see he was sorry she would be leaving. 'I'll see if I can arrange it.'

'Thank you.'

23

After the battle at Arras began, the hospital was swamped with injured men. Some of them were pilots. Everybody knew that the Flying Corps was suffering awful losses at the hands of the German jastas. Only the lucky ones ended up at the hospital, however. Most of those shot down were killed.

The wounded were brought by motor ambulances from the dressing stations at the front. Many had lost limbs that had been severed by shrapnel from exploding shells. Others were gassed or blinded, or burned or shot. Elizabeth was no longer shocked by their injuries. If she was shocked by anything it was by how quickly the terrible became commonplace.

When she found time to visit the pilot he was conscious, but delirious from the morphine, and as usual was not aware of her. Without the morphine, the pain of his injuries would drive him mad. She sat beside the bed with her hands on her lap. She wanted to hold his hands, but the pressure of her touch would cause him pain. She had brought a book of poetry with her and she read to him from it. Sometimes she thought the sound of her voice penetrated his mind, and for a little while he was still. It was almost as if he was listening. He seemed to turn towards her and her heart beat faster.

She had come to believe that he was William. She said to him the things she had wanted to tell him when she went to Shoreham. She hoped that on some level he understood.

She prayed that he forgave her.

Later, his body began to twitch convulsively as if he was dreaming. Some mumbled sound came from his ruined mouth. She leaned forward to try and catch his words, but she could make no sense of them. She spoke to him again until he became quiet, her eyes blurred with tears.

When she left, the man in the next bed was awake. She went to his side. 'Are you alright?' she asked quietly.

'My legs hurt.'

She felt his brow. He was hot with fever. He had been burned in an attack with flame throwers during an attack that had been repelled, but initially his injuries had not seemed too serious, and he had lingered for three days in a hospital near the front, where his wounds became infected. Since then, both of his legs had been amputated. It was unlikely that he would survive. He had an all too familiar look about him. Elizabeth sat with him until he fell asleep, and by then she was too tired to move and she fell asleep herself, with her head resting beside his shoulder. In the morning he was dead.

Later that day, Elizabeth volunteered to drive an ambulance to the front to collect wounded men from the dressing stations. When they arrived at the field hospital she discovered that one of the wounded men was a pilot who'd been shot in his right shoulder. It was a nasty wound, but he was better off than the other men they were collecting, and on the way back he sat in the cab with Elizabeth, while Margaret, the Canadian nurse who went with her, rode in the back. The pilot's name was Stringer.

'Which squadron are you from?' Elizabeth asked him.

'Number twenty eight.'

She recognised the number with a jolt. 'There's another pilot from your squadron at the hospital.'

'You mean the chap who was burned?'

'Yes.'

'How is he?'

'He's very ill. I expect you know that nobody's quite certain who he is?'

'Yes, so I believe… Hasn't he said anything yet then?'

'No.'

'Poor devil.' Stringer lit a cigarette. 'It's the worst thing that can happen, you know. Getting burned I mean. We all think about it. Of course none of us ever talks about it.' He lapsed into brooding silence and avoided looking at her, as if he was ashamed of his admission. His eyes were dull, almost sunken.

'I think everyone has their particular fear,' Elizabeth said. 'A lot of the men in the trenches are afraid of being gassed.'

He threw her a quick, grateful look. 'It isn't so much the thought of being killed. We all know it could happen, of course, but it's just something that has to be accepted. One simply hopes to be able to do one's bit first, I suppose. But burning…' He shuddered. 'How bad is he? The chap in the hospital, I mean?'

'He doesn't feel any pain,' Elizabeth said, thinking that was what Stringer meant.

'When we heard about the crash, we were all so relieved to hear one of them had survived,' Stringer told her. 'But then we heard nobody could tell which of them it was. It makes you think.'

'Did you know either of them?' Elizabeth asked.

'You mean Wright and Reynolds? Yes, both of them, actually. Actually I was supposed to be on the patrol that day, but I wasn't well. Good thing too as it turned out. The others were all shot down.' He frowned and his foot tapped a rapid tattoo on the floor of the cab. He muttered something under his breath

'What did you say?' Elizabeth asked.

'What? Oh, it's just something Reynolds said in the mess. There was a bit of a scene at dinner one evening. Reynolds told the CO to his face that the brass were all fools.'

There was an undercurrent in Stringer's tone that Elizabeth couldn't quite put her finger on. A sort of resentment coupled with grudging respect. He wouldn't look at her, his eyes darted this way and that, as restless as his foot. 'Why did he think that?' she asked.

Stringer looked at her and laughed unnaturally. 'Oh, Reynolds was like that. Odd fellow you know. Difficult.'

'Really?' She kept her tone neutral. 'In what way?'

Stringer shrugged and winced, then put his hand to his shoulder. 'He was a bit of a loner, I suppose. Didn't mix well. And he was pretty quick to voice his opinions. Most of the chaps thought it was a bit off. Bad for morale and all that.'

'I see.'

Stringer fell silent and then suddenly said, 'Anyway, he was right about the brass. We all knew it I suppose. We lose men everyday. They keep sending us up in those bloody two-seaters and we haven't a chance.' He was shaking, his tone vehement. And then he looked at her guiltily. 'Sorry. I shouldn't be telling you any of this.'

'Don't worry,' she said. 'Do you know what happened when Lieutenant Reynolds and the other pilot were shot down?'

'I heard all about it. Plenty of the men in the trenches saw the entire thing. Reynolds and Captain Wright were flying Nieuport scouts. They were meant to be escorting the patrol, but they were attacked by an entire squadron of Albatrosses. The two-seaters were shot up pretty quickly. I'm sure Reynolds and Wright did their best, but they were hopelessly outnumbered. They were both shot down near the lines. I suppose you know that one came down on our side. Some artillery chaps managed to get the pilot out, but the plane was hit by a shell so nobody could tell afterwards which one it was.'

'I heard the other one crashed on the German side,'

Elizabeth said. 'Is that right, do you think?'

'Oh, yes. They saw it go down from the lines.'

'You don't think there's a chance the pilot might've survived?'

Stringer shook his head. 'If the Huns had caught him we would have heard about it by now.'

'He might have escaped.'

'Anything's possible, I suppose,' he said, though she knew as well as he did that it was unlikely.

After they arrived at the hospital, Elizabeth was kept busy with the wounded. Towards evening she asked which ward Lieutenant Stringer had been sent to. He was sitting in a chair by the window when she found him.

'Hello again,' he said, pleased to see her.

'How are you feeling?'

'Oh, alright, you know. I'm having an operation in the morning. Apparently I'll make a full recovery. Two months at the outside, I'm told.'

He sounded cheerful, but the haunted look in his eyes remained. 'I'm glad for you,' Elizabeth said.

'Yes, thanks.'

'I expect you'll get some home leave, won't you?'

He nodded. 'Yes. It'll be good to see everyone again.' He looked in his pocket for a cigarette and offered one to Elizabeth.

'We're not allowed to smoke on duty.'

'Of course. Sorry.' He seemed troubled, distant.

'Where do you live?' Elizabeth asked, thinking he'd like to talk about his home.

'Worcester,' he said. 'It'll feel strange to go back there. I suppose life goes on much as it always did. My father's with one of the banks. He's on the board. My mother's always busy with her committees and so on.'

'Do you have any brothers or sisters?'

'Two sisters. I'm the youngest. They're both married now, but they live in the town.'

'You must be looking forward to seeing them.'

'Yes.' He frowned. 'I can't imagine it somehow, you know. After all this.' He laughed self-consciously. 'I expect it'll be the other way around when I'm there, and I won't be able to imagine coming back here again.'

He put his hand to his shoulder and Elizabeth wondered if he wished his wound would not heal so readily. He looked at her and seemed to guess what she was thinking. He looked away.

Later, she went to see the pilot, and found Stringer there. He was looking intently at the bandaged figure lying in the bed.

'Do you know who he is?' she asked him

He looked at her and shook his head. 'I'm afraid not. I thought I might, but it could be either of them. Will he live?'

'Nobody thought he would survive this long, but he has. He must have a very strong will.'

'Reynolds was like that. You could sense it about him.'

'Yes.' She realised Stringer was watching her.

He was embarrassed to be caught. 'I'm sorry. It's just I've heard people say you knew Reynolds. Before the war.'

'Yes I did.'

'Do you think it's him?'

She nodded, and he looked again at the figure in the bed. 'I think you might be right, you know. I don't know why exactly. I'm very sorry.'

'Thank you.'

After Stringer went back to his ward Elizabeth stayed for a little while. For once the pilot was peaceful. She was glad for him, and yet she knew that it might be a sign that he was giving up.

She went outside for a cigarette. There was a small garden in the middle of the buildings where patients could sit outside. Somebody was smoking a cigarette. He wore a long coat. One of his legs was in plaster and a pair of crutches leaned against the seat. He seemed lost in his own thoughts and she didn't disturb him, but after a little while she felt him watching her. She finished her cigarette, and would have gone inside again, except the man was still staring at her.

'Are you alright?' she asked him.

'Liz?'

He struggled to his feet, using his crutches for support. Her heart was pounding. As he came closer she could see his face beneath the peak of his cap. He was thinner and his eyes had the same glassy, hollowed look as Stringer's.

'I thought I must be imagining things when I saw you,' he said. 'You look different. But it is you though, isn't it?'

'Yes.'

They looked at one another, neither of them quite able to believe in the other. And then Christopher smiled.

'I'm so glad to see you, Liz.'

24

For seventy two hours William had been travelling north. During daylight he spent most of the time hidden in woods, where he concealed himself in the sparse winter undergrowth as best he could. He slept fitfully, waking often because he was cold, or because he imagined that he heard voices. After his plane crashed he'd seen German soldiers on their way to the wreckage, and he didn't know if they were looking for him or had assumed he was dead. He had no clear recollection of the crash itself, only the tops of the trees rushing to meet him. He thought he must have blacked out, and when he came to he was lying on the ground, and it was raining fire. The wreck of his plane was lodged in the woodland canopy above him, where it had come to rest. The trees were burning. He'd managed to crawl clear of the fire. His leg ached badly and there was a gash in his scalp that had left his hair matted with blood, but otherwise he seemed to be uninjured.

He saw the soldiers soon afterwards. They were crossing a field towards the thick pall of smoke rising from the woods. He watched them until they passed him, and then he went in the opposite direction. Since then he'd travelled at night, following the roads away from the front. Progress was slow. His leg ached badly and he had to rest often. Other than the cold and the worry of being caught, his primary concern was food. He was constantly hungry, though at least water was easy enough to find in the many streams running through the area.

At the end of the third night he found a place to sleep among a copse of trees. He woke to the sound of voices and the rumble of wheels and horses' hooves. No more than twenty yards from where he lay hidden, a column of German troops with artillery were passing by on their way to the front. The column came to a halt for some reason and the soldiers took the chance to light cigarettes or to eat something. Their uniforms were clean, which meant they were fresh troops; reinforcements for the trenches. Many of them were older men. One of them said something and another in his group laughed, a deep guttural sound. The one who'd spoken left the others and came into the trees, making his way straight towards the place where William was hidden. He was a big man with a beefy red face and a rifle slung over his shoulder. As he came closer William took his pistol from his pocket and cocked the hammer.

He thought about what would happen if he killed the soldier. Others would come after him and they had horses. He would be caught and shot. One of the soldier's companions called out something and coarse laughter erupted among the others. The soldier grunted a reply and, putting down his rifle, he shrugged off his pack and dropped his trousers, then squatted beside a tree a few yards from where William lay. When the soldier was finished he returned to the others, leaving the pungent stink of his shit behind, and soon the column started off again and their voices faded and were gone. For twenty minutes, until the last of the column had passed, William didn't dare to move.

As darkness fell again he continued north. He stopped at a stream to drink and rest his leg. He gulped down all he could to fill the gnawing emptiness in his stomach. He knew the relief wouldn't last long. Before an hour had passed he'd be pissing it away again.

When the pain in his leg had eased he continued on his way. It was cloudy and there were no stars visible. Now and then squally showers fell and made his clothes damp. A freezing wind came up and chilled him to the bone. He knew he had to find food, and if he was going to walk all the way to the Dutch frontier without being caught he would need to get rid of his uniform. When he saw a glimmer of yellow light in the darkness he changed direction and climbed through a hedgerow to cross a field. The mud stuck to his boots, and in his weakened state, it made every step an effort. When he reached the far side of the field he saw that the light came from a window on the ground floor of a farm house. He watched it for a little while and then crept towards a barn across the yard.

The barn had wooden doors, which creaked when William opened them and set a dog barking furiously somewhere close by. Alarmed, he slipped inside and took the pistol from his pocket, waiting to see if anyone would come. After a few moments the dog stopped barking, but William waited a little while longer before he put the gun away and began to feel his way around.

The air smelt of hay and dry dirt. As his eyes adjusted to the darkness inside, William could see byres and stalls. An animal breathed heavily through its nostrils and moved restlessly; hooves on hard packed earth. He found a box filled with straw and potatoes. He put some in his pockets and then found another box that held apples. He ate one straight away and shoved more in with the potatoes. Further on he felt in the hay byres and touched something warm and soft. It moved and he recoiled as a hen exploded from the hay, squawking with alarm. Outside, the dog began barking again. More hens flapped around him, and he tried to grab one of them, but their feathers were soft and slippery. He felt something smooth and warm, and when he realised they were eggs he stuffed them in his pockets. Outside, the dog's barking had become frenzied, and he knew it was bound to bring somebody from the house to see what was wrong. Quickly he made his way to the door and slipped outside again.

As he crossed the yard a door opened, spilling light from the house. William heard a questioning grunt, but by then he was around the corner, already swallowed by the darkness. Too late, he glimpsed a shape looming in front of him and then something wrapped around his face and arms. He struggled briefly before realising he'd run into clothes drying on a line. Hurriedly, he snatched at some trousers and a shirt and then plunged through a hedge into a field. His leg gave way and a bolt of agonising pain caused him to cry out, but he forced himself up and stumbled on.

On the other side of the field he stopped to get his breath. To his surprise there was no sound of pursuit. The barking dog had fallen quiet again. After a moment he felt in his pocket for the eggs. Two of them had broken when he fell, but he scooped out the yolk and albumen and ate it, then cracked the other two and sucked out their contents. Afterwards he ate two apples, but decided to keep the potatoes until he could cook them. The thought of hot potato, smoky from a fire, made his mouth water.

He walked on for half an hour until he came across the ruined remains of a barn. Though part of the roof was missing, he found a corner where it was sheltered and dry. He took off his uniform and exchanged it for the clothes he'd taken from the farm, and then he sat down in the corner to rest. Within minutes he was asleep.

*****

When he woke, the grey light of morning revealed broken rafters and crumbling masonry. His leg was painfully stiff and he was cold and hungry again. As he struggled to his feet, William froze. A stockily built man stood in the gap where there was once a door. He was roughly dressed and unshaven, and beside him on a rope leash was a large brown dog that eyed William warily. In the crook of his arm the man carried a rifle.

'Bonjour,' William said. His French was passable but he knew he would never pass for a native.

The man didn't respond. He looked at the discarded uniform on the ground and the clothes William now wore beneath his coat. The rifle remained in the crook of his arm. Though William didn't feel threatened yet, he was aware that pilots brought down in occupied territory couldn't rely on the local population for help, since the Germans would shoot anyone caught assisting the enemy.

Keeping an eye on the rifle, William bent down to rub his stiff leg and at the same time he pretended to lose his balance and stumble. The man took a step toward him, and then stopped as William took out his pistol and pointed it at him. For several seconds neither of them moved.

'Anglaise?' The man questioned.

'Oui, Je suis Anglaise.'

The man nodded, but otherwise didn't react. Keeping the pistol trained on him, William stepped closer and gestured that he should move aside. The dog growled, but the man said something sharply and it fell quiet. In the light of day William saw that the barn was on the edge of a large, sloping grass field. It was very early and the air was cold and damp. Thin mist shrouded the countryside and pale cloud blanketed the sky. It was as if the colour had been leached from the landscape. At the eastern end of the field was a wood. William gestured to the rifle and held out his hand. Warily, the man handed it over, and William began to back away. After he'd gone a short distance he turned and limped to the edge of the trees. When he looked back the man hadn't moved. William held the rifle aloft so the man could see it, then placed it on the ground before slipping away into the woods. Once he was out of sight, he changed direction to head north again.

In order to put some distance between himself and the man with the dog, William travelled by daylight, though he was careful to stay away from roads. Around midday he made his way deep into a wood and risked lighting a fire. The flames cheered him up, and when the fire was reduced to hot embers he buried his potatoes and sat against a tree. An hour later he was tossing a scalding potato from hand to hand. The skin was tough and blackened, while the white flesh was steaming hot and soft. He'd never tasted anything so delicious, though he wished he'd kept an egg to crack over it.

When he set off again it was with the realisation that he would never reach the frontier without help. Either he would starve or else be caught by the Germans and shot as a spy. He decided that he must find a town, where he stood a better chance of finding food and some means of transport. Towards evening he came across a sign indicating the way to Cambrai. He knew from there he ought to be able to reach Lille, and then perhaps he could find a way to get to Bruges. He reached the outskirts of the town as it was getting dark, and found a place to sleep in the shelter of a stone wall.

In the morning William walked into the town. It was still early, but already the market held in the square was busy. Nobody paid him any attention. As he passed a shop window he was surprised by his own reflection. An unkempt and unshaven labourer dressed in rough working clothes stared back at him.

Everywhere William looked there was food, though the shortages caused by the war were apparent. There were a few skinny chickens and ducks for sale, and a rabbit or two. One stall sold offal and bones to make soup. Others displayed home-grown produce, but the vegetables were poor quality. The people were taciturn, and argued over the price of a cabbage. Their faces were pinched, their eyes sharp as they searched for a bargain. As he wandered among them, William was careful not to meet anybody's eye. He tried to look as if he had a purpose, while he waited for an opportunity to present itself. He considered trying to steal money, perhaps by pretending to bump into somebody.

After walking around the market once he found himself back where he started. Old men sat at tables outside cafés, drinking whatever passed for coffee, and smoking pungent cigarettes while they watched the women shopping. One of them stared at him. He imagined nothing would escape them. Suspicion was etched into their lined and weathered features.

He walked through the market again, and thought this time he had to make a move. He passed a stall where a young woman was arguing over half a pig's head with a man wearing a bloody apron. William found it difficult to follow their rapid speech, but he gathered she was deriding the quality and price of his meat. She made as if to turn away in contempt, but the butcher regarded her impassively and merely shrugged. The woman hesitated, her mouth drawn in a tight line, and then offered him half of what he was asking. As they bargained, William loitered, and when an agreement was reached he saw her take money from her pocket to pay for the parcel that she put in her basket. As she turned to leave, she caught William's eye for an instant. He looked beyond her as if searching for somebody. Suspicious lines creased her brow, but then she brushed past him and merged with the crowd. After a few moments William followed her.

He kept his distance. The woman was perhaps in her mid-twenties, small and dark haired, with pale olive skin Though there were purplish smudges beneath her eyes, she was pretty, William thought, or could have been if she'd been well fed and wore decent clothes, instead of a shapeless long coat and heavy boots. She stopped at a stall selling turnips and swedes and produced something from her basket. He couldn't see what it was, but she bargained with the stall-holder until a trade was agreed.

His plan was to follow her until she left the market, then walk quickly up to her in some street where there were no people and steal her money. He didn't like the idea very much, but he didn't have a choice. Suddenly the young woman stopped and turned to look directly at him. Her expression was suspicious, even accusing, and he knew it was no good, that she had somehow guessed his intention. Abruptly he turned away and tried to vanish among the press of people. At any moment he expected to hear a shout from behind, and then people would look at him and move out of the way and he would be exposed. He pushed through them, determined to get away, aware that he was making himself conspicuous. People threw him angry looks and muttered as he rudely barged past. He knew he ought to slow down and behave more naturally, but he couldn't quell his rising panic. He grasped the butt of the pistol in his pocket. He just wanted to get away, and he cursed his stupidity for going there.

Eventually he was free of the stalls and he walked rapidly along the edge of the square, back in the direction he had come from. Before he'd gone a dozen steps a car appeared, coming along the street towards him and it was followed by a lorry full of German soldiers. For an instant William froze before he turned to a shop window and pretended to look inside, his heart racing. He wondered how they'd known about him, and thought he must have been betrayed. He thought of the young woman, but realised it couldn't have been her to bring the soldiers so soon. He must have been seen on his way into the town earlier, or perhaps even the day before. In the end he supposed it didn't matter. All that mattered now was what he was going to do.

Watching the reflection in the shop window, he saw the lorry stop and soldiers clambered from the back while an officer in the car shouted orders. Some of them ran to take up positions at the exits from the square, blocking William's escape, while the others set up a machine gun in front of the church steps which they trained on the people in the market place. Everybody looked on in silence. William searched in vain for another way out of the square.

A man and a woman were brought from the lorry. They

were wearing civilian clothes and their hands were tied behind their backs. The officer began to address the crowd. Speaking in French he said the two prisoners had been tried by a military court and found guilty of being saboteurs, and since they were from the town their punishment was to be carried out there as an example to others. When he'd finished, six soldiers formed a line in front of the prisoners. An order was given and they loaded their rifles and raised them to their shoulders. There was a pause. The prisoners looked resigned to their fate. The final command was given and a ragged volley of shots echoed across the rooftops and the prisoners crumpled to the ground. The officer approached and took out his pistol, and two shots rang out.

It was all over in a matter of minutes. As soon as the execution was over the soldiers began to return to the lorry. One of them looked curiously at William as he passed. Their eyes met and something made the soldier hesitate, perhaps sensing William's nervousness. Suddenly, the young woman William had followed earlier approached them, her expression tight with anger. Certain that she was about to accuse him, William started to take out the pistol, but the woman saw the movement and a warning flashed in her eyes.

'There you are you lazy pig!' she said angrily. 'I thought I told you not to come back until you have done a day's work and earned money to put bread on the table for your children!'

Startled, William regarded her blankly. She continued to berate him furiously, but her eyes said something else. She took his arm and roughly shoved him as if to herd him in front of her.

'I should have listened to my mother! She told me you were a worthless pig like your brother and your father!'

The woman went on scolding him, her words an almost indecipherable torrent. The soldier, who moments earlier had been suspicious, now grinned with amusement, and then shouldering his rifle he continued on his way towards the lorry.

The young woman continued her stream of remonstrations, but she flicked her eyes towards the closest street leading from the square, and William did his best to look sheepish as he allowed himself to be hectored away. Two old men at a nearby table chuckled as he passed. Behind him, William heard the lorry's engine start up, then the meshing of gears.

Only when they were safely away from the square did the young woman look back to be sure there was nobody close by. 'Do you speak French?'

'Yes. A little'

'We must get away from here.'

After that she didn't speak to him again until they were a mile from the town.

25

When they were safely away from the town the young woman looked at William's leg. 'You are limping. Are you hurt?'

'It's just bruised, I think. It happened when my plane crashed.'

'You are a pilot?'

'Yes. I was shot down a few days ago near the lines.'

They had left the main road and were walking on a rutted lane flanked by hedgerows on either side. The coat that the young woman wore was too big for her and made her seem small and vulnerable, though there had been nothing vulnerable about the way she had come to his aid in the market.

'I want to thank you for what you did back there,' William said. She made a movement of her shoulders that was not quite a shrug. 'How did you know I was English?'

'You do not look French,' she said. 'And when I saw you in the market you were acting strangely. Were you following me?'

'I'm afraid I was planning to steal your money,' he admitted.

'That is what I thought.'

He was surprised. 'Why did you help me if you knew?'

'I would not have helped you if I thought you were only a common thief. I thought perhaps you were a spy. Though not a very good one.' The faintest hint of a smile touched the corners of her eyes.

'The people who were shot... were they spies?'

'They were from a village near here. They had been sending information about the Germans to the British.'

'What you did was very brave,' William said. 'And very dangerous.'

'I am French. This is my country.'

She spoke matter of fact, as if anyone would have done what she had, but William knew it wasn't true.

'What will you do now?' she asked him.

'I'm trying to make my way north. I want to get to the Dutch frontier.'

She regarded him sceptically. 'You will not get far looking like that.'

'I'll stay away from towns in the future.'

'How will you eat?'

'I expect I'll manage somehow.'

She stopped, and took a loaf of bread from her basket and offered it to him. 'Here, you must be hungry.'

Though it was almost more temptation than he could bear, he refused. 'You've already put yourself at risk for me. I can't take your food as well.'

'If you do not eat you will not get to the frontier. Anyway, I have more.' She showed him her basket. 'Every morning I go to the market to trade eggs and sometimes cheese for other things we need. One loaf less won't make any difference.'

Unable to resist any longer, William thanked her and tore off a chunk of the loaf. The crust was still warm and crispy though the bread was heavy and chewy.

'When did you last eat?'

'Yesterday.' He told her about the farm where he'd stolen eggs and potatoes.

'Here.' She gave him a piece of sausage, which after a moment's hesitation he accepted gratefully.

'Where do you live?' he asked her.

'On a small farm near here. If you want, you can come

there with me. You can rest your leg. You need some proper food and I can find some clothes that fit you better.'

'I can't ask you to put yourself in any more danger after what happened to those poor devils in the square.'

'There is a war,' she answered simply. 'If we are to drive the Germans from France, we must be prepared to resist them.'

The prospect of shelter and food was appealing, and William knew if he was going to get to the frontier he needed her help. 'Alright, thanks,' he agreed. 'But I'll only stay for a few days and then I'll go.'

'As you wish.'

When they continued on their way the woman told him that her name was Helene Lisle, and that the farm where she lived belonged to her husband's parents. When the Germans invaded Belgium he had left her there to look after them and had gone to join the army.

'We did not know the Germans would get this far, otherwise I would not have stayed,' she said.

'Where would you have gone?'

'To our home in Rouen. I was a schoolteacher there. We had only come here to visit Jean's parents.'

'Where is your husband now?'

'He is dead.'

'I'm sorry.'

She didn't speak again until they came to a farm track that led through the fields towards a farmhouse and some outbuildings some distance away.

'It would be better if Jean's parents do not see you,' Helene said. 'I will take you another way to the barn. There is a loft for the hay where you can stay without them knowing you are there.'

William hesitated, concerned at the need for secrecy.

'It is alright,' Helene said. 'They are old, that is all. They will worry if they know.'

He felt there was something she wasn't telling him.

Briefly he wondered if he could trust her, but then he reminded himself that she had saved his life and he felt guilty for doubting her. 'Alright,' he said.

She led him away from the track to a wood, and eventually they emerged from the trees to approach the farm from another direction. A hedgerow hid them from the house until they reached the back of a barn, where there was a narrow wooden door.

'Wait here,' Helene instructed. 'I will make sure there is nobody inside.

While she was gone, William had a chance to get a better look at the farm. The buildings were made of old brick and timber and had a neglected, mean air. The roof of the house was poorly patched and a corner of one wall bulged where it had sagged. Ancient, faded paint flaked from the wooden doors and windows, and around the buildings weeds and nettles grew unchecked, smothering abandoned rusted implements and a pile of crumbling bricks and rotting timber. It was barely a farm at all, William guessed, just a few acres from which its inhabitants scratched a meagre living, huddled in a depression in the land beneath a leaden sky.

After a few minutes Helene returned. 'Come. It is alright. There is no-one there.'

Inside the barn the light was dim and the air musty with the mingled smells of animals and old hay. Helene ushered him towards a wooden ladder that led up to a shadowed loft.

'I will come with some food when I can. Albert and Marie go to bed very early, until then you must be very quiet.'

'What if somebody comes?'

'Albert is too old to climb the ladder. If you are careful he will never know you are here.'

Once again, William hesitated. It occurred to him that he was putting his life in the hands of a woman he barely knew, and yet without her he would almost certainly have been caught back in the town. He began to climb the ladder, and at the top found a space about thirty feet long and twenty wide. It was partially filled with hay and could be accessed by a pair of wooden doors that opened above a yard outside. He went to a corner and made a kind of bed for himself, piling the hay around so that if anyone came up the ladder he couldn't be seen, then he put his revolver close to hand and lay down. Within minutes he was asleep.

*****

When William woke it was almost dark. He climbed down the ladder into the barn and stood still for a few moments, allowing his eyes to become accustomed to the gloom. The doors were closed. A horse regarded him from a stall, and in another were two cows. Fat brown hens pecked at the dirt floor. He went outside to the back of the barn and relieved himself at the edge of the field, being careful not to be seen from the house. The rain had stopped, but it was very cold, and the wind made him shiver. To the south, flares cast a glow above the horizon.

When he returned to the loft he sat by the hay doors. Between cracks in the boards he could see the house on the other side of a yard. A light showed in a downstairs window and occasionally he saw signs of movement. He pictured Helene and her husband's parents sitting down to eat their evening meal, and wondered if Helene would tell them about the spies the Germans had executed in the square that day. It made him uneasy to think that her parents-in-law were oblivious to his presence, and yet by being there he was putting them all in great danger.

An hour after dark, the yellow glow of a lamp showed in one of the upstairs rooms, and shortly afterwards was extinguished again. Another hour passed before William heard the creak of the doors. He went to the ladder and peered into the darkness, and after a few moments Helene climbed up and passed him a pot.

'Be careful,' she said quietly. 'It is hot.'

They sat in the corner he had cleared and she gave him a spoon that she took from her pocket.

'I am sorry I took so long. I had to wait until I was sure Albert and Marie were sleeping.' She gestured to the pot. 'Eat. And then we will talk.'

The smell of the food when he lifted the lid made his mouth water. 'What is it?'

'It is made from beans and other vegetables. A little pork. Whatever we can find.'

William tasted it. The gravy was thick, with a strong flavour of garlic and herbs. There were vegetables that he couldn't identify, and small nutty things that he thought were acorns. Helene told him that things were bad in the towns. The Germans had gone to the farms and stolen the animals and crops and the people had very little left to sell. But at least the people on the farms could forage for food in the fields and the woods.

'Did the Germans come here?' William asked.

'Yes, in the summer. They took everything.'

'What about the animals down there?'

'Albert managed to hide them in the woods. Every morning he takes them away again in case the soldiers come back and then brings them here at night. We manage, but it is difficult.'

He paused between mouthfuls of stew, stricken by guilt that he was eating their food, but she urged him to finish it. When he had finished every scrap she went to the ladder and climbed down into the barn, and when she returned she had a bottle of wine and two mugs.

'The Germans did not find this,' she said as she poured the wine. 'How long have you been a pilot?'

'I learned to fly before the war, and I volunteered for the Flying Corps at the beginning.'

'The German aeroplanes fly over here sometimes. You can even see the pilots looking down at us. Albert worries that one day they will see his cows.'

They must be low, William thought, if they can see the pilot. 'Is there an aerodrome near here?'

'Yes.'

'How far is it?'

'A few kilometres. Five, six maybe.'

He leaned back against the wall and stretched out his leg carefully.

'Does it hurt?' Helene asked.

'A bit.'

'Let me look at it.'

'It's alright.'

'You should let me see it,' she insisted. 'My father was a vet. When I was young I used to help him.'

Reluctantly, he undid his trousers and pulled them down, and she knelt beside him and struck a match so that she could see. His thigh was badly bruised, the flesh purple, fading to dark green and an ugly yellow colour at the edges. He saw her looking at the old scars and ridged tissue. When the match went out she gently felt with her hands, applying pressure while she watched his reaction. He winced now and then, the pain like the thrust of a knife.

'This is an old injury,' Helene said eventually. 'What happened to you?'

'An accident. I was caught in a harvester when I was a child.'

'It must have been very bad. Has it always troubled you?'

'Sometimes.'

'The bruise is bad, but nothing is broken. I think perhaps there is a weakness. It will heal again if you rest, but if you do not it may get worse.'

He thought that she was right. Since the crash, the pain hadn't improved and he was limping more, but he had already decided he couldn't stay there. 'I have to reach the frontier.'

'As you wish.' She picked up the empty pot. 'I must go. In the morning I must go to the market. If you are here when I return, I will bring you some food.'

Her manner had become brusque, as if his decision to leave offended her. 'Thank you,' he said. 'For everything.'

She went to the ladder, only glancing at him quickly before she climbed down. 'Goodnight.'

'Goodnight.'

A few moments later he heard the creak of the door.

******

When William woke it was pitch black. He didn't move, sensing that somebody was close by. He opened his eyes a fraction and saw a shape right beside him. With a quick movement he reached for his revolver with one hand and at the same time grabbed hold of whoever was there. Helene stared at him, her eyes wide. The revolver was pointed at her face, the hammer cocked.

'What are you doing?' he said, his heart pounding as he released the pressure of the trigger. 'I could have killed you.'

'I did not want to wake you. I brought you some things.' She gestured to a bundle.

The tension slowly flowed out of him. 'What time is it?'

'Early. It will be light soon.'

'How long have you been here?'

'Not long. A few minutes.'

He saw she had brought him clothes and a pair of shoes.

'They belonged to Jean,' she said. 'There is soap also. You will find a stream in the woods where you can wash without being seen.' She fished two hard boiled eggs from her pocket and a piece of bread. 'There is more food with the clothes. I must go to the market now.'

He took the food and thanked her.

She nodded and went to the ladder. 'Good luck,' she said.

As she climbed down he went to the edge of the loft. He wanted to say something more, but he didn't know what. At the door she slipped outside and from the hay doors he watched her cross the yard. He thought she would look back one more time but she didn't, and then she reached the corner and vanished from sight.

A few minutes later William gathered the things Helene had brought him. He wished he had something to write with so that he could leave a note, thanking her again for risking her life to help him. Outside, the night was giving way to a grey dawn. The fields were shrouded in mist. He made his way to the wood and found a small stream at the bottom of a steep bank. He climbed down carefully using small trees and roots protruding from the ground to stop himself falling. When he reached the bottom he found the water was icy cold, but he stripped off everything and scrubbed himself clean and shaved with a razor he found in the bundle of clothes Helene had brought him.

When he'd dressed again, William buried the old clothes in a shallow pit, and while he ate the eggs and bread he felt something in the pocket of his jacket. It was a tin containing cigarettes and a roll of money. He counted the notes, and then sat down and lit one of the cigarettes. While he smoked he thought about the money. It must be everything Helene had. He resolved that if he survived the war he would come back and find Helene one day, and somehow he would repay her for everything she'd done for him.

When he finished his cigarette he got up to go. It was much more difficult climbing up the bank than it had been getting down, and when he was halfway up William thought he should have walked along the stream and found an easier way. By then though, he decided he may as well carry on. As he neared the top he reached for a tree to haul himself up, but as he did his foot slipped and he lost his balance. For a moment he wavered, but then he began to slither backwards. He twisted around to try and regain his footing, but instead his momentum pitched him forward and he fell. There was nothing he could do other than try to slow his descent as he rolled and tumbled towards the stream. He grabbed for handholds, that tore his skin, and tried to dig his heels into the ground, but it was too slippery to get a hold, and then suddenly he slammed into the earth at the bottom. A sharp flash of agony knifed through his injured leg. He stifled a yell and lay on his back, breathing hard and looking up at the tops of the trees.

Ten minutes passed before William tried to move. He broke off a sapling that was strong enough to take his weight, and using it as a cane began to limp painfully along the edge of the stream until the bank gradually flattened to a shallow slope. After that it took him another hour to get back to the barn.

*****

Soon after William managed to climb up to the loft again, he heard the barn doors open. He cleared some hay aside and peered down through the cracks in the floorboards to see an old man moving about below. He was thin-faced with lank strands of grey hair clinging to a grizzled scalp. One arm hung uselessly at his side, the fingers of his hand frozen like a claw. He fetched a stool and set it down beside one of the cows, and then placed a pail beneath its udder and, resting his head against the animal's flank, he began to squeeze milk into the pail with long, rhythmic squirts. As he milked the cows the old man mumbled to himself, a low muffled monologue of which William could only make out the occasional word or phrase, but which seemed to be an incessant grumble against the injustices he'd borne throughout his life. When he'd finished the milking, the old man collected eggs from the hay around the barn and left. A few minutes later he returned and led the cows and the horse outside, and William watched from the hayloft as the little procession plodded through a field toward the woods.

Later he saw an old woman came out of the house to throw scraps to the hens that had left the barn and were now pecking in the yard. She was heavy, her face set in a perpetual scowl. She spent part of the morning in a room beside what William assumed was the kitchen. The windows were open and he could see her washing clothes in a tub, and afterwards she put them through a heavy ringer and hung them on a line at the end of the yard. When she was finished she went to a small building at the end of the house, and though he could see her moving about he couldn't tell what she was doing.

When Helene returned at midday, she crossed the yard and went into the house. When the old woman saw her she stopped what she was doing and hurried after her, though neither of them spoke. Half an hour later Helene came to the barn. William went to the edge of the loft, and when she looked up and saw him her eyes widened in surprise, though he had the feeling she was also pleased. She glanced over her shoulder to make sure there was nobody around and then quickly climbed the ladder.

'Why didn't you leave?' she asked, keeping her voice to little more than a whisper.

'I fell down the bank by the stream,' he said.

'Are you hurt?'

'It's my leg.'

'Let me see.'

She felt the bruising while he gritted his teeth and sweat popped on his forehead.

'Can you walk?' she asked.

He shook his head. 'Not very well.'

'I will bring something that will help later.'

As she turned to go he held her arm. 'Wait.' He dug in his pocket and gave her back the roll of money he'd found earlier. 'It looks as if I won't need this.'

She hesitated, then took it. 'I will come when it is dark.'

For the rest of the day William sat by the hay-doors, where he could see outside. He watched Helene go out into the fields carrying a basket, and later when she returned it was full of things he assumed she'd gathered from the hedgerows and woods. Later, he saw her cutting wood and carrying it inside, and afterwards he glimpsed her digging in a garden. She worked without seeming to stop. But what struck him most of all was that she never spoke to the old couple, nor they to her. In fact she went about her work almost as if they didn't exist, though several times William saw the old woman scowl at Helene's back and mutter something under her breath.

Late in the afternoon he heard the sound of engines, and soon afterwards a dozen Albatrosses passed by about half a mile away. They were losing height, and he thought they must be returning from a patrol to land at the aerodrome Helene had told him was nearby. Seeing them made William realise that, for now at least, the war was over for him, and he admitted to feeling a certain degree of relief.

At some point William fell asleep. He woke up when the old man brought the animals back to the barn. By then the light had faded and it was raining. William watched the house as he had the night before, and some-time after the lights were extinguished he heard the creak of the barn doors and went to the top of the ladder to help Helene. She had brought more stew, made from vegetables and some sort of fatty meat, and when he'd finished eating they shared a cigarette and she poured wine into his mug.

'It is one thing we have plenty of,' she said and told

him it was made from the grapes that grew on the vines in the garden.

'Tell me about your husband's parents,' he said.

'They do not like me.'

'Why?'

'Jean was their only child. I met him when I came to the town to work for a few months. I told you, I was a teacher.'

'I thought you lived in Rouen.'

'Yes. And afterwards I went back there. Jean followed me. He asked me to marry him. At first I refused because I did not want to live here. But Jean said he wanted to stay in Rouen. He did not want to live like his parents. He wanted to make furniture and open a shop where he would sell it. He was very good at making things.

'When we got married, Albert and Edith would not come to the wedding. They said they could not leave the farm. I knew they blamed me for taking their son from them. They said that without him to help them they could not manage alone. Of course, Jean felt guilty for leaving them, but he hated it here. He said even if he had not met me he would not have stayed. For three years we were happy. Sometimes Jean went to visit his parents, but I never went with him. And then one year he asked me to come. Jean's business was doing well and we were thinking of starting a family. He wanted to persuade his parents to come and live in Rouen, and he thought if I came they would change their minds about me. I was not so optimistic, but I agreed for Jean.'

'And you were caught here when the war started?'

'Yes. And now you see how it is with Edith and Albert. They blame me for everything. They think I took Jean away from them and that it is my fault he is dead. They hate me.'

'But they let you live here?'

'Only because they need me to do the work,' Helene said dispiritedly.

'Why do you stay?' William asked. 'I mean, I know you can't get back to Rouen with the war on, but you could go and live in the town couldn't you?'

'What would I do? There is very little food, people must look after their own families.'

'What about when the war is over?'

'Then I will leave. Until then we are stuck with each other.'

And with him too, William thought. He had no choice other than to stay there, and yet how long could he remain without his presence being discovered?

'You are worried about them,' Helene guessed.

'Yes,' he admitted. 'What will they do if they find out I am here?'

'You do not have to worry that they will betray you. They are afraid of the Germans, and anyway if they betray you then they betray me also. They do not like me, but they need me here. But it would be better if they did not know.'

'What about the extra food?'

'There is enough for us all. I have always done the cooking because I cannot stand the food Edith makes. And it is me who goes to the market. They will not notice.'

He wondered if Helene was right. He thought she was less certain than she pretended to be, and he remembered how she had reacted when he told her he was leaving, and now he understood that she had wanted him to stay. He imagined her life there, having nobody to talk to, knowing that Albert and Edith hated her. She was lonely, he thought.

Helene took something from her pocket wrapped in a cloth. 'This will help your leg.'

'What is it?'

'A poultice. It is made from herbs.'

She pushed up his trouser leg and applied a thick, pungent, dark paste to his bruised skin, and then she bound the whole thing tightly with a strip of cloth.

'I can stay for a little while if you would like?' she said

when she was finished.

'Don't you have to get up early to go to the market?'

'It is not late. Usually after Edith and Albert have gone to bed I sit up by myself.' She settled herself back into the hay. 'Do you want to have another cigarette? We could share one if you like.'

He lit one and passed it to her.

'Will you tell me about yourself?' she asked.

'What would you like to know?'

'I don't know. Where did you learn to speak French?'

'At the school I went to. But it was a long time ago.'

'Do all children in England learn French at school?'

'No. Only at public schools, which is like a private school here.'

'Ah. Then your family is rich?'

'My parents are dead.'

'I am sorry. Do you have brothers or sisters?'

'No. Do you?'

'Two sisters, yes. Both older. Are you married, William?'

'No.'

'But there is somebody you love in England? A girl?'

'Why do you think that?'

'Because you are nice-looking, and I think you are a good person. Why wouldn't there be somebody?'

'There isn't,' he said. 'Where are your family?'

'They are still in Rouen, as far as I know.' She was silent for a moment and then said, 'I am sorry. I should not ask you so many questions.'

He realised that he must have sounded evasive. 'It's alright,' he told her. 'I'm just not used to talking to anyone like this.'

'Why not? Don't you have friends in your squadron? Is that what it is called?'

'Yes it is. And no, there isn't anyone really. I don't know why. I suppose since the war began I've kept to myself.'

'Why?'

'It just seemed easier that way. I think I decided I'd have more chance of surviving if I didn't rely on anybody else.' He gave a wry smile. 'Obviously I was wrong.'

'Yes,' she agreed, smiling back at him.

She began to tell him more about herself before she was married. She grew up in a large house outside the city. Her father's work took him to all the local farms. They were not poor but they didn't have much money. On Sundays, if the weather was fine, they would have picnics by the river, or sometimes her father would hire a boat.

William liked listening to the sound of her voice. There was a moon outside and the grey light that seeped through the boards cast her face in deep angular shadows. Eventually she said that she ought to go.

'Goodnight, William.'

'Goodnight.'

He heard her climb down the ladder and then the creak of the door, and when he looked outside saw her cross the yard. When he lay down in the hay to sleep he found himself trying to picture her husband, and imagined them at their wedding together, laughing and drinking wine, looking into one another's eyes, and later when they were alone, the whispered intimacies of lovers.

And then, when he closed his eyes he thought of Elizabeth and wondered where she was.

26

Elizabeth held the door open, but Christopher hesitated. His eyes were filled with dread.

'Are you alright?' she said.

'Yes, of course. I'm sorry, it's just …'

He didn't finish whatever he meant to say. Instead he visibly gathered himself together. 'Where is he?'

'This way.'

She led him through the ward. It was late. She had brought him when most of the men would be sleeping, though perhaps it was a mistake. That first night, when they'd met again in the hospital garden, and she'd told him that William was at the hospital too, he wasn't as surprised as she'd expected.

'Do you know I've been dreading this moment for years. I always knew I'd run into him somewhere or other. I think I'm actually glad. Where is he?'

'He's in one of the wards. He's very badly injured.'

'But he'll be alright won't he?'

'I don't know. His plane crashed and caught fire. He was burned over most of his body.'

Christopher had paled visibly. 'My God. I've often wondered about him, you know. I thought he must have joined the Flying Corps. But I always thought he would be alright. I don't know why, really.'

The following day he'd asked to see him.

When they reached the pilot's bed, Elizabeth stood aside and watched as Christopher approached. His face was cut by shadows accentuating his gaunt, hollowed appearance. She knew he had nightmares at night, beating at imaginary flames and crying out in terror. He woke drenched with sweat, the veins in his temples standing out like cords. It was the old horror of burning come back to haunt him, only now it was far worse. She thought that was partly why he wanted to see William, to face his own demons.

He turned to her. 'Is he in pain?'

'No.'

'When he was brought here... after he crashed. What was he like then?' Christopher asked. 'Was he aware of what had happened?'

'He was given morphine at the front,' she said, understanding the reason for his morbid questions.

'We're all given revolvers, you know. In case we're shot down on the other side. But a lot of chaps swear they'd use it on themselves rather than burn. I've often wondered if any of them do. Will he live?'

'No,' Elizabeth said quietly. 'He's dying.'

The plan to send him home had been abandoned. He wasn't expected to last more than a few more days.

They went outside and stood in the shelter of a doorway, watching the rain falling steadily. The guns continued to pound at the front. They were saying the battle at Arras was a success, though in fact the Germans had already retreated to stronger positions before the attack began. In the air though, the British squadrons were being decimated. If Christopher hadn't been wounded he would probably be dead, Elizabeth thought.

'Did you ever see William again after we came back from France?' Christopher asked.

'No. I tried to find him, but it was hopeless. I had no idea where he might have gone. Then when the war started I thought he might have volunteered for the Flying Corps and so I asked a friend of my mothers' for help. Her husband knew people at the war ministry.'

'Did you find him?'

'I learned that he was at a camp at Shoreham on Sea.' She explained how she'd gone there and sent William a letter and had stayed for two days waiting for his reply which never came.

'When I went back to London I decided I wanted to do something useful.'

'So you became a nurse?'

'Yes.'

And you never heard from William?'

'A few months later I found out that he never received my letter. By then he was in France. For a long time I tried to forget. I told myself that he wouldn't want to hear from me anyway. I imagined he hated me and I didn't blame him. But as the war went on, and so many men were killed, and everybody began to realise that it wouldn't all be over quickly, I couldn't stop thinking that he might be killed and I would never get the chance to tell him that I was sorry. In the end I asked to come to France.'

'You mean William was the reason you came here?'

'Yes. At least in part. But I was too late.'

'God, I'm so sorry, Liz. I had no idea. You must love him a great deal.'

'I didn't always know how much. But yes, I do.'

She couldn't hold back her tears any longer. Despite everything, and though they hadn't seen each other for so long, she still felt closer to Christopher than perhaps anyone. There was a part of her that was still the young, innocent girl she'd once been. He put his arms around her to comfort her, and she sensed his need for her too. They clung to one another. Beyond them the rain continued to fall like a veil of grey, keeping the bitter world at bay.

*****

317

The funeral was held at a village church outside Amiens. Ordinarily when men died they were buried in a cemetery close to the hospital, but Elizabeth asked for permission to make other arrangements. She wanted William buried somewhere she thought he would have liked. The graveyard was surrounded by a stone wall, and beyond it were fields, and a lane that ran through the village. The names of the dead on the gravestones were a record of the history of the village stretching back through generations. In the oldest part they were worn smooth and covered with moss, some of them broken, others leaning at a crooked angle. Centuries old oak and chestnut stood guard, and though the sky that day was grey and forbidding, in the summer to come they would provide leafy havens of shade. It reminded her of the churchyard in Scaldwell where William had once taken her.

As the coffin was lowered into the ground, the curate prayed, his words whipped away by the wind. Elizabeth and Christopher were the only mourners. When it was over, the curate shook their hands and offered his sympathies, then left them and hurried back towards the comfort of his church, his cassock flapping like the wings of the crows in the trees.

Elizabeth told herself that when the war was over she would come back every year to put fresh flowers on the grave. As they walked back to the gate she took Christopher's arm. He used a cane and could only walk slowly.

'I still think about Sophie a good deal you know,' he said.

It was the first time he'd talked about her. The first time either of them had really broached what had happened.

'When I think of the way I behaved, it seems almost impossible that it was only a few years ago,' he continued. 'I look back and it's like remembering one's distant childhood. I don't mean that I'm trying to excuse my actions because of youth. Only that I don't think I'm the same person that I was then. It's the war I suppose. None of us are the same.'

Elizabeth thought she understood what he meant. Had she never become a nurse, never come to France, she would be a different person than she was now.

'We shouldn't have gone to Cannes, you and I,' Christopher said.

'No.'

'At the time I believed it was for the best. I thought if I was gone, Sophie would accept things more easily. I even imagined I was being noble in a way because I thought it was unfair of me to hide her away somewhere and have her as my mistress but never give her the respectable marriage she wanted. But it was cowardice really. I see that now. I loved her. I should have married her and the hell with convention and position and all the rest of it. It seems so useless and unimportant against everything that's happening here.'

He sounded bitter. Full of self-recrimination.

'You shouldn't take all the blame yourself,' Elizabeth said. 'I encouraged you to go to Cannes. I'm as much to blame for what happened to Sophie as anybody.'

He made a gesture, dismissing her claim. 'I behaved abominably towards you too, didn't I?'

She thought of their first night together on the train. The crushing humiliation she'd felt at their perfunctory lovemaking. But he wasn't thinking of that. He meant when they returned to England and he left again, only leaving her a note.

'It was all a terrible mistake,' she said.

Margaret, the Canadian nurse, had driven them to the village in an ambulance. On the way back to Amiens she stopped at a café to let them out.

'We'll walk the rest of the way,' Elizabeth said.

'Okay. I'll see you when you get back.'

They went inside and sat at a table in a corner. When

the waiter came to take their order, Elizabeth asked for water as she was on duty later. Christopher asked for a large whisky.

'Henry's joined up, by the way,' he said as he lit a cigarette. His drink arrived and he emptied half his glass in a single swallow. 'He's somewhere in Lincolnshire apparently, learning to fly.'

'He always wanted you to teach him didn't he?'

'Yes.' He drained his glass and signalled for another. 'I thought about trying to talk him out of it, but I realised there was no point. He wouldn't have listened to me. I suppose you're surprised to hear me say something like that.'

'Why would you think that?'

'It's not the done thing is it? We're meant to put a brave face on it all. Do our duty for King and country and all that.'

He smiled cynically, and when his drink arrived he emptied his glass without even looking at it. When he lit another cigarette Elizabeth saw that his fingers trembled slightly.

'I met a pilot from William's squadron,' she said. 'His name was Stringer. He told me that William wasn't very popular. Apparently he was very critical of the Flying Corps brass.'

'Was he? Yes, I can imagine him being like that. Good for him. They are bloody fools you know! My squadron was losing men faster than they could be replaced before I came here. The new chaps were lucky if they lasted two weeks. Did you know they won't let us have parachutes?' He snorted with bitter derision. 'They think it would encourage us to abandon our planes unnecessarily, and so men are condemned to burn to death.'

He was angry and disillusioned, and she guessed he hadn't told anyone how he felt before. He cursed the generals as much as he did the German Albatross jastas, and she let him get it out of his system.

'Thanks,' he said eventually.

'What for?'

'For listening. I know I'm not the only who thinks this way, but of course nobody says anything. That's why you told me about William isn't it?'

'I always thought you were alike in many ways,' she said.

'Yes, I suppose we were. I'm sorry everything went wrong you know. I thought a lot of William.'

'Yes, I know.'

'I'm glad that we've met again, Liz.'

'I'm glad too, Christopher.'

'I wouldn't like to think I might ever lose you again.'

'You won't,' she said. 'We'll always have each other.'

'I don't mean just as friends, Liz,' he said quietly.

She didn't answer.

'Look, I know this isn't the right time to be saying any of this. I know you're terribly upset, but I could be leaving again soon and who knows if I'll ever get another chance.'

'It's alright, I'm not upset,' she told him. 'I thought I would be, but I think I've cried all my tears. When William was first brought here I think I always knew deep down that he wouldn't survive.'

'You always talk as if it you're certain it was him. Are you really?'

'I don't think it matters.'

'No, I suppose not. And that's what I'm trying to get at. I know you loved William just as I loved Sophie, but they're gone now. We can't change that can we? But we're here, Liz, we're alive.' He reached across the table and took her hand. 'I love you. I want you to marry me when this war is over.'

'Once, I would have given anything to hear you say that,' Elizabeth said. 'It was all I dreamed of, for you to think of me like any other woman. To love me like any other woman.'

He released her hand, hurt evident in his expression. 'But you don't feel that way now?'

'I don't know how I feel. I love you because I've always loved you. But perhaps we ought to accept that what we feel for one another is a different kind of love.'

'Is it? Perhaps we were simply too young before. We've both made mistakes, but that doesn't mean we should make those same mistakes again. It should make us all the more determined to recognise that it isn't too late for us.'

But she couldn't give him an answer then. She asked for time to think, and he said that of course, he understood.

That night two men in Elizabeth's care died. One of them was a captain from Staffordshire, a burly man of forty whose moustache was as red as his hair. He died without a sound. Though he'd been awake when Elizabeth made her first rounds, when she returned two hours later he was gone. The other was a young subaltern who had lost both his legs. She had seen other men with similar injuries. His legs were blown off high above the knee, and it was a miracle he'd survived the initial shock and loss of blood. She sat with him and talked to him about anything that came into her head. They wanted to listen to her talk about England, about things they knew, and they wanted to listen to a woman's voice, feel the touch of her hand. One minute he was watching her with frightened unblinking eyes, and when she looked again the life had gone out of them.

After her shift ended, Elizabeth went to Christopher's ward. His bedclothes were knotted about his body and his brow was damp from sweat. He muttered in his sleep, and now and then tossed fitfully. After she'd straightened his bed she drew up a chair and sat beside him. She held his hand and spoke quietly to him. The anguished look he wore gradually eased, and the lines in his brow were smoothed and he seemed to sleep peacefully.

Christopher's wounds were healing and it wouldn't be long before he was returned to duty. She knew he was afraid, though he would never admit it. She thought about everything he'd said. She thought he needed her, that she represented the hope of a future. If she gave him that, she was glad. She remembered something her mother used to say about notions of romantic love having nothing to do with marriage. Perhaps she was right. She did love Christopher. Not the same way she'd loved William, but it was love nevertheless. She wanted him to live. Suddenly she saw them as they could be one day, married and living at Pitsford House together. She believed that they could be happy.

In the morning, when Christopher woke, Elizabeth was still there, though she had fallen asleep herself. When he tried to make her more comfortable she woke up and smiled when she saw him. Outside the rain had turned to snow.

27

Outside, the snow was half a foot deep on the fields. In the woods and along the hedgerows, frozen clumps fell from the trees with muffled thuds. At dawn, rooks circled like black scratches against a grey sky.

As he left the barn, William shivered at the bite of the wind. He began to hurry towards the trees. Sleep still fogged his mind and the snow dragged at his feet. When he reached the stream he washed and shaved in the frigid water, scraping his skin with the razor, pulling out the hairs by their roots. At least it woke him up. The cold made his leg ache, though Helene's poultices had healed the bruising, and he no longer walked with a limp. When he was dressed again he sat on a fallen log to smoke a cigarette, and only then did he register his footprints in the snow. Hurriedly he climbed back up the bank and went to the edge of the trees. His tracks cut a vivid slash in the pristine white of the snow leading back to the barn.

'Christ!' he muttered. 'You bloody idiot!'

How could he have been so careless? For almost a month the Lisles had continued their existence oblivious to his presence in their barn. And now he may as well have put up a sign to tell them he was there.

There was nothing he could do except go back to the barn. He walked in his own footprints, though he didn't know what good it would do. Soon Albert would come to milk his cows, and then he would take the animals to their hiding place in the woods and he would see the tracks.

When William reached the hayloft again, Helene had already left for the market. He could see her footprints on the track that led to the road. After a few minutes, Albert appeared and plodded to the barn. As usual he set about milking the two cows, muttering his litany of complaints to an uncaring God, and afterwards collected the eggs and returned to the house. When he appeared again he was carrying his rifle in the crook of his good arm. He set off along the track, his breath clouding in the frigid air. Sometimes when he went hunting, Albert would return with a rabbit or a pigeon or two, or even a pheasant, though Helene said that it was getting harder to find anything to shoot. Except Germans, she'd added with dark humour, and they were tough to eat.

Though he'd been given a reprieve, William wondered why Albert hadn't taken the animals to hide them in the woods, but then he realised it was because of the snow. There was no point, because if the Germans came they would see the tracks. For the moment William was safe. He looked hopefully towards the sky. Perhaps fresh snow would fall and obscure his footprints, or perhaps the temperature would rise and the snow would melt.

Helene had brought him some books, and for a while he tried to read Madame Bovary, but he couldn't concentrate. Instead he sat by the hay doors overlooking the yard, listening to the sounds coming from the dairy where Edith was making butter. Now and then he got up and went to the back of the barn where there was a hole in the brickwork. His tracks remained; a stark testament to his presence.

Towards midday, Albert returned carrying a pair of rabbits. He came into the barn and threw the corpses onto a block he used for chopping wood. He'd already gutted them, but now he took one and held it down with his foot. He removed its head and made a slit along the front legs and with one movement pulled back the skin from the body. He dealt with the second rabbit in the same way, and when he was finished he wiped the blade of his knife and nailed the skins out to dry. As he was doing this Helene came back from the market, her face pinched from the cold. She went into the house and a few minutes later came to the barn.

'What have you got there?' she asked Albert.

'Rabbits,' he grunted without looking at her. 'The snow makes them easy to see.'

He wiped his bloody hands, then went to the water-trough behind the barn. As Helene looked up to the loft William whispered to her urgently.

'I went to the stream this morning. He'll see my tracks in the snow.'

Her eyes widened as she understood, but it was too late. Albert appeared at the door.

'Helene! Come here,' he hissed.

'What is it?'

He gestured. 'Come outside and look.'

William went to the far end of the loft, where he could hear them talking.

'Someone has been here,' Albert said.

'Yes, I was going to tell you.'

'Tell me? Tell me what?' The old man sounded suspicious.

'This morning when I came out of the house, I thought I heard something. I saw a man. I think he had been trying to get into the barn. When he saw me he ran away back to the woods.'

'Who was he?' Albert said in alarm. 'Was he a German soldier?'

'No. I don't know who he was. Just somebody looking for food I expect. I don't think he will come back again.'

There was a short silence as if Albert thought Helene's story sounded all wrong to him, but he couldn't decide why she would make up such a thing. 'What makes you think he won't come back?'

'He looked frightened. He is probably miles away by now.'

But Albert wasn't reassured. He went to have a closer look at the tracks and then followed them a little way before he turned back to Helene. 'You say he ran away, this man?'

'Yes.'

'There is only one set of tracks. He went back in his own footprints. Why would he do that?'

'I don't know. Perhaps it was easier for him.'

Albert stared at her. Finally he trudged back to the barn, and when they went back inside he gestured to the rabbits. 'You can cook those for supper.'

'Perhaps I should keep one of them. I could sell it at the market tomorrow,' Helene said.

'Don't do that. Cook them both. It is a long time since we had rabbit.'

'Are you sure? Perhaps I should ask Edith.'

Albert scowled. 'I am sick of eating stew filled with scraps and acorns, and lately there seems to have been even less than usual. I say cook the rabbits and let us eat a decent meal for once.'

'Alright. If Edith is angry with me - too bad. It will be too late then.'

The old man gave her a sly grin as if they were co-conspirators, his earlier suspicion suddenly forgotten. 'Yes that is right, it will be too late. You are a good girl, Helene. I always said you were a good girl.'

She picked up the rabbits and went across the yard to the house, and after a moment Albert followed her.

That night, Helene was late coming to the barn. When she finally arrived, she sat by the hay doors smoking a cigarette while William ate. He'd come to look forward to her nightly visits. No, it was more than that. He relied on her. She was his only human contact. She brought him food and cigarettes, books to read, news of the outside world. It struck him that she looked very tired. Now and then she peered outside.

'What are you thinking about?' he asked.

She gave a wan smile. 'Nothing.'

'You look tired. You don't have to stay with me.'

'No, I want to. I'm glad you are here.'

'Are you?'

'Of course.'

'Life would be much simpler if I weren't. And you would get more sleep.'

'But I would be lonely. Since you came, I have somebody to talk to.'

He saw her shiver. 'Why don't you come away from there? The wind blows through the gaps.'

'I am alright.'

'You keep looking at the house. Is everything alright?'

'Perhaps I am a little nervous because of what happened earlier.'

'I'm sorry about that. It was stupid of me.'

'It does not matter.'

'That was quick thinking, your story about seeing somebody. Do you think he believed you?'

'I don't know. It was the first thing that came into my head.'

'It reminded me of the day in the square, when you suddenly appeared out of nowhere and started telling me I was a lazy, good for nothing pig.'

She smiled. 'You see, what a nag of a wife I would be. Poor Jean.'

'I think he was very lucky. You must miss him.'

'Yes, but you cannot always look back in life, I think.' She peered at him. 'Can I ask you something?'

'Alright.'

'Why don't you ever talk about your life before the war?'

Her question surprised him. 'I don't know. What would you like to know?'

'That is what you always do.'

'What do I do?'

'You answer a question with another question.'

'I don't mean to.'

She shrugged. 'Perhaps it is better if I do not stay long tonight.'

Suddenly he wanted her to stay. 'Don't go yet. You can sleep if you like. I'll wake you before morning.'

She hesitated, then sat down again beside him. He put his arm around her so that she could lean against him.

'Have you ever loved somebody?' she asked.

He didn't answer at first. He thought of what she'd said about him never talking about himself and he knew it was true. 'Yes,' he said eventually.

'Will you tell me about her?'

'Her name was Elizabeth.' He paused, wondering where to start, how to explain what he'd felt. Then he began to tell her about that summer before the war. As he spoke it all came back to him with startling vividness, and though it ended in pain and tragedy he thought his life since then was like a landscape bleached of colour. A lonely, solitary vigil. Until now.

*****

In the morning, William heard Albert open the barn doors. Helene had already gone and he was half asleep, buried beneath the hay in a corner of the loft. He heard Albert moving about as he fetched the pail to milk the cows, but then there was silence, and after a moment he heard the unmistakeable creak of the ladder. William lay very still, listening intently and imagined the old man standing at the top of the ladder peering into the gloomy space. He tried to remember if he had left anything lying around that would give him away. Helene had brought clothes and a blanket for him over the weeks but he normally took care to keep them hidden underneath the hay. So long as Albert didn't climb all the way up and start poking around, he would see nothing out of the ordinary. After what seemed like a long time the ladder creaked again as Albert climbed back down.

Straight away William crawled to a place where he could peer down into the barn through the cracks between the boards. Albert fetched the milking stool and soon William heard the sound of milk splashing against the pail. But something was different, though it took William a few moments to realise what it was. For once, Albert didn't mumble his complaints against the world, and it seemed to William that there was something unnatural about the way Albert sat. There was a tension in his shoulders he had never seen before, as if Albert was self-consciously aware that he was being observed.

Only after Albert had gone did William get up and look around. He saw what Albert would have seen, nothing more than hay scattered on the floor. But then by the doors he saw a flash of colour. It was the red leather cover of the book that Helene had given him to read; Flaubert's Madame Bovary.

For the rest of the morning he kept a watch on the house to see if the Lisles' behaved any differently from normal. Once, he glimpsed a movement at Helene's bedroom window and he was sure it was Edith.

When Helene came back she went into the house, and shortly afterwards she came across the yard to the barn. As soon as she came in the doors William whispered to her to be careful.

'I think Albert saw something. He climbed up here today.'

A worried frown creased her brow, and then with a nod she went back outside again. For the rest of the day she stayed away. Now and then William caught a glimpse of Edith at the door of the house, or half hidden behind a window as Helene went about her work. He had the feeling the old woman was watching her.

That night, Helene didn't come to him until after midnight. He was very hungry. She gave him a hunk of bread and some cheese, and while he ate he told her what had happened that morning.

'Did they say anything to you?' he asked.

'No, but they are suspicious,' she said. 'When I came back from the market Edith went through my basket to see what I had. She doesn't usually do that. Then after we finished our meal tonight I saw her look in the pot when she thought I wouldn't notice. I think she wanted to see how much was left.' As Helene spoke she unwrapped some cold chunks of meat. 'I saved this from my plate when they weren't looking.'

'I can't eat your food,' William said.

'You must. You need to keep up your strength.'

'So do you.' He took the meat and divided it in half, and told her he would only eat his share if she ate too.

'I have been thinking. I do not think they know you are here,' Helene said.

'What makes you so sure?'

'I know them. Edith has never trusted me. If I am ever later than usual coming back from the market, she asks me where I have been. She wants to know everybody I have talked to.'

'What do you mean?'

'At first when I came here she always went to the market with me. She didn't want to let me out of her sight. She was afraid that I would meet a man and leave them. Once she saw me talking to a man who worked in the market and she called me a whore.' Helene smiled sardonically when she saw that William still didn't understand. 'I think they suspect that somebody is coming here at night. My lover.'

But William didn't think it mattered what their suspicions were. 'If I stay here they're going to find out sooner or later,' he said. 'I've been thinking too. Tomorrow when you go to the market I want to come with you. I'll leave first and wait for you along the track.'

Helene was alarmed at the suggestion. 'It is dangerous for you to go into town.'

'I'm not going to the town. I want you to show me how to get to the German aerodrome.'

'Why do you want to go there?'

'I want to see what it's like. How well guarded it is. I want to see if it would be possible to steal a plane.'

Helene stared at him incredulously. 'You cannot be serious!'

'Why not? Our own aerodromes aren't very well guarded. Why would they be? They're miles behind the lines, so the only thing people worry about is being attacked from the air. I imagine it's probably the same for the Germans. It's at least worth a look. Even if taking a plane is impossible, I might learn something useful.'

'If you are caught the Germans will shoot you as a spy.'

'If I stay here that might happen anyway. If the Lisles' find out about me, you don't really know what they'll do.'

Helene didn't reply, but her silence confirmed that William was right. He felt for her hand in the darkness. 'Don't worry. I just want to have a look anyway. I'll be back by tomorrow night.'

'You promise me that you will come back?'

He felt her eyes on him. 'I promise.'

'Alright. I will show you the way.' She got up. 'I should not stay tonight.'

Reluctantly, he agreed. He said goodnight and listened to her climb down the ladder, then went to the hay doors and saw her cross the yard. Afterwards he watched the window of her room. The house was dark, but for a second he thought he saw her looking back at him.

In the morning, he left an hour before dawn. During

the night it had rained and the snow was gone, the ground turned to mud. He waited near the road for Helene, and when she arrived she gave him a map she'd drawn to show him how to find the aerodrome. For the first part of the way they went in the same direction. As the sun rose, the cloud began to break up, and in the distance they saw aeroplanes heading towards the lines. Helene was quiet, her mood seemed pensive. When they reached an intersection where their routes parted, she warned him that there were often German troops on the road and he must be very careful.

'Don't worry,' he assured her. 'I'm not intending to let myself be caught. I'll see you tonight.'

She stared at him fiercely, almost desperately. Suddenly she kissed him, pressing her mouth hard against his.

'I will be waiting for you, William.'

She turned on her heel, and walked quickly away from him before he could respond. And then he called out her name and she stopped and looked around.

'I'll be back, Helene. I promise.'

She nodded once, a smile touched her lips and then they both went their different ways.

He kept away from the roads, using the woods and hedgerows to keep out of sight. Quite soon he didn't need Helene's map because he saw a dozen Albatrosses returning from a patrol, no doubt to refuel and reload their guns, one of them trailing a thin stream of smoke. When he heard their engines he hid among some trees, and watched them until they vanished below a wooded rise no more than half a mile away.

The aerodrome was in a large field beyond the rise. On one side it was bounded by trees and on the other were the hangers and tents where the mechanics and riggers lived. William found a place to conceal himself and settled down to watch. The single approach road was guarded and there were soldiers posted around the perimeter, though not in great numbers. Two sentries patrolled the wooded side of the field, and whenever they met they paused to talk for a minute or two. They looked bored, and carried their rifles over their shoulders with the air of men who don't expect to have to use them. William timed them, and found that when they separated it took them about three and half minutes to reach the furthest extremes of their patrols before they turned to walk towards each other again. For that three and a half minutes on a dark night, William thought it would be possible to dash across the field to the hangars without much risk of being seen.

He also counted six anti-aircraft positions, which reinforced his idea that the Germans expected any threat to come from the air. He could see mechanics working on machines in the hangers, while the Albatrosses he'd seen earlier were being refuelled and re-armed on the field. Several men who looked as if they might be pilots were standing chatting and smoking outside a wooden building, which he assumed was their mess. After about an hour, more men came outside, and one who appeared to be their leader began to walk back towards the waiting planes. The others followed, and dispersed to their various machines, and one by one their engine's burst into life and the planes began to take to the air. As they passed overhead, William lay on his back to watch them. How many British planes would they send down in flames before the day was over, he wondered?

He kept watch on the aerodrome for most of the day, and by the end of it he knew there were several two-seaters based there, as well as the Albatrosses. As the light began to fade he decided that he'd seen enough and he slipped away through the trees.

On the way back to the Lisle's farm, William kept to the fields and hedgerows until he reached the place where he'd left Helene that morning. After that he walked along the road, though he listened out for the sound of any approaching motor. Perhaps it was because he was distracted by thoughts of Helene that he didn't see the soldiers sooner. He rounded a bend in the road and had already gone another ten yards before he saw a group of them, less than fifty yards away. His reaction was instinctive. He stopped dead and one hand went to the pistol in his pocket. By then he'd taken in the lorry jacked up at one corner, and the wheel lying in the grass. The soldiers were standing around smoking and talking, in no hurry to mend the broken wheel. Their rifles were propped against the side of the lorry. One of them saw William and for a few moments he seemed unconcerned. Even then, William might've got away with it if he'd brazened it out and walked on nonchalantly, but his behaviour made the soldier curious. He called out something and William decided to run.

As he climbed through the hedgerow, William heard shouting. In front of him an open field stretched toward a distant wood, and he realised that for several hundred yards he would be completely exposed. By then, however, he had no choice and he began to run. His leg began to hurt immediately, but he gritted his teeth against the pain and ran as quickly as he could. He was afraid that the distance was too great. His heart was pounding, sweat dripped into his eyes and his breathing was ragged. He was out of condition from being cooped up in the barn for so long and it seemed to take an age to reach even a third of the way across the field. He heard a shot from behind, followed by a ragged volley, and as he felt bullets whiz by in the air he changed direction.

The soldiers continued to shoot as he weaved and dodged towards the trees. He risked looking back and saw that all but one of them had stopped chasing him. He thought they had given up, but he was wrong. The next shot passed so close to his head it sounded like the whine of a mosquito. He dropped to a crouch and dodged to the left as two more shots were fired, both kicking up dirt within feet of him. He looked back again and saw that the soldiers

335

who'd given up the chase were now taking their time, and aiming carefully as they tried to bring him down. Only one still pursued him and he was much closer.

William dived to the ground and rolled, and as he came onto his knees he took out his revolver and aimed with both hands before squeezing off three shots. Taken by surprise, the soldier chasing him threw himself to the ground, and straight away William got to his feet and started running again. He did the same thing again twenty seconds later, though this time he only fired a single shot to conserve his ammunition. Each time, he managed to gain a little distance, and finally he managed to reach the trees, and gasping for breath, plunged into the undergrowth.

As soon as he was out of sight William changed direction. Bullets thudded into the trees wide of their mark. Ahead of him was a long downward slope, the ground carpeted by drifts of rotting leaves, sparse winter limbs all around, the light clear and silvery. As he ran, the slope became steeper and he gathered speed. He skidded and stumbled, somehow managing to leap over fallen boughs as he wind-milled his arms to keep balance. He heard the sounds of pursuit behind him as the soldier crashed into the woods, then a muffled curse. He risked looking back and immediately fell.

When he hit the ground the air was driven from William's lungs. He slithered down the bank and something hard jabbed into his ribs. A shot rang out but the bullet passed harmlessly overhead, and then abruptly he came to rest in a hollow. For a second or two he was stunned, and then he heard the soldier plunging down the slope after him. He looked around and saw that the lip of the hollow would conceal him for a few seconds. Ahead of him another slope rose towards a ridge, but if he went that way he would be exposed. The only cover was a tangled thicket nearby, but even as he stumbled towards it, William changed his mind and threw himself flat on the ground behind a tree, gambling that the soldier would expect him to have run for the thicket, and so that's where his focus would be. A second later he heard the soldier skid to the top of the hollow and stop, and then there was silence.

After what seemed like forever, the soldier worked the bolt on his rifle and climbed cautiously down into the hollow. William hardly dared to breathe. Sweat ran down the back of his neck. He heard the soldier take a step nearer. And then another. He imagined the soldier's rifle trained on the thicket, his finger on the trigger ready to shoot. Very slowly, William raised his head a few inches. The soldier was no more than a few feet away. As he took another step, William moved, and at almost the same instant the soldier realised his mistake. He began to turn, swinging his rifle around at the same time, but William was quicker. He raised his revolver and fired, and the soldier staggered. One hand flew to his throat where blood spurted from a wound and he fell backwards, dying. His legs kicked, and then a gargling sound came from his throat before he lay still.

William approached carefully. The dead soldier was young. No more than twenty. The sound of faint voices carried through the woods, and quickly William turned and began to climb the other side of the slope. He moved from tree to tree, and they didn't see him until he was near the top. A few shots were fired, but by then he was lost to them. He ran on at a slower pace. The sounds of pursuit dwindled until they faded with the dying light, and William slowed to a walk through the comfort of deepening shadows, his hands trembling.

*****

By the time he reached the Lisle's farm it was very late. A sliver of moon revealed the silhouette of the house in utter darkness, the yard outside thick with shadows. William waited for a little while, listening for any sound that shouldn't be there. When he was sure that it was safe he made his way to the back of the barn and slipped quietly inside. He waited for his eyes to become accustomed to the dark. The animals snuffled and moved in their stalls. A wary hen clucked. The ladder creaked as he climbed. All he wanted to do was lie down in the hay and sleep.

The hayloft was empty. He'd hoped Helene might be there. From the hay doors he peered across the yard to the window of her room, but it was too dark to see anything. He heard a sound from nearby and glimpsed a movement in the darkness, but as he reached for his gun he heard Helene's voice.

'William?'

She was sitting in the furthest corner, where the darkness was thickest. He went to her as she stood up.

'I thought you weren't coming back.'

'I ran into some soldiers.' He told her what had happened. 'After that I saw lights on the roads and I heard dogs. I think they were looking for me. I found a stream and walked in it for about a mile to put the dogs off my scent.'

She felt his clothes, which were still wet. He was shivering with cold.

'You have to get dry. Take these things off.'

He didn't argue with her. He was freezing. While he sat down and undid his boots she took off her coat and piled hay into the corner. When he undressed she turned away. She put his wet clothes in a pile.

'I will bring you something else to wear in the morning.'

Though he wrapped a blanket around himself the cold had entered William's bones. He couldn't stop shaking.

'Are you hungry? I brought some food. It was hot when I came but it will be cold now.'

'I'll eat it later.' His teeth were chattering.

'Lie down,' Helene told him.

She lay beside him and covered them with her coat and

some of the hay, and then wrapped her arms around him to keep him warm. Every now and then he would shiver violently and she would hold him tighter. Gradually, he absorbed the warmth from her body and his breathing grew more even and regular, and eventually he slept.

When William woke, he felt Helene's arms around him, her breath on his face. Her eyes were open, watching him.

'I thought I had lost you,' she murmured.

He kissed her. She helped him undo the buttons and clasps of her clothes. In the darkness her body was shadowed and mysterious. He placed his hand on her hip and felt the curve of her waist, the flat plane of her belly. Her skin was smooth, her beasts soft. Men are built for pragmatism, he thought, for work and hardship and strength, all straight lines and angles, while a woman's form promises succour and comfort. Refuge from a hostile world. He lowered his lips to her throat and she put her arms around him and shifted her position to let him lie between her thighs. He entered her and they moved together slowly as they kissed. Heat burst on her skin as if the blood in her veins had turned to fire. He continued to move, kissed her eyes and her mouth and her neck. She breathed in rhythm with their movements and then she stiffened against him and her hands gripped his shoulders tightly. Slowly, the intensity of the moment passed and he felt her body soften and grow languid. She murmured his name and then exchanged places, making him lie on his back. She put him inside her again and moved her hips. He looked up at her and she bent forward to kiss him, her hair soft against his chest, and after he came she lay beside him and for a little while they slept.

Helene stayed until it was almost dawn. When they woke she asked him about the aerodrome and he told her what he'd seen.

'I think it would be possible to steal a plane at night. The best time would be an hour before dawn. I'd cross the lines while it was still dark and land as soon as there was enough light.'

'Will you take me with you?'

He didn't hesitate. 'Yes.'

28

Edith ladled stew into two bowls and carried them to the table. She set one down in front of her husband, who peered at it with sullen resentment.

'What is this?'

'It's your supper, what do you think it is?'

He stirred the thin gravy, pushing aside the vegetables. 'There is no meat.'

'We cannot eat meat every day. Have you forgotten there is a war going on.' She threw him a warning look, but the old fool didn't notice.

'Why didn't you put that pigeon I shot today in here?'

'Phah!' Edith made a dismissive gesture. 'That thing was nothing but feathers and bones. I have seen bigger sparrows than that sorry excuse for a pigeon.'

Albert would have protested again, but as Edith sat down she kicked him hard in his shin, and he looked at her with pained surprise. Finally he saw the look in her eyes and comprehension flooded his expression. Guiltily, he glanced at Helene, and seeing her watching them curiously he lowered his face to his bowl and began spooning stew into his mouth.

Idiot! Edith thought. Barely an hour ago, she'd told him that they would eat the pigeon later after they went to their bedroom. These days he could not remember anything. His head was like a rusty bucket full of holes.

Edith did not see why they should give precious meat to Helene, when it was clear she would only take it to the man she was hiding in the barn. Look at her sitting there! Whore! There was no way of telling how long the bitch had been deceiving them. The thought of her waiting for them to go to sleep every night so that she could sneak to the barn made Edith so furious she did not dare lift her eyes from the table. If Helene saw her face, she would know instantly that her secret had been discovered.

It was all Edith could do to keep her mouth shut. To think the harlot has been rutting like a sow in heat, while her poor Jean lies cold and dead without even a proper grave. How could she do this to them after they had taken her into their home and given her food to eat, and a warm bed in which to sleep, while their son, their poor son, lay dead?

'I saw Monsieur Roussel at the market today.'

Edith looked up in surprise, her furious thoughts momentarily dispelled by Helene's comment. 'Roussel the builder?' she said, wondering why Helene should mention such a thing when it could be of no possible interest.

'Yes. He told me he has very little work. They are finding it difficult to feed their family.'

'Then perhaps he should not have had so many children,' Edith said scornfully. 'That wife of his seemed to have a different brat in her belly every year, as I recall.'

'I don't know about that,' Helene said. 'But his eldest boy was with him. He is fourteen I think. He looked like a very strong boy, and Monsieur Roussel said he is a very hard worker. I think if somebody were to give the boy his keep in return for work, they would do very well from the arrangement.'

'I have seen that boy,' Edith said. 'He is a runt. I do not think anybody would get much work out of him.'

'He didn't look like such a runt to me,' Helene murmured.

Why was she going on about this boy, Edith wondered? It was no concern of theirs what problems the Roussels' may have. Who did not have problems these days?

'Is there more?' Albert demanded suddenly, having finished his stew.

Edith got up and fetched the pot from the range. She put the remaining spoonful into Albert's bowl.

'Is that all there is?' Helene asked when she saw the pot was empty.

'What do you mean?' Edith said. 'You haven't even finished what is in your bowl yet.'

'I just wondered.'

'You always make too much,' Edith said flatly. 'From now on I will cook the meals.'

She smiled maliciously to herself. There, she added silently, what will he eat now, eh? Perhaps he will not be so keen to fuck you on an empty belly!

After supper, Edith and Albert went up to bed as usual. Edith brought out the bread and the still warm pigeon from the cupboard where she had hidden it and divided it between them. Albert ate greedily, fat running down his chin while he sat up in bed. Edith placed a chair beside the window where she could see the yard.

'I went to the stream in the woods today,' she said.

'What for?' Albert said, his mouth full of food.

'Somebody has been going there,' she said, ignoring his question. She had found signs of regular visits. Broken bushes, footprints. 'He has been here for weeks. Perhaps longer. Why would he hide in our barn for so long?'

Albert scowled and shrugged. 'I don't know.'

'He must be afraid of something.'

'What?'

'What do you think? The Germans.'

Albert stopped eating and looked worried. Edith had been thinking about it. She was sure she was right. 'He could be a spy,' she said. 'Or a deserter.' This, she thought, was the most likely answer. Helene was hiding a German deserter. It was bad enough that she would open her legs to

343

another man, but to whore herself to a Hun was unthinkable. Now she had put them all in danger. Whoever it was she was hiding, you could be sure that when the Germans discovered him they would all be shot. She saw the same thought had occurred to Albert. He had forgotten about his food entirely.

'What should we do?' he said.

'That is what I am trying to decide.'

After a while she got up and turned off the lamp. Shortly afterwards they heard Helene come upstairs and go to her room. She moved around and then there was silence. She was listening to make sure they were asleep, Edith thought. And then she would go to the barn as she had every night since Albert had seen the tracks in the snow.

But though Edith remained by the window she didn't see Helene, and they didn't hear her leave her room. Something was different that night. But what? Perhaps Helene had guessed they were suspicious. Or was it more than that? What was it she had said about the Roussel boy earlier? Something about him being willing to work in return for his keep. Why had Helene mentioned such a thing? A suspicion took hold in Edith's mind and as she considered it she began to think it made sense. Albert grunted and snored. Even though her talk of German soldiers had frightened him, he had fallen asleep. Well, let him sleep for now. It would give her time to think.

An hour passed before Edith heard Helene quietly open the door to her room. A moment later she heard the creak of a board on the landing outside and she knew Helene was listening to check they were asleep. Soon afterwards she heard the creak again, and then from the window she saw Helene cross the yard carrying something in her hand. It was a bundle or a bag. Getting up from her chair, Edith went to the bed and woke Albert.

'Get up,' she said when he opened his eyes. 'Get dressed and come downstairs. Hurry!'

Without waiting for him she went next door to

Helene's room, though to Edith it had always belonged to Jean. Even now, when she saw Helene's things, her heart hardened a little more. It was like a piece of rock inside her chest. When Jean went away to Rouen, she had died inside. It was because of Helene that he went. That whore had stolen her son and turned him away from his own parents.

She checked in the drawers and found that some of Helene's clothes were gone, and some of Jean's too.

Downstairs in the darkness, she went to the cupboard and took out Albert's guns and put them on the table. She loaded them by feel, and when he came down she put the rifle into his hands.

'She is going to leave with him,' Edith hissed. Albert looked at her uncomprehendingly and she saw she would have to explain it to him. 'If they are caught by the Huns, she will tell them where she lives and the soldiers will come. You know what that will mean.'

Albert nodded fearfully, and then he turned and went to the door.

*****

When Helene slipped into the barn, William was waiting for her. 'I brought you some food,' she said and gave him bread and cheese. Edith would be angry when she discovered it was gone, but it didn't matter anymore what Edith thought.

'Thanks.' William began to eat. 'Are the Lisles' asleep?'

'I think so. I listened at their door but I couldn't hear anything.'

'You look worried,' he said.

'I think they know.'

'Did they say something to you?'

She shook her head. 'No.' It was the look she'd seen in Edith's eyes earlier. Perhaps she shouldn't have said anything about the Roussel boy, but despite everything Helene couldn't just walk away without trying to do something to help them. Well, she had done all she could. It was up to Edith and Albert now. She thought that Jean would not blame her for what she was doing, he would have wanted her to leave while she had the chance.

They were very different, Helene thought, comparing Jean to William. She knew Jean had loved her fiercely. From the first time they met, she'd sensed his need to be loved. He had been starved of it. He told her later that from that first day at the market, he'd resolved that he would marry her. When a person loves another like that it is difficult to resist, as she had discovered. She knew William didn't love her the way Jean had. There was something about him that was almost unreachable, she thought.

When he'd finished eating, William asked if she was ready. She picked up the small bag she'd brought with her containing a few personal things, while he checked the chamber of his pistol and put it in his pocket.

They went out the back door of the barn and joined the track a hundred yards from the house. Helene looked back towards the farm, relinquishing that part of her life. There was no sound, no movement, and for some reason she couldn't fathom that made her uneasy.

They walked briskly towards the road. There was a cold breeze and occasionally cloud hid the moon, plunging them into thick darkness.

They'd almost reached the road when Albert stepped out in front of them from behind the tree where he had concealed himself. He pointed his rifle at William's chest.

'Stop there!' he said.

'What are you doing?' Helene demanded. Instinctively she stepped in front of William.

Albert ignored her and gestured with the gun. 'Move away from him.'

The mixture of fear and malice she heard in his voice

worried her. She tried to reason with him. 'Albert, listen to me. This man is a British pilot. He has been fighting the German soldiers who killed your son.'

'Shut your mouth! I told you to move away!' The old man was surprised, but after a moment he seemed to decide it made no difference that William was British. 'Do you know what the Germans will do if they find him here?'

'They won't find him. He is leaving.'

'But you are going with him. The Huns will catch both of you and then they will come here. Now do as I say and move away from him.'

'What are you going to do?' He didn't answer her, but Helene guessed his intention. 'If you shoot him,' she warned, 'you will have to shoot me too.'

He stared at her. 'Do you think that I won't?'

'But then what will you do? You and Edith will be alone. You cannot manage without me.'

'What do you care what happens to us?' Albert accused. 'You would have left us.'

'No,' she said. 'Is that what you think? I was not leaving. I was only going to show this man the way past the town, that is all.'

'You are lying,' Albert said, but there was note of uncertainty in his tone.

'I am not lying.' She knew he was thinking and she pressed home her advantage. 'Albert, if you let this man go, then I promise you that I will stay here. Everything will carry on as before.'

Albert appeared to waver. 'Alright,' he agreed finally. 'You stay and tell him to go.' He stood aside and gestured to William with the gun.

But Helene knew he was lying. Albert was a selfish coward, and she knew he would kill William rather than run the risk of him being caught and betraying them. She half turned to William and saw that his hand was in the pocket where he'd put his pistol. She spoke in English so that

347

Albert wouldn't understand. 'He will kill you.'

'What did you say to him?' Albert demanded. 'Get away from him! Get away, I said!'

But at that moment Helene reached out and swept the rifle aside. There was a shot and a flash from the barrel, and at the same time she saw William take out the revolver and point it at Albert, even as he worked the bolt to reload.

'Stop,' William said.

Albert froze. He had ejected the spent cartridge and a new one was in the breech. He stared at them both with rheumy eyes wide with fear, but Helene saw at once that Albert believed William would kill him, because that is what he would do if their situations were reversed, and she knew what he would do.

'No, Albert!' she cried. But it was too late. The old man shoved the bolt home and began to swing the barrel around. A shot cracked in the air and Albert staggered. He looked surprised. The rifle fell from his grasp and he reached out for support, and finding nothing there he fell to the ground.

William lowered the pistol, and for a moment neither of them moved, and then Helene knelt down and put her hand to Albert's neck to feel for his pulse.

'He's dead,' she said. As she looked up she glimpsed a movement in the darkness and realised she should have known Edith would not have stayed at the house. She shouted a warning, but as William began to turn there was a flash and the report of a shot, and he threw his arms out and fell backwards onto the ground. Helene scrambled for Albert's rifle which was lying on the ground beside her, but even as she laid her hands on it, Edith approached and working the bolt to reload, she levelled her gun at Helene's head.

Hatred burned in Edith's eyes. She looked at her dead husband. 'It was not enough that you took my son! Now you have taken my husband! Whore!' She spat a gob of spittle into Helene's face.

'I did not take Jean from you,' Helene said quietly as she wiped her cheek. 'He would have left even if he had never met me.'

'Liar! You are a whore and a liar!'

'You can curse all you like, but you know it's the truth. You talk of love, but you did not love Jean. You only wanted him to stay here so he would look after you when you are old. You didn't care what he wanted. If you loved him you would not have done this.' She gestured towards Albert and William, who lay motionless behind Edith. 'Do you think Jean would be proud of what you have done? He would hate you for this!'

'Do not speak of my son!' Edith screamed at her furiously. 'If he was here, he would have killed this man with his own hands. And then he would kill his whore of a wife too!' She stepped closer and aimed the gun at Helene's face. 'I will send you to hell where you belong!'

Helene stared at her. 'Then do it. I would rather die than spend another minute living with you.'

The shot was loud. Helene flinched, but she didn't feel the bullet. Edith's gun fell to the ground and the old woman crumpled. A few feet away William was still lying on his back, but in his hand he held the pistol. He fell back again, his face creased with pain, his skin pale. When Helene reached him, she felt for his wound. His clothing was soaked with blood beneath his left shoulder, and when she undid his shirt and put her hand inside he stiffened and groaned.

'The bullet has gone all the way through,' she said, feeling the exit wound in his back. There was a lot of blood. It pumped slowly between her fingers. 'Can you sit up?'

'I'll try.'

She helped him and then went to Edith's body. The old woman lay on her side, her eyes open but lifeless, her thin lips drawn back in a grimace over yellowed teeth. Quickly Helene tore the old women's dress to make a bandage, and tied it as tightly as she could around William's chest to stop the bleeding. When she'd finished she helped him to stand.

'Can you walk?'

Beads of perspiration popped on his brow even though it was cold. He nodded, his eyes glazed with pain.

'I'll boil some water at the house and clean the wound properly.'

But William grabbed her arm. 'We can't go back. Somebody might have heard the shots. And I need a doctor. We'll carry on as we planned.'

'But you are hurt.'

'If I can make it to the aerodrome, I'll be alright.'

'Can you fly a plane like this?'

'I think so. Get the gun.' He struggled to his feet. 'We have to hurry.'

*****

From the edge of the trees, William watched the sentries stop to smoke. The tips of their cigarettes glowed red in the dark. They stamped their feet to keep warm and spoke in low voices punctuated by muffled laughter. They were careless, certain of another night of boredom.

He turned to Helene. 'Ready?'

She nodded, though she looked worried. It had taken them much longer to get to the aerodrome than he'd planned. The dressing Helene had put on his wound had stopped most of the bleeding, but William was in considerable pain. The last mile had been the most difficult. He'd had to rest frequently, and even now the world swam and blurred around him, though he tried not to let on. He knew if he didn't follow his plan through now, he never would. He needed a doctor, and it was unlikely that he could make it back to the Lisle's farm.

Two hundred yards of open grass lay between where they were crouched and the hangers. There was a moon, and once they left the cover of the trees they would be committed. They had to reach the other side before the sentries turned to come back. They had timed it. To be safe they could only count on three minutes, and suddenly William doubted that he could make it.

'William,' Helene said. 'The sentries. We must go.'

He saw they had started their patrol again but he hesitated.

'What is it?' she said.

'It's too dangerous.' He took Helene's hand. 'Go back to the farm. If you bury the bodies nobody will know.'

'What about you?'

'I've got to try.'

'Then I will come too,' she said resolutely and he knew she wouldn't change her mind.

'Alright.'

She helped him to his feet and he put his good arm around her shoulders. They began to walk across the field as quickly as they could, but before they had covered a third of the distance William knew they would never do it. The hangars seemed impossibly far away and already the sentries were half way to the ends of their patrol. All it would take is for one of them to glance in their direction and they would be discovered.

'Wait,' he said and when Helene stopped he took his arm from her shoulder. 'We can go faster this way.'

She looked doubtful, but he started to walk and then to run a little. The pain was agonising. Sweat soaked his hair and ran into his eyes, and he was swaying like a drunkard. After a moment Helene caught up with him. She looked back.

'They're almost there.'

He picked up his pace. He saw the hangars through a black fog, and once he stumbled, but somehow managed to stay upright, though he felt strangely disconnected from his legs and knew he was losing consciousness.

'Just a little further,' Helene said, her voice tense.

He forced himself on for her, because her life was in his hands and he owed it to her. From somewhere he found reserves of strength. The hangars were very close. No more than fifty yards. He ran faster, and then finally they were there and he collapsed in the shadows.

'It's alright,' Helene said as she looked back across the field. 'They didn't see us.'

He tried to smile, but he felt light-headed and thought he would be sick. He lay still, feeling his heart pumping too fast, and he took long slow breaths. His shoulder felt like there was a fire burning deep inside somewhere. He was hot all over. They remained hidden where they were until William felt strong enough to move again. He thought that he must have passed out for a few minutes because he couldn't remember how long they had been there.

Eventually, with Helen's help, William struggled to his feet and told Helene to follow him. They made their way to the front of the hangar. It was dark inside. He waited, listening for any sound that would give away the presence of a sentry. From somewhere nearby he heard voices, but inside it was silent. The planes stood in pairs facing out to the field. There were four of them, three Albatrosses and a two-seater. He led Helene to the two-seater and showed her where to put her foot to climb up to the rear cockpit. The observer's cockpit was fitted with a machine gun, which was armed. William hoped that meant the plane was also fuelled. He showed Helene how the machine gun worked.

'If anybody tries to stop us, cock it and pull the trigger.'

She nodded.

When he climbed up to the pilot's cockpit, William found that the controls seemed much the same as a British plane, and once he'd found the switches for the magneto and the fuel he climbed down again and went around the front to prime the engine. As he reached up to turn the prop he felt something give in his wound, then warm stickiness oozed down his side and he knew he was bleeding again. Outside the hangar, the moon appeared through a break in the cloud and the field was washed in pale grey light. He looked up at Helene.

'It's now or never.'

'Then it's now,' she replied.

He switched on, then went around to the front again and took hold of the prop and pulled down as hard as he could. The engine exploded into life, and as quickly as he could manage William climbed up to the cockpit and opened the throttle. As the plane rolled out of the hangar, William saw the sentries across the field standing motionless, too surprised to move. He turned to face the runway and as the plane began to quickly gather pace the sentries shouted out and began to run, un-slinging their rifles at the same time. A shot rang out. William ignored them, focusing his attention on the grass ahead. He glanced at the gauges and began to pull back on the stick. Another shot was fired and the bullet hit one of the wings. The sentries were only fifty yards ahead and to their left, and both of them had had the presence of mind to stop running so they could aim their rifles properly. William willed the machine to lift off the grass, afraid that the sentries would find their target. Suddenly, he heard the heavy bark of the machine gun behind him and clods of dirt flew up around the sentries. Helene fired another burst and both sentries threw up their arms and were spun around, and then the plane was past them and began to lift from the ground.

When the wheels cleared the treetops, William looked down at the figures running all over the aerodrome. He saw flashes from rifle fire and the machine gun barked again as Helene fired off another, long burst.

*****

As the night faded with the sunrise, William began to take the plane down. They had crossed the lines ten minutes earlier, and below them the country was unscathed by fighting. He was eager to land before they were taken for an enemy scout and set upon by an early patrol. He was feeling faint again and his shoulder had begun to throb, the pain coming in waves. He wasn't sure how much longer he could remain conscious.

He chose a grass field bounded by a road to put the machine down. As he approached, he felt the wheels skim the top of a hedgerow and then they hit the ground. The plane bounced and wobbled and then the wheels touched again, and this time William shut the throttle down.

As soon as they stopped he switched the engine off, and as the sound died he leaned back and closed his eyes. A lark hovered overhead, and for once the guns were silent, and all he could hear was its song. From the road came the sound of an approaching engine, and peering across the field he saw a lorry approaching at speed.

'We'd better get out before they start shooting at us,' he said. As he struggled from his seat he turned to Helene. Her head was resting against the back of the cockpit and her eyes were closed. 'Helene?'

He felt her neck for a pulse. Her skin was cold to the touch, and though he couldn't see where she'd been shot he knew she was dead. With difficulty he climbed down onto the grass. An intense weariness overcame him and he sat down. On the other side of the hedgerow the lorry had stopped and soldiers were climbing out. Somebody shouted orders and they began to clamber through the hedge holding their rifles in front of them cautiously. There were half a dozen of them in khaki led by an officer holding a pistol. William closed his eyes.

He heard voices. Somebody said that he wasn't wearing a uniform and then another said there was somebody else in the plane.

'Hands up, Willy!' one of them called out.

Willy. It struck him as amusing and William smiled to himself.

'What's he think's so funny then?' a voice wondered.

Somebody said he was bleeding. William felt the sun on his face, and something wet, which he realised were tears. He heard one of the soldiers climb up on the plane.

'Bloody 'ell, it's a woman. She's dead, sir.'

'Get her down, will you corporal.'

And after that, William heard nothing.

29

As Elizabeth reached for the ward door, her ring caught the light. Christopher had written to his mother to ask her to send it. The ring, a diamond solitaire, had belonged to his grandmother. With a stab of guilt Elizabeth slipped it from her finger and put it on a silver chain she wore around her neck. She told herself that wearing jewellery was against the rules anyway.

The nurse on duty was Margaret. She smiled when Elizabeth came into the ward. 'Hello. I know who you've come to see.'

'Is he awake?'

'I shouldn't think so. But you can go and see for yourself if you like. He's down there at the end.'

Elizabeth hesitated. 'How is he?'

'They think he'll be alright. You know they operated on him this morning?'

'Yes.'

'Are you alright?' Margaret asked, looking at her with concern.

'To tell the truth I'm a bit nervous,' Elizabeth admitted. 'When I heard the news I could hardly believe it. I still can't.' She looked along the ward. 'I think I'm afraid that it won't really be him. That there's been another mix-up.'

'I can understand that. It must be very strange to think that you've buried somebody you care for, and then discover that he isn't dead after all.'

'Yes, it is.'

'You needn't worry though,' Margaret assured her. 'I talked to the Captain who brought him in. Apparently he was drifting in and out of consciousness, but he told them who he was. Apparently there's no doubt.'

'Have you spoken to him?'

'Not yet. He was asleep when I came on.'

Still Elizabeth hesitated, but she couldn't explain to Margaret that she had other reasons to be nervous. She didn't know how William would react when he saw her. For all she knew he hadn't thought of her for years, or perhaps he had, and he hated her. She wasn't sure which would be worse.

'Liz, can I ask you something?' Margaret asked tentatively.

'Yes, of course. What is it?'

'When you were nursing the other chap... the pilot you thought was Lieutenant Reynolds... it was obvious that he meant a great deal to you. I didn't know you well then, and I didn't like to ask, but I've always wondered if... well, how well you knew each other.'

'You mean were we lovers?'

'Gosh, that does make me sound terribly nosy doesn't it?'

'It's alright,' Elizabeth said. 'And the answer to your question is, yes. But it was all rather complicated. We were young. I became very mixed up. There were others involved, you see, and it all ended terribly.'

'You knew Christopher before the war too didn't you?'

'Yes. He and William were friends.'

'Oh dear.'

'Yes,' Elizabeth said wryly.

She found William sleeping. He was pale, but that was to be expected after losing so much blood. He looked thinner than she remembered too, but otherwise he hadn't changed a great deal. His arm and shoulder were heavily bandaged, but as Elizabeth already knew, the wound was clean. He was lucky the bullet hadn't hit a bone. She reached out to touch him, as if to assure herself that he was really there.

She hadn't been certain how she would feel when she saw him. When she'd nursed the burned pilot, her feelings had been complicated by the almost certain knowledge that he would die. She had pitied him as she would anybody so terribly injured. She'd also thought she loved him, but the reality was that she loved a memory. It was an echo of the past.

Now she wondered if perhaps after such a long time, and faced with the man William was now, her feelings might have changed. In a way she hoped that they had because she was engaged to be married to Christopher. Yet she was also afraid of that possibility. When she gazed at his face, however, there was, after all, no confusion, no troubling doubt. Only a welling tide of relief that he was alive, and the absolute certainty that she loved him, just as she always had.

*****

The café where Elizabeth had arranged to meet Christopher was on the corner of Rue Paris, in the old part of the town, not far from the hospital. It was small, and though it did a steady trade with the local people who were its regular clientele, it was never really busy. A few streets away there were several places that stayed open until early in the morning. They hired bands that played ragtime and were filled with soldiers on leave from the trenches.

Christopher was already waiting when Elizabeth entered. He stood up and kissed her cheek.

'Am I late?' she said. 'I'm sorry, we were busy today.'

'That's alright.' He took her coat and they sat down. 'Can you have a drink or do you have to work again tonight?'

'No, I'm off until the morning. Can I have Vermouth

please?'

Christopher gestured to catch the attention of the owner who was behind the counter. 'Un Vermouth, et un whisky, s'il vous plait.'

'Oui, Monsieur.'

'Have you been waiting long?' Elizabeth said, noticing Christopher's empty glass.

'No. A few minutes, that's all.'

He was drinking a lot lately, she thought. 'What happened today?'

'I saw Faversham. I've been given my own command.'

She didn't know what to say. He'd told her that he expected to be given another posting, but she'd hoped he would be sent back to England to train new pilots or something.

'You don't look very pleased, Liz,' he said. 'It'll mean a promotion in due course. Major Christopher Horsham. It has a rather distinguished note, don't you think?'

He was putting a brave face on it, Elizabeth thought. Perhaps that was what she was expected to do as well, but she knew he was hiding what he really felt. 'I'm sorry, I can't pretend to be pleased that you're going back to the fighting.'

'Don't worry. We all have to do our bit, you know.'

'You're forgetting that I'm a nurse. Every day I see what happens to people who do their bit. And they are the lucky ones.'

She sounded bitter. It happened to everybody sooner or later. Disillusionment set in, the futile questioning. Nothing changed, and sometimes she wondered if anything ever would. Perhaps the world would keep fighting until there was simply nobody left to fight. Christopher emptied his glass and signalled for another.

'I'm sorry,' she said. 'I must be tired I expect. Don't take any notice of me. Tell me about your posting.'

'That's the spirit. Anyway, you needn't be so glum

about it. I haven't told you the best part yet. It's a completely new squadron. We're getting the new SE5s.'

She had heard of the Flying Corp's new plane. The pilots were all talking about it as the answer to their prayers.

'It seems the brass have decided at last to take a leaf out of the Hun's book. They're equipping entire squadrons with the new machines,' Christopher went on. 'And by all accounts they're more than a match for the bloody Albatrosses.'

He seemed genuinely enthusiastic, even excited by the prospect, which puzzled her. She thought it must be for her benefit, so that she wouldn't worry about him.

'Don't,' she said quietly.

'Don't what?'

'Don't pretend like this. I know how you really feel about going back to the fighting. I don't want you to pretend for my sake. I want us to be honest with each other.'

'Yes, I can see how you'd think that,' he said. 'Sorry, I should have realised. But the truth is everything is different now, Liz. The SE5 will turn the tables.' He appeared to actually mean it.

'Can these planes really make such a difference?' she wondered.

'Absolutely! Fifty six squadron proved it. They were the first to get them. They shot down four Albatrosses on their first outing.'

His new found confidence confused her. 'I'm sorry, I expect I'm just being selfish because I've become used to us being together.'

'Yes, of course, I feel the same way,' he said. 'But the chateau where we're going to be based is only about ten miles from here, so I'll still be able to get back and see you.'

He ordered more drinks and they asked for a plate each of the café's speciality cassoulet.

'I went to see William earlier,' she said.

Christopher reacted. He reached into his pocket for his

cigarettes even though he had just put one out. When he met her eye again there was a hint of trepidation in his gaze. 'I thought you must have. I didn't like to ask. How is he?'

'He had an operation on his shoulder, but apparently he'll make a full recovery.'

'Good.' Christopher twirled his glass and stared into its contents. 'You must have had a lot to talk about.'

'I didn't speak to him. He was asleep.'

'Oh, I see.'

'I don't even know if he'll want to see me when he wakes up.'

'I suppose that's possible. But you will at least try I expect?'

'Yes.'

'Of course. Will you tell him that you tried to find him?'

'No,' she answered, having already decided.

He was surprised. 'Why not? After all, you came to France because of William. Why wouldn't you tell him the truth?'

'Because there's nothing to be gained by telling him now,' Elizabeth said. 'And he's only part of the reason that I came here. I do want to see him. I want to tell him that I'm sorry because I think I behaved terribly once, and I suppose the truth is I'll never feel comfortable until I've done that. But everything has changed now, Christopher.'

'Has it?' he asked. He glanced at the engagement ring on her finger again, and suddenly Elizabeth understood why he had been so determinedly positive about his new posting. She guessed what he was about to say.

'Liz, when I asked you to marry me, you believed William was dead. We both did, otherwise I would never have asked. But I feel it would be wrong of me to hold you to our engagement if you feel differently now.'

He was being noble, Elizabeth thought, doing what he thought was right and honourable. That was why he pretended to be so pleased about his new squadron. But she knew him and despite what he said, she understood he needed her. He talked about their future often, about the things they would do when they went home. He even talked about children. She sometimes thought that without this vision of their future life he wouldn't be able to carry on. She knew then that her own feelings and desires were unimportant. Once, her selfishness had resulted in terrible consequences, but she would not repeat the mistakes of the past. Though she loved William, she would never reveal her feelings to anyone.

'You don't have to hold me to anything,' she said. 'Because I want to marry you. I want to be your wife, Christopher.'

He looked into her eyes and she could see how much he needed to believe her. But he still doubted her. 'Can I ask you something?'

'Of course.'

'What did you feel when you saw him?'

A flippant response sprang to her mind, but Elizabeth knew that he would see through it and so she tried to be as truthful as possible. 'I felt the love that anybody would feel for an old friend, and sorrow for the way I behaved.'

'Then you're not in love with him?'

'No, Christopher, I'm not in love with him.'

He smiled. 'I can't tell you how glad I am.' He squeezed her hand tightly.

After their meal they walked to the hotel where Christopher had been staying since he left the hospital. The concierge on the desk glanced at Elizabeth disapprovingly as they crossed the lobby, but she had long since given up caring what people thought. She spent the night with Christopher whenever her shifts allowed, perhaps twice a week. Old fashioned notions of propriety seemed pointless in the midst of the war.

When they reached his room he asked her if she

wanted a drink.

'Yes, alright. A small one please.'

He poured her a whisky and brought it to her. 'I'd like to see him, you know.'

'William?'

'I want to explain. Apologise, I suppose.'

She was surprised, and yet when she thought about it she didn't know why she ought to be. They had been friends. Good friends. That was the point wasn't it? What made it all such a betrayal.

'Will you tell him for me that I'd like to see him?'

'Of course.' She got up and kissed him. 'I'd better not have any more. I've got an early start.'

She went through to the bedroom and undressed. When she got into bed she turned out the light. She knew Christopher wouldn't come through yet. He always stayed up late drinking whisky. He was avoiding her. Or perhaps it would be more accurate to say that he was avoiding physical intimacy. The first time she'd stayed with him after he asked her to marry him, he had tried to make love to her but couldn't. He blamed his wound. He said the drugs affected him. She hadn't minded of course. But when it happened several more times, she realised it wasn't his wound. He worried about it, apologised repeatedly, but even though she did everything she could to reassure him, she knew he felt humiliated by what he saw as his failure. It was the war, she told him. They would have all the time in the world for that sort of thing when it was all over, when they were married. He was grateful to her. Now he avoided the situation altogether by waiting until he thought she was asleep before he came to bed.

She sensed he was standing in the doorway watching her. Her eyes were closed and she breathed evenly. After a little while he undressed and got into bed beside her. She waited for him to put his arms around her but he never did. She thought he was afraid she would wake up. After a few minutes she turned around and let her arm fall over his chest, still feigning sleep. Eventually he kissed the top of her head.

When she woke it was pitch black. Christopher was mumbling and thrashing his arms about. Elizabeth got up and turned on the lamp. She fetched a damp cloth and mopped his brow. He was feverish, the bedclothes twisted tightly around his body. She untangled him and then lay beside him and held him.

'It's only a dream,' she whispered. 'You're safe now.'

She thought on some level he must hear her and understand. Gradually he quietened down, as he always did. When she was sure he was sleeping she kissed him and went to the window to look outside. She thought about their conversation earlier. Christopher had asked her if she was in love with William, and when she said that she wasn't, she knew she ought to have told Christopher she was in love with him, but she hadn't. He'd offered to break off their engagement, and she had told him there was no need because she wanted to be his wife, but she hadn't said that she was in love with him then either. It struck her that she'd never said those words to Christopher, and she wondered if he'd noticed.

He was sleeping peacefully at last. It would be morning soon, she thought. She might as well get dressed and go back to the hospital.

30

The day room was quiet. A man sat alone in a corner with a book open on his lap, though often he gazed into an invisible distance, and he hadn't turned a page for half an hour. Two others, one of them whose left leg ended just below the knee, played chess. They were hunched intently over their game, neither of them speaking other than an occasional murmur of quiet admiration for a move the other had made. William occupied one of four chairs that had been arranged around a table beside a window, fussed over by a nurse who spoke with a Canadian accent.

'You really shouldn't be out of bed so soon,' she said as she examined his dressing. 'I'm sure this must hurt.'

He winced as she moved his shoulder. 'I just can't lie there doing nothing. Anyway, it'll get better just as quickly here as in the ward won't it?'

'I suppose so. But you'd better get back before the doctor comes around later or I'll get into trouble. We have to take special care of you. Everybody's talking about you, you know.'

William was aware of the attention he was attracting. People had been coming up to him in the ward all morning, and though he knew they meant well he didn't want to talk to anybody. It was why he had come to the dayroom.

'Is there anything I can get for you?' the nurse asked.

'No, I don't think so. Unless you've got a cigarette?'

She took a packet from her pocket. 'You can keep them if you like. I've got some more anyway.'

'Thanks,' he said gratefully. 'I'm afraid I don't know your name.'

'It's Margaret.'

'Are you Canadian?'

'Yes. I'm from Ontario. My parents are from Scotland originally. I've never been there myself, but I'd like to go when the war is over. Have you been there?'

'No, I'm afraid not.'

The nurse told him about the town where her mother was born. It was on the west coast somewhere, little more than a village by the sound of it. He half listened to her, imagining mountains and lochs.

'Well, I ought to be getting on,' she said. 'I expect I'll see you later. Just try not to move your arm at all.'

He thanked her, and when she had gone he gazed out of the window. In the garden two patients wearing khaki coats over their pyjamas were sitting on a bench in watery sunshine. They were smoking, neither of them talking.

William took a cigarette from the packet the nurse had given him. He tried to strike a match, but it was difficult to manage with his arm bandaged up and he dropped the entire box, scattering matches all over the floor. He looked at them helplessly and suddenly was engulfed by a rush of frustrated rage.

'Shit!'

The other patients looked at him curiously. He hurled the cigarette packet angrily at the window, and when it fell harmlessly to the floor he looked around for something more substantial. He wanted to smash the glass into a million fragments, but there was nothing close enough to reach. Then all at once, the anger that had consumed him so suddenly, drained away and he slumped in his seat.

The chess players resumed their game, while the reader picked up his book and turned a page before his attention wandered again and he gazed off into space.

William heard the nurse come back into the room, her

heels clacking on the floor. Without saying anything she crouched at his side and began picking up the matches he'd spilled. He supposed she'd seen enough not to be unduly worried by something like this. He thought of Helene sitting still and cold in her seat. He'd wanted to ask about her when he woke up, but for some reason he couldn't. Perhaps he didn't want to believe she was dead. He thought that was it. He recalled the coldness of her skin when he touched her. With her eyes closed she had almost appeared to be sleeping.

'There was a woman with me when I crashed,' he said at last. 'Do you think you could find out what happened to her?'

The nurse didn't reply. He realised she wasn't actually the Canadian nurse. It was odd the way she kept her face turned away from him. She seemed familiar though he couldn't put his finger on why. 'Are you alright?' he asked.

'Yes…. I'm afraid the woman you asked about was dead when you were found.'

Her voice prompted a jolt of recognition. She turned towards him and he saw it was Elizabeth. He was dumbfounded. He felt as if he were in some kind of surreal dream. For several moments neither of them spoke, and then she passed his cigarettes and lit a match for him. He knew he ought to say something, but he felt incapable of speaking.

'I'm sorry, William… Did you know her well?'

He found his voice. 'Yes. She helped me after I crashed. She saved my life. Do you know where they will have taken her?'

'I'm not certain. There's a cemetery near here where she might have been buried. I'll find out for you.'

'Thank you.' He should have been there, he thought. He realised that her grave would be unnamed, just a cross among rows of others. Nobody knew who she was. He looked away, back out towards the garden. He wanted to ask Elizabeth how she came to be there. He wanted to ask a hundred questions, but none of them would form into words.

'I shouldn't have come like this,' Elizabeth said in response to his silence.

She thought it was his reaction to her, he realised. A rebuke. Fractured images flew into his mind and fled. A dance somewhere, years ago now. The two of them walking outside in the summer air. In the hay-barn where they lay together, her eyes closed, naked, arms around him, whispered endearments.

He didn't hear her get up, and when he turned to look she had reached the door. He found his voice again. 'Would you tell somebody her name. It was Helene. Helene Lisle.'

At least her grave would be marked. He remembered that she had family in Rouen. At least when the war was over they would be able to find her.

'Yes, alright,' Elizabeth said.

'Thank you.'

He heard her open the door, and then her heels as she went along the corridor.

*****

He felt tired later and went back to the ward to sleep. When he woke he walked the corridors of the hospital looking for Elizabeth. He found her working in another ward, and for a few minutes he watched her, unobserved. She looked tired and thinner than he remembered, but he supposed the same could be said of him. Nevertheless she often smiled as she tended the men in her care and stopped to speak to them. He slipped away before she saw him, disturbed by the things he felt for her.

When he saw her again it was late. She had gone outside at the end of her shift and was smoking a cigarette in the garden. When he opened the door she looked to see who it was.

'Do you mind if I join you?' William asked.

'No. Of course not.'

She helped him light a cigarette and they stood in uneasy silence. 'How long have you been here?' he asked in the end. Like strangers he thought, passing the time.

'About nine months now.'

'I was posted nearby before I was shot down,' he said. 'Strange to think that you would have been here then.'

'Yes. I suppose it is.'

Occasionally he'd daydreamed, or perhaps fantasised was a better term, that one day they would meet again. He'd always thought it would be in England. Somehow or other he would have made a success of himself by then and he would see her with Christopher across a crowded room. Perhaps a restaurant. Their eyes would meet and she would react. A small shock of recognition. Then she would turn to Christopher and say something and he would look across the room. He never knew what happened after that.

He realised belatedly that she had said something to him. 'I'm sorry, what did you say just then?'

'I asked how your shoulder is feeling?'

His hand went to it automatically. 'Oh. It's alright. A bit sore. I was lucky apparently.' He saw another silence stretching ahead of them.

'William,' she said, sounding abruptly resolute. Like somebody taking a breath before leaping into the unknown. 'I want to say I'm sorry for what happened...' Elizabeth hesitated, groping for words or else simply uncertain of how he would react. And then having already begun, she appeared to cast her doubts aside and spoke in a rush.

'I know you must have hated me and I don't blame you. I don't know how to explain it, and I don't why you should forgive me, but I want you to know I regret it. I was stupid and selfish.'

She paused, looking at him with a sort of beseeching expression. Almost pleading. It made him realise that she had thought about this for a long time. Perhaps even rehearsed it. He was taken aback that she wanted his forgiveness and that it appeared to mean so much to her, but he was uncertain exactly what she was apologising for.

'I convinced myself that it was all for the best,' she went on. 'I told myself it would be better for Sophie if Christopher left, but I wasn't thinking of her really, I was thinking of myself. I couldn't admit it though.'

He understood that she had lived with the belief that Sophie's death was her fault. 'You couldn't have known what Sophie would do,' he said.

'Perhaps not, but that doesn't absolve me. We came back, you know, as soon as your telegram arrived to tell us about Sophie. We caught the next train, but by then you'd already left.'

'There was no reason for me to stay,' he said.

'Of course, the fire,' she said, though that wasn't really what he meant. 'I'm so sorry, William.'

'It's alright.'

'No it isn't. I wish it had all been different. I wish Sophie was alive, and I wish I'd had the courage and decency to talk to you and at least try to explain things that day. But I was a coward and I've always regretted it. I suppose we all do foolish, hurtful things in our lives. The important thing is to recognise them and learn from them. Don't you think? Perhaps then, if we can, we can make amends.'

'Yes, I think you're right,' he said and her relief was visible.

'You can't imagine how it feels to finally say this... I've wanted to for so long...'

Her sorrow was genuine, William thought. All this time he had tried not to think about her, but deep down he had wondered how she had felt when she and Christopher received his telegram. He was glad that she was affected by what happened. She hadn't forgotten it all, or worse, dismissed it as if it had been a thing of no consequence, which is what he'd imagined during the moments when he thought the worst of her.

Only then did he realise that he had imagined this scene, perhaps in his sleep. It always ended with Elizabeth confessing that she loved him, after all. He smiled wryly to himself at the vanity of such foolish dreams.

'It's alright,' he said. 'It's alright.'

*****

The following morning Elizabeth came to see him in the dayroom, and this time it was easier between them.

'They're saying you're bound to get the MC,' she said.

'Who are 'they'?'

'People. Everybody. Haven't you heard anything?'

'Actually, I'm seeing somebody later on today. From HQ,' William said. 'I think his name is Jarvis.'

'You must be pleased.'

William thought of Helene and wondered what he should be pleased about. People came up to him wanting to shake his hand. They said it was wonderful that he'd stolen one of the Hun's planes from under their very noses like that. He wanted to tell them that if it wasn't for Helene he would never have survived.

'Can I ask you something?' he asked, changing the subject.

'Of course.'

'I was wondering about Christopher. How he is?'

She was glad that he'd asked, he saw. He supposed she didn't know how he felt after all this time. It was as if she let out a breath that she'd been holding in.

'He's fine. He's a pilot too. In fact he was wounded. He's here.'

'Here?' William looked around, his heart racing, surprise and other darker emotions leaping, half expecting to see Christopher standing at a doorway.

371

'In Amiens,' she said quickly. 'He was discharged from hospital. He'll be leaving again in a few days, actually. He's been posted to a new squadron. We're engaged to be married.'

She had blurted it out in a rush and William wondered why she seemed so anxious. Her news surprised him, but only because he'd assumed they would already be married.

'Congratulations.'

'Thank you.'

He took out a cigarette and offered her one.

'I can't, I'm on duty.' She struck a match for him. 'He'd like to see you before he leaves. If you want to.'

He thought about it for a moment. 'Yes,' he said truthfully. 'I'd like that.'

*****

That afternoon, Margaret, the Canadian nurse, came to tell William that Major Jarvis had arrived to see him. She showed him to an office used by one of the doctors. He knocked and went inside.

'Ah, Captain Reynolds, I presume? Jarvis. Pleased to meet you. Do sit down. Do you smoke?'

'Thank you, sir. But actually it's Lieutenant Reynolds.'

'Not any more it isn't. Hasn't anybody told you? You've been promoted, old man.'

'No, I wasn't aware of it.'

'Well, never mind.' Jarvis made a casual gesture and lit their cigarettes. 'I don't suppose the good doctor will mind us fogging up his office. I'm only borrowing it, you see.'

The room was cramped. Files and papers clogged every surface, overflowing from the battered wooden desk onto the floor. A number of leather bound medical texts occupied a shelf, though one had been removed and was lying open on top of some papers. Jarvis peered curiously at an illustration of a pair of human lungs.

'Remarkable,' he observed. 'I understand that the war

has advanced medical knowledge considerably, you know. I suppose it just goes to prove that there's a positive side to any situation.'

Jarvis smiled. His lips were thin and unusually pink, his eyes a pale watery blue. William could think of no response to his remark, though he thought of the young infantry lieutenant occupying the bed next to his own. Would he be consoled by the knowledge that, while the loss of half his innards might be distressing for him, it would nevertheless yield interesting information for medical science?

'Speaking of medical matters,' Jarvis continued. 'How's that shoulder feeling? I understand you're recovering very well.'

'Apparently I was lucky,' William said, his mildly ironic tone going undetected.

'Jolly good. Better than being six feet under, I expect. You're something of a Lazarus.'

'Sir?'

Jarvis peered at him. 'Hasn't anybody told you that either? You're supposed to be dead, Reynolds. There was a bit of a mix-up. Actually, I don't suppose you know any of this, do you? The thing is that when you were originally shot down, the rest of your patrol bought it too. There were no survivors. Except the chap who was flying the other Nieuport. What was his name?'

'Wright.'

'Yes, that's the fellow. Anyway, he came down on our side of the lines, but his plane was hit by an enemy shell. There was no way to tell which of you he was. He was badly burned, you see.'

Looking back, the last William remembered of Wright was his plane trailing smoke. 'You said he survived, sir?'

'Yes. But not for long I'm afraid. He died after a few days, but the official records show that he was you. It seems somebody made a bit of a cock-up. Somewhere nearby,

Reynolds, there's a grave with your name on it. Which is why I'm here. Partly anyway.'

'I'm sorry, I'm not sure that I follow your meaning.'

Jarvis leaned back, smoke wreathed about his head. 'It's quite simple. We have to decide what to do with you.' He surveyed the mass of papers in front of him then began clearing a space, stacking everything to one side. When he was satisfied, he opened a plain folder and produced a pen and a bottle of ink.

'You've pulled off something of a coup, Reynolds. Not only have you managed to return from the dead, which by itself might have made an interesting side story for the press, but you've done it in rather a spectacular fashion. It's never happened before, you know. One of our own swiping a bloody plane from right under the Hun's noses. I expect they must be hopping mad about it. It's a shame you didn't get an Albatross of course. I suppose there weren't any?'

'The Albatross is a single-seater, sir.'

'What? Oh, yes, quite. The woman who was with you. I'll get to that in a moment. First things first, though.' He took the top off his pen and poised it over a blank sheet of paper. 'Now, I'd like you to tell me everything that happened to you from the moment you crashed. Try not to miss anything out.'

As William talked, Jarvis made notes. Occasionally he would ask William to clarify something, or to wait while he caught up. He was interested to hear about the execution William had witnessed in the square at Cambrai.

'A man and a woman, you say?'

'Yes. Helene told me they were accused of being spies.'

'Helene? I take it she was the young woman who escaped with you?'

'Yes.'

'How did you meet her?'

He described what had happened in the square. How

she had pretended to be his wife scolding a lazy husband. He found he could recall every detail. The feel of his hand gripping the revolver in his pocket, the questioning look of the young German soldier before Helene suddenly appeared, and then his own surprise at finding himself berated by this angry, nagging woman with blazing eyes. He saw her as clearly as if she were standing before him at that moment, and then he thought of her again the last time he'd seen her when her head had rested against the side of the cockpit, her skin pale and cold to his touch. The words caught in his throat. Jarvis looked up.

'What happened after that?'

'She took me to the farm where she lived.' He went on to explain how Helene had hidden him in the barn.

'Her parents weren't aware of your presence?'

'They were her husband's parents.'

'Ah, yes. He was killed, you say?'

'Yes.'

'Why didn't she tell them about you?'

'Because she wasn't sure how they would react.'

'You mean she thought they might report you to the Germans?'

'She didn't know what they would do.'

'She didn't trust them?'

'It was just the kind of people they were. They were old. Helene didn't actually get on with them very well.'

'Really? Why not?'

'I think they resented her. They imagined she was to blame for taking their son away.' William was suddenly annoyed by Jarvis's questions. 'Why are you asking me all this?' he demanded.

Jarvis looked up. 'If you wouldn't mind continuing, Captain,' he said coolly.

Reluctantly, William continued. He described how he began to form a plan to escape after he had visited the German aerodrome, but things almost went wrong when the

Lisles had discovered his presence. 'After that, I thought it was best to leave straight away.'

'And you decided to take Helene with you?'

'Yes. We left that night. But the old man, Albert, confronted us before we reached the road.'

'Confronted you?'

'He had a rifle.'

William related everything that happened, ending with him shooting Madame Lisle.

Jarvis was shocked. 'Good God! Was the old woman dead?'

'Yes.'

'But you believe their intention was to kill you, in order to prevent Helene leaving them to manage alone?' There was a faint but unmistakeable note of incredulity in Jarvis's tone. 'Even though they resented her?'

'I have no doubt of it. It wasn't only that that they didn't want her to leave, they were afraid of what would happen to them if I was caught.'

Jarvis studied what he'd written thoughtfully. 'What exactly was your relationship with this young woman, Reynolds?'

'What do you mean, sir?'

'I think you know what I mean. You know how these country folk can feel about certain things. Family loyalty and so on. After all, this woman was their son's wife.'

'Their son was dead,' William reminded him.

'Quite.' Jarvis lit another cigarette and got up from his seat to stand at the window. 'As I mentioned, your escape has caused quite a stir. The newspapers want to write about you. You're to be awarded the MC by the way.' He paused. 'We've been considering the idea of a tour.'

'A tour?'

'Public relations, Reynolds. Send you back to England, arrange speaking engagements, newspaper interviews and so on. Give the public a chance to see a genuine hero. It's not the sort of thing we go in for ordinarily, of course. But the fact is, the Flying Corps has had rather a difficult time of it during the past few months. We're desperately short of pilots, and it isn't quite as easy to attract new recruits these days. Everybody's heard rather too much of Von Richthofen and his merry men, I'm afraid. A story like yours might provide us with some much needed publicity in our favour. At least that was the idea. To be frank, I'm not so sure now.'

Jarvis came back to the desk and lifted a corner of his notes. He seemed to make up his mind and offered a pink, watery smile. 'I think we'll leave it there for the moment, Captain.'

William stood up, realising that he was being dismissed.

'Just one other thing,' Jarvis said as William reached the door. 'I think it would be best if you don't talk about any of this for the moment. I'm sure you understand. You haven't told anybody I take it?'

'No, sir.'

'Jolly good. Better to keep it that way then, I think. You carry on resting that arm and I'll come and see you again shortly. Thank you, Captain.'

*****

Helene had been buried in the cemetery outside Amiens. Her grave was marked with a simple wooden cross that had now been inscribed with her name and the date of her death. William imagined a life they might have had together after the war was over. He thought they could have been happy. He would have loved her. She had brought something to life in him again, made him see that love and pain go hand in hand, and without them both, life is meaningless.

Before he left, William looked for Wright's grave, though he supposed it would be his own name on the grave until somebody sorted out the bureaucratic mix-up, if they ever did. He thought he would send a letter to Wright's family, so at least they would know the truth. Perhaps one day it would give them some comfort to visit here and know their son had received a proper burial. But though he walked back and forth among the rows of crosses he couldn't find one that bore either his name or Wright's. Perhaps there was another cemetery.

That evening, Elizabeth came to see him again and this time she brought Christopher with her. William shook his hand.

'Hello, Christopher.'

'Hello, William. I'm glad to see you again.'

He was saddened at Christopher's appearance. Though he'd thought Elizabeth looked tired, and he was sometimes taken aback by his own drawn appearance when he used a mirror to shave, Christopher had the haunted look many pilots took on after a while. It was in their eyes, a kind of bleakness.

Whatever lingering uncertainties remained regarding his feeling towards both Elizabeth and Christopher, they finally dissipated at that moment. William knew that what had hurt him as much as anything, was that when they'd left he had felt rejected. He thought if he could have them both as his friends again he would be grateful. He didn't regret knowing them or having loved them in their different fashions, any more than he regretted loving Helene. If he regretted anything, it was only the years in between, when he had forgotten how to feel much at all except a profound loneliness that had threatened to corrode his soul.

31

Elizabeth paused at the door. The chair where William often sat by the window in the day room, was empty. One of the men who could normally be found playing chess looked up from the paper he was reading. His usual opponent had been sent home, though all the pieces were set up on the board ready for a game.

'Hello,' the man said. 'If you're looking for Reynolds, I think you'll find him outside.'

Though he smiled at her, Elizabeth thought she detected the merest hint of resentment in his tone, as if there couldn't be any other reason for her to be there these days. She started to say that actually she wasn't looking for William at all, but the man had already returned to his paper.

'Thanks,' she said and he looked up again and gave her a cheery smile that proved her wrong. It was guilt, she thought. She was afraid she wore her feelings for anyone to see.

She found William in the hospital garden. He was sitting alone in the spring sunshine, carefully flexing his arm. His wound was healing quickly. She watched him from the doorway, unobserved. This is how it would be, she thought. Watching him from a distance, her feelings held close. She wanted to go to him, to touch him. It was almost an overpowering urge, but she could live with denial just to see him, to know that he was alive and well. She tried to convince herself of that, and yet just as when she tried to imagine the future, when they were all back in England, she found that she couldn't.

When she joined him he turned to her and smiled. She lifted her face to the sun to mask an ache of longing. 'It's wonderful to feel the sun isn't it?' she said.

He looked toward the cerulean sky. Barges of cotton cumulus drifted with the breeze. He frowned.

'Why do you look like that?'

'It's nothing.' He shrugged. 'A bad habit. It's a good day for flying.'

'Oh, I see.' The war. Everything revolved around the bloody war! Even a sunny day couldn't be enjoyed for its own sake. Sometimes Elizabeth wondered if people would ever be the same again.

'Christopher's leaving tomorrow,' she said. 'He's booked a table at a club in the town. Will you come?'

'Of course.'

'Do you remember his brother, Henry?'

'Yes. He was at Pitsford for a little while when I was there.'

'That's right. Anyway, he's here, in Amiens. He's been posted to Christopher's squadron.'

'I remember that he wanted to fly. How long has he been in France?'

'He only just arrived. It's his first posting. Christopher's pleased, I think. He says he is anyway.'

'What do you mean?'

'I think he's worried too. I met Henry yesterday. I haven't seen him for years, but of course he's completely grown up now. He's very keen to fight.'

They were all like that when they arrived. A mixture of bluff and bravado masking their true feelings. Most of them had heard enough to have the good sense to be nervous. You could see it in their eyes, no matter what they said. But there were still some like Henry, for whom the whole thing was a glorious adventure. King and Country. Honour and Duty. Young men, Elizabeth thought, often didn't value their own lives until the moment when it was about to be taken away.

She became aware that William was looking at her with a slightly puzzled frown. 'What is it?'

'I was thinking about what you said, about not seeing Henry for years. Wouldn't you have seen him at Pitsford?'

'Oh, I see. Actually Christopher and I didn't see each other for quite a long time,' she said.

'Oh? I thought...'

'No. After we came back from Cannes, Christopher was very upset about Sophie. We didn't meet again until Christopher was wounded.'

'You mean here, at the hospital?'

'Yes.'

She could see him thinking about that. She knew he must've assumed that their engagement was the natural result of the intervening years together. It would be so easy to tell him the truth, Elizabeth thought. She only had to explain that she'd tried to find him and had travelled to Shoreham and eventually to France because of him. But she wouldn't do that. 'It's strange how things work out, sometimes,' she said.

'Yes, it is. I'm glad.'

'Are you?'

'Yes, for you. Both of you.'

'Thanks.'

They sat in silence for a little while. She wanted to ask him where he'd gone after he left Pitsford. What had his life been like before the war? Had there been another woman? Had he fallen in love again? Had he hated her?

'Are you worried about Christopher,' he said.

She realised he'd been watching her and had misunderstood her silence. A guilty flush burned her cheeks. 'Yes, I am,' she said. 'Can I ask you something? Are you frightened when you fly?'

'Everybody is. Some people cope with it better than others, but I think it gets to everyone in the end.'

'I think Christopher is afraid. Perhaps I shouldn't be saying this. I know he wouldn't want me to. Do you remember at Sywell, when poor Nigel Wentworth was killed?'

'Yes.'

'Of course you do. That was a stupid question. The thing is I'm sure it affected Christopher. He has nightmares. He dreams that he's burning.'

'A lot of men worry about that. It's the worst thing that can happen.'

'It didn't help that when he first came here...' Elizabeth stopped herself.

'What happened when he came here?'

'There was a pilot who was badly burned. Actually he was from your squadron.'

'Do you mean Wright?'

'You know about him?'

'The mix-up. Yes.' He thought for a moment. 'Of course, you must have been here then, were you?'

'Yes.'

'So you thought Wright was me?'

'Yes. It disturbed Christopher, I think. He said something like he never thought it could happen to you. Somehow he took it as a bad sign.' She felt him looking at her and wondered if he was going to ask her if it affected her. If he did, she doubted she could conceal her feelings.

'Have you got a cigarette?' she asked suddenly to distract him.

'I thought you weren't allowed to smoke on duty?'

'We're not. So you have to promise not to tell anyone.'

'Alright.' He smiled and struck a match.

'Your arm is getting better isn't it?'

'Yes.'

'I suppose you'll be sent back too,' she said, and as she spoke she was suddenly struck with a terrible fear of losing them both.

'I don't know. There's talk of sending me home on some sort of tour. They seem to think they can use me to encourage new recruits.'

'That's wonderful!'

'Do you think so?'

'Yes, of course. They couldn't send you back here again afterwards could they?'

'I suppose not.'

'You don't sound very pleased by the idea. Surely you're not the type to think it's your duty to stay here?'

'It isn't duty.'

'What then?'

'I don't know exactly. Responsibility perhaps. I don't mean to my country, so much. I'm talking about sticking it out because everyone has to, don't they? Like Christopher.'

'If you talk that way, you may as well say you should all stay here until there's nobody left on either side. Until everybody has been killed.'

He seemed surprised by her vehemence. 'It isn't only that anyway. It's the whole idea of being used to recruit others. I'm not sure I want to do that. And I don't like the idea of being made out to be a hero. I'm not. It's Helene they should write about if they want to write about somebody.'

It was the first time Elizabeth had heard him mention Helene since he asked what had happened to her.

'Will you tell me about her?' she asked.

He began to tell her what had happened to him after he had crashed. Elizabeth visualised the barn where Helene had hidden him. She imagined them drawn to one another in the darkness of their secret existence, sharing their loneliness, and she understood that something had happened to him there. She was glad that he'd found somebody who had filled the emptiness in his soul that she was certain she had helped create.

*****

To celebrate his last night in Amiens before taking up his new command, Christopher had arranged a table for them at the Café Chat Noir in the old part of the town. The interior was smoky and dark, with tables arranged around a dance floor in front of a stage where a band of Negro musicians were playing rag-time. From the moment they arrived, people were dancing and waiters went to and fro, carrying bottles of chilled champagne and bowls of mussels cooked in white wine and cream. Many of the men wore uniforms. There were both French and British, and a few Australians and New Zealanders. It was a popular place for the flyers based at aerodromes to the east and west, for whom Amiens was closer than either Paris or the coast.

'I've never been here before,' Margaret said, looking around with bright, excited eyes. She had managed to get the night off to go with them and was wearing a blue dress that went with her eyes, and hugged her figure in a way that drew men's gazes. Especially that of Christopher's brother, Elizabeth thought, as Henry's adoring eyes followed Margaret's every movement.

'What do you think of it, Henry?' Christopher asked.

Henry tore his gaze from Margaret to look around at the women wearing jewellery and silk dresses that clung to their bodies. They smoked and drank as much as the men. Outnumbered as they were, they could dance the entire evening away with a different partner for each tune if they wanted. At the next table a young woman who wore her long, almost jet-black hair loosely, threw back her head and laughed at something a young captain whispered in her ear, his hand resting on her thigh. She kissed his cheek and then his ear, the tip of her tongue pink and shocking as she teased his lobe. Her ruby lips moved as she whispered some promise or other.

'It seems alright,' Henry said, imitating worldly

insouciance that wasn't, however, matched by the tug of disapproval on his young features. He glanced at Margaret as if worried that such sights might offend a lady, or what in the realms of his inexperience, he imagined constituted a lady.

A waiter brought champagne and whisky, and Henry emptied a glass of the latter quickly. He immediately stifled a choking sound and turned bright red.

'Steady on, old man,' Christopher said.

'Good grief, where on earth did they find that awful stuff?' Henry exclaimed to cover his embarrassment.

'I adore this tune,' Margaret said as the band began playing again. 'Henry, will you come and dance with me?'

'I'd be honoured, Miss Weston.'

'It's Margaret,' she protested, laughing at his formality. 'You'll make me feel old calling me that.'

Henry blushed. Margaret led him onto the floor and they were swallowed up among the other dancers.

'He seems so young,' Elizabeth commented. Margaret was no more than four or five years older than Henry, but he looked like a schoolboy next to her, which in fact he had been until quite recently, she thought.

'Yes,' Christopher said heavily. He emptied his glass and signalled to the waiter for another. 'He reminds me of myself when I was that age. Do you remember?'

'It seems a long time ago.'

'I wonder what he'll be like in a few months time?'

Or if he'll even be alive, Elizabeth thought, finishing Christopher's unspoken thought. She squeezed his arm and he smiled at her.

'Christ, I mustn't get bloody maudlin this early on in the evening must I? Anyway, I shouldn't worry about Henry after reading his flight instructor's report. He was top of his class, you know. A 'natural pilot' in his CO's words.' Christopher looked at his watch and peered through the crowd towards the door. 'I wonder where William is? He did say he was coming didn't he?'

'Don't worry, he'll be here. Why don't you dance with me?'

'Alright.'

As they danced, Christopher relaxed a little. He smiled and chatted with her and exchanged cheerful helloes with some people he recognised, though Elizabeth knew it was partly an act. William arrived just as they returned to their table.

'There you are!' Christopher exclaimed shaking his hand. 'I was beginning to think you weren't coming.'

'I'm sorry I'm late. I forgot the name of the club and it took me a while to find it.'

'Well, you're here now, that's the main thing. Sit down and have a drink. What would you like? Whisky?'

'Yes, thanks. Hello Elizabeth,' he said.

'Hello.' William kissed her cheek, and for a moment she caught the scent of his cologne. She felt herself blush for no reason and her heart was racing. As they parted she saw Margaret watching her.

'And you know my brother, Henry, of course. You've met before, though it was a long time ago now,' Christopher said.

William and Henry shook hands. 'How are you, Henry?'

'Very well thanks. I must say it's a thrill to meet you again. I've heard all about your exploits of course. I thought it was absolutely splendid of you to pinch one of the enemy's own machines.'

'I expect Elizabeth's told you that Henry's been posted to my squadron,' Christopher said as he filled everyone's glasses. 'To old friends.'

'Yes. Old friends.'

They ordered supper, and while they ate Margaret told them about her life in Canada. She had grown up in a hotel owned by her parents, which had provided her with an interesting childhood. Perhaps to get her away from an environment where she came into contact with so many disparate characters, her father sent her away to school, but when she came home for the holidays she was allowed to work in the hotel. She knew how to cook as well as any chef, and her experience on the desk meant she could run an office.

As the evening went on they talked of anything but the war. Christopher seemed to be in good spirits, and he told Margaret how he and William had built an aeroplane together once.

'We all knew each before the war. I expect Elizabeth's told you. We used to drive all over the countryside going to dances.'

He was drinking too much, Elizabeth thought. She saw William glance at her questioningly.

'It was always the same crowd we'd see. Everybody drinking and dancing and nobody caring about anything but having fun.'

There was something ghoulish about Christopher's reminiscing. Sophie's ghost walked in the empty landscape behind his eyes.

'They were all such good people. So full of life. Do you remember Harry Thwaites?' He looked at Elizabeth and William in turn. 'He was always a good chap. And Bunny Rogers.' He turned to Margaret. 'There were four of us who used to go about together all the time. Liz and William were sweet on one another in those days. And there was another girl, her name was Sophie.'

There was an uncomfortable pause in the atmosphere around the table, like the needle slipping on a gramophone record.

'I remember hearing her name once,' Henry said, frowning as he tried to recall where.

Christopher clapped him on the shoulder. 'I'm pretty sure you never met her, Henry. It's a shame. I should've introduced you to her. She was an absolutely wonderful girl. I'd never met anyone like her.'

Henry looked confused and Elizabeth felt sorry for him. Henry didn't think it was quite the thing for his brother to be waxing on so much about another girl when he was engaged to be married. She pushed back her chair and excused herself, and Christopher looked at her guiltily.

Margaret went with her to the Ladies room. 'Am I missing something here?' she asked.

'It would take too long to explain,' Elizabeth said.

Margaret offered her a cigarette. 'You're in love with Captain Reynolds, aren't you?'

'Is it so obvious?'

'It is to me. Does Christopher know? Is that what all that was about back there?'

'He knows I used to be. I don't know what he's doing.'

When they returned to the table, Christopher was still talking about people he knew before the war, though now his mood was sombre. 'Harry Thwaites is dead,' he said abruptly. 'Bought it last year on the Somme. And Bunny too. I met somebody from his regiment. Bunny was having something to eat when a shell exploded right where he was sitting. There was nothing left of him at all. Just a spray of blood and bits of flesh. Nothing bigger than your fingernail, by all accounts.'

Elizabeth put her hand on his arm. 'Christopher, are you alright?'

He focused on her with bleary eyes. 'Sorry, I'm ruining the party aren't I? It's just that it's terrible to think they're all gone now.'

'I know what you mean,' Henry agreed. 'Several of the chaps I knew at school have been killed. I'm going to think of them every time I go up in my kite. It'll put me in the right frame of mind when we meet those blasted Huns, and when I see one of them going down in smoke I'll think; there goes one for poor old Kingsley or Chalmers.' He turned to William with an earnest look. 'I expect you can't wait to get back into the thick of it can you, Reynolds? I say, is it true that when you pinched one of their planes you shot up their aerodrome for good measure?'

'I was too busy trying to stay in the air to do anything like that,' William said.

'You had somebody with you though didn't you? Actually it was a woman wasn't it? That's right. It's coming back to me now. The chap I spoke to said he knew one of the men that found you when you landed. According to him the woman was already dead, but she'd used up half a belt of ammunition before she was hit. I must say, it makes me laugh to think of all those Huns running around getting shot up by one of their own machines.'

William didn't say anything, but Elizabeth could see that he was affected by Henry's tactlessness, and she was grateful when Margaret suddenly insisted Henry dance with her.

'Sorry about Henry,' Christopher said when they had gone. 'He's a bit enthusiastic I'm afraid.'

'It doesn't matter,' William said.

'Liz told me that young woman saved your life. I'm sorry, old man.'

'Thanks.'

'This is meant to be a happy occasion, but between me and Henry we're managing to put a terrible damper on things. From now on there's to be no more of this depressing talk. I promise. I tell you what, why don't you two go and have a dance together? That'll do the trick.'

'I haven't danced for a long time,' William said.

'It's like riding a bicycle. You never forget. Anyway, Liz won't mind if you step on her toes, will you?'

She smiled though her heart was thudding. 'Don't feel you have to, William. Anyway, I expect you have to be careful with your arm don't you?'

'I think I can manage. Anyway, the more I use it the

quicker it'll get back to normal, I'm told.'

She stood and they went to the dance floor. She was conscious of Christopher watching them, and at first they were stiff and a bit awkward together.

'It feels a bit strange doesn't it?' William said.

'Yes it does.'

The tune ended and they let go of one another, but almost immediately the band began to play a foxtrot.

'We can go back to the table if you like,' William said.

'I'd rather stay.'

He put his arm around her and they began to dance again. 'Does he talk about Sophie very often?'

'No. I'm sure he thinks about her though. He loved her.' It occurred to Elizabeth that William must be wondering if history was repeating itself; that she was in love with a man who didn't return her feelings.

When the tune ended they went back to the table and Christopher asked her to dance with him.

'It's wonderful to see William again, don't you think?' he said when they were on the floor. 'And for us all to be together like this.'

'Yes, it is.'

He smiled at her. 'Are you enjoying yourself, darling?'

'I'm happy so long as I'm with you.'

'Are you really?'

'Of course. Don't you believe me?'

'You wouldn't rather be with William?'

'How can you ask such a thing?' she said. 'Is that why you were talking about Sophie and the four of us going out?' She saw that she was right.

'I'm sorry. I wanted to see how you both reacted.'

'You mean you were testing me,' she said angrily.

'No, not the way you think, Liz.'

'How am I supposed to think then?'

'You're angry.'

'Yes, I'm bloody furious. How dare you do that to

me?'

'I only did it because I know you were in love with William. I don't want you to feel you have to stay with me, that's all.'

Her anger faded. For an instant she was tempted to tell him the truth. But what was the truth? She loved William, but in the morning Christopher was going back to the war. She had known him all her life and she loved him too. Perhaps not in the same way, but no less powerfully. 'Surely you must know that I love you.'

Relief flooded his eyes and he gripped her hand tightly. 'I'm sorry,' he said. 'Of course I do. And I love you.'

'And when this war is over we're going to be married.'

'Yes, yes we are.'

*****

When they arrived back at the hotel, Elizabeth got ready for bed while Christopher poured himself a whisky. After a while she got up and went to find him. He was standing beside the open window in the sitting room.

'Come to bed,' she said.

He finished his cigarette and let it drop to the street, watching it explode in a shower of sparks. 'I thought you were asleep.'

She didn't answer, only took the glass from his hand and led him away from the window. He went with her and in the bedroom undressed and got into bed. He kissed her, but then broke off.

'I'm sorry, Liz. I don't know what it is. Too much to drink I expect.'

'It doesn't matter,' she told him. 'I just want to be here, the two of us together.'

'I just feel... I don't think I'm being fair to you.'

'We have our entire lives in front of us,' she told him. 'Most couples are separated by the war. They only have letters to keep them going. At least we can be together. Nothing is more important than that.'

'I suppose you're right,' he said.

'Of course I am.'

He put his arm around her. 'You are the most amazing person, Liz. One day when this is all over we'll have a wonderful life. I can see us at Pitsford with three or four children. We'll have picnics by the river, all of us together.'

'Yes, of course we will.'

'It'll be marvellous. I do miss the place you know. I suppose one takes these things for granted most of the time, but being over here makes me appreciate it more. I often think of the woods. Do you remember what it's like there in the spring, with the bluebells like a painting by Monet?'

'It's beautiful,' she said, remembering how they'd roamed there as children before he went away to school.

'There's a glade somewhere in the middle, a great open space with a huge fallen tree where we used to play. We had sticks as swords. I'd be king of the castle and fight you off.'

'You'd try,' Elizabeth said, laughing as she remembered. 'I'd knock you down often enough.'

'Yes you did, didn't you? That's why I liked you so much, I think. You weren't like other girls.'

'Wasn't I?'

'No.'

He was quiet for a little while. And then he said, 'I feel I can't keep going sometimes, you know. The only thing that gets me through is thinking about you and I together when this is all behind us. I don't think I'll ever want to leave again, you know.'

She didn't answer. He stroked her hair. Her eyes leaked tears and her throat was tight.

When he fell asleep she got up and went into the other room. She sat by the window staring outside. When she heard him cry out, an hour had passed. He was dreaming, the bedclothes were twisted tightly around him and his arms were flailing as he mumbled incoherently. She sat beside him and stroked his brow.

'Shhh, it's alright, Christopher. I'm here.'

He was hot, bathed in sweat. The sound of her voice began to calm him. She talked to him about Pitsford, describing every room as she remembered them. She made it sound as if they were there together, walking through the house, hand in hand, ready to begin their lives together again. It was late afternoon, perhaps in the autumn, and the fires were lit, the flames reflected on the polished glass and silver. Eventually he slept peacefully.

32

'Whisky?' Colonel Faversham asked.

'Yes, thank you, sir.'

Faversham poured two glasses and gave one to Jarvis. They lit cigarettes and sat on opposite sides of the fireplace. The house was near St Omer. It belonged to a factory owner from Paris who had grown up in the area, though for now the army had requisitioned its use for the Flying Corps.

Beyond the large windows at the end of the room, the grounds shone wetly beneath an overcast sky, though the cloud had begun to break, parting like muddy scum revealing depths of blue.

'He actually killed them?' Faversham said, referring to Albert and Edith Lisle.

'Yes, it rather shocked me too,' Jarvis confessed. 'Though in fairness I gather he didn't really have a choice.'

'No, I suppose in the circumstances he didn't,' Faversham agreed, though his tone was heavy with reservation. 'Nevertheless, no matter how you dress it up, shooting dead a couple of pensioners hardly lends his escape quite the note we're after, does it? And one of them a woman too.'

'Quite.'

'It's a pity though.'

'We could still use him of course.'

'I don't see how.'

'He hasn't told anybody about any of this, and I told him not to, for the time being. It would simply be a matter of editing his account of events somewhat. I was thinking that perhaps if Reynolds didn't mention the Lisles at all, it would simplify things.'

Faversham sipped his whisky, which was a rather decent single malt. 'What about the woman? What was her name did you say?'

'Helene.'

'Yes, that's it. We have to account for her somehow or other.'

'He could simply say that she hid him until they escaped, which is true after all.'

Faversham considered the suggestion. 'Was there something going on between them do you think?'

'I wondered that myself actually. I get the feeling that there may have been, yes.'

'That puts rather a different complexion on matters don't you think? After all, we've only got Reynolds' account of what actually happened. If he was mucking about with somebody's wife, who's to say what really went on.'

'Yes, I see what you mean, sir. I must admit the same thing occurred to me. Though to be fair, he needn't have told me anything about the Lisles. If there was more to it than he's letting on, you'd expect him to keep quiet about the whole thing.'

Faversham considered this argument. 'What we must consider, Jarvis, is the benefit versus the risk. Before we send Reynolds back to England to drum up some favourable publicity, we have to weigh the positive effect on recruitment, against the negative effect if some unpleasant truth were to get out.'

'Unless it was to come from Reynolds himself, I don't see how that might happen, sir,' Jarvis countered. 'The others involved are all dead.'

'I agree. Then our decision rests on whether or not Reynolds is the sort of chap we can rely on. What do we know about him?'

'He seems steady enough. Perhaps a bit shaken up from his experiences, but that's to be expected. I'm sure it will pass. He was at Oundle, I believe.'

'Well, that's something. Not a first rate school, of course, but quite acceptable. What about his family?'

'I'm afraid we don't know. Reynolds is rather vague concerning them. His parents are both dead.'

'Siblings?'

'None, sir.'

'Who was his last CO?'

Jarvis consulted his file. 'Thompson. Number twenty-eight squadron.'

'Go and speak to him, Jarvis. See what he has to say.'

'Yes, sir.'

Faversham emptied his glass and looked at his watch. 'I think I'll get Smith to saddle my horse. Work up an appetite before dinner. I believe we're having game pie this evening. I'm very partial to a decent game pie. Would you care to join me, Jarvis?'

'Thank you, sir. I'd like that very much.'

'Excellent. Come along then, we'll get somebody to find you a horse.'

*****

It was midday when Jarvis arrived at twenty-eight squadron. The adjutant showed him to the CO's office.

'I hope you don't mind me dropping in like this.'

'Not at all,' Major Thompson assured him. 'Would you like to stay for lunch?'

'That's very kind of you. Perhaps we could talk first?'

'Yes, of course. Cigarette?'

'Thank you.' Jarvis took a cigarette from the offered box and accepted a light. 'I want to ask you about a chap who was under your command. Lieutenant Reynolds as he was then, though it's Captain Reynolds now. MC.'

'Ah yes. I've heard all about his exploits, of course. I suppose you have to admire the cheek of a fellow who steals one of the Hun's machines from under their noses.'

'Yes, well that's exactly the point, you see. It's the sort of thing that we feel it might be to our advantage to make the most of. Play the whole thing up in the newspapers and so on. It might help us to persuade a few more men to volunteer for the Flying Corps.'

Thompson nodded. 'Yes, I can understand what you mean.'

'We're considering sending Reynolds on a sort of speaking tour of England. Civic receptions, that sort of thing.'

'I see.'

'That's why I'm here really. I'd like your opinion of the fellow.'

Thompson leaned forward and tapped his cigarette on the edge of an ashtray. 'Is this an official enquiry, may I ask?'

'No, not at all,' Jarvis assured him. 'Simply a chat, off the record, so to speak. I want you to feel you can speak freely.'

'It's just that I wouldn't want to blemish a chap's record in any way.'

'Of course. Perhaps I should tell you that we have certain reservations about Reynolds. Nothing to do with his actions, you understand. It's simply that we must be careful to make certain he's suited for what we have in mind. We don't want him saying the wrong sorts of things to the newspapers.'

'No, I can see that. Well, in that case if I were to be perfectly frank with you, I'd have to say that I think your concerns would be justified.'

'Really?'

'He was never very popular here amongst the other chaps. Kept very much to himself. Bit of an odd fish actually. Wouldn't let the men service his machine and so on. Insisted on doing everything himself. He rather gave the impression that he imagined he was a cut above everybody else. Damned opinionated with it too.'

'Opinionated? In what sense?' wondered Jarvis.

'He was prone to criticising his superiors. Not only me, but the General Staff. Didn't agree with the way the war was being pursued. Quite frankly, Reynolds didn't know his place.'

Jarvis wasn't surprised by Thompson's remarks. His own initial impressions of Reynolds had always been that Reynolds might be more of a hindrance to their aims, than a help. He thanked Thompson for expressing his views openly.

'Not at all. Now, how about that lunch before you leave? The patrols ought to be back about now. You might like to speak to some of the men.'

'Yes, I'd like that. How are things in this sector at the moment by the way?'

'Oh, I think we're managing alright. Naturally, I'd like to have some more experienced pilots, but I should think everybody's in the same boat.'

'I'm afraid so.'

'Mind you, I haven't enough planes for the pilots I've got at the moment. Is there any chance we might get some of the new machines?'

'The SE5s? Unlikely I'm afraid. They're all being sent to the new fighter squadrons as quickly as we can make them.'

'It's just that my chaps are having to fly without an escort, you see.'

'Yes, I sympathise, but I shouldn't worry too much, once we've got enough of the new machines, I think you'll find the enemy won't have things all their own way. I'll mention your concerns, though,' Jarvis assured him.

'Would you? I'd appreciate it. Not that I'd want

anyone to think I'm complaining, you understand. I realise we must all do the best we can.'

'Naturally.'

'Now, here we are.' Thompson held open the door to the officer's mess. 'I believe we're having beef today. Can I offer you a drink, Jarvis?'

'Thank you. I'll have a whisky if you don't mind.'

'I'm afraid we've only got Bells, will that be alright?'

'Absolutely. Though I might have a dash of soda with it in that case.'

33

The clerk in charge of records didn't appear at all surprised by William's request.

'So you want to know where you're buried, sir. Though it isn't actually you, of course.'

'Yes, that's right. The records ought to have been changed to show that it's Captain Wright.'

The clerk's expression was sceptical. 'I doubt that. But let's have a look. If you'd like to wait here I'll see what I can find out. Would you like a cup of tea or something, sir?'

'No thanks, Sergeant.'

'Right then. I'll be as quick as I can.'

In fact he was gone for more than an hour, and William had begun to think the man had forgotten about him. Eventually, though, he returned and his smile was evidence of success.

'I was right about one thing, sir. The records haven't been changed, but I'll put in a request right away to get it done. There's a bit of a backlog as you can appreciate, sir. It's the lucky ones' get their own graves, but even then you can never really be sure who they're burying. A bit of this and a bit of that. I suppose it doesn't really matter though does it, sir. Dead is dead, as they say.'

'I expect you're right.'

'Bit of a funny one this, though. Unusual. No wonder you couldn't find the grave. It's not in the cemetery that's why. He was buried in a village just outside Amiens.'

The records clerk showed William the documentation,

though it told him nothing other than what he'd just heard.

'Do you know why he was buried there?'

The clerk shrugged. 'No idea, sir. Perhaps you could ask at the hospital. Somebody there might know. He wasn't French was he?'

'No. Not as far as I know, anyway.'

'Well, I'll leave you to it then, sir, shall I?'

'Yes, thanks for your help, Sergeant.'

'Pleasure, sir.'

When he got outside William lit a cigarette. He decided to go to the village right then and see the grave for himself. After returning to the hospital he managed to find an ambulance that was returning to the front and cadged a lift. He arrived late in the afternoon. The village was little more than a handful of cottages that had grown up in the protective folds of the landscape, sheltered from the elements. A hollow by the river that trapped the heat. It was June and the weather had changed. A single dusty road was the only way in or out of the village. It passed beneath shady trees and ran alongside a low hill where a wall made of grey stone surrounded the churchyard.

'I can wait if you want, but only for a few minutes,' the ambulance driver offered after William climbed out.

'No, it's alright, thanks. I'll walk back.'

As the ambulance drove away a brown dog roused itself from a patch of shade and ran after the vehicle barking half-heartedly, and then duty done trotted back and collapsed in a panting heap. The sound of the engine faded to silence.

He climbed the path to the empty churchyard. The most recent graves were at the back behind the church, where the view over the wall stretched across fields and woods of dark green. He could see the red roof of a farmhouse in the distance. From the woods came the staccato echo of a woodpecker, and from the other direction the rumble of guns.

He found the grave under the branches of a yew. The headstone was made of polished marble, inscribed with his name and the dates of his birth and supposed death. He looked around. It was a peaceful place, a green idyll far from the war. It reminded him of Scaldwell. He sat down to think. He wondered if it was Elizabeth who'd arranged for him to be buried there, though it was odd that she hadn't said anything. He wondered why.

By the time William arrived back at the hospital it was late in the afternoon. While he was packing his things, Elizabeth came into the ward.

'I've been looking for you,' she said.

'I went for a walk.'

She watched him fold his clothes. 'You're leaving?'

'Yes. My orders came this morning. I was going to tell you.'

'Are you going back to England?'

'No. I've been posted to a new squadron.'

She tried to hide her reaction, but he thought some things are impossible to conceal. She looked away so he wouldn't see the tears she held back.

'Elizabeth…'

She looked at him and tried to smile, wiping her eyes. He thought about the grave where Wright was buried and he wanted to go to her and put his arms around her, to hold her and feel the softness of her hair, breathe the scent of her skin. Neither of them moved.

*****

They met at seven o clock at the hospital gates and walked towards the town. Elizabeth was quiet. When he glanced at her she was looking at the ground, her brow creased in angry lines.

'They shouldn't be sending you back,' she said at length. 'I've heard that other men who've escaped after they crashed have been treated as heroes.'

'They're desperately short of pilots,' William said, though he suspected there might be other reasons for the decision to keep him in France.

'Then they must need experienced men to train new ones. Surely you've done your part.'

'No more than anyone else.'

'It just doesn't seem fair.'

'There's something else,' he said. 'I've been posted to Christopher's squadron.'

She stared at him in disbelief.

They went to a café where they had been once or twice since Christopher left. The owners were friendly and the food was good.

'Christopher will be glad to see you,' Elizabeth said when they were sitting at a table in the corner. 'You can look after one another.'

'How is he?'

'I worry about him. Now I'll have to worry about both of you.'

The café was busy with people who had stopped for a drink and a snack on the way home from their work. Like everywhere else, there were very few men under the age of forty five. The women worked at jobs that would have been the realm of men before the war. The owner's wife brought them a bottle of Bordeaux.

'When did you last hear from Christopher?' William asked, offering Elizabeth a cigarette.

'He writes every few days. I think things are difficult. He says the new planes are very good, but there still aren't enough of them.'

'It will get better,' he said, trying to reassure her.

'Will it?' she said sceptically. 'I've heard that our squadrons have been attacked by as many as thirty German planes at a time.'

William had heard the stories too. The German jastas

had developed a new tactic of concentrating their numbers where they were needed, sometimes flying missions en masse. The pilots referred to them as flying circuses because of the garish colours the German's painted their machines.

'They've had the upper hand, but it's changing,' he said. 'The SE5 is making a difference and I've heard Sopwith are making a bigger version of the Pup. With the new French Spads and Nieuports arriving as well, the tables are turning.'

'Do you really think so?'

'Yes,' he said. He could see she wanted to believe him, and by all accounts what he was telling her was true, though the new planes weren't arriving in sufficient numbers yet, and there was a serious shortage of experienced pilots.

Despite William's efforts to be positive, Elizabeth was unusually quiet during their meal, and no matter how hard he tried to take her mind off the war he couldn't lighten her mood. She looked tired, he thought. Though on the surface she was still the young woman he'd once known and loved, she had changed. She rarely laughed. A memory came back to him of the day he'd taken her flying and shown her Scaldwell. If Christopher hadn't been waiting for them when they returned he would have asked her to marry him. Would that have changed anything he wondered? It seemed to him that too many things in life went unsaid, and opportunities for happiness were missed and later regretted.

'I went to Thierry this afternoon,' he said.

Her eyes widened in surprise and she put down her fork. 'How did you know?'

'So it was you. I thought it might have been. I wanted to find out where Wright was buried so that I could write to his family.'

'I suppose you're wondering why I didn't tell you.'

'No,' he said. 'I don't think I am.'

They looked at one another, their silence speaking more than words could ever express. The colour of

Elizabeth's eyes had always fascinated him; the startling clarity of green that made him think of light on the surface of the sea, illuminating the depths underneath. In some ways there was nothing more intimate than gazing openly into the eyes of another person. One felt exposed in a way. Nothing could be hidden. It made his heart race. He felt an overwhelming sense of relief. A kind of freedom.

They smiled at one another as if sharing their thoughts.

'There's something I want you to know,' Elizabeth said. 'When we were in Cannes, Christopher and I both knew we'd made a mistake. When I look back now, I see how heartless I must have seemed to you. I can't excuse what I did. I'm not even sure I can explain it entirely, but I think you knew I was in love with Christopher, or at least imagined myself to be. You asked me more than once if I was and I denied it. The truth is, I'd been in love with him for years. But it was more an idea than an actual feeling. All I ever wanted was for him to feel the same way about me. But he never did. He never saw me the way he saw other girls. The way he saw Sophie. And then I met you and without even wanting to, or realising or understanding what was happening, I began to fall in love with you. I was very confused.'

William listened to her speak, watching her mouth, her eyes, the way she fiddled with her wine glass. The ring she wore, Christopher's ring, flashed in the light.

'After we came back I tried to find you,' Elizabeth continued. 'I tried everything I could think of. But you seemed to simply vanish. I didn't know who to ask, but I tried everyone. Nobody knew anything.'

He thought back. The weeks after the fire were unclear. 'I went to Birmingham,' he said. He'd worked for a coachbuilder and then an engineering firm. He had lived in lodgings and nine months of his life had disappeared in a black haze. Eventually he began to think about flying again, but shortly afterwards the war began and he had decided to join the Flying Corps.

'Yes, I know. You were sent to Shoreham.'

He was surprised that she knew, and then she told him how she'd travelled to Shoreham and sent a letter to the camp and waited for a reply that never came. 'I didn't receive a letter.'

'You'd already gone by then, but I only found that out months later. My letter was returned. By then I was living in London, training to become a nurse and you were in France.'

As he struggled to absorb what Elizabeth was telling him, it struck William how arbitrary life was. How fickle timing and circumstance could turn a person's life toward a hitherto unforeseen direction. It was as if the forces that governed their existence had conspired to keep them apart, but still, somehow, they came to be sitting together at a table in a café in Amiens. He could understand how the Greeks had believed the gods meddled in men's affairs for their amusement. And perhaps they weren't finished yet. Though he and Elizabeth were only separated by the width of a table, they were bound by loyalty as surely as if they were chained. The table may as well have been a chasm.

Elizabeth told him about the day the burned pilot was brought to the hospital and the confusion over his identity. 'I wanted him to be you, because the alternative seemed to be that you were dead. And when he died at least I had sat beside you and told you the truth, and I clung to the idea that you heard and understood everything I said.'

'What did you say?' he asked, wanting to hear her speak the words.

'That I love you. That I've always loved you.'

Did any other phrase in language express so much of what was truly important in life, William wondered.

Elizabeth looked at the ring on her finger. 'When Christopher asked me to marry him, I agreed because in a way I love him. I love him like a friend I've known all my life. But more than that I agreed because I believed I would never see you again, and Christopher was alive and he needed me. He still needs me. He needs to believe in me.'

William understood what she was saying, but he already knew it. There was solace, at least, in the knowledge that he loved her and that she in turn loved him. He smiled and reached across the table for her hand and that was enough.

34

JULY 1917

The barrage on the German positions had been going on for nearly a week. A thousand guns were raining shells onto the ground that rose towards the ridge overlooking Passchendaele, with the intention of destroying the heavy enemy fortifications. The German artillery were responding and had put up a balloon to assist their gunners, and it was this balloon that William and Henry were about to attack.

It was a quick raid, meant to take the Germans by surprise so that they would have no time to winch their spotters down to safety or telephone one of the aerodromes to summon a squadron of Albatrosses. Unless they were unlucky enough to run into a patrolling jasta, William hoped they would slip across the lines and complete their mission and be back in time for lunch.

Henry was on his right as they climbed for height on their own side of the lines using the cloud for cover. The Hispano Suiza engine in his SE5 growled steadily as the altimeter climbed above ten thousand feet. The plane was steady and had proved to be fast in a dive. It could out climb an Albatross, though it was not quite so quick in a turn. The Lewis gun above the top-plane was loaded with standard ammunition, but the Vickers mounted on the cowling in front of William was loaded with incendiary bullets, designed to ignite the helium in a balloon and make it burn.

He entered heavy moisture-laden cloud, and for a few

minutes he couldn't see Henry, but he trusted him to hold his course. Henry had taken the place of William's normal wingman, who was giving the other two pilots in William's flight some shooting practise. They were replacements for Kirk and Wilson, who had both been shot down within a week of each other.

At thirteen and a half thousand feet the cloud thinned, and then moments later William flew into bright sunshine. Automatically he looked all around, searching for enemy planes. The greatest danger when flying was being taken by surprise. Both sides habitually patrolled close to their effective ceilings, using cloud and the sun to their advantage, always hoping to pounce on vulnerable two-seaters working at lower heights. For the moment he couldn't see anything. To the north, a slab of heavy, dark cloud covered the landscape at about five or six thousand feet. Between there and his current position the drifts of cloud were layered at varying heights, and in between were oceans of blue. It was a landscape of a thousand hiding places, where danger could lurk unseen until it was too late. Far below, the earth was a dull canvas of muted greens and browns. In the air, the dimensional perspectives were reversed. The cloud made towering mountains and deep valleys and endless plains that stretched to the far horizon.

Henry's plane emerged from the cloud and William checked his compass before changing course to follow a bearing that would take them over the lines south-east of the ridge. They sailed on through clear sky, accompanied by the reassuring note of the engine and the wind humming in the wires. He looked over the side of his cockpit at the ruined swathe of the Ypres Salient. Flattish, waterlogged land being churned to more mud and craters in preparation for yet another momentous battle. Explosions appeared silently, like ripples on a muddy pond.

William began to look for the balloon and soon he saw it far below. There would be a basket underneath with a crew reporting by phone to the artillery below. If they were alert, one of the crew would have his glasses trained to the sky searching for danger.

William gestured to Henry, who had already seen their target anyway. They had a method for attacking balloons. Because they had to attack at such a low height they took it in turns. On the first run Henry would stay up at around ten thousand feet to keep watch for enemy planes and draw them off if any should arrive. Both jobs were dangerous in their own ways, so after William had made two passes - if the balloon hadn't been destroyed - they would change places. Henry had argued the point, saying that he ought to go first because he needed the experience. The truth was, he simply wanted to claim the 'kill' for himself. He had already shot down five German planes and he was keen to add a balloon to his score. But in this case, William had overruled him.

William cocked his guns and scanned the sky for a final time. There was nothing there. At least nothing he could see. As he pushed the stick forward and opened the throttle to maximum his heart was hammering. He felt alert in a way that he never did at any other time. Every nerve ending, every ounce of sinew and muscle, every electrical pulse of his brain was sharpened and focused on what he was about to do. He was aware of the plane as if he were part of it. He could feel the vibrations from the wires and the frame running through the stick and the pedal, felt the power of the engine as the growl of the firing pistons became a roar. The wind tore at his face and the humming of the wires became a wail of protest. Fear and excitement became one. He was appalled and exhilarated at the same time. In front of him, the balloon grew rapidly larger and clearer, the ground took on more and more definition. In a few minutes he would kill or even be killed himself. The thought struck at his bowels, a momentary terror threatening to cause him to lose control of his functions. Then all at once there was no time to think of anything but what he had to do, and a curious calm descended over him.

The balloon crew on the ground were nervous that day, it seemed. Before he was within range, William saw the first puff of dark smoke unfurl in the air ahead of him. Others soon followed, but the anti-aircraft gunners were struggling to find their range and the explosions never threatened him seriously. He was more worried about the threat of being hit by the machine guns on the ground, but he couldn't think about that. He concentrated on his target. Already the ground crew were winding in the cable and the balloon was losing height. He attacked from above at a steep angle. When he pulled the trigger the Vickers barked and tracer flashed in a line dead into the centre of the balloon. He was aware of the figures in the basket, the flash from their rifles as they fired back at him, and then as he roared past, he twisted around to see if the balloon was burning. Though he knew he'd hit it, the balloon appeared undamaged, and he pulled back on the stick and banked to port to come around for another pass.

On the ground, the machine guns opened up. Above the noise of his engine, William heard the crack of bullets in the air. He lined his sights up on the balloon and opened fire early, a long burst that once again seemed to score a direct hit, though there was still no sign of fire. At the last moment, instead of climbing past his target he levelled off and reached for the Lewis gun to fire a burst into the belly of the basket. A figure threw up his arms and toppled over the side, and for an instant William felt both exultation and horror. But still the balloon refused to burn.

He looked up, searching for Henry, and glimpsed him circling in position. He should climb and exchange places, William thought, but by the time he did that the balloon would be very low and Henry ran the risk of being an easy target for the machine guns. He made a decision and banked in a steep turn, pushing the nose down again. If he didn't get it this time they would break off the attack and run for home. For a third time the balloon filled his sights, and this time he started shooting as soon as it was in range. He followed the tracer in a straight line with the throttle wide open. Bullets hit his wings and splinters of wood flew off a strut, but when he glanced at the damage the wires were intact. He held his course. The crew were plainly visible, one of them waving his arms and frantically gesticulating to the winch party below, while another aimed his rifle. The tracer found its mark, but nothing happened. William kept his finger on the trigger, and as he got closer the balloon seemed to fill the sky until he thought he'd left it too late to break off. As he banked hard to port he was aware of a pale, terrified face, and at the same time he saw a lick of flame grow like the petals of a flower unfolding. There was an explosion, and the balloon collapsed on itself and fell in burning fragments. William felt the heat on his face and feared it would burn him too, but then it was behind him and he pulled back on the stick and began to climb and turn for home.

When they landed, Henry jumped down from his cockpit and pushed brusquely past one of the mechanics. He ripped off his goggles and strode to William's plane.

'You were supposed to exchange places after your second run,' he said angrily.

'If I had, it would have been too low,' William answered.

'I could have got it,' Henry insisted petulantly. 'That would have been my first balloon.'

'It doesn't matter which of us pulled the trigger,' William pointed out. 'We had a job to do and we did it.'

But he knew Henry didn't see it that way. Henry turned and stamped off towards the chateau like a child who'd lost his favourite conker.

*****

'There you are,' Christopher said, turning from the window as William came into the room. 'It looks as if it's clearing.'

Outside, the rain was easing. The solid sheet of grey that had severely restricted flying since the beginning of the attack at Passchendaele was fading to a heavy drizzle. Since William's balloon busting mission four days ago the squadron had only flown two patrols.

Christopher gestured to a chair and poured himself a drink from a decanter on his desk. 'Whisky?'

'Just a small one thanks.'

The library of the sixteenth century chateau where the squadron was based, served as Christopher's office. There was a large fireplace, and two of the walls were lined with shelves filled with books. Since his posting there, William had spent his spare time, such as there was, reading Proust and Voltaire.

'Thanks.' He took the drink Christopher gave him and they both lit cigarettes.

'If it continues to clear like this we'll be flying in the morning,' Christopher said. 'HQ are desperate to know what's happening. I gather the entire thing is a complete mess.'

'I can't believe they went ahead with the attack in this weather,' William said. 'You can imagine what it must be like out there.'

'Yes, well, I expect these things are planned well in advance. If there's a delay the element of surprise is lost.'

'I very much doubt that there's any such thing as surprise anymore.'

'You're probably right. Anyway, the fact remains that the reconnaissance squadrons will be up as soon as the weather breaks, and that means the Huns will be out to stop them. I think we can expect to be busy. At least Henry will be pleased for another chance to add to his score.'

'Yes, I expect so,' William said.

Christopher gave a wry smile. 'You're not overly fond of him are you?'

'He's a good pilot,' William said diplomatically. 'And a brave one.'

'He can also be a pompous ass.' Christopher smiled. 'You don't have to respond to that. Henry may be my brother, but that doesn't make me blind to his shortcomings. I had to speak to him the other day, actually. I don't like his attitude towards the men. I heard him giving some poor fellow what for. He was complaining that his gun had jammed and putting all the blame on this young fitter. He said he'd have him on a charge if it happened again.'

Though William hadn't seen the incident himself, he wasn't surprised. He recalled the first time he'd met Henry years ago at Pitsford. He'd thought him a bully then for the way he used his position against people who couldn't defend themselves for fear of losing their jobs.

Christopher emptied his glass and lifted the decanter. 'Another?'

'I'm fine thanks.' Christopher was drinking a lot, William thought, but then Christopher wasn't alone in that respect. When William had passed the room they used as a mess earlier, most of the pilots were sitting around reading or playing chess, all of them drinking. Over the past few days they were often drunk before dinner, and then afterwards there would be drinking games and music until the early hours.

'There's no news of Hunt, by the way,' Christopher said, referring to a pilot who'd been seen to go down a few days ago. One of the others thought he might have managed to land and there had been speculation he might evade capture and turn up again one day.

'Are we getting somebody to replace him?'

'Yes. He ought to be here tomorrow. I had a letter from Elizabeth this morning,' Christopher said. 'She sends her love.'

'Thanks. Send mine back would you.'

'Yes, of course.'

'Is she alright?'

'Yes I think so. She's working very hard. They've been overrun with wounded since this latest push.'

'You must miss her.'

'Yes.' Christopher frowned and looked out of the window at the rain. 'I was hoping to get up for a night to see her, with this weather. But it's not really possible at the moment. Anyway, I expect she's been run off her feet.'

'How long before you're due some leave?'

'Leave?' Christopher sounded despairing. He shook his head at the impossibility of the idea. 'I find it's best not to think about it. I try and take each day as it comes.' He picked up an envelope from his desk and William saw Elizabeth's handwriting on the front. 'About the only time I can contemplate any sort of future is when I write to Liz. I often talk about Pitsford, what it will be like when we're living there again. I can almost believe it will really happen.'

'Of course it will.'

'I wonder if you believe that? I can't help thinking it's a dream. A fantasy. I want to believe in it, but I don't think I really do.'

There was a worrying fatalistic note to some of the things Christopher said, William thought. He sometimes talked as if he'd given up hope for the future, though never if any of the others were present.

'Can I ask you something, William? As friends?'

'Of course.'

'After you crashed and you met that woman who helped you… what was her name?'

'Helene.'

'Helene. Yes. Liz said something to me. She thought you might have been in love with her. I'm not asking if you were, it's none of my business, of course. But I know you cared for her. I couldn't help wondering, in that case, whether you ever considered staying there?'

'Staying?'

'Yes. I suppose Hunt going down made me think of it. I mean, if he did manage to get away and found somewhere to hide from the Germans like you did, he could simply stay there until the war ends.'

It was an extraordinary idea William thought. 'Would you do that?'

'It's difficult to know unless one is in that situation, but if I'm absolutely honest I think I would consider it.'

'Perhaps. But I think in the end you'd try to escape.'

'You seem very sure,' Christopher said. 'Is it so wrong to think of one's own life, one's future? I mean it's not as if I'm one of those fellows who didn't join up at the start. I think I can claim truthfully to have done my duty. Nobody would ever know, after all. How could they?'

'You would know,' William said, and he was vaguely surprised to acknowledge that apart from practical considerations, it was why he'd never thought of doing what Christopher was suggesting.

Christopher acknowledged that he was right with a wry, almost bitter smile. 'Yes, I suppose I would.'

By morning, the weather had cleared enough to allow flying. A blustery westerly shook the tops of the trees and patches of cloud fled across the sky, casting shadows on the land. The planes were assembled on the still wet grass, and as the pilots came down from the mess, Christopher gave his flight leaders their final instructions.

'Our job is to protect the observer squadrons in our sector from the enemy. We're rotating with other fighter squadrons nearby, so there ought be one lot in the air at all times. It goes without saying that everybody needs to keep a sharp lookout because the Huns are bound to be out in force too.'

William joined the three other pilots from B Flight. 'Hemming and Chalmers, you're my wingmen. Chalmers on my starboard side. Beresford, you're protecting our backs, alright?'

Beresford was the youngest of them, a boy of eighteen with red hair and protruding teeth. He responded eagerly. 'You can rely on me, sir.'

William knew he didn't have to worry unduly about Hemming, but the other two still lacked experience. 'Good luck, then,' he said. 'And remember to stay close. If we get into a fight use your speed. Dive and zoom! Do you understand me? And don't fly in a straight line for longer than you have to!'

Suddenly there were a hundred things he wanted to remind them, instructions he wanted drummed into their brains until they were second nature. But he knew there was nothing more he could do. 'Time to go,' he said.

'Tallyho!' called Chalmers, and as he went to his plane called to Beresford. 'I say, save me a Hun if you get the chance! I'm the only one here who hasn't opened my score yet and it's damned embarrassing.'

But his bravado failed to quell a waver in his voice, or keep the terror from his eyes.

The engines were started and the steady roar of a dozen V8's filled the air. Wreaths of smoke and the smell of oil and petrol were whipped away by the breeze. While the pilots waited for their machines to warm up, they checked their guns and controls. Elevators dipped like gladiators bowing their heads, ailerons flapped up and down.

Finally, the first machines began to move across the grass. As they gathered speed they were followed by the next two, and then two more. When it came to William's turn he gestured to Chalmers and they followed the others. He looked over his shoulder to see Beresford and Hemming safely off the ground. Blood surged like a tide through his veins. All around them the horizon widened and the landscape opened up, with its patterns of field and hill and river and road.

They played follow-my-leader, climbing ever higher as Christopher led them on a course towards to the lines. Cloud formations drifted white and grey against the blue of the sky from three to twenty thousand feet. The higher they climbed, the more unreal the ground seemed as woods and buildings and the Ypres dissolved into a puddle of greens and brown. As they reached seventeen thousand feet and took their places in a 'V' formation they passed over the salient below. To them the battlefield was nothing more than a swathe of dun coloured nothingness. They had no idea of the vanished roads, the swamp of mud that the land had become in the rain where men and horses drowned and sank without trace, sucked down by the quagmire.

Far below the SE5s, the two-seaters of the reconnaissance squadrons lumbered over the battlefield to report the disaster and direct artillery fire onto the German positions, and from the north-east came the Albatross jastas intent on shooting them down.

William saw the enemy planes when they were at about fourteen or fifteen thousand feet heading straight for a cluster of half a dozen two-seaters observing a stretch of the ridge. The air was pockmarked with puffs of grey from the anti-aircraft fire, and now and then intermittent layers of cloud obscured both the ground and the two-seaters. It was the cloud that made the Albatrosses impossible for the two-seaters to spot.

William counted six of them. A knot tightened in his stomach and he flicked off the safety on his guns. He looked around, wondering why there were only six of them. Above there were clouds and blue sky, and the sun dazzled him. Something felt wrong, though he couldn't see any other enemy machines. Ahead, he saw a flare rise in an arc from Christopher's plane. Christopher banked and put his nose down, and the others began to follow. William hesitated. The flare was like a beacon. He had an uncomfortable premonition and wished he could speak to Christopher and urge him to hold back. But if they waited, the two-seaters wouldn't have a chance. He searched the sky again but couldn't see anything. Then he banked and changed course to follow the others, and the rest of his flight followed suit.

After that there was no time to think. The two-seaters spotted the Albatrosses and broke and ran. As the Germans closed for the attack, the SE5s in turn tore down on them. William singled out a target painted green and red. The wires complained with their banshee howl and his engine thundered. He saw Christopher open fire first, and at almost the same moment William's target filled his sight ring and he pressed the trigger in a long burst. The German pilot reacted almost instantaneously, banking hard and pulling his nose up to escape, but Hemming was there to cover that side and let off a bust of fire before rolling away and zooming up.

For a few minutes there was mayhem. Planes rolled and turned, zoomed and dived every-which-way. Tracer carved deadly tracks across the sky. One of the two-seaters went down on fire, but the others took their chance and escaped while they could. An Albatross broke off and dived towards the east helped by the wind. The one William had attacked desperately tried to gain height and when William followed, the German used his faster turning ability to try and bring his twin Spandaus to bear, but Hemming caught him with a burst from his Lewis as he flashed underneath. The Albatross slipped over and began spinning towards the earth.

It seemed that the SE5s had the upper hand, but suddenly tracer flashed over William's head and he heard the thud of Spandaus and bullets raked his port wings. Reacting instinctively, he stamped on the rudder bar and pushed the nose down. As he dived, he threw the stick across and half rolled, then changed direction to twist in the other direction. The guns followed him, and a machine already at full speed whizzed over his head. More tracer appeared over his wing. The engine roared as he pulled up, trying to use his speed to escape. Only then did he look around and see the sky full of flame-red Albatrosses. They were everywhere. Two of them were trying to box him in, both shooting at once. He dived again while bullets punched holes in his machine. The plane shuddered and shook. His heart raced. He realised they'd been tricked, lured down to be attacked by twenty or thirty planes that must have been waiting high above, like falcons searching for a kill.

He was down to seven thousand feet. He pulled back on the stick and zoomed up again, half rolling in a vertical turn. The sky was marked with smoking trails. Half a mile away an SE5 plummeted towards the ground, pursued by three Albatrosses. A moment later it was engulfed in a sheet of flame and exploded into fragments. A red shape flashed past and instinctively William opened fire then dived again. It was every man for himself. Planes were fighting everywhere. A cloud formation offered cover and William flew into the thick of it, hoping he wouldn't meet another plane in the middle. He emerged into clear sky. An Albatross flew overhead and he reached for the Lewis and put a burst into its belly, though there was no time to see what happened to it.

He wondered how many of them would make it home. Then again he heard the thud of Spandaus and threw his plane to one side and dived.

35

It was raining outside and a stiff westerly had blown up. A heavily overcast sky brought the onset of evening and the world beyond the window was uniformly grey. Water ran down the glass in streams, blurring the view, though Hemming continued to stare outside. William wondered if he really saw anything out there, or was his gaze fixed on some internal landscape of his own.

He looked around the room at the others. Two of them stood in front of the fire smoking, another sat nearby, hunched over his knees, clasping a drink in both hands and gazing into the flames. Occasionally one of them would attempt to dispel the mood by making some remark, and the others would look up and perhaps manage a murmured response or a sympathetic smile before retreating again to their private thoughts. Corporal Baker moved among them asking if anyone would like another drink. He spoke in a quiet reverential tone, like somebody in a church. It was Baker who'd thought to light the fire. Not so much because it was cold as to try and brighten the atmosphere a little.

'Can I get you something, sir?' he asked, approaching William.

William almost declined, but then realised his glass was empty. 'Thanks, I'll have another whisky.'

'Right you are, sir.'

'Baker,' William said as the steward turned away. 'Do you know whether the CO has come down yet?'

'Yes, sir, he's in his office.'

'Don't worry about that drink. I think I'll go and see him for a minute.'

Christopher shouldn't be alone, William thought. God only knew what was going through his mind.

He crossed the hall and paused outside the library door before knocking and going inside. The fire had been lit, again thanks to Baker, William guessed, and the flames did their best to cast a cheerful glow. Christopher was sitting at his desk with the telephone and a half empty whisky bottle beside him. For a moment he didn't move. The light from the fire flickered in his eyes, but otherwise he might have been a statue carved from wax. His flesh had a greyish pallor and the shadows accentuated the sunken, lifeless look in his face.

'Christopher?'

He gave a start. 'William, it's you. Come in. Would you like a drink?'

'Don't you think we ought to join the others?'

'Yes, I suppose you're right.' Christopher gestured to the phone. 'I was hoping to hear something. There's always a chance some of them came down on our side.'

'Baker will tell you if there's any news.'

Christopher didn't move. 'Six men, William. Half the squadron in a single day. I should have known it was a trap.'

To lose so many men was bad enough, but that one of them was Christopher's brother was more than anybody should have to bear. 'You're not to blame, Christopher. None of us saw them.'

'That's not the point though is it? The responsibility is mine. I led everyone down. I should have seen them. They were just waiting for us to make a mistake and I played into their hands.'

'We don't know that it was planned,' William argued. 'They might just as easily have come across us by chance. It was simply bad luck on our part.'

'Bad luck?' Christopher's mouth twisted into a

mirthless smile. 'Six men killed, seems a little more than bad luck.'

'You know what I mean,' William said, and then he spoke firmly, trying to shake Christopher from his mood. 'Besides, you have to think of the others. They have to go out again tomorrow, and somehow you have to get them over this.'

Christopher blinked in surprise, but then he made a visible effort to pull himself together. 'You're right, of course.' He got up from his desk, though he couldn't disguise his weariness, like a man with a weight on his back that he would carry for the rest of his days. He smiled, but his eyes were empty and it occurred to William that he was close to the limits of his endurance. He'd seen the signs often enough to recognise them. Men who wore a perpetually haunted look, who had lost hope. To a lesser degree he saw the same expression in his own eyes each morning when he shaved. He saw it in them all.

'Christopher,' he said. 'I'm sorry about Henry.'

'Thank you.'

When they joined the others, Christopher asked Baker to serve dinner. They took their places around the table, unable to ignore the empty chairs. Christopher stood up to address them and William thought it was to his credit that Christopher conveyed the sorrow and regret that they all felt, while at the same time managing to summon a rallying tone.

'We have lost brave men today. I'm not going to give you a speech about duty and making a sacrifice for one's country and all that. I suppose that's why we're all here, but I'd prefer to simply remember our friends. I'm proud to have served with them and I'm proud to have known them. And when we go out again, we ought to think of them and pray that we do our work as bravely as they did, because I think that is the best way that we can honour them.'

When he finished there was silence. William was the first to stand up and the others quickly followed.

'I give you absent friends,' Christopher said, which the rest of them echoed before emptying their glasses.

When they sat down again the mood altered. Some of the tension dissipated. Christopher's speech and their toast had given them an expression for the things they all felt.

They were served chicken soup, and though none of them had much of an appetite they at least began to talk, rather than sit in deathly silence. They spoke about what had happened, and as they recounted moments of the fight they became excitable as they tried to make sense of it.

'I saw Beresford get hit,' Hemming said. 'A Hun got on his tail and I saw him twisting and turning, trying to get away but it was no good. He should have zoomed up, the bloody fool! If he'd done that he might have got away!'

He sounded angry at Beresford, though William wondered if it was really an expression of the guilt they all felt because they had survived.

'I was busy dodging Huns myself so I didn't see it all, but the next time I looked he was going down in flames,' Hemming added.

'Atherton was on fire as well,' one of the others chipped in. 'Did anybody else see him? He jumped. I watched him climb out of his cockpit and crawl back toward the tail. The whole front of his machine was blazing by then. He just sort of rolled over the side, and I saw him spinning as he fell. It must have taken an absolute age for him to get all the way down. Do you think he would have known about it?'

He looked around the table, hoping somebody might give him an answer, a sort of ghoulish eagerness in his eyes, as if Atherton's fate was his own personal demon, his secret terror. He looked at Christopher as if he might provide an answer. And then one by one they all turned to Christopher. He appeared not to have heard and was concentrating on eating his soup. In silence they witnessed the tremor in his hand. He stared at his trembling spoon as if by force of will he could stop it, but he only seemed to make it worse and soup splashed onto the tablecloth. Frustrated, he put his spoon down. When he became aware that they were all watching him, they hurriedly averted their eyes as if they'd been caught in some voyeuristic indecency.

'It's actually not very good soup,' William said in an attempt at humorous irony.

Christopher managed a grateful smile. 'Did anybody see what happened to Henry,' he asked. He sounded almost embarrassed, as if he didn't want to give the impression that Henry meant more to him than any of the others.

Hemming said, 'The last I saw of him there were a pair of Huns on his tail, but they all flew into a cloud. I don't know what happened after that.'

The door had opened without any of them noticing. A voice said, 'Atherton was supposed to be watching my back. He ought to have flown his kite right into one of those damn Huns. At least that way he could have taken one of them with him.'

It was Henry, still wearing his flying gear, and spattered with mud and oil, but otherwise unharmed. They regarded him with astonishment as he took his regular place at the table and gestured to Baker.

'Bring me a beer, steward, and fetch me some of that soup. I've been stuck at the back of the bloody trenches for half the afternoon and I'm famished.' He looked around at the others with a vexed expression. 'I know I'm a bit late, but you might have waited for me before you started.'

'We didn't know,' Christopher said, finding his voice at last. 'What on earth happened to you?'

'Do you mean to say that nobody telephoned? I crashed near one of our artillery units. My kite was pretty well smashed up, but I managed to get out alright. You ought to get hold of their commanding officer and lay a complaint if they didn't tell you. They were pretty unhelpful all round actually. I had to more or less find my own way back here.'

It was only then that Henry seemed to fully take in the fact of the empty chairs at the table.

'Good Lord, where's Davies and Wetherby? They haven't all bought it have they?'

'I'm afraid so,' Christopher said. 'We thought you had too.'

'What? Not likely! I got one of those Huns that were on my tail, by the way. Did anybody see him go down?' He looked around the table, but nobody spoke up to offer confirmation. 'Surely somebody must have seen it?' he insisted, sounding irritated. 'When I came out of the cloud he was right below me. I dived on him and put a burst right into his cockpit and he just rolled over and dropped away like a stone. Dead as a dodo I shouldn't wonder. I don't see how you could all have missed it.'

'I expect we were all quite occupied at the time,' Christopher said quietly.

'But I'm sure I saw one of our own planes nearby at the time.' Henry looked at each one them, as if he suspected somebody of deliberately trying to deprive him of the credit for his victory.

'It might have been one of the chaps who didn't make it,' Hemming suggested helpfully, at which Henry scowled.

'What rotten luck. It isn't fair.' He turned to Christopher. 'Do you think they'll take my word for it at HQ? You'd vouch for me wouldn't you?'

'Why don't we discuss it later.'

For a moment it seemed that Henry would continue to press his point, but the significance of the five empty chairs penetrated his mind at last. Reluctantly, he let the matter go. 'Where's that damn steward with my soup?' he demanded irritably.

*****

The following morning Christopher informed the pilots that the attack at Passchendaele had, for the moment, been called off. Due to a combination of the continuing bad weather, and the fact that every plane in the squadron was damaged, the squadron was grounded.

'In the circumstances, I've decided that since we could all do with a break, we ought to go to Amiens for the night,' he added.

His announcement was met with a rousing cheer, and later that morning they set off in the squadron's tender and checked into the hotel where Christopher had stayed after he left the hospital.

'I managed to get hold of Elizabeth earlier,' Christopher said as he and William went to their rooms. 'She's going to meet us later at that club we went to once, do you remember?'

'Yes, the Chat Noir.'

'That's it. I can't tell you how much I'm looking forward to seeing her. I must have re-read every one of her letters fifty times, I should think.' Christopher laughed at himself. 'I sound like a schoolboy smitten with his first love don't I? Speaking of which, Margaret's coming too I believe. Henry's been writing to her, you know. I think he may have been smitten himself.'

They reached William's room, which was on the same floor as Christopher's.

'The girls won't be able to get away until quite late. We may as well go as soon as you're ready and we'll have dinner.'

'Alright,' William agreed. 'Give me an hour to have a bath and get changed.'

In the privacy of his room he thought about Elizabeth. He wanted to see her, and yet a part of him dreaded it. He imagined being close to her, having to smile and talk politely and yet being unable to touch her, to hold her. It would be a kind of torture, but not seeing her would be infinitely worse.

When he was ready he stared at his reflection in the mirror. He was pale and there were dark circles under his eyes. He looked like a ghost, he thought.

The Chat Noir was just as busy as the last time they'd been there. The men were glad to be away from the aerodrome, even if it was only for a night, and they were determined to make the most of it. Within minutes of their arrival, Hemming and three others were competing to impress a pair of French girls, who clearly enjoyed the attention lavished on them. They were all laughing and talking at once, insisting on having the next dance and ordering more champagne as soon as a bottle was empty, even though the prices were bordering on extortionate. Henry didn't join in, however, but often glanced at his watch and peered anxiously towards the entrance.

When Elizabeth and Margaret arrived, Christopher got up eagerly. 'It's marvellous to see you again, Liz,' he said, hugging her.

She was aghast at his appearance, though she tried to hide her reaction and kissed him. 'I'm sorry it took us so long to get here. We got away as soon as we could.' She looked around at them all with the same expression of shock, before kissing William's cheek. 'Hello again,' she said.

'Hello.' For an instant they looked into one another's eyes and he felt a jolt of longing that he was sure must be obvious to everyone, though Christopher gave no sign of having noticed.

'Thank goodness you could come, Margaret,' Christopher said. 'Henry's been looking at his watch all evening.' He turned to his younger brother. 'Well, aren't you going to say hello?'

Henry blushed and threw him a furious look as he offered his hand. 'Hello Margaret. It's awfully nice to see you again.'

She smiled and kissed his cheek. 'It's nice to see you again, Henry. Will you take me for a dance?'

'Of course,' he said, crimson from her kiss, and led her off to the dance floor.

Christopher pulled out a chair for Elizabeth. 'Have you been working hard?'

'We've been absolutely snowed under since Haig began this latest push at Passchendaele. I can't imagine why that man hasn't been replaced. He must be either an immense fool, or the most callous man on earth.'

'Are things that bad?'

'I can't tell you the stories we've heard from the wounded. Thousands of men forced to attack through mud that came up to their thighs, terrified of being sucked down while the Germans shot them to pieces with their machine guns.'

She looked washed out, William thought. She was under as much strain as they were.

'Yes, we've seen some of it ourselves,' Christopher said as he poured her a glass of champagne. His hand trembled and some of it splashed onto the table, but he laughed it off. 'I seem to have got the shakes. Can't get rid of it. Come on, Liz, drink up. You too, William. We've come here to forget about the war for a little while. We ought to have some fun.'

Elizabeth hesitated, but then picked up her glass and resolutely emptied it.

'That's the ticket,' Christopher said, and then he and William followed suit and he filled their glasses again.

After that they did their best to pretend there was no war, and it seemed that everyone in the club was intent on doing the same thing. They were determined to have fun, to drink and eat and dance as if it were the last evening in their lives, and underneath it all they knew that for any one of them it might well be. Couples could be seen kissing in dark corners. Laughter and music drowned out any real attempt at conversation, even if there had been anybody who wanted to talk.

At the squadron's table, whisky and champagne flowed ceaselessly. Seats were found for the two French girls, and their over-eager suitors insisted they join them for supper. Some of the men asked Margaret to dance and she was only too pleased to oblige. William watched her on the dance floor, laughing out loud at some outrageous flattery, while Henry looked on trying to give the impression that he didn't mind. When she returned he was attentive, holding out her chair, making sure her glass was filled, his adoring eyes stuck to her like glue, and yet a minute later she would be whisked away again by one of the others. They were all drunk, except Henry. Though he drank as much as anyone, while the others became more boisterous, Henry became increasingly introverted and sullen.

Christopher encouraged Elizabeth to dance with Hemming and the others, and he took his turn with the French girls. William danced with them too and also with Margaret, and he drank whatever was poured into his glass, but he avoided Elizabeth. He watched her whenever he thought nobody would notice, and longed to be somewhere quiet with her where they could be alone. Sometimes their eyes collided, and for an instant they looked at one another with a kind of helpless, desperate intensity.

In the end their avoidance of one another became too obvious to go unnoticed. As Christopher refilled their glasses he followed William's gaze towards the dance floor where Elizabeth was dancing with Hemming.

'She's wonderful isn't she?' Christopher said, his eyes glassy with drink.

'Yes, she is.'

'Do you know, I don't think I've seen you two dance together yet. You'd better ask her or she'll think there's something wrong.'

'I haven't had a chance,' William said. 'Somebody

always beats me to it.'

'Well here's your chance. Hemming's had enough I think.'

The tune ended and Hemming drunkenly stumbled, then apologised profusely as Elizabeth laughed and led him towards the table.

'What are you waiting for?' Christopher urged.

William got up to meet her. She glanced quickly at Christopher. 'Can I have the next dance?' William asked.

'Of course.'

As the band began to play another tune he put his arm around her.

'I thought you were going to ignore me all evening,' Elizabeth said.

'It wasn't because I wanted to.'

'I know.' They began to dance, moving easily among the other couples.

'This was the first tune we ever danced to,' Elizabeth said. 'Do you remember?'

He realised that she was right. He could picture the hotel, the light spilling into the lane outside. He looked into her eyes. He remembered kissing her and going to the barn where they made love for the first time. He knew without asking that she remembered too. For a little while they didn't speak. He drew her closer, wishing the dance would never end. Nothing existed except the two of them.

William glanced towards the table and saw Christopher watching them. His expression was unfathomable, and then he smiled and raised his glass in a toast.

'How long has he been shaking like that?' Elizabeth asked.

'Not long. He's under a lot of strain.'

'He looks as if the life is being drawn out of him little by little.' She sounded despairing. 'You all do.'

'We had a bad fight yesterday. We ran into some Albatrosses. Lots of them. They surprised us and we lost five of our men. Christopher thinks it was a trap and he blames himself.'

Her eyes widened. 'Is it true?'

'That he's to blame? No. He's a good CO and a good pilot. But I think his nerves have just about had it.'

They danced in silence, but now Elizabeth seemed lost in her own thoughts. She clung to him, but wouldn't look at him. Finally, when the music ended, she met his eyes with a look of utter bleakness.

'You're going to be killed,' she said despairingly. 'You're all going to be killed.'

*****

It was very late when Elizabeth and Christopher returned to the hotel. They left the others at the club, and when Elizabeth managed to get Christopher to his room, he sat on the edge of the bed and gazed at her blearily. He held out his hand to her and she sat beside him. He put his arm around her shoulder and kissed the top of her head. 'I love you, Liz.'

She smiled. 'And I love you.'

He leaned back and kicked off his shoes. 'I just want to sit here with you quietly. Is that alright?'

'Yes, of course.' She leaned against him. She could hear his heart beat as he stroked her hair. She knew he didn't love her really. He needed her and she was there for him.

After a while he fell asleep, and she got up and covered him then went through to the other room. She didn't feel like drinking any more. Instead she sat alone in the darkness.

*****

Henry left the club with Margaret, who was drunk. She said goodbye to the others one by one and gave them each a kiss as if they were boys lining up to be tucked into bed, and she their nurse. She became teary.

'Look after yourselves, all of you,' she said, engulfed by a wave of affection that even included the two French girls.

When they were outside, Henry took her arm. 'Can you walk alright?' he asked her, sounding concerned. 'I could try to find a taxi if you like.'

'Don't worry, it isn't far. Besides, I've got you to help me haven't I?' She breathed deeply and seemed to sober up a little. As they walked through the streets she peered at Henry's grim expression. 'Are you annoyed with me, Henry?'

'What? Good lord, no! Of course not! If I'm annoyed it's with those other fellows. It's intolerable that they behaved the way they did towards you. I'll speak to them when we get back about showing proper respect to a lady.'

She wondered what they'd done that had upset him. Whatever it was, she hadn't noticed. The fresh air was clearing her head a little. The letters Henry had written to her were sweet. He had proclaimed his feelings in lush prose that he probably imagined was poetic. She didn't mind though, it made her blush sometimes to think that he obviously thought of her as virtuous and innocent.

'What is it like where you live?' she asked.

'It's beautiful, actually. It's called Pitsford House, in Northamptonshire. I can't wait to show it to you.'

'What does your father do?' she asked, wondering when she'd agreed to go to Northampton with him.

'He's in parliament. He spends a lot of time in London of course, but my mother lives at Pitsford quite a lot. I expect she'll be very pleased to have another lady for company.'

'Another lady?'

'When we're married.' He stopped and turned towards her, his face serious. 'I expect you know I'm in love with you. I didn't mean to ask you like this, but I can't stand it seeing those other fellows behaving the way they were. They wouldn't do it if we were engaged. Please say you'll think about it, Margaret.'

'Oh,' she said, too surprised too think how else to respond. She glimpsed a figure along the street, and with relief saw her opportunity to avoid Henry's proposal. 'Look, there's William! It is you, isn't it?'

'Hello,' William said as he came upon them. He smiled, looking curiously at them both as Margaret eagerly took his arm.

'We may as well all walk together,' she said.

'Yes alright,' he agreed, though he noticed Henry's scowl of displeasure.

At the hospital gates they said goodnight to Margaret. She kissed them both and told them to be careful. Tears sprang to her eyes.

When she had gone, William and Henry continued to the hotel. William lit a cigarette and offered one to Henry, though Henry declined brusquely.

'I hope I didn't interrupt anything just then,' William said.

'As a matter of fact you did. I was about to ask Margaret to marry me.'

William wondered why Henry sounded so put out, though when he thought about the way Margaret had grabbed his arm, he guessed what had happened.

When they reached the hotel, Henry said he was going to find the clerk. There was a light on in the bar beside the reception desk and William imagined Henry intended to drown his sorrows. 'Goodnight,' he said.

Henry muttered something in a surly tone and went off.

To hell with him then, William thought.

*****

Elizabeth heard a door open in the corridor. She got up

and went through to the bedroom. Christopher was asleep. She undressed and put on her nightgown. For once he was sleeping peacefully. Perhaps it was because he'd had so much to drink.

She went back to the other room and sat by the window. In a few hours it would be light. She would go back to the hospital and the wounded, and Christopher and the others would go back to their aerodrome. She wondered if William was asleep. She wanted to see him. She thought about the terrible thing she'd said to him earlier and wanted to explain that she hadn't meant it.

She slipped outside and stood at his door. She raised her hand to knock but then dropped it again. Why was she there? Was she thinking of William or was she thinking of herself?

Along the corridor a door opened from the stairs and Henry appeared. He paused at his door, searching in his pocket for his key and then he looked up and their eyes met. Neither of them spoke, and then Elizabeth returned to Christopher's room. 'Goodnight,' she said at the door, and Henry muttered some reply.

As she took off her robe to get into bed, Christopher spoke to her. 'There you are. I woke up and you weren't here.'

'I couldn't sleep.'

She lay down and put her head against his chest.

36

Outside, the sky was beginning to lighten. The street shone wetly in the rain and wind rattled the windows. There would be no flying today, William thought. He was already dressed.

After he left his room, William waited in the hotel lobby for the others. Henry was the first to appear, and when he saw William he strode towards him.

'You've got a damned nerve!' he said accusingly. 'I thought my brother was meant to be your friend!'

'What are you talking about, Henry?' William said, completely taken aback

'I saw Elizabeth coming from your room last night!'

'What on earth are you talking about?'

'Don't try to deny it, Reynolds. I know what I saw.'

Behind them, Christopher came down the stairs. William lowered his voice. 'Keep your voice down unless you want the whole place to hear you,' he warned. 'Whatever you think you saw, you're mistaken, and I'd advise you to keep it to yourself. If you say anything to Christopher, you'll be doing more harm than good. Do you understand?'

'Do you think I was intending to tell him?' Henry said with scathing astonishment. 'Clearly you think nothing of Elizabeth at all other than as some plaything for your own revolting desires, otherwise you wouldn't risk her reputation like this. If you've any shred of decency you won't so much as look at her ever again, otherwise I promise you'll have me to answer to.'

Though William still had no idea where Henry had got the idea that Elizabeth had visited his room, there was no time to respond. As Christopher approached, William did his best to look as if nothing was wrong.

'Good morning,' Christopher said. 'Any sign of the others?'

'Not yet,' William replied. 'We were just wondering whether one of us should go and fetch them.'

Christopher looked at them both as if he detected some hidden undercurrent. Abruptly Henry turned away.

'I'll go and see where they are,' he muttered.

As Henry strode off, Christopher watched his brother with a concerned expression. 'Is there anything I ought to know about?' he asked. 'Henry seems a bit irritable.'

'It's alright,' William assured him. 'I think I might have annoyed him, that's all. He walked Margaret back to the hospital last night and I think I might have happened along at the wrong moment.'

'Oh, I see.' Christopher frowned. 'I think he's quite smitten, isn't he?'

'He does seem to like her.'

'Unfortunately, I'm not sure his feelings are entirely reciprocated, though Henry appears determined not to acknowledge the fact.' Christopher stared after his brother with a contemplative, serious expression, and then he looked at William and seemed to snap out of whatever he was thinking. He took out his cigarette case and offered one to William.

'I don't like the look of that weather.'

'No,' William agreed. 'It doesn't look as if it's going to clear up very quickly either.'

'Well, I don't suppose anyone will mind very much.'

During the drive back to the chateau, the men were quiet. They seemed to sense unspoken tensions, which wasn't helped by Henry's obvious black mood.

Eventually, Hemming made a comment. 'You've got the devil of an expression, you know. If I'd left that club last night with Margaret, I'm sure I wouldn't have such a long face.'

'It's Miss Weston to you!' Henry snapped.

'Actually, Margaret insisted that I call her by her first name,' Hemming said, sounding miffed.

'I think you ought to leave it, old man,' one of the others muttered.

After that they drove in uncomfortable silence.

By the time they got back the weather had worsened, and it was clear there would be no flying at all that day. The men passed the time in the mess or else went to their rooms. William read Proust, though he couldn't concentrate at all. He kept thinking about Henry's baseless accusation, and was worried that he would say something to Christopher. In Christopher's current state of mind he couldn't imagine what effect it would have on him. In the end, William went to Christopher's office, where he found him standing at the window gazing outside at the slanting rain.

'Have you got a minute?' William asked.

'Yes of course, come in. Actually I'm glad you're here, I want to talk to you. Would you like a drink?'

'Yes, alright, thanks.' He watched Christopher pour a single glass. 'Aren't you having one?'

'No, I don't think I will at the moment.' He gave William his glass and took out his cigarettes. 'I've just heard they've decided to renew the attack at Passchendaele.'

'When?'

'Tomorrow. I'm going to send four men to St Omer tomorrow to pick up some new planes. We'll be getting some new pilots over the next few days. I think Henry can go.'

'Who's going to stay behind?'

'Myself, you, and I thought Hemming.'

'Alright.'

'Apparently the Huns have replaced the balloon you shot down. HQ want us to do the job again, I'm afraid. Hemming would be a good man to go with you, wouldn't he?'

'Yes, he knows how to keep a cool head.'

'That's what I thought.'

'Will you be coming?'

Christopher gazed out of the window again for a moment before replying. 'Yes.'

He didn't seem to have anything else to add and William saw his chance to talk about his exchange with Henry earlier. 'Christopher,' he began. 'When you came downstairs this morning, did you overhear Henry and I talking?'

Christopher held up a hand to stop him. 'Before you go on, there's something you ought to know. I'm going to tell Henry this later too, by the way. The fact is, I'm breaking off my engagement with Liz. I was writing to her before you came in, actually.' He gestured towards a letter on his desk.

'So you did hear.'

'Not really, no. But I gathered something was wrong so I spoke to Henry after we got back.'

'What did he tell you?' William demanded. 'Actually you don't have to say anything. The point is I don't know where he got the idea. It isn't true.'

'I know it isn't,' Christopher said calmly. 'My decision has nothing to do with whatever Henry mistakenly thinks he saw. I should have done this some time ago. We're meant to learn by our mistakes, aren't we? I can't change what happened in the past, but I can at least try to make amends.' He held out his hand. 'I want you to know that I think of you as my friend, William. I always will.'

'I'm glad.'

'I hope there are no hard feelings between us?'

'Of course not.'

'Good. Now, I'm afraid I have a few things I must get

finished, if that's alright. The burden of being a CO, and all that. I'll see you at dinner.'

*****

That evening in the mess, Christopher announced that the attack at Passchendaele was to be renewed and that he wanted Henry and the others, except Hemming, to fetch some new machines from St Omer.

During the meal he picked at his food and drank very little. Now and then he managed the trace of a smile when somebody said something that caused the others to laugh uproariously. William worried about him. Though he seemed to have stopped shaking there was a kind of remoteness about him that was disquieting. Eventually, after the remains of their main course were cleared away, Christopher folded his napkin and stood up.

'I think I might forgo pudding. There are some things I must attend to. Paperwork and so on.' He looked around at table at them all, as if there was something more he wanted to say. The men waited uncertainly as the silence lengthened, but in the end he offered a slight smile. 'I suppose I just want to wish you all luck, gentlemen. Goodnight.'

A chorus of goodnights followed him, and then at the door he paused and looked directly at William and gave a slight nod before he left the room. When he was gone, an uneasy silence lingered. The men glanced at one another with questioning, puzzled expressions.

After a moment William got up. He had a sudden feeling that something was wrong. Without a word he strode to the door.

'Where are you going?' Henry demanded. William ignored him, but Henry got up and followed him. 'I asked you a question.'

The door to Christopher's office was closed and when

William knocked there was no answer. 'Christopher!' He tried the handle and found it was locked.

'Wait a minute, damn you!' Henry said coming up behind him and catching his arm. 'Can't you leave him alone? I should have thought you've done enough.'

'Let go!' William said.

'Dammit Reynolds...'

William hit him, and Henry staggered backwards just as the others came to see what the trouble was. Ignoring them all, William stood back and kicked at the door, and as the wood splintered and gave way the sound of a gun shot came from inside.

Christopher lay on the floor, a pistol close to his outstretched hand. A dark pool of blood was soaking into the carpet as it pumped from a wound underneath his chin. His foot twitched convulsively and a bubbling sound came from his frothing lips.

'He's alive,' William said as he quickly took off his jacket and then tore his shirt to make a pressure bandage. He turned to the others, who'd followed him inside, and who now stood looking on in horror.

'Fetch a car!' William said. 'Hurry!'

As somebody ran from the room, Henry went to Christopher's desk, where he picked up sheet of paper. He read what was written on it and then stared at William accusingly before crumpling the note and putting in his pocket.

'He must have been cleaning his gun,' he said.

37

There was still an hour before dawn. Outside it was dark, but in the hangar the two SE5s stood beneath electric lights. The damage they had sustained two days earlier had been repaired by cannibalising parts from some of the other machines. Sergeant Chambers looked on as William inspected the plane he would be flying.

'Was there any damage to the engine?' William asked.

'It was a write-off, sir. We had to get a new one sent to us.'

'We'd better start her up anyway.'

He climbed up to the cockpit while Chambers took hold of the prop. The engine fired at the first try. William let it run for a few minutes until he was satisfied and then he switched off and climbed down.

'Have the guns been sighted?' he asked.

'Yes, sir. The Vickers is loaded with incendiaries.'

'Good.' William looked at his watch and wondered where Hemming was.

'Is there any news about the CO, sir,' Chambers asked.

'No, I'm afraid not. He was alive when he left here, but that's all I know.'

'I hope he's alright, sir.'

'Yes. So do I.'

William wondered what the men had heard. The official line was that it was an accident, but he doubted that anyone believed it. He glanced at the time again and was about to send somebody for Hemming, when Henry arrived.

'What are you doing here?' William asked. 'You were supposed to go to St Omer with the others.'

'I changed places with Hemming. He wasn't feeling well.'

'He looked alright last night, what's wrong with him?'

'I don't know. What does it matter anyway?'

'I don't suppose it does,' William said, though he didn't believe Hemming was really ill. He wondered what he should do. He didn't like the idea of taking Henry with him after what happened to Christopher, but if he ordered him to stay behind, Henry would be bound to take it as a personal affront. Despite everything, they still had to manage to get along somehow. William knew there was a good chance he'd be asked to take Christopher's place, and the last thing he needed was Henry carrying a chip on his shoulder.

'Actually, I wanted to talk to you,' he said, taking Henry aside so they wouldn't be overheard. 'I wanted to ask you what was in the note you took from Christopher's desk?'

'What note?' Henry stared at him insolently.

'I saw it,' William said. 'We both know it was there, but if you want to pretend there wasn't one, I won't argue. The point is, I hope you understand that what Christopher did had nothing to do with what you imagine you saw at the hotel.'

'I don't know what you mean. What happened was an accident. He was cleaning his gun.'

'He'd had enough, Henry,' William persisted. 'It could happen to any of us.'

Henry regarded him with a flat, cold look. 'Shouldn't we go before it gets light?'

It was pointless trying to talk to him, William thought. He thought again about ordering Henry to stay behind. After what happened to Christopher nobody would question his decision and there would be no question of a slight against

Henry, but he doubted Henry would see it that way.

'If you're worried about the mission, I can go by myself,' Henry said loudly.

Some of the men overheard and glanced their way, and William wondered if in some way Henry was trying to compensate for Christopher's actions. It was getting late, and the sooner they set off, the less likelihood there was of running into a patrolling jasta. He knew if he denied Henry the chance to go he would take it as a public humiliation, and admitted he had no choice.

'Alright,' he said.

The planes were pushed outside onto the grass. The sky was beginning to lighten, black fading to grey. The guns had been silent for most of the night, but they would start up again soon when the attack was renewed. At least if they could destroy the German balloon they might save the lives of a few men.

'We'll do the same as last time,' William said as he and Henry walked out onto the field. 'I'll attack first while you cover me. If I don't set fire to it, we'll change places.'

Henry looked at him, anger flashing in his eyes. He was about to protest, but evidently changed his mind. 'Whatever you say. After all, I expect they'll make you CO now, won't they,' he said nastily.

William was again tempted to send him back. It was too late though. It was almost light already. He reached his own machine and climbed up, and then, as he settled into his seat nodded to Chambers to prime the engine.

'Good luck, sir, see you for breakfast.'

'Thanks,' William said, and flipped on the switch. 'Contact.'

The engine fired, shattering the dawn.

*****

The recent un-seasonal heavy rain had passed and the

day dawned with the promise of fine weather. The night sky faded to blue, and as the sun scorched the horizon, the verdant land unfolded far beneath the wings of William's plane. Away from the lines, dusty roads and lanes dissected fields and meadows, skirting thick woods of beech and oak and farms whose ochre roofs were visible from miles around. In the middle of it all was a ruined swathe of mud, where two armies faced each other and no building or tree was left standing.

The balloon rose with the dawn into the still air, a bloated sausage tethered to the ground a thousand feet below. The course William set took them across the lines to the south, so that they approached the ridge from the east with the sun behind them to hide them from the observer. At fifteen thousand feet, William searched the sky for enemy planes, and seeing nothing he signalled to Henry and began to dive. The engine note climbed and the wind sang in the wires. At ten thousand feet he saw Henry level out to cover him, and then he was on his own, hurtling ever closer to his target. He cocked the guns and fixed the ring on the balloon, and watched it grow bigger with every second.

His heart was racing, blood pumping through his veins in a rushing tide. He thought of Oundle, a schoolroom dusty with chalk, shafts of sunlight slanting through the tall windows, and the sonorous tones of a master reciting Ovid. He used to look out of the window to a glimpse of green fields beyond the town, where the path followed the banks of the river to Fotheringhay. Then his thoughts fled to Scaldwell, where three oaks stood on the green and the church stood on a low hill where he'd taken Elizabeth that day to show her his parents' grave, so that she would know where he came from.

On the ground, the gun crews began to shoot at him and the sky filled with unfurling clouds of smoke. He looked up to check where Henry was, and it didn't surprise him that he was nowhere to be seen. It was too late to do anything about it. If he was quick he would see to the balloon quickly enough and then he would zoom up and head back to the lines before the jastas had a chance to come after him. What excuse would Henry give when he got back, William wondered? Some fault or other with his engine no doubt, though nothing would be found.

The balloon was almost in range. William gripped the trigger and waited.

EPILOGUE

JULY 1920

From the air the Northamptonshire countryside is a rural idyll of gently undulating fields and woods. Beneath a blazing sun hay is loaded onto carts and wheat is being harvested. The workers pause at midday to rest in the shade and eat their dinner. Children run off to play hide-and-seek, or to splash in the streams where they try to catch fish.

Pitsford House stands proudly isolated within a sea of green, approached by a long driveway flanked by leafy trees. A motor car travels along the drive and stops outside the house, and a figure gets out from behind the wheel and climbs the steps to the entrance.

When she takes off her hat, Elizabeth reveals that she wears her hair short. She goes inside without ringing the bell. As she crosses the hallway her heels click on the floor. She passes Morton, who is going in the opposite direction, and she smiles warmly as they greet one another.

'Good afternoon, Miss Gordon.'

Hello, Morton. Is he outside?'

'I believe he's on the terrace, Miss.'

'Thanks.'

At the doors leading to the terrace, Elizabeth pauses. Christopher is standing with one hand in the pocket of his jacket. He's wearing a pale suit with an open-neck shirt. In profile he looks just as he did before the war and Elizabeth feels a momentary sense of sadness. Some instinct alerts him to her presence and he turns to her and smiles. The right side of his face is scarred and slightly twisted. He is partially paralysed. His right hand is useless and he has a limp when he walks, but at least he is alive. It is, in fact, a miracle that he is alive.

'Hello, Liz,' he says. 'Would you like a drink before lunch?'

'Yes, please. Can I have a small gin?'

She doesn't offer to get it herself. He wants to do things even if it takes him a little longer than somebody else. He jokes about his disability, but she knows that it eats away at him. It is a permanent reminder of what he did. It's worse whenever he thinks of Henry, who was killed in October, two months after William disappeared.

They sit outside on the terrace for a little while. Christopher tells her that he's thinking of going into business.

'Land is all very well, and of course I wouldn't ever want to sell, but the fact is, I need another income if I'm going to keep this place up. I think things will only get worse with all these new taxes they're talking about.'

'What will you do?'

'Funnily enough, I'm thinking about something to do with aviation. It's the future, Liz.'

She is surprised under the circumstances. For a moment neither of them speak, reminded of William.

'Are you still going to France?' he asks eventually.

'Yes. I'm leaving next week.'

'Liz…'

'What?'

'It's just that I hate the idea of you living like this,' Christopher says tentatively. 'Always hoping that someday he'll turn up.'

She smiles. He cares about her, she knows that. He thinks she is allowing her life to drift by. She opens her bag and takes out an envelope, a letter addressed to her. 'This came ten days ago.'

He looks at the envelope. There is no return address but the postmark is Canada.

'Look inside,' she tells him.

He takes out the single sheet of paper and reads what has been written on it.

Dear Elizabeth,
I will be at the churchyard in Thierry on the eighth.

Christopher looks at her with a puzzled frown. 'It isn't signed.'

'No.'

'Is that all there was?'

'Yes.'

He reads the lines again as if it might offer some other clue as to who sent it, as Elizabeth has done a hundred times. 'Do you recognise the handwriting?' he asks.

'No. But I never saw his handwriting.'

He stares at her. 'Liz, this could be from anyone. If it was him, surely he would have said more.'

But she has thought about it a lot. He wouldn't know anything about her. She might be married. She might even be dead. If not from the war, then from the influenza epidemic.

Christopher sees that she will not be dissuaded. 'And what if it isn't him?'

'Then nothing will have changed,' she says.

*****

On the morning of the eighth, Elizabeth leaves the hotel early. It is the same one where Christopher stayed after he left the hospital. The previous evening she had dined alone in the dining room. Every time the door opened she looked up, her heart beating wildly, but she was always disappointed.

A taxi takes her to Thierry. She sits silent and tense, her bag containing the letter on her knee. Now that she is here, she can't believe that he will come. She thinks it is a mistake. She imagines she will spend the entire day waiting fruitlessly in the hot sun. She doesn't know what to tell the taxi driver, but decides she will tell him to come back for her at six o clock. If he hasn't come by then, she will accept that he isn't going to.

The village is just as she remembers it. She looks eagerly at the church and the surrounding graveyard. When the taxi stops she pays the driver and hurries to the gate. Her heart is racing and she cannot control the hope that suddenly consumes her. At the gate she looks toward the tree at the back where his grave is, and of course there is nobody there. The graveyard is empty, as deep down she knew it would be.

When she opens the gate the hinge creaks. She walks slowly along the path, and when she is level with the church she stops. She sees there is somebody leaning against the tree in the early shade, which is why she didn't see him before. He sees her and turns to face her and steps out onto the path. For a few moments they look at one another, twenty yards apart. He smiles, and though she would like to smile she cries instead, though she does not know why, because she has never been more happy.

He begins to walk towards her. She manages a single step before she breaks into a run.

ABOUT THE AUTHOR

Stuart Harrison grew up in England, but now lives in the Bay of Islands, New Zealand. He is the author of five previously published novels, including The Snow Falcon which was translated into twelve languages and became an international bestseller when it was released in 1999. A new version of The Snow Falcon, completely rewritten and revised from the original, has been released, in conjunction with The Flyer, as both a print book and ebook.

The Flyer, which took two years to write, is certain to appeal to everyone who enjoyed The Snow Falcon. More information about Stuart and his work can be found at www.stuartharrison.com where the author can also be contacted.

BOOKS

Published by Harper Collins in the UK:

The Snow Falcon, 1999
StillWater, 2001
Better Than This, 2002
Lost Summer, 2003
Aphrodites Smile, 2004

Published in 2012 available from online retailers:

The Flyer
The Snow Falcon (Revised)

More coming in 2013 writing as both Stuart Harrison and Stuart C Harrison. See my website for details.